## Richard Dacre and The Murder Room

**⟫⟫** This title is part of The Murder Room, our series dedicated to making available out-of-print or hard-to-find titles by classic crime writers.

Crime fiction has always held up a mirror to society. The Victorians were fascinated by sensational murder and the emerging science of detection; now we are obsessed with the forensic detail of violent death. And no other genre has so captivated and enthralled readers.

Vast troves of classic crime writing have for a long time been unavailable to all but the most dedicated frequenters of second-hand bookshops. The advent of digital publishing means that we are now able to bring you the backlists of a huge range of titles by classic and contemporary crime writers, some of which have been out of print for decades.

From the genteel amateur private eyes of the Golden Age and the femmes fatales of pulp fiction, to the morally ambiguous hard-boiled detectives of mid twentieth-century America and their descendants who walk our twenty-first century streets, The Murder Room has it all. **⟫⟫**

## The Murder Room
### Where Criminal Minds Meet

**themurderroom.com**

**Richard Dacre (pen name of Donald Thomas) (1926–)**
Donald Thomas was born in Somerset and educated at Queen's College, Taunton, and Balliol College, Oxford. He holds a personal chair in Cardiff University. His numerous crime novels include two collections of Sherlock Holmes stories and the hugely popular historical detective series featuring Sergeant Verity of Scotland Yard, written under the pen name Francis Selwyn, as well as gritty police procedurals written under the name of Richard Dacre. He is also the author of seven biographies and a number of other non-fiction works, and won the Gregory Prize for his poems, *Points of Contact*. He lives in Bath with his wife.

*By Donald Thomas*

Mad Hatter Summer: A Lewis Carroll Nightmare
The Ripper's Apprentice
Jekyll, Alias Hyde
The Arrest of Scotland Yard
Dancing in the Dark
Red Flowers for Lady Blue
The Blindfold Game
The Day the Sun Rose Twice

*As Francis Selwyn*
Sergeant Verity and the Cracksman
Sergeant Verity and the Hangman's Child
Sergeant Verity Presents His Compliments
Sergeant Verity and the Blood Royal
Sergeant Verity and the Imperial Diamond
Sergeant Verity and the Swell Mob

*As Richard Dacre*
The Blood Runs Hot
Scream Blue Murder
Money with Menaces

# Money with Menaces

Richard Dacre

An Orion book

Copyright © Richard Dacre 1989

The right of Richard Dacre to be identified as the author of this work has been
asserted in accordance with the Copyright, Designs and Patents Act 1988.

This edition published by
The Orion Publishing Group Ltd
Orion House
5 Upper St Martin's Lane
London WC2H 9EA

An Hachette UK company
A CIP catalogue record for this book is available from the British Library

ISBN 978 1 4719 0451 6

www.orionbooks.co.uk

*Author's Note*

The events of *Money with Menaces* occupy two months in the career of DCI Sam Hoskins, from early January to early March. Canton and Ocean Beach are a creation of the novelist's imagination. Their police forces, politicians and citizens exist only in fiction. In one sense, Canton is any city. In the near future, it may be every city.

# ONE

# Hi-jack

# Chapter One

Morning traffic was building fast on the outer ring-road, according to Coastal Radio travel news at five to eight. On the Eastern Causeway it wove and parted like a Road Race pin-ball game. Feeder lanes curved and joined, peeled off and spiralled through an industrial mist of January dawn.

There was ice in the air. No question of that. It chilled the fume-vapours of the steelworks to a haze the colour of nicotined bar smoke. But above the urban traffic lanes a concrete arch of the Causeway Flyover and its coiling approach roads patterned the cold ocean sky. In its pin-prick brightness their lines had the artistry of cathedral vaulting.

From several hundred car radios the same tough-chinned voice predicted a cold day of bright intervals and squally showers, heavy at times on the western coast from Ocean Beach to Sandbar. Drivers on the Eastern Causeway heard the radio pips for eight o'clock. Across the rivulets and marshland of the Eastern Levels, Canton city centre appeared distantly. Its new finger-towers of white and grey tiles dwarfed the Edwardian belfries and spires.

The maroon Saab, with its high tail and the bunched muscular span of its wide chassis, hung back a little in the nearside lane. A roof-rack sign proclaimed PENINSULAR 24-HOUR PARTS AND RECOVERY. Its driver kept an even distance behind the white Ford Transit. The car and the van turned off, like formation partners. They crossed the Causeway Flyover and glided down towards the coastal moors. Ahead of them corrugated steelwork sheds at Atlantic Factors rose vast and gaunt as old airship hangars.

The outline of the Transit rode tall and square above the Saab's windscreen. Through one of the van windows at the rear, the back of the driver's head appeared, anonymous as a wooden block.

With the sweep of a dancer, the Saab began to glide closer. On the right-hand door at the rear of the Transit the inset black handle with its lock was clearly visible. A blue wave-patterned logo of the Atlantic District Health Authority filled the adjacent panel. In dull metallic warning, the reinforced bumper of the maroon car caught the offside corner of the white Ford, as if the youthful driver of the Saab had misjudged his angle of overtaking.

The front passenger in the Saab frowned and edged forward a little with excitement. He spoke sidelong to the driver.

'Watch his corner, now. If it jams on his tyre, we shan't take him anywhere.'

'He won't need nudging much more,' the driver said confidently. 'I reckon we've got his attention. Watch out.'

He looked quickly in his mirror to see the state of the traffic behind.

'You two in the back,' he said sharply to his other passengers. 'Get dressed up! Masks on and heads down. And gloves. Don't forget gloves.'

There was a moment of fumbling and fitting. Then Pluto the Pup and a Mouse-Mask with the sewn-in rubber smiles of corpses confronted him in the mirror. Big Piggy sat beside him, pressing eagerly towards the windshield.

'Right,' said the teenage driver calmly, pulling on his Foxy Grandpa face, 'here we go, then.'

He was up behind the white van again, the lettering TRANSIT and the blue oval with its FORD signature almost at the top of his own windshield. There was a harder jolt that threatened to throw the Saab back into the car behind. Pressed metal caught again in a dismal squeal, like a power saw cutting against the grain of a plank. The orange hazard lights on the van began to flash as it lost speed.

'I'd say he felt that,' said the front passenger in the Saab, as if to himself. 'I think he knows we'd like a word.'

Big Piggy leant forward a little from the rear seat.

'Take it easy, Tommo. He could be retired police driving for a firm like that. He could have two-way radio.'

'They don't have radio,' the front passenger said quietly. 'Not on their Transits. Only on the ambulances. I checked that. Any case, he's a bit too naughty for retired police. Watch it, Steve. He's pulling in.'

They were well beyond the flyover now, where the hard shoulder began again. The square white shape of the Transit with its low-slung chassis had turned off the carriageway. It stopped with its hazard lights still pulsing. The Saab drew up immediately behind it. There was a moment's pause, as there always was after such impacts. The van driver got used to the idea that the collision had really happened. Aggravation and delay settled on him like a cloud. He got down carefully on the passenger side of the cab, screened and protected from the speeding traffic. Slowly, fumbling in his pocket for documents, he walked back towards the Saab, now stationary a foot or two behind his own vehicle. He was a short, dark-haired forty-year-old with pebble lens glasses, his breath condensing in the raw morning air. He did not look like retired police.

'What's this game?' he shouted ahead of him, righteous in his innocence. 'You stupid little bugger! What's this game, then?'

The boy behind the wheel of the Saab got out. As he faced the advancing pebble lenses, hidden from the road by the height of the Transit, he was the larger of the two. The driver of the van stopped, seeing the palsied corpse-smile of the rubber Foxy Grandpa. He looked quickly behind him, as if he might break into a run. But Big Piggy had wwalked round the front of the Ford and the driver could see no escape. Foxy Grandpa came one way and Big Piggy the other until the three of them stood by the side of the van, concealed from the road. There was another shield-logo on the panel of the Ford Transit and a neat scroll with the words ATLANTIC DISTRICT HEALTH AUTHORITY. CANTON DIVISION.

Foxy Grandpa took another step forward. In his long shabby coat he might have been a youthful wino from Martello Square or the Pier Head.

'Hi, Jack!' he said, the smile audible under the Disneyland death mask.

'My name's not . . . '

But the long-coated boy was not to be put off. From a baggy pocket of the overcoat he slid a gun that looked like a child's toy, stained and worn.

'Hi, Jack!' he said again, amiable but insistent. 'It's a hi-jack!'

The man stared at them.

'You gone bloody mad?' He gestured at the logo on the side of the Transit. 'This is a hospital van! There's nothing here for you.'

'Pharmacy van,' said the boy with the gun. 'Pharmacy is what it is, Jack. And what this is, Jack, is a Colt forty-five. Sawn-off barrel. Blow your head apart like a melon at this range. See? And what the other gentleman's showing you is a real sharp carver. Go through you like it was slicing tender cooked turkey. Any bother, Jack, and you could easy be carrying your nose home in your hanky. All right? That help to make things clearer, does it, Jack?'

Big Piggy and Foxy Grandpa were already herding the driver back into his cab. Pebble Lenses tried to stand his ground, a last defiance born of self-respect. Big Piggy moved forward another step, the knife still concealed from view of the traffic by the parked van and the flap of his coat. He drew the carver out and tucked its point towards the man's chin, easing him inside the van.

'All right,' the van driver said morosely, 'there won't be any bother.'

'A little ride,' Big Piggy said, tickling the man's dewlap with the steel point, letting a spearmint breath into his face. 'That's all. You'll be home for lunch. Unless, of course, you'd prefer to be a hero. In that case, Jack, they'll find you down here and your head somewhere on the bridge up there. All right? Got that?'

The man said nothing. Big Piggy pressed against him.

'Got that?' he asked savagely. 'Have you?'

The van driver nodded, so far as the blade would permit.

There was just room for two of them in the cab of the Transit beside the driver. The button-nosed Mouse-Mask slid across the front seat of the maroon Saab behind the wheel. Big Piggy and Foxy Grandpa, with his wolfish grin and rimless specs, kept their faces down as they sat close to the driver at the dashboard of the Transit. A moment later the white Ford van with its scraped rear wing eased out into the flow of traffic. The new driver of the Saab behind eased off his Mouse-Mask. Foxy Grandpa sighed and looked at his watch. It had taken less than a minute. The best yet.

'Round the circuit and back out to the country,' said Big Piggy with the carver. 'You don't really want to be a hero, do you, Jack? I mean, you don't get paid for being a hero, do you?'

'No,' said the man numbly.

'That's better, Jack,' said Foxy Grandpa, eyes on the road. 'You could be famous by this evening. You could have your picture in the papers.'

Big Piggy sniggered. 'Supposing, that is, you still got something left to take a picture of!'

'You talk too much!' Foxy Grandpa said sternly. 'Now, Jack. Signal to turn off on the Sandbar road. Pull into the nearside lane. That's the trick. Nice and easy. No need for you to get hurt unless you want it.'

The nicotine-coloured haze of Atlantic Factors fell away to their left. They drove for several miles on the country road. It ran inland behind Canton, Lantern Hill and Ocean Beach, inland from executive villages. Twenty miles on, beyond anything that Foxy Grandpa had in mind, it would come to the flat spit of Sandbar with its little harbour and wooded hills rising behind the quayside. The maroon Saab followed close behind the van. Beyond the urban motorway the Sandbar road was quiet. It was the commuter routes from coastal suburbs, Lantern Hill and Ocean Beach, that were jammed at eight o'clock in the morning. Big Piggy fell silent as the bare and dripping winter trees grew denser. Foxy Grandpa gave the orders.

'In here,' he said suddenly, indicating a makeshift lay-by, puddled and muddied under the overhanging boughs. The driver turned the van, bumping over the rutted gravel, and stopped the engine.

'Let's have the key to the cupboards in the back,' Big Piggy said.

'They don't give us keys to the back. We don't need 'em.'

Big Piggy fitted his Disney mask a little straighter and sighed.

'I think Jack wants to be a hero, after all,' he said to Foxy Grandpa. He touched the flat steel of the blade to the side of the man's face gently and turned to his companion again. 'Wouldn't you say he wanted to be a hero, after all?'

'Look!' said the van driver furiously, 'they don't give us keys to the cupboards! We don't need 'em and we don't want 'em! It's just delivery, see? The surgeries and pharmacies got keys at the places we deliver to. Right? You want to get at the things in the back, there's a wrench and a hammer in the tool-box down there. If it makes any difference!'

'That's better, Jack,' said Foxy Grandpa with the gun. 'More like it. Hands on the steering column now. One either side.'

The driver had given up long ago. They had no trouble with him. Foxy Grandpa took two lengths of white nylon cord. Pebble Lenses made no objection as they tied his wrists either side of the steering wheel. Indeed, he moved aside a little to make their task easier. Jack was not the stuff of which heroes were fashioned.

'Key to the back doors of the van, Jack,' said Foxy Grandpa reasonably. 'Don't tell me you haven't got one, otherwise I'll start getting cross with you.'

'On the ring with the ignition,' said the driver sourly. 'In the column.'

Foxy Grandpa retrieved it.

'You're a good boy, you are,' Big Piggy said admiringly. 'We might take you on our next little outing.'

The driver said nothing. The two Disney masks got out, standing concealed behind the van as a single car passed and vanished towards Sandbar in a fading drone. The winter morning was quiet again. From the boot of the Saab they took a light steel bar, the size of a ceiling lath, tapered at one end.

Mouse-Mask reversed the Saab and turned it round, its open boot conveniently close to the van. Big Piggy unlocked the rear doors of the Transit with the driver's key.

'Right,' said Foxy Grandpa to the others. 'Use the pick again. Smash the locks on the compartment.'

The Transit van's interior had been fitted out with cup-boards, like the kitchenette of a camper. On the double-doors of each cupboard a simple padlock held the handles together. It was a half-hearted precaution against casual theft. Mouse-Mask and Big Piggy slid the bar under the handles, wrenching them off together with the lock. As they did so, the van alarm erupted in a shrill pulsing whistle. According to the mythology of crime-prevention, the teenage robbers would take fright and run at the sound. But the youth of inner-city Canton were not part of the punters' mythology. None of them took the least notice of the siren, as they worked intently to pass out the shoe-box size pharmacy cases.

Pluto the Pup, in jacket and pleated skirt, kept watch on the driver while the others opened the boot of the car and made more room for the cases inside.

They retrieved the steel pick. The Saab was loaded in two minutes, the alarm on the Ford Transit still pumping out its whooping blasts. The last of the Disney masks piled back into the car. There was a moment of slithering and skidding on the grit as the wheels locked. Then the maroon car shot clear on to the tarmac of the road, heading back fast the way it had come. Half an hour later the alarm on the Transit expired, unnoticed. The silence was so intense that the hospital driver, tied to his steering wheel, could hear the chatter of sparrows in a hedge on the far side of the winter field.

# Chapter Two

'Park here a minute,' Chief Inspector Hoskins said.

He sat contentedly in the passenger seat of the Ford Sierra, a bulky greying man of indeterminate middle-age. The blue-tinted glasses gave a veiled scepticism to his round eyes. Sergeant Chance drew up by the Cakewalk promenade of Ocean Beach. The sea front tarmac shone black with the rain of the winter day. A storm had been gathering all morning and had broken an hour before lunch. Under heavy Channel cloud, the world lay trapped in January murk.

'Hang on a minute,' Hoskins said. 'We could be quite a while in conversation with the lovely Billy Catte.'

He opened the car door against the force of the wind, strolled across the Cakewalk and disappeared into the cream-painted stone of the public conveniences by the pier. The wide promenade itself and the Beach Lawns that ran down the centre of Bay Drive were empty, as if the blustery wind had swept them clear of people. The parked car rocked a little under the force of the Atlantic gusts. Across the deserted sands came an insistent scrabbling of the slate-grey sea, somewhere between high and low water. The wet uncovered shore glimmered bleak and colourless in the cloud-light.

Sergeant Chance, a large fresh-faced young man with a flattened mop of black hair, tuned the car radio to Coastal Radio News and found that he was almost too late.

'Coastal Radio News at one-thirteen on Wednesday the fifth of January,' said the voice of the tough-chinned optimist. 'The Labour Group on Canton city council plans to challenge the government's latest rate-capping directive in the courts. Canton Lambs Football Club manager, Rory Roberts, promises that the club's present deficit of eighty thousand pounds can be made good by the new sponsorship deals agreed with Peninsular Trucking and the Blue Moon Leisure Complex at Ocean Beach. Reports are coming in of an armed robbery on a van belonging to the Atlantic District Health Authority. Neither the authority nor Canton Hospital Security has yet confirmed that the van was delivering drugs from the hospital pharmacy to chemists' shops and doctors' surgeries. Saturday's Winter Garden Concert, featuring the

Hangman's Children and Eight O'Clock Walk, has sold out. Black market tickets are reported to be changing hands at several times their face-value. Canton police have warned fans to beware of forgeries.'

Sergeant Chance reached out to turn off the summary.

'And finally,' said the voice, as if daring him not to listen, 'local business tycoon, Councillor Carmel Cooney, owner of Peninsular Trucking and Blue Moon Leisure, is in the news a second time. To challenge the policies of the council's ruling Labour group, Mr Cooney has threatened to resign his safe Conservative seat at Hawks Hill and enter the current by-election contest in the Canton Dock ward, which had the city's largest Labour majority before the death of Councillor Tom Robens last week. Ms Eve Ricard, vice-chair of the Labour group, dismissed the challenge as a "stunt" and defended the council's policies on education, police, racism, equal opportunities and sexual harassment. With the time at one-fifteen *this* is Clegg Jones. And *that* was Coastal Radio News this cold and blustery Wednesday lunchtime. Coming up next, the Foolish Things, "Young Misses in love with Old Hits" . . . '

Hoskins was walking back across the promenade, the wind whipping and snapping at his coat-tails. The radio burst into song and a promise of Memory Lane.

> When the moon hits your eye,
> Like a big piece of pie,
> That's am-or-ay . . .

Chance turned the switch and Hoskins opened the car door.

'Right, my son. If you're ready, we'll go. And that thing is supposed to be on police frequency, not *Housewives' Choice*.'

'I was having my break,' Chance said unapologetically. 'Entitlement. What's more, Cooney's bailing out the Canton Lambs and he's standing for the Dock ward by-election to screw Eve Ricard.'

Hoskins appeared not to care. A thin rain began to blow in from the sea as they crossed by the bulb-hung arch of the New Pier entrance and walked towards the town. The Chief Inspector turned up the collar of his coat.

'Cooney's a big boy now. Our friend Billy Catte should be enough for me this afternoon.'

Beyond Bay Drive's expanse of wet black tarmac, Rundle

Street was bright with neon alphabets. Most of the street, leading inland from the New Pier, was occupied by fish restaurants closed for the winter and gaming-machine arcades open every day of the year. The letters rippled above the glass fronts in the fruit-gum colours of Lucky Penny, Gold Digger and Mr Cat's Prize Bingo. With every change of neon, a skeletal cat in top hat and tails was lit up from feet to whiskers in radiant electric-blue.

At the sea front end of Rundle Street, the Edwardian shops and pubs had been reconstructed in cherry-coloured brick. The Cakewalk Bingo and Social Club boasted a flight of steps and cinema doors at one side of Catte's premises. A notice reserved the right to refuse admission. So far as Hoskins knew, that right had never been exercised.

Ignoring the grander entrance, Hoskins led the way in past the plate-glass swing-doors of Mr Cat's Lucky Penny Arcade. An Atlantic squall hit the Cakewalk and the seaside streets. Rain smacked and ran against the plate-glass, painful as hailstones upon the face.

Like all the other arcades in the street, the ground floor of Mr Cat's Prize Bingo was a single concourse bathed in hard fluorescent light. There were several tellers' booths with armoured glass, where the clientele could change its money. A couple of uniformed security guards stared out at the rain-swept street with conspicuous indifference. None of Mr Cat's winter patrons looked like troublemakers. There were half a dozen pensioners in baggy overcoats and scarves, several shabbily dressed young mothers with pushchairs investing their social security benefits in Diamond City and Silver Dollar.

Down the aisles, the gaming-machines stood like sleek and flashing spaceships. In their coffins of armoured glass, Aztec Gold and Bullion Raid offered a waterfall of small change poised on a shelf-edge, as if about to pour over at the next drop of a punter's coin. But it would be a long while and many coins later before that happened. A handwritten notice had been taped to the glass. DO NOT BANG. ALARM FITTED.

Sergeant Chance nodded at a video game across the aisle. A death's-head and a redhead in green tights had been scrolled on the black glass with loving suggestiveness. 'Xenophobe. Seek out and destroy all hostile and alien life-forms.'

'You reckon we could do him under the Race Relations Act, if all else fails, Sam?'

Hoskins glowered at the painted glass with its girl in green tights. He strode bulkily towards the door at the back of the arcade.

On a winter afternoon the staff of the Lucky Penny almost outnumbered the customers. Apart from the young women in the tellers' booths and the two security guards, the machines were served by Mr Cat's Kittens. Hoskins counted half a dozen of them, each in her middle teens. All were dressed in cherry-red. Three wore tight singlets and extremely short cheer-leader skirts. The others had the same singlets but with pants of a tight bikini cut instead of the little skirts.

'Fems and Toms, I'd say,' Chance marked the difference for Hoskins' benefit. 'Bit on the cheeky side in both cases.'

'Yes,' said Hoskins bleakly. 'Then, I suppose you'd know, wouldn't you?'

Before Chance could reply, Hoskins pushed his way past a single-parent family and reached for the handle of the office door.

'That's private, there! You want the other way out, squire.'

Though not appearing to notice their approach, the two security men had headed them off.

Hoskins fingered out the dim green plastic of his warrant-card.

'Registered security firm, are we?' he asked pleasantly. 'Or just doing Mr Catte a personal favour?'

'More of a favour, boss,' said the second man obligingly. 'Only it looks better with the caps on.'

'And the baseball bats?' Hoskins asked in the same pleasant voice.

'Only for show, boss,' the first man said. 'Play fair now. Half a dozen young tearaways could come bursting in and do this place any time.'

Chance walked round them and tapped at the door.

'Must help to stop the pensioners and pregnant mums from vandalising the one-arm bandits,' he said approvingly.

Standing back, he waited for Hoskins to lead the way into Catte's office.

Billy Catte rose from his sagging leather chair in the corner, a cup of instant coffee in his hand. His office had the dimensions of a prison cell. It was bleak as a communal shower. The only window in its distempered walls looked out on to the alleyway at the rear of Rundle Street and had been fitted with steel bars as protection. Faintly, as if from the next room, a Walkman portable cassette player filled the smoky room with the lilting chorus of operatic Verdi, 'Va, pensiero, sull ali' dorate . . . '

'Mr Hoskins?' he said cagily. 'You want to see me? You could have rung up and said. Only I got paperwork to get through this afternoon. If I don't, then my taxes is late and your wages ain't paid.'

'We don't phone in advance, Mr Catte. Contrary to policy.'

Catte was a dark burly man with a nose that seemed broader from having been broken long ago. He had the makings of an amiable bruiser but the slight protrusion of his eyes suggested indignation rather than amiability. With his cropped springy hair and arched brows, he looked perpetually surprised at the malice of the world. Just then, it suited his tone.

'You're not saying I've stepped out of line, are you, Mr Hoskins? Because I most certainly have not.'

Hoskins unloaded one of the steel-frame chairs stacked in a corner and nodded to Chance to take the other.

'I'm not saying you've done anything. It's what other people tell me. So me and Sergeant Chance are going to sit down here with you and get this sorted. Right?'

'What people? What things?'

Catte watched them shift their chairs into place. As yet he did not sit down. He stood over the two policemen with the plaintive bewilderment of the innocent. Behind him rose a tall grey safe of hardened steel with a broken lock. Above it, a machine service calender from Manchester showed two naked and sun-toasted girls splashing through the shallows of a Pacific beach. The ashtray on the desk was full and there were two unwashed cups next to a tarnished electric kettle. Of Catte's paperwork there was no sign beyond an imported and badly creased paperback which promised *Elaine Cox, A Well-Reared Tomboy*. The book lay spread, cover upwards, on the desk. Hoskins picked it up, turned it and glanced at the type. The pages exuded the pleasures of private reformatory management. He winced and put it back.

'You think we could have that music off, Mr Catte?'

'No,' said Catte bluntly. 'I like a tune. Helps me think. Just because the punters and the yobs want bongo rubbish don't mean I can't have something decent in here. What people and what things?'

Vibrant and gathering intensity, La Scala sang of its homeland, 'Del Giordano la riva saluta . . . '

'Social services, Mr Catte,' said Hoskins, as if he regretted the inconvenience. 'They're the people complaining. We have to take notice of them.'

Billy Catte sat down. He scowled but turned the volume of the music a little lower.

'Look!' he said. 'I got bloody Income Tax inspectors. I got bloody Customs and Excise with their Value Added Tax. I got bloody fire regulations. I got bloody gaming laws. I got bloody planning restrictions!'

'And now you got bloody social services,' Chance said brightly. Hoskins frowned.

'But why?' Catte spread out his hands, appealing to them at the injustice of the whole thing. 'Tell me why?'

'Because you've also got Melanie Paget out there, dressed up in hot-pants and tight sweater.'

'So? Fifteen. She can work a few hours if she wants. Same as she might deliver newspapers. And there's nothing wrong with that uniform unless someone's got a dirty mind. Just a bit of a lark. She's not wearing any less than she would be on the beach in summer. If she wants to stick it out a bit, that's strictly up to her. I'm not running a kindergarten.'

'You know the machine arcade owners' code of practice? No one under eighteen allowed in?' Hoskins asked.

Billy Catte had considered the question long ago. He shrugged.

'That's for punters, not staff. Staff can be any age. Any case, I don't belong to their poxy association.'

Hoskins nodded, as if he understood.

'Fair enough, Mr Catte. So that just leaves me one problem. Am I going to do you under section three of the Gaming Act, 1968, or section two of the Children and Young Persons Act, 1933? Or possibly both? Maximum, two years' board and lodging at Her Majesty's expense. What would you think, Mr Catte?'

Catte's expression was unchanged by the bad news. He appeared to think for a few seconds, as if out of respect for Hoskins.

'What I think,' he said at last, 'is that you and your

boyfriend here can go and do one another inside-out for all I care. And anything else you got to say, you can say to my brief.'

'Jack Cam would that be?' Chance asked innocently.

Billy Catte glowered at him.

'For what it matters to you, son, it's Claude Roberts, as you'll bloody soon find out if this keeps up.'

Hoskins intervened. 'I'm not talking about her age, Mr Catte. And I don't care if she goes round in a mini-skirt or hot-pants. Your trouble is that if she's caught here, working during school hours, then it's a free ride to the Crown Court for you.'

But Catte was unimpressed.

'So?'

Hoskins sighed again, as if with strained tolerance.

'In case you hadn't heard, my friend, holidays ended last week. School is back. They don't knock off till four this afternoon. It's now just short of two. All right?'

'That!' said Billy Catte scornfully. 'It's Wednesday afternoon. They have hockey on Wednesday afternoon. She don't do hockey. Ask her dad.'

Hoskins nodded.

'Social services and the DHSS are going to be asking her dad about that,' he said reassuringly. 'That and a lot of other things. And you still look like top billing for the Crown Court, my friend. There's a string of complaints like this.'

Catte was still unmoved.

'Apprentice is what she is,' he said. 'And in that case it don't matter whether she's here or school.'

Sergeant Chance grinned at the absurdity of it.

'Apprentice? Old Claude Roberts tell you that, did he? In that case, you need Jack Cam even worse than you look!'

He got up and opened the office door a few inches. Melanie, the long fair hair slanting across a knowing face, was clearing out cigarette ends and gum-wrappers from under the machines with a long-handled broom. Chance closed the door and sat down.

'Apprentice!' He grinned again as if admiring Billy Catte's pluck. 'She's on the brush, that's all she is. See for yourself!'

Catte stood up. He took the kettle and began to mix instant coffee for himself with a well-used spoon.

'You want to be witty, Sergeant Chance, you go and do it

with Claude Roberts. And unless you can show me why not, I want the pair of you out of these premises now. And if you think I got this far in life to be stopped by some pouftah or lessie in the social services, you got another think coming.'

Hoskins made no attempt to move.

'You've got me wrong, Mr Catte,' he said quietly. 'I don't think it's the social services that'll finish you.'

'Then what's all this garbage for this afternoon?'

Hoskins looked at him with faint curiosity.

'You want to use your imagination, Mr Catte. Suppose there's a real rumpus now, which there will be if you don't start seeing sense. Who's going to be the one that's really cross with you? Not me. Not Mr Chance. Not the social services. It won't be pouftahs and lessies, that's a promise. They've got unions and rules. Knock off at five o'clock and go home for the night. But if you start acting half-smart, and there's inspectors crawling over every gaming arcade and club in this town, it's going to be down to you. And who's going to suffer most? Not a little man like you. It's Mr Cooney and his friends that're going to find themselves up to their necks in investigations and inspections. Now, I can't say how they'll feel about it. But I'd bet a fiver it'll be you out the front of the class and touching your toes as an example to the rest.'

Billy Catte sipped his tepid coffee.

'You don't stop trying, do you, Hoskins? It don't get through to you, does it? If you come here to quote laws and regulations, you could have saved yourself the petrol. For all I care, the two of you and the social services and the rest of it can go and piss up a rope together. I don't discuss laws with you any more than I talk about taxes with the tax inspector. I got an accountant that does that. And I got Claude Roberts to talk about laws with you. Right?'

'That's silly,' Hoskins said gently. 'It's just making trouble.'

But Catte was in command now.

'Is it? You listen to me. Suppose you go back to your social services pouf and tell him to bring charges. What happens? Letters go to and fro to see if I'm doing what he thinks I'm doing. You'd be lucky to get a warrant this side of next Christmas. So then there's charges. And after that it goes to some pimply young wanker in the prosecution service. Another six or twelve months while he gets his head out of his pants and decides if it's worth going on with your charges. And he won't because he'll see he's on a hiding to nothing. But even if he does, there's a three-year queue for the Crown Court. So all you're telling me is that I might end up in court in about five years time, if I'm unlucky. That's nothing to the concern I've got about very likely having to have a hip-replacement. And if that happens as well, I shan't be available for court till after you've retired. Still, meanwhile, I'm doing very nicely in the trade.'

Billy Catte took another sip of grey coffee, pulled a face, and abandoned the cup on his desk. Then he continued.

'And there again, Mr Hoskins. Even if I do get taken to court, my brief'll be smarter than yours. No offence, but I can afford better. Quiet word with his lordship the judge beforehand. Custodial sentence not appropriate. Young Melanie called in evidence, twenty years old by then, supposing you can still find her. Not going to do much for your side, is she? She might tell a story in the dock that you wouldn't like one bit. Being harassed by the social services and made to say things that weren't true. Not going to sound too clever, is it? So if the worst happens to me, I reckon it's a slap on the wrist for being a naughty boy and home for tea. That being the case, why don't you fuck off, leave me alone, and earn your wages by catching some criminals for a change?'

Hoskins felt his face growing warm. 'Two years in gaol is what we'll be asking for.'

But Catte shook his head. 'For Melanie being here on her sports afternoon? And by then, Mr Hoskins, the queues for the prisons is going to be even longer than the ones for the hospitals. You think I got time to care about your poncing rubbish when I got my health to worry over?'

'There could still be room for you. Supposing you don't take a warning in time.'

Billy Catte smiled at last, reminiscently. He was going to win this round, and he knew it.

'That's the trouble with warnings, Mr Hoskins. Years ago, you tell some young thief or yob what the law is and he could go to prison, he'd watch his step. People don't think like that any more. Man gets done for fiddling his tax or his VAT. If I was on a jury I'd vote not guilty and stick to it. No disgrace any more. Just bad luck. Being caught isn't what it was. Could happen to any of us. There was some poor old mug from the government on telly the other night. Said we shouldn't prosecute firms that fouls the rivers and breaks the law because if we fined them they wouldn't have the money to clean themselves up. Sensible attitude, I call it. Glad I voted for his lot.'

'Court and prison could happen to you,' Hoskins said grimly. 'That could be arranged.'

But Catte laughed out loud.

'We'll see, if the time comes, Mr Hoskins. You go and have a word with old Claude Roberts. Write and tell me how you get on. And, if you don't mind, I'll let you out of the office door at the back. Not good for business to have faces like you tramping through the front.'

A few minutes later Hoskins and Chance stood among the dustbins and split plastic of rubbish sacks at the rear of the Rundle Street arcades.

'The girl,' said Chance bitterly. 'I say we have a go at her.'

'Not without a female officer present, my son. Not in this day and age. What if young Melanie takes her boss's side? Brings accusations. You fancy charges of unlawful touching up? We've seen her there, Jack. Time and date confirmed. That's enough for the moment. She's only one of a dozen, according to our DHSS friends.'

They walked down Rundle Street and into the town centre of Ocean Beach. Forlorn and abandoned a fortnight after Christmas, the unlit and rain-drenched street decorations swung and clattered in the squally breeze. Where the narrow street opened out in the wide seaside square of The Parade with its department stores and central gardens, Chance paused. They were by a shop that sold remainder books, cards and stationery.

Hoskins turned. Chance was smiling at a girl behind the shop counter, just inside the window. She turned, her face brightened, and she opened and closed the fingers of her raised hand in a lethargic 'Ciao!' She was about nineteen or twenty, Hoskins supposed, a petite figure in spike-heels, sweater and smooth jeans tight enough to show thighs hardly thicker than a man's upper arm.

Chance put his face to the glass of the window and mouthed a few words. The girl nodded. Her golden blonde hair lay in a loose sweep to her shoulders. Her face, Hoskins thought, was that of a sulky elf, the hair spilling forward as she leant towards the window. There was a little too much mascara on the lashes of her hazel eyes. Her nose was rather too big and the weaker chin gave her a prim and sullen look.

'It's Julie,' Chance said, grinning at Hoskins and then looking back again.

'Is it? I see.'

Julie turned to take money from a customer, showing in profile a flat stomach and the backward jut of hips that seemed to flaunt extreme youth. The dye of the blue jeans was washed out, perhaps when they were shrunk on her. Their fit was tight enough to draw sheaves of creases behind her knees and across the backs of her thighs. Every stitch of her underwear seemed contoured through the thin denim seat. Hoskins went back towards Chance.

'She part of your caseload, is she?'

Chance grinned again.

'She could be on to a promise, Sam. I mean, if she plays her cards right, she could be the future Mrs Chance.'

'Oh.' Hoskins nodded and looked at her again. 'The real thing at last.'

Jack Chance, of course, would go for such a vision as Julie. Like a hungry pigeon after a dropped sandwich. Hoskins saw her as a rather old-fashioned girl, reminiscent of the 1960s and the Bardot cult. Modern girls of her age and class, it seemed to him, dressed either like paratroopers or Popeye the Sailor. Chance pushed open the door.

'All right, then, Julie?'

'I had to go shopping at lunch,' she said, the voice a half-educated whine much as Hoskins had expected.

'I wasn't here then anyway. Get something nice?'

'I got a present for Danny's birthday. A jumper from round the corner.'

'That's great,' Chance said. 'See you after seven.'

He edged back and closed the door, having stayed firmly between Hoskins and the girl.

'You must introduce me next time,' Hoskins said casually.

Chance gave him a suspicious look.

'So long as you don't fancy yourself, Sam. I'm in there with a winning line. She's a nice girl. I mean Julie is a really nice girl.'

'Yes,' Hoskins said wearily. 'Yes, of course. Anyone could see that.'

# Chapter Three

North of Canton, between the valley's facing slopes, the afternoon's storm had cleared a little. Winter sun caught a brief gap in relays of slate-wet cloud. It touched the bald hump of hills in the distance. On those moorland heights, heather and scrub had withered in cold December rain to a Gold Flake tobacco-brown. There was a gust of wind and the cloud snuffed out the watery sun. As the breeze fell away, a lower rain-sky darkened the valley opening beyond the Northern Quadrant sweep of Canton Ring-Road. Patrolman Terry Cross looked at himself in the car mirror from under the slashed peak of his cap with its white nylon cover. He put the lapel microphone to his mouth.

'Nothing this end, boss,' he said lazily. 'Not a sign. You don't think they took the cut through to the motorway over the Crest road?'

'No,' said Wallace Dudden's voice irritably. 'We've got the junction covered both sides with the video. Traffic Control's certain that the car and occupants must be in the Mordaunt Lane area. Could be parked somewhere. Outside a pub, more than likely. They left the Hope and Anchor north of Mordaunt village about five minutes ago. A right carload of little monkeys. Well pissed after lunch by the look of it. We don't want slaughter on the motorway or in the city centre. Landlady, Mrs Preece, thinks it was a Citroën saloon. Reddish.'

'Nothing here, sarge.' Cross worked the last of a cheese sandwich from behind his teeth.

There was a murmur over the airwaves as Sergeant Dudden turned to talk to someone else in the control room. Then he was back.

'Best thing is, Terry, you and Bob McPhail drive north on the valley road. Turn off down Mordaunt Lane a hundred yards or so. Set up a road check near the junction with the valley road. For public consumption, it's called a road safety survey. That'll stop 'em one way. I've got another mobile with Jock Craigmiller and Harry Matthews in it, heading for Mordaunt Lane the other way from the M42 junction at the Crest. That just about puts the cork in the bottle. And don't be bashful about it. Mr Clitheroe wants high profile on drink-and-driving until the festive season's laid to rest.'

'Right-o, boss,' said Cross philosophically. He crumpled the sandwich wrapping in his lap and tucked it into the glove compartment. Then he turned to Bob McPhail in the seat beside him. McPhail put his cap on and pulled a face at himself in the wing-mirror.

'You fancy looking the other way when they drive past, Terry?'

'What I don't fancy,' Cross said, 'is sick all over these car seats and the inside of the limo stinking like a four-ale bar for the next week. Or stinking of bulk purchase disinfectant by courtesy of the motorpool cleaners. Like driving a mobile casualty department after that lot's been over it.'

He let in the clutch and they moved off smoothly from the concrete bridge spanning the two-lane arterial road of the Northern Quadrant. Driving away from the city, Cross followed the valley road. Tall spruce trees clothed the nearer heights, the winter woods bare and grey like rockface. Further up the valley were the white toy-houses of scattered hill farms, the tin roofs of quarry buildings, the tall transmitters of Coastal Network Television and the Radio Canton mast. This bleak northern edge of Canton might have been the industrial foot-hills of the Pyrenees or the Apennines. But already the new look-alike estates of Clearwater programmers and software salesmen had claimed the first of the lower slopes.

'Who's coming the other way to meet us?' McPhail asked.

Cross scowled and pulled out round a faltering motorbike. 'Jock Craigmiller and Harry Matthews.'

'And the best of luck,' McPhail said sardonically. 'I wouldn't mind them getting there first. I've had enough of asking sir to blow into the little bag this Christmas. Eleven positives in six thousand breathalysers. Road blocks, aggro, kicks up the arse from the public, shouted at, spat on, and all for what? Waste of everyone's time.'

The green eye on the dashboard blinked with a steady click-clock as Cross signalled to turn right into Mordaunt Lane.

'Season of goodwill,' he said casually. 'Divorce rate goes through the roof and domestic wounding hits the top of the chart. Nothing like Christmas together for bringing out the homicidal streak in Mr and Mrs Average.'

He pulled in a hundred yards or so along the lane to Mordaunt, a field-gate on one side and a tall bank of woodland on the other. A mist like the warm breath of cattle hung above the dank ploughland beyond. Drawing the car into the space by the field-gate, Cross parked it conspicuously and unclipped his seat-belt. Wallace Dudden's traffic check was in place. McPhail looked over his shoulder towards the rear of the car.

'I'm going to take one of the welcome signs and put it up ahead, Terry. If Wallace Dudden's right, we could end up being rammed head-on by this carload of comedians. You stay put here in case they see us and try to do a bunk.'

'Any luck,' Cross said, 'they'll go the other way. Motorway has to be more likely than Mordaunt Lane. If that happens, Jock and Harry can have the glory.'

McPhail grunted. He went to the boot of the car and took out the familiar blue sign with its white lettering.

STOP

POLICE VEHICLE CHECK

He walked away to position the sign about thirty yards from the squad car, while Cross turned on the blue pulse of the roof-lamp and the hazard lights. As McPhail propped the sign in place on the grass verge, he listened for the sound of a car engine approaching. There was nothing except the distant murmur of traffic on the main valley road. It seemed that Jock and Harry must be having the pleasure of this one.

He was about to turn away when he heard a car door being closed gently with a muffled click. Walking softly towards the bend in the lane, McPhail saw a maroon flank of pressed steel through the twigs that overhung from the raised hedge. He put his mouth close to the lapel microphone.

'Romeo Four. Suspect vehicle parked in Mordaunt Lane about one hundred yards from the valley road junction. I'm going down a bit closer. Try and see what they're up to. Tell Terry Cross.'

'Understood Romeo Four. Watch yourself. There's probably a few of them in it. Hang back a bit until Charlie Five gets to you.'

McPhail walked forward cautiously in the raw mist of

the winter afternoon, between the tall hedges of the narrow country road. It was not his terrain. The streets of dockland Peninsula or the arterial stretches of the motorway were home ground. Countryside was different. Unpredictable and tricky. Bramble-thickets and cow-pats.

There were three or four faces in the maroon-coloured car.

'Romeo Four. Could be the one we want. Looks like several of them inside. One of them just got back in, probably out for a leak. Over.'

'Understood Romeo Four,' said Wallace Dudden's voice again. 'Just watch them, Bob. Chat them up, if necessary. Nothing stronger. Wait for Jock and Harry to get down Mordaunt Lane to join you. Give us the number and we'll check the SP.'

McPhail walked closer to the red car. They were talking and laughing to one another, paying him no attention. Whichever one had got out of the car was back inside now. That made it easier. He put his mouth to his lapel and talked to his condenser microphone again.

'Romeo Four. See if you can check registration number E4800 PMY. Red saloon. Looks like a Saab. That's it, sarge, I think I'm spotted. I'll go and have a friendly chat. No point standing here like a spare part.'

McPhail felt the wet gritty mud of the narrow road through his soles as he went casually towards the car. He tapped on the driver's window. The boy inside wound it down and looked at him, surprised and amused by the sight of the patrolman's cap with its white cover. McPhail listened for Cross starting the white Rover patrol car to come to his assistance. Dudden would see to that.

'We're carrying out a road safety check on Mordaunt Lane,' McPhail said quietly to the driver. 'Just routine. This your vehicle, is it?'

'For what it matters to you it is,' the driver said. McPhail let it go.

'So long as you're driving it.' He took out a notepad. 'You've consumed intoxicating liquor in the past two hours, have you?'

The boy could hardly check his laughter. 'You think I'm pissed?'

'If he's not pissed,' said a girl from the back of the car,

'he's been wasting good money. You feel like asking for a refund, Raz?'

McPhail put his hand out.

'Ignition key,' he said sharply. 'And don't muck me about. You've got a patrol car both sides of you.'

The boy shrugged, took the key from the ignition and handed it out through the window.

McPhail took a step back, giving room for the car door to open.

'Now get out of the car.'

The boy shrugged again, as if it were all the same to him. He pushed the door open and pulled himself out.

'Now turn round,' McPhail said. 'I'm taking you to the other car.'

The teenager was tall and fair-haired with a high colour and the hint of a dimpled 'sonny boy' face. He looked back once at his friends in the silent car. Their bravado seemed knocked cold. Doubt was settling on them.

McPhail and the boy walked without speaking for about ten yards to the curve in the road. Then from behind him McPhail heard the whining suction of a car thrown into reverse. Some clever little bugger had sparked it across. Or else there was a second ignition key. Probably not a key, McPhail thought. Cars were stolen with the only one available.

'You and your friends really fancy trouble, don't you, son?' he said for the boy's benefit.

The engine faded and then roared in confident forward gear. McPhail saw it coming, puddle-water and grit from the surface of the lane flying to either side of its broad tyres. The engine-note rose, gears changing up in a fury of acceleration. McPhail and the boy in his custody turned to opposite sides of the lane, McPhail moving towards the patrol car and the safety of the field-gate. But the second driver of the Saab knew what depended on him now. Freedom or a cell that stank like a vulture's crotch, while the world went on without him. Six or seven years with a real Crown Court stone-face handing it out.

McPhail turned to look back once. Though he went for the hedge, there was no escape through its packed twigs. The heavy maroon car caught him at flashing speed, its nearside corner striking the small of his back as he stumbled, lifting him several feet in the air like a gored matador. The speed of the Saab was such that the nearer edge of the windshield caught him again as he fell. McPhail wheeled in the air again and went headfirst into the packed stone of the roadway. Coat flailing, he landed with a thump and was still. It happened with a speed that tricked the eye, like a practised croupier flipping over a pack of cards.

Ignoring the boy who stood pressed against the other hedge, the driver of the Saab gathered speed as Terry Cross pulled the patrol car out to cut off the route of the escape. The Saab driver saw the white Rover moving and tensed his foot on the brake. The maroon car slithered side to side in the muddy lane like a toboggan in a chute of ice. Cross got out on the far side of the car just before the Saab hit its rear wing and bounced to a halt.

'Stay where you are!'

But by the time that Terry Cross had walked back six feet to the rear of the damaged patrol car, the driver of the Saab was out and on his feet.

'You asked for this!' he shouted furiously. 'You good as asked for this on bended knees! You stupid bastard!'

'Stay where you are! This road is blocked in both directions.'

Cross took a step closer with a look of confidence he could scarcely have felt.

'Get back!'

'Don't be a silly bugger,' Cross said more quietly.

There was no indication that the second boy caught these words. His hand came up with the snout of the sawn-off Eley revolver. The lane rang hard and cold to a sharp rasping explosion. Cross went back against the damaged wing of the white Rover and slid to a sitting position. The lane rang a second time to the same hoarse metallic bark.

The gunman got back into the car and drove against the snapping twigs of the hedge to get round the damaged police Rover. The first driver of the Saab was running to catch them. The second boy waved him on and watched him get into the Saab.

A moment of utter stillness was broken only by a liquid whispering from the damaged patrol car. A drip that grew to a trickle had begun to gather from the ruptured fuel tank beneath the tail. The boy who had shot Terry Cross went back to the wrecked car. The policeman's body lay hatless against it, his head down as if in a doze.

'You bastard!' the boy said softly, his teeth clenched with the fury of what he had been made to do by Cross' stupidity. 'You brainless bastard!'

The others watched him, as if frightened to speak. He towered over them in his fury. Holding out the Eley at arm's length in a double grip, he fired into the spilling petrol. There was a spurt of grit from the lane as the crack of the revolver rang and reverberated across the cold ploughland. He fired again and the hammer hit the cartridge casing with a dead click. But the first shot had taken effect after all. There was a dancing flame, like the brandy on a Christmas pudding. As he ran back towards the Saab, the buckled patrol car emitted an exhalation no louder than a gas fire igniting. But already the flames were cradling the dented metalwork and the body of Patrolman Terry Cross. A thin spiral of oily smoke drifted up above the winter lanes and the skeletal trees of the ploughed fields.

None of them spoke. There was no hysteria, scarcely any surprise, only the quiet precision of deep shock. They had done something which they had always supposed they might have to do, sooner or later. A quiet sobriety settled on Wallace Dudden's 'carload of monkeys'. The teenage gunman slid in behind the wheel with the fair-haired 'sonny boy' in the passenger seat. Gently, as if not to disturb the thoughts of his companions, he started the car and moved off down the lane. Behind him, he was aware of an explosion of some kind from the wreck of the burning Rover.

'Suppose he wasn't dead?' said the girl in the back numbly.

'They were both dead,' the young gunman said. 'I saw that one close up. Right between the eyes. He went down like a ton of bricks.'

'You can't know!'

'Shut it, all of you,' the driver said. 'What's done is done. You get that ignition key back, did you, Raz?'

'It was in his hand when you hit him. Could be in the ditch. They might find it when they start going over the place. Maybe not for a day or two.'

'That's it then,' the boy at the wheel said. 'This car goes. This afternoon. Well out of sight.'

On the valley road, they filtered into the traffic moving towards Clearwater and a suburban dual-carriageway that ended on Atlantic Wharf. The afternoon was brighter, a thin white cloud behind the lower slant of the sun. Like the silver umbrella of a photographer's studio, it turned the disc of light to a circlet of blinding fire, shining directly and painfully into the eyes.

'It wasn't our fault,' the curly-haired front-passenger said quietly. He was the calmest of them all now. 'Not what we wanted. If we'd put our hands up, not one of us would see the light of day again for eight or ten years. Not with what we've done. Them or us. Like war. We never used the gun before. But there was always a risk we'd have to. Tommo did it for us. Remember that. We owe him. All of us. Next thing is to lay hands on ready money.'

'Now?' The third boy, who had taken no part, asked the question doubtfully.

'Now,' the driver said. 'Before they find out what's done. Before they get organised. When that happens, you won't hardly move in this town. Agreed?'

'I don't know,' said the boy in the back. As they crossed over the Northern Quadrant Flyover and came down into Clearwater, he began to cry silently. The girl put her arm round him and cuddled him.

Then she leant towards the adolescent gunman in front of her.

'You fool!' she said gently. 'What d'you think your dad's going to do when he hears about this?'

He grinned at her in the mirror.

'Much the same as your cow of a mother's likely to do with you,' he said scornfully. 'How're they ever going to hear anything, unless we tell them?'

Four miles off, above the pink tarmac of the Mall, its Viennese domes and clock-tower of City Hall, its white government offices and Memorial Gardens, Sergeant Dudden looked at the VHF receiver that was bringing him the news. He waited for Craigmiller to finish.

'You'll have fire service,' he said, responding mechanically. 'Ambulance with resuscitation equipment. Divisional back-up. You'll have three cars with you in about five minutes. Bloody hell, Jock, what's happened down there?'

The receiver emitted a bleep, like a warning from a life-support system. Craigmiller's voice sounded clipped through the Rice Krispie static.

'Don't know, boss. A bomb could have gone off, for all I can see. That's what it looks like. And it could have been an ambush. If we're lucky, Bob McPhail might hold on. It's so close at the moment, we can't hardly tell. But he's got to have doctors and hospital, boss. Quickly.'

# Chapter Four

In the fading light of the dank January afternoon, the Chief Inspector and his sergeant walked back across the windy sea front of Ocean Beach to the parked car. Hoskins handed Chance his folded copy of the *Canton Evening Globe*. Its headline was page-wide in thick banner-type: BONNIE AND CLYDE M-WAY DRUGS HAUL.

'Bonnie and Clyde!' said Hoskins grumpily. 'Will you look at that nonsense. Seems one of the little bastards was a girl.'

Chance handed it back.

'Lunchtime news said it was a delivery from the infirmary. Nothing about a drugs haul. That's your mate Gerald Foster and our friends of the press.'

Hoskins shivered as an ocean squall caught them across the wrinkling surface of the shadowed tide. The rain had blown over but the late afternoon wind from the Channel was piercingly chill.

'Yes,' he said. 'Still I don't suppose they knocked off a hospital van just to get a load of bed-pans and bandages. Thing about Gerald Foster, most of what he writes is guesswork. But almost every time he guesses right. That's journalism for you.'

Chance started the car.

'If you was going to stop off in Lantern Hill for any reason, Sam, I could pass an hour or so here. Run you over there and then come back.'

A brief image of Lesley crossed Hoskins' mind: the firm pallor of the hips, the sleek breasts and back, the rather sulky self-possession of the face with its pudding-basin crop of straight fair hair and parted fringe. He tried to dress the image suggestively in translucent bedroom lingerie, even in the utilitarian costume of black cotton briefs and thin sweater. Then he remembered that her Wednesday afternoons were occupied. Community Centre crèche for working mothers. Refuges for battered wives. The good works of a feminist conscience, he supposed.

'No, my son,' he said firmly. 'You had your canteen break a couple of hours back.'

Chance hummed to himself as they followed the sweep of Bay Drive and turned up Clifton Hill. The little hotels were dark and shuttered after the brief Christmas season. The ice cream parlour stood locked and empty. Only the filling-station at the top was lit, its forecourt wet and wind-swept.

'It was different when you was witness-tickling out Lantern Hill,' Chance said.

'She wasn't a witness, Jack. Someone she lived with was killed. That's all.'

'Not much she wasn't!' Chance said quietly, as if to himself. 'And you should have seen your face when you come back from taking evidence off her! Looked like you put your hand in your pocket for a hanky and come out with a fifty-quid note.'

They crossed the roundabout at the top of the hill and joined the dual-carriageway of the Canton Link. The sun was lower. Its glare of molten silver turned the Atlantic horizon-line to a fuzz like wind-blown spray. The inland terrain across which the colourless brilliance fell was lit sharply as a silhouette. Hoskins realised with surprise that he could pick out individual rooftops miles away in Lantern Hill or Orient. On the western coast, the bays and cliffs in shadow were already dark as twilight. A long frothing sea, the colour of suds, was driving in with a broad cold sweep of running waves. The wind had not yet turned the shallow tide to storm. But Hoskins had known this coastline all his life. The storm was coming. He had no doubt of that.

Jack Chance was not one to give up easily.

'So what's on until seven o'clock?'

Hoskins continued to stare at the sea.

'I've got last night's tapes to listen to. The pirate radio merchants on the *Hit-Back Show*. Last night they gave out four names. Two assistant tax inspectors, one traffic warden, one social worker. Gave their full names, addresses, car numbers, who the wives are, where the kids go to school. Anyone who's got a grudge against them, and wants to hit back, can go looking. And he'll know just where to look.'

Chance picked up speed on the Canton Link. 'Just bloody silly,' he said. 'The whole thing.'

'But effective,' Hoskins said. 'There was one of the senior tax people last month. Sour as vinegar and mean as a stoat with the trembling tax-dodgers. Reckoning was, he used to excite himself by trying to make business ladies cry. Anyway, he was senior enough for his mail to be opened by his office secretaries. So one of 'em opens an envelope addressed to him and inside there's a bondage magazine, all leather and halters. And there's a note addressed to him by his Christian name. Dear John, it says, thanks for the loan of the mag. I thought it might be safer to send it back to you at work, seeing you don't want the wife opening it by accident. Do you want the spanking photos back now or can I borrow them a bit longer? Something along those lines.'

Chance snorted at the absurdity of it.

'Someone's been having you on, Sam!'

'Got it from the secretary herself, my son. Deborah Cameron, as was.'

'They'd all know it was a wind-up.'

'They might,' Hoskins said. 'They probably would. But he's always going to be remembered as the man who got porn in his mail. And he's probably a stoat with his juniors, too. They won't let it drop easily. Not too difficult to ruin a reputation so long as there's one person with a real grudge against you. You got promoted and he didn't. You got a better office than him. Or your secretaries think you act like Heinrich Himmler. Or you treat one better than the other, so there's jealousy.'

'It's dead lead,' Chance said scornfully.

Hoskins shrugged. 'Mud sticks, my son. They're all going to laugh their heads off behind his back. Jokes about "Mr Bound-to-Please". In this case, they decided to transfer the bloke to another tax district. After that, almost everyone believed it.'

'Neat,' Chance said.

From behind a grey bank of cloud the shafts and bars of the low sun caught the ocean like stage spotlights with a pale smoky gold of Christmas tinfoil.

Hoskins roused himself from images of Lesley as they came on to the Northern Quadrant.

'Sod it!' Chance said suddenly. The illuminated panel on the overhead gantry was flashing 40. The one beyond that advised 20. Then the hazard lights on the cars in front began to flash through the twilight as the drivers halted in a patient queue.

Hoskins sat with his arms folded, staring at the inexplicable traffic jam ahead.

'My dad reckoned it was all the bright politicians and civil servants of the future that volunteered for war in 1914. All killed in a few months. Affected the breeding stock of the ruling-class, he used to say. Meant we had to make do with thick-heads in charge from then on. I think of that every time I'm stuck on this joke of a motorway. Two lanes! Imagine any-one deliberately planning a two-lane motorway. Hardly room to mend a pothole without closing the thing down. No one in this country's been able to design anything properly for the past fifty years. Now, you take kitchen equipment . . . '

Chance tapped his fingers irritably on the steering wheel of the Sierra. They had passed the Clearwater interchange. It was several miles to the Mount Pleasant turn-off. Ahead of them on the east-bound carriageway nothing moved. The red procession of tail-lights, two and two, was halted down the mile or more of slope that ran behind Taylors Town and Orient. There must be three or four miles of puffing exhaust pipes and drivers in shirt-sleeves trying to mimic the thrusting young executive. Along the urban motorway the sodium glow of the concrete lamp-standards outshone the twilight. Beyond this bronze fluorescence the world had gone black.

Jack Chance sighed and pretended to listen to Hoskins on Design. They were on the higher section of the Northern Quadrant, level with the fields on one side and Clearwater's Lady Margaret Estate on the other. Traffic moved with insolent freedom in the west-bound lanes. Beyond the thick wooden rails of the motorway fencing, the estate roads were empty of parked vehicles and the few passing cars sped tan-talisingly past and out of sight. Chance looked at his watch.

'We could have stayed down the Beach after all, Sam. This lot's going to be stuck here half the night.'

Hoskins ignored him. He turned on the courtesy-light and did his best to absorb the *Canton Evening Globe*. Presently he seemed to brighten up at what he read.

'There's a bloke in here reckons we'll be under water a hundred years from now,' he said cheerfully. 'He calculates all the city from Barrier to Orient and inland to Mount Pleasant has to be about twelve foot under.'

'They just built new houses down Barrier,' Chance said moodily.

'And the family page is getting riper. Man impersonated sister-in-law to catch rapist, Canton court told. And the one that never notified his mother's death. Kept the body in the airing-cupboard. Went on drawing her pension. He's pleading poverty. There's quite a good one-parent family's DHSS fraud. Claiming benefit at two addresses simultaneously. And that three-in-a-bed case is still going on at the Crown Court. Chap that came back and found his missus in bed with another woman.'

'Couldn't tell the difference in the dark,' Chance suggested glumly. He glared at a scrap wagon on the hard shoulder. Its engine cowling was wet and the steam of a boiling radiator rose in drifts through the orange lamplight. Hoskins continued to read happily from the court case.

'That's more or less what the bloke's saying. Couldn't tell one from the other. Seems they don't believe him. His missus says it's happened before. No wonder Gerald Foster sells copies with yarns like that. He's wearing hand-made suits now. Let's see what other little gems of family life we've got.'

'Hang on, Sam,' Chance said suddenly. 'What's going on over there?'

'Where?'

'Over there. Hard shoulder. Far side of the other carriageway.'

Hoskins turned the corner of his newspaper aside. Two young men were climbing over the wooden rails of the four-foot barrier fence. They seemed to have come from the narrow strip of grassland dividing the urban motorway and the sodium-lit streets of Clearwater's Lady Margaret Estate.

'Could be a knock-off,' Hoskins said. 'Looting houses on the estate. Making a quick exit across the fast lane. Can't imagine a foot-patrol chasing 'em across that.'

The two youths stood on the white line dividing the hard shoulder from the lanes of the west-bound carriageway. Unlike the jammed east-bound traffic, the Ocean Beach commuters were moving freely and fast.

'They're going to make a run for it!' Chance said. 'Cheeky little sods!'

Almost at once, the first of the youths set off in a diagonal sprint towards the grey metal crash-barrier of the central reservation. The other followed, by instinct rather than judgment, through the moving traffic of the west-bound lanes. Several vehicles began to swerve and weave, as if to avoid the second runner, then disappeared towards Ocean Beach and Sandbar in a whining protest of car horns.

Hoskins reached to open his door.

'Get on the blower, Jack. Tell Traffic Division we've got blood sports on the west-bound carriageway. They can get a patrol down that side easily enough.'

Putting down his folded newspaper, he slipped out of the passenger door and moved forward between the lines of stationary vehicles on the east-bound carriageway. The two runners were now in consultation on the narrow grass-strip of the central reservation with its grey low-level crash-barrier.

'Sam!' It was Chance shouting from behind him. 'Watch it! The tall one's carrying a shotgun!'

At the same moment Hoskins saw for himself the twin barrels of the weapon that one of the runners was carrying. The fugitives turned, hearing Chance's shout. Hoskins crouched and moved forwards behind the outer line of cars. The police Sierra was in the fast lane of the Northern Quadrant. There came a blast that ended with a sound like a handful of hard-flung grit and the crackling of shattered glass. He heard the second barrel, the pellets of shot scattering on the tarmac road surface.

'Get back, Sam! They've seen you!'

Hoskins crouched at the rear of a Toyota Corolla. But there was nothing more. Edging across to the hard shoulder, he saw the two youths scramble over the bars of the motorway fence and drop down on the far side. Hoskins raced after them and tried to do the same. He was astride the fence when he heard a crack that echoed round the night sky of the urban ring. A fragment of wood splintered somewhere on the fence-rail, ten or twelve feet from him. By the time that he landed on the wet grass in the darkness, the two figures had sprinted across the little field and were in a half-lit stretch of new housing beyond. He saw them take a corner and disappear. Even before he got to it, there was the slamming of car doors, the grinding of an engine out of gear, and then the fading sound of the vehicle as it raced somewhere towards the city centre and the docks.

Hoskins turned back, feeling his trouser-legs wet from

the grass. He walked slowly and uncomfortably. Chance was standing on the hard shoulder by the fence.

'I sent the news to Division. They want us back now. No hanging about here. Straight back.'

Hoskins looked about him at the stationary traffic.

'Someone ought to stay and show 'em what's what, Jack. There's a real firearm out there. Apart from the shotgun. Took a bit out of the fence. Somewhere along there. They'll need proper lighting, metal detector and a team to search for the bullet and the cartridge case. Might be on the hard shoulder but more likely in the grass.'

'Tactical Support Unit, Sam, armed and ready,' Chance said. 'They're bringing 'em down the west-bound carriageway and then closing the ring-road both sides. I told them we'd had shots fired. But we're to go straight back as soon as this lot starts moving. Armed officers only. Clitheroe's orders. And, by the way, a lorry driver had a word on his radio with one of his mates up front. Seems a transporter came down the Hawks Hill approach, ploughed right across the motorway and blocked all three lanes about half an hour ago.'

'What a mess,' said Hoskins bitterly. 'Look at this lot! Anyone get caught in those shotgun blasts?'

Chance shook his head as they got back into the Sierra. He closed the door and reached for his seat-belt.

'There's a Mini without a windscreen but the girl's all right. Wheeled her on to the hard shoulder until the pick-up gets here.'

'We ought to be staying here to show the support group the lay-out,' Hoskins said, still grumbling as the first sign of movement appeared far along the lines of halted cars.

Chance started the engine. 'I gave 'em the exact location and details. Armed officers only, Mr Clitheroe says. Very emphatic, the message that came over.'

The traffic began to edge forward at last, gathering speed until it was trundling at ten or fifteen miles an hour. Then the frustrated mortgage-payers of Clearwater and Hawks Hill began a demented Grand Prix race towards the evening paradise of the semi-detached and the double garage. Hoskins turned in his seat and saw, on the three lanes of the opposite carriageway, a trio of white Rovers with their blue lights revolving, headlamps on full beam and sirens whooping. He turned round again.

'I reckon I counted at least four Desperate Dans in black suits and carrying telescopics. Probably bag something for the pot.'

'Nothing else coming down that side,' Chance said. 'They must have closed it. Should manage to block the rush-hour traffic in both directions. Can't have been easy to arrange.'

# Chapter Five

The headquarters building of Canton City Police rose beyond the public gardens of the Mall and City Hall. Its bull-nosed oblong, topped by radio masts and disc receivers, gave it the air of a concrete battle-cruiser. At the nearer end stood the main lobby of plate-glass, rubber plants and reception counter. At the far end was a side-door by the motorpool. The combination lock opened in response to a correct tune played on computerised buttons beside the steel frame. There was no lift at this entrance. The stairs to the fifth floor CID offices were quiet and deserted in the early evening, removed from general use. Leaving the parked Sierra, Hoskins and Chance began their climb.

The fifth-floor corridor was empty as their shoes squealed on the new vinyl tiles. Hoskins turned at the door of his office, before his companion could disappear into the sergeants' room next to it.

'First of all, young Chance, get something down on paper about that motorway fiasco. I want it tidied away.'

'What about Catte?'

'My undivided attention later on,' said Hoskins grimly. 'Right now, I'd get a real lift from seeing those truculent little sods on the motorway banged up.'

He went in and closed the door behind him. With the time of arrival noted in his duty diary, he folded his arms on the high window-sill and stared out across the city. Half an hour ago he had been shot at twice. He told himself that it happened. It was true. And it had left no more impression on him than being snowballed by urchins in the street. He felt so exhausted that reality was ceasing to affect him. And that was dangerous.

Nor was there much comfort in the visit to Ocean Beach. Hoskins began to see Billy Catte's point of view. The whole discussion had been futile. Catte was right about that. Whatever the truancy patrol or the social services might think, Melanie Paget and Taylors Town Comprehensive School had nothing more to offer one another. But the law, in the shape of Superintendent Ripley and Clitheroe as ACC Crime, still wanted Billy Catte. Not so much on behalf of Melanie Paget but as a matter of public policy. There was a feeling abroad that Billy Catte was long overdue. To Hoskins, such feelings spelt trouble.

He stared out across the city. In his mind, he composed one report on the visit to Ocean Beach and another on the Northern Quadrant 'incident', as it would soon be known. The corner-room allocated to him was across the corridor from Superintendent Ripley with the CID sergeants' room between them at the end of the building. On the other side was a room whose door carried the message POLICE SURGEON. KEEP LOCKED.

Hoskins had two windows. The present one looked inland towards the affluent ridge of Hawks Hill, where the gardens had mature trees in them and the roads were quiet between high walls and gabled roofs. By this time of night in January the hill was nothing but a pin-prick map of street-lights. At the city's verge, beyond Clearwater, the terrain opened out into the long industrial valley edged by the first slopes of a mountain landscape. A toy castle with conical turrets, a Pre-Raphaelite design of the 1870s from a mediaeval tapestry, rose distantly among the trees. To the nearer side of Hawks Hill was the beginning of Mount Pleasant, the fortress tower-blocks of council tenants, where the single-storey pubs with their thick roofs of concrete slab and slit windows to reduce breakage had the appearance of air-raid shelters left over from Hitler's war.

The other window was the one Hoskins preferred. It showed the real Canton, built on a wide alluvial foreshore that was almost below sea-level. Ahead of him stretched the civic centre and the pink tarmac of the Mall with its memorial gardens and cherry trees now dark with early frost. City Hall and the Museum in their slabs of pale Edwardian stone were topped by domes and flying chariots in bronze like Parisian pavilions for a long-forgotten world fair. Beyond them, the buses and department stores of Great Western Street led down to Atlantic Wharf and the protective bank against the sea, the route upon which the railway had been raised.

A hundred years before, east of the Wharf, Dutch engineers had constructed a barrier against the tides. It had given its name to the thousand shabby rows of back-to-back houses sheltered by it. The Barrier district once provided a work-force for the ships and the coal trade. To the western side of Atlantic Wharf lay Peninsula and the docks, the flat com-pacted silt jutting out to form a bay or natural harbour. Between Hoskins and Peninsula was the final district of Canton proper: the narrow streets and little houses, the clubs, pubs, and restaurants of Orient. Its name had come from the first overseas trade of the city docks, long before the coal or the development of the city's 'Chinatown'.

Hoskins' one sentimental indulgence was this brooding upon the city where he had been born and where, without a doubt, he would die. The rest of the British population seemed to have become a race of nomads, moving house every eighteen months, chasing after jobs or schools from Bradford to Ealing, to Wrexham and Stirling. Bloody point-less, Hoskins thought. The phone rang.

'Sam? That you? Gerald Foster. I'm down the *Western World* night-desk and I'm getting more horse manure from your press office than I can ever remember. What the hell's going on, Sam?'

'Nothing's going on, Gerald. I've just this minute took my coat off. Had a difference of opinion with some teenage yobboes about half an hour back. That's all.'

'Don't give me that, Sam! I'm talking about a police patrol driver and his mate, shot dead apparently, between Clearwater and Mordaunt.'

Hoskins felt as if the floor had collapsed under him and he had fallen five storeys to the basement.

'I've just been out there,' he said softly, as if that would make their deaths untrue. 'There was some young thick-head waving a shotgun. He fired it and missed. And the one with his Lone Ranger kit missed as well.'

But he knew Gerald Foster. He knew Foster was going to be right.

'Been out where, Sam? I'm talking about this afternoon. Earlier on. They brought two of them into the infirmary about half-past three. One shot dead and burnt beyond recognition. The other in a hell of a mess. No confirmation that he was shot as well or what happened to him. No one's saying if he's alive or dead now. I can't afford to get it wrong on tomorrow's breakfast-tables, Sam. Come on.'

Hoskins sat down at his desk.

'Wait a minute, Gerald. I've just come back from the Northern Quadrant. There were two yobboes loosing off a shotgun and another firearm in a tail-back of stationary traffic.'

'When was this?'

'About half an hour ago.'

'That's the third lot today,' Foster said incredulously. 'The hospital van held up by gunmen on the Eastern Causeway this morning. PCs McPhail and Cross shot in Mordaunt Lane this afternoon. And now this lark of yours. You reckon it's all the same bunch?'

'Bob McPhail and Terry Cross? You sure?'

'Where the hell have you been this afternoon, Sam?'

'Questioning a witness down the Beach. With Jack Chance.'

'No one tried to raise you?'

'No reason they should, Gerald. I was booked out down the Beach. Interviewing a client. Hang on.'

At that moment Chance knocked and entered in a single unceremonious movement. He stood on Hoskins' regulation square of russet carpet, urging haste in frantic dumbshow.

'Sam?' Foster's voice quacked at the far end of the line.

'Gerald, I've got to go. I'll find out what I can and call you later tonight.'

He put the phone down before Foster could draw breath.

'Those little bastards!' Chance was huge with anger, the only time Hoskins could remember it. 'They killed McPhail and Cross. The two Paddies on the cars.'

Hoskins looked at his hands. 'That was Gerald Foster. Same thing. Two of them shot.'

'One shot, one run down on purpose,' Chance said more calmly. 'And it's Ripley's office straightaway. Preferably with a story about what took so long getting back from the Beach.'

Hoskins got up and they crossed the corridor. As Ripley's door opened, Hoskins understood why the fifth floor had seemed deserted. They were all in the Ripper's office. Standing room only. There was the dark-moustached Edwardian-poisoner face of Clitheroe, the new ACC Crime. There was Superintendent Maxwell Ripley, a tall grey man in his middle fifties, blunted and worn by experience. He seemed to droop and pant a little like a beagle at the end of a long hunt. It was common knowledge that his retirement was now two years away and he was nursing his blood pressure. All the Ripper wanted was a quiet spell to coast home. There were DCI

Tom Nicholls and DCI Betteridge, Clitheroe's 'left-hand men', as the description went. Wallace Dudden, Dave Tappin and Stan McArthur were there from the sergeants' room, next to DI Clarke and DI Perceval, newly made up. They stood motionless along the far wall, staring at Hoskins and Chance, like school prefects posing for a team photograph.

'Where the hell were you, Sam?' It was almost a snap from Ripley, showing the ACC Crime that here was a super who could manage men. Behind his own desk, with the framed photograph and the personal ruler, the Ripper was in command.

'Down the Beach trying to get evidence from Billy Catte.' Hoskins gave the excuse for a second time in as many minutes. 'Where I was supposed to be.'

'You know the score?' Clitheroe asked gently.

'I do now.'

'Good,' Clitheroe turned away. 'Carry on, Mr Ripley.'

Hoskins interrupted without apology.

'The score also includes two guns fired on the Northern Quadrant about half an hour ago.'

'Northern Quadrant? The Tactical Support Unit call?' Clitheroe narrowed his eyes to a squint. 'Do I take it that it was you and Jack Chance out there?'

Hoskins nodded. 'A couple of athletes, probably robbing houses on Lady Margaret Estate. When noticed, they made a dive across the motorway. No one's going to follow them across lines of speeding traffic in the west-bound lanes. They had a car parked down one of the country roads beyond. Nothing on the east-bound motorway could move an inch. Two breakdowns blocking the hard shoulder for good measure. We could have stayed and put the Support Unit in the picture.'

The tension in Clitheroe's face suggested a personal affront.

'After what happened earlier this afternoon, I will not have unarmed officers facing armed fugitives. The press and the politicians would crucify us if something else went wrong now.'

Hoskins shrugged. 'Tactical Support won't find much to do out there now.'

'And Mr Hoskins was shot at twice when he went after them over the barrier-rail,' Chance said loyally.

Ripley touched both ends of his cylindrical ruler, raised it, and lowered it into place again.

'Did you get a proper sight of them, Sam?'

Hoskins shook his head.

'Not a good one, Max. Youngish, one with dark hair, the other fair. Tall rather than short. Five-ten to six foot. Eighteen to twenty years old. Had their backs to me mostly. I'd say they were probably the same ones as this morning. You don't usually get imitations that fast.'

'The landlady behind the bar of the Hope and Anchor at Mordaunt village,' Tom Nicholls said, 'Mrs Preece. One of them came in and she wouldn't serve him. Probably under-age and certainly drunk already. He wanted a couple of quarts to take away. She saw him go back to the car and drive off. That's when she phoned us.'

'Did she recognise any pictures?'

Nicholls shook his head. 'Derek Holland took her through several albums this afternoon. About half a dozen faces might have been him but she couldn't say. We're checking them out. Couldn't remember his clothes either. Thought the car was a red Citroën.'

'And the car?' Hoskins asked.

'McPhail radioed in the number before he approached them. It's a Saab, not a Citroën. The punter who had it stolen was sobbing down the phone to the desk sergeant about a week ago. After today, I should think it's either down the bottom of the Railway Dock or else folded into a neat square down the Western Reclaim scrapyard.'

Superintendent Ripley let out a long breath.

'As it stands we've had two armed incidents on the urban motorway and two policemen shot dead within the past ten hours. That's something more than an emergency. And we've got our friends of the press baying at the gates. In an hour, at most, there has to be a statement. I don't suppose it's got to make the national news tonight. But Coastal Network Television has to put out something at half-past ten on the local news.'

'Saying that we have the situation in hand,' Hoskins suggested blandly. They all looked at him. Ripley glowered, his shaven gill a blueberry flush.

Clitheroe intervened. The thin poisoner-moustache looked neat as black velvet.

'Drugs,' he said precisely. 'Did your fleeting glimpse of these two fugitives suggest that they might be graduates of the school of pharmacy, Sam?'

Hoskins shook his head. Clitheroe could scarcely conceal a certain satisfaction at the bad news he was about to break.

'That pharmacy van this morning was carrying everything. There were pills that would do no worse than keep you on the bog for a day or two. And there were also quite a few constituents to be used in prescriptions. Try a taste of them as they are and they'd kill you stone dead.'

There was a moment's silence as they absorbed this.

'Four tearaways and a vanload of pharmaceuticals,' Clitheroe went on. 'If they should start marketing them as they are, which is about their level of skill, you'll be picking up bodies from all over the city.'

Hoskins shook his head. 'I doubt it. These yobs have come on a bit in the last year or two. They may not know the technical details but they can soon find someone who does. What worries me is the thought that they're amateurs.'

'Amateurs?' Clitheroe's suspicion suggested that Hoskins might be joking.

'Amateurs,' Hoskins said again. 'No sense of self-preservation. They could have been killed doing that motorway dash. They don't care. And that van hi-jack this morning. It could have gone wrong at any minute. Easily. Police patrol could have pulled up on the hard shoulder. They'd have shot their way out then, easy as this afternoon. And the minute someone gets in their way another time, they'll shoot again. Bloody mad. A professional villain wouldn't go near them. Professionals don't hi-jack a van and park it in a lay-by in full view while they rob it. A good professional would tie up the driver and dump him, drive the van to a yard or a lock-up garage, loot it, then get rid of it. You wouldn't so much as see it again.'

Ripley sat back in his chair, ignoring Hoskins' comments. 'That blasted Northern Quadrant's been nothing but trouble. Traffic piles up in a few minutes. Blocked every morning and every evening. Chaos end to end. Breakdowns on the hard shoulder. Our cars stuck in the tail-back with all the others. The assailants get fed up, abandon their stolen vehicle. They simply step over the line and catch a bus on the nearest street, while our drivers wait in a two-mile queue. There was an exercise at Hendon last year, based on that very premise. Places like the ring-road could end up as a villain's paradise.'

He folded his arms as if challenging contradiction. Then he turned his ruler round.

'I've had Gerald Foster on,' Hoskins said. 'He knows Terry Cross was killed but he said there was some doubt about Bob McPhail.'

Ripley shook his head. 'McPhail wasn't certified dead when they got him to Canton emergency. Someone had a life-support machine on standby. But he was dead already. Head injuries. Terry Cross was shot twice but the first one must have killed him. The bullet went in above the left eyebrow and exited at the back of his head. Mordaunt Lane is taped off. We've found two cartridge cases so far but no bullet. Looks like a forty-five filed to fit a four-five-five.'

'Amateurs,' Hoskins said with morose satisfaction.

There was a moment's silence.

'So what comes next?' Nicholls asked.

Clitheroe sat down on the corner of Ripley's desk.

'It's not usual for ACC Crime to take direct charge of an inquiry. But the murder of two of our officers by armed robbers isn't a usual event. I shall take responsibility for this.'

'What about the Press?' Hoskins asked. 'They've got to hear something from us.'

Clitheroe shrugged.

'Political decisions have to be taken, Sam. Do we tell them to warn the public to watch for signs of danger on the motorway, thereby stoking up panic? Do we announce armed patrols in unmarked cars? Do we put surveillance cameras on every lamp-standard for twenty or thirty miles around? If we do, then who's going to monitor them all? There's no money to call in the special constabulary and pay overtime. We don't want another cock-up like GCHQ. Expensive equipment to monitor four million phone-calls at a time – only to realise you need thousands of people to do it.'

Ripley shook his head.

'And if we go hell-for-leather after a gang of teenagers,' Clitheroe went on, 'how many resources get diverted from elsewhere? The next time a little old lady down in Barrier gets her house turned over, how do we respond? Do we just send a nice young woman in police uniform with victim-support leaflets because the big hairy CID bottoms that should be pressing her best chair-seats and clinking her tea-cups are riding shotgun on the M4? Next time we get a rape complaint, do we ask the subject if she wouldn't mind deciding she enjoyed it after all because that would free more of us for motorway surveillance?'

There was a silence. Clitheroe nodded, as if he had expected it.

'We don't do any of those things, so far as I'm concerned. Instead, we catch these bastards and put them away for as long as possible.'

It was half an hour later when the meeting broke up and Hoskins returned to his office. Before sitting down to his report, he picked up the phone and dialled the *Western World* night-desk.

'Gerald? Sam. I've just come from the meeting. They were both killed. McPhail as well. But he was run down by a car, not shot.'

'I know,' Foster said, 'I got confirmation from the infirmary press office at last, Sam. Thanks anyway. You fancy the Porter's Lodge tomorrow? Twelvish? Buy you lunch.'

'At a price,' Hoskins said sceptically.

Foster laughed. It was the first time Hoskins had heard anyone do it that day.

'You want to get out of Division, Sam. Making you cynical. Nice little number in the security industry might suit you.'

'Balls,' said Hoskins glumly.

Gerald Foster gave a sigh. 'If you say so, Sam. See you tomorrow. Take care.'

Hoskins drew the report form towards him. A siren from one of the patrol cars howled along the Mall, past the domed and deserted City Hall, echoing across the darkened bus bays of King Edward Square. It dwindled over the Town River bridge with estuary mud-flanks gleaming sodium-bronze in the street-lights. Its warning faded among the little streets of Orient with their take-aways and New China Supermarkets, their betting-shops and house-clearance furniture, laundrette and twenty-four-hour funeral service. More powerfully than the Last Post and the full police honours of burial, the electronic requiem of the car siren bore the grief for McPhail and Cross to Peninsula and Barrier, Hawks Hill and Mount Pleasant, Lantern Hill and Harbour Bar.

# Chapter Six

For several months Hoskins had scarcely entered the headquarters canteen at lunchtime. Despite his years in the
Division, it was a place where he felt alone. Jack Chance
and the sergeants had their corner. Maxwell Ripley grew
increasingly preoccupied with Clitheroe, the new ACC
Crime. Tom Nicholls and the others had never been more
than acquaintances. Hoskins' private life was simple and
self-contained. He had been a widower since another man's
motorway miscalculation fifteen years before. 'Solitary as an
oyster.' The phrase from his childhood reading seemed to
describe him now. His habitat was the flat in the 1930s Queen
Anne brick of Lambs Chambers, overlooking the green space
of the Lambs Acre Memorial Ground. Throughout the week
the turf was open and silent. Then, on Saturday afternoons
in winter, the stands roared for a litany of great names in
rugby football. Wasps and Harlequins, London Welsh and
the Barbarians, Cardiff and Blackheath.

Dangerously for a policeman of his sort, his few loyalties
lay outside the Division. Gerald Foster of the *Western World*,
his friend in the fifth-form of Canton Grammar School.
Harold Moyle, another fifth-form bravo, now headmaster of
Shackleton Comprehensive School. Lesley Wiles, the object
of his 'witness-tickling' as Chance called it, on the heights
of Lantern Hill overlooking the placid dock water of the
Peninsula. Despite their original earnest pledge of indepen-
dence, each depended on the other now more than it was
wise to acknowledge.

In driving-coat and leather gauntlets, Hoskins walked across
King Edward Square, past the driverless custard-yellow buses,
on his way to lunch with Gerald Foster. The rain of the
January morning had cleared. Blue sky and streets dark with
moisture reflected a pale winter brilliance. The Porter's Lodge
was in the commercial and banking area of Canton. Narrow
streets ran past it. At one end lay the mudflats and sluggish
tides of the Town River. At the other were the candy-striped
blinds and Edwardian art nouveau of the Great Western Street
department stores.

Foster was waiting in one of the dark wooden booths of the

mock-Gothic pub of the 1890s. Before the coming of steam-tugs, it had been a lodge where the dock porters waited in a sawdust bar to unload the sailing barques that came upstream to the city's heart. The Lodge offered Hoskins anonymity. Policy salesmen and bank clerks packed it with a rumble of lunchtime conversation. No one else from 'A' Division ever set foot there so far as he knew. Its interior was chocolate-dark mahogany brought from Brazil with the old coffee trade on the river wharf. The gloss on the polished wood had the electric sheen of a silk dress. Hoskins felt at home with the frosted leads of the windows and the coloured glass of bottles lining the mirrored bar. The white stucco of the dado with its Tudor roses had long since darkened to a creamy brown under the pall of tobacco smoke which never seemed to clear. It suited him. There was comfort in the warm tobacco-fogged air.

Foster, a short and thick-set figure with a bunch of dark hair greying and brushed back hard, raised a hand from his booth as Hoskins pushed open the mullion-windowed door of the Victoria Saloon.

'You must have had a pig of a day yesterday, Sam,' he said philosophically as Hoskins sat down. 'I had no idea I was breaking bad news when I phoned.'

Hoskins settled himself in the corner of the tabled booth, which had the air of a narrow four-poster bed. He looked about hopefully for a waitress.

'Not to worry, Gerald. It's the Ripper that wants your arse over a barrel, not me.'

'What for?'

Hoskins paused. A girl in her porter's uniform of bowler hat, blouse, tall boots and black tights took Foster's order for two plates of sausage and mash with pints of Jupp's Special Brew. Foster studied the rear of her long elegant thighs and the graceful movements of her young legs as she crossed to the bar and the serving-hatch.

'I'd wheel her trolley for her any time,' he said thoughtfully. 'What's up with the Ripper, then?'

Hoskins watched beer being drawn.

'That Bonnie and Clyde headline of yours in yesterday's lunchtime edition. Ho-ho-ho! All a big joke. Loveable Canton scallywags. Meantime, two of our lads with a wife and kid a-piece are having their heads taken off by the evil little bastards. Failed to amuse our Mr Ripley.'

'Stuff that, Sam! No one knew two of your chaps were about to get killed. We went to press hours before that. How is old Ripley, anyway?'

Hoskins watched the beer approach, followed by sausage and mash.

'Counting the days until Bournemouth, Gerald. Less than two years to go. Almost got a demob chart on his wall. Still, since Clitheroe arrived, at least he's stopped filling up his in-tray with brochures for Eventide Homes.'

Foster grunted and reached for the mustard pot.

'Beats me why the hell he wants to go to Bournemouth. I did the Labour Party Conference there last year. Thought it was a right dump. Light industry springing up everywhere and half the unemployed of Liverpool hiding from the dole investigators. And how's Jack Chance?'

'Found true love down Ocean Beach. Slim long-haired, little-girl sort of girl. I reckon he'll need garden shears to get her jeans off. The tightest fit I've ever seen. Jolly uncomfortable, I should have thought.'

'That's Jack Chance all right,' Foster said through a mouthful of sausage.

The warm lunchtime vapours of the bar enclosed them. Standing-room was soon packed with pin-striped brokers and tastefully painted companions, thrusting young account managers and hopeful clerks. The rumble of talk and the cigarette smoke rose to the stained dado above the Brazilian mahogany.

'Just toss the dog a bone, Sam,' Foster said presently. 'What's the thinking in the Division about yesterday's set-to?'

'Depressed is what the thinking is, Gerald.' Hoskins shook his head and drained his beer. 'The entire force stretched to busting and then this happens. Trouble is, as I keep saying to deaf ears, yesterday was down to amateurs. That's what scares me most. Shoot first and think about it afterwards. As for that pharmacy van, take a sniff at some of the contents and you'd be a goner in about three minutes.'

'Has that been broadcast?'

'It will be tonight,' Hoskins said. 'The other thinking in Division seems much the same. These young clowns have no experience, no knowledge, no finesse. But they've seen all the films on the telly about how you knock off armoured trucks and the rest of it. They think they can do it. Truth is, they haven't a clue. They are teenage amateurs and bloody dangerous with it. Worse still, they seem to be armed to the teeth. Shotgun and what one of 'em told the pharmacy driver was a forty-five Colt. Forensic says there's no such gun, outside the movies. Whatever it is, though, it killed Terry Cross. These buggers are going to shoot their way in and out, because that's the way it's done on the silver screen.'

'Clitheroe thinks that?' Foster asked respectfully.

'We all do, Gerald. Last night I watched two of them do a runner across a busy motorway. Tyres screaming and punters snarling. I suppose the little sods were too stoned or pissed to care. Worse still, they might have been cold sober and still not caring. Turns out they did it all for about fifty quidsworth nicked from a house on the Clearwater estates. Give me a long-term professional villain any day, Gerald.'

'Still,' Foster said, 'one bad day like that isn't exactly a crime-wave.'

'We don't need it, Gerald. We had a crime-wave here before that started. There's the Hot-Rodders and the Chains trying to wipe each other out in cars and on bikes respectively. The last Blue Moon concert was like the Battle of the Somme and there's another one coming this Friday. And then it takes an armoured brigade to police the Saturday football. There's the home draw with Fulham this week. Tom Nicholls is doing the rounds. Telling the corner-shopkeepers down Vestry Road to close for the day and board their windows. Mind you, there's a handy off-licence on the corner of Lockbridge Park that reckons it's going to stay open anyway.'

'Use a bit of Public Order Act, Sam. Tell 'em it's either ticket-only fixtures or close 'em down.'

'They did ticket-only with the Newport game the other week. And there was still twenty-three fans in the casualty department after it. One bloke helped to take a friend to casualty, only to get knifed by some joker while he was talk-ing to a nurse. And one of the house-surgeons was attacked with a chair-leg by a nineteen-year-old wino who'd got his eye on the medicinal brandy. I tell you, Gerald, you need to be fighting fit to survive a hospital visit in this town.'

Foster pushed his plate away.

'That's the infirmary for you,' he said. 'Everyone goes private now. Everyone that can afford it.'

'You can't go private, Gerald. Not when you're lying on the pavement down Vestry Road, ten o'clock Saturday night, end of a broken bottle or a Stanley-knife stuck in your face, pint of your blood all over someone's boots. Not the time to start explaining to the para-medics that you're actually a private patient and not one of the mob.'

'Can't see how yesterday makes that sort of thing worse, Sam.'

Hoskins watched a black-stockinged, straight-skirted office girl smoothing closer to her escort.

'Yesterday was an invitation, Gerald, to all the other budding gangsters in Peninsula or Mount Pleasant. Get tooled up and hi-jack a few vehicles like they do in Belfast. Hit these poufy-voiced wankers from the smart offices. The ones with the company cars and the expenses, houses up Hawks Hill and kids at private school. Wouldn't you feel like that if you lived in a high-rise or some flop down the docks? I bloody would. And, of course, I'd take on the police at the same time.'

Foster shook his head, as if it were all beyond him.

'You want to come in where it's dry and warm, Sam. Bloke like you that's made DCI has to be in demand. But decide on it now, not when you're fifty-five or sixty.'

'I do all right, Gerald.'

Foster pulled a face of weary scepticism.

'Yes,' he said sardonically. 'Looks like it, doesn't it? Still, if you nail whoever killed Terry Cross and Bob McPhail, you could be in with a chance.'

Hoskins shook his head. 'That's Clitheroe's case, Gerald. He says so. Direct command.'

Foster stared at him. 'Sod that, Sam! This is made for you. Last time a policeman was killed was John Stoodley. And you caught the bugger who did it. Clitheroe's a chair-polisher.'

'I've got work on already, Gerald. Making sure Billy Catte doesn't employ girls who ought to be at school.'

Foster continued to stare. 'This is a bloody scandal!' he said, stupefied. 'It needs talking about!'

'Not in the columns of the *Western World*, if you don't mind, Gerald. What I've got may not be much of a job, but I'd like to keep it.'

The two friends walked back together as far as the concrete and glass fortress of Rockwell Press on King Edward Square, housing the *Western World* and *Canton Evening Globe*. Foster paused by the shallow steps leading up to the rank of glass entrance panels.

'Talking of Billy Catte, Sam, word is you've been aggravating him.'

'You know how it is, Gerald. I keep in touch, as they say.'

'Really is under-age girls working for him, is it?'

'Something like that.'

'Not that I owe you one today, Sam. But I'd say you're looking in the wrong place. Try the Totty-Boxing at the Realito Club. You'll find it down the Peninsula. Billy Catte's promoting it, I hear.'

'I don't need telling where the Realito is, Gerald. What's Totty-Boxing?'

'American sport, Sam. Texas mainly. Two young ladies in a ring with gloves on and not much else. Smacking hell out of each other while the fans lick their lips and twinkle.'

'Dunno, Gerald. Par for the course nowadays. Carmel Cooney had a couple of dark-skinned models wrestling in mud at his last charity show. Had the Mayor of Ocean Beach and his chaplain in the audience. All clapping like mad. The ladies got the right to join in all the sports nowadays, Cooney says. Reckons he's just an Equal Opportunities employer.'

'I think you'll find this is a little bit more than wrestling in mud, Sam. Bit of under-age in it, too. I'm not saying there's necessarily enough in it for you to give Billy Catte a tug. But if you reckon to sort him out, you are going to need all the help you can get.'

Hoskins rubbed his gloved hands briskly together.

'I gathered that from previous friendly chats with him. Apart from "piss off" and "I want my brief" Billy Catte seems a bit short on conversation. Noticed a bit of under-the-counter literature on his desk. Could tell us something about his social values, I daresay.'

'Right,' Foster said enthusiastically. 'See you soon, young Hoskins. Take care crossing the road.'

Hoskins walked slowly back down the pink-tarmac'd Mall, past the dove-grey domes of City Hall with their flying charioteers in black bronze. The arched Edwardian windows of the ground floor showed a glimpse of high stucco'd ceilings, a hint of the lofty chanceries of Europe in 1914. This suggestion was soon dispelled by the box-files of Mount

Pleasant rent demands and stickers inviting the citizens to pay their local taxes promptly by credit card. Hoskins wondered how much local tax Billy Catte paid. Perhaps he might look into that.

Back in his office, he rang Jack Chance in the sergeants' room.

'Everything there is on Billy Catte, my son. In here, as soon as.'

Ten minutes later, Chance said, 'We back with all this lot again, are we?'

Hoskins tapped a sequence on a plastic keyboard beside his desk. He stared at the orange lettering on the grey display screen.

'We are, my son. Mr Catte may be right about taking two years to get him to court. But that's supposing he's out, on bail, awaiting trial.'

'Right!' said Chance enthusiastically, seeing the neatness of it.

Hoskins peered at the shimmering orange script.

'Suppose, however, charges of some gravity had to be brought. Not just Melanie skiving off hockey. I don't see us agreeing to Billy Catte on bail. Nor a judge neither. Danger of witnesses being intimidated. Not to mention the fact that Mr Cat's Prize Bingo seems to have a villa or two in Spain to which he might abscond. I'd like to know how the money got out there to buy that little home-from-home.'

'Right!' said Chance again.

Hoskins pressed a second key and the pattern on the screen changed. He nodded at it approvingly.

'I don't think Mr Catte is going to be quite so witty about how long it takes to get him court. Not if he's got to spend the time banged up in the remand wing of Canton gaol.'

'Enough there, is there?'

'Nope.' Hoskins sat back. 'Got the evening paper, have you?'

'No. What for?'

'I could have had one off old Gerald Foster just now,' Hoskins said. 'See if you can raise one in the sergeants' room, or somewhere.'

'Wallace Dudden does the horses. He'll have one. What're we after, Sam, exactly?'

'Totty-Boxing for a start,' Hoskins said.

'What Boxing?'

'Totty-Boxing down the Realito Club. Gerald Foster says it's all the rage there just now. I want the details.'

'Is it what I think it is?' Chance asked suspiciously.

Hoskins shook his head.

'No, my son, I shouldn't think so. There's not much can keep up with an imagination like yours.'

Chance shrugged. He sauntered out to find an evening paper with the assumed limp-wristed gait of one whose more delicate feelings had been snubbed.

# Chapter Seven

Next evening, Hoskins rode against the rush-hour on the Metro-rail from Lantern Hill. It had been a difficult afternoon. For some reason that he failed to guess, Lesley had played the educated and emancipated young woman, the pitch of her voice setting his nerves on edge. It would sometimes be like that, Hoskins supposed, now that their relationship had passed its bland and courteous stage of the first few months. It crossed his mind that she might be brooding on similar doubts about him in the aftermath of their meeting.

As the Metro-rail carried him level with the house-roofs of Orient, he pictured the pearly sleekness of her tall firm figure, the fair hair in its aggressively and perversely plain pudding-basin crop and its long parted fringe. Then the rubber-shod carriages slid into their platform, alongside the main station of Canton Central, on the railway bank above Atlantic Wharf. This rampart had been the city's defence against the sea a century before. Now it divided the shopping centre from the inner basins of the docks.

Emerging from the subway, Hoskins looked for the Sierra with Chance at the wheel. There was no sign of it. He bought a *Canton Globe* and stood under a lamp near the taxi rank, reading Gerald Foster on the Dock ward by-election and the growing appeal of community politics.

The rush-hour had dwindled and the city centre was closing for the night. Along a redeveloped Churchill Avenue, parallel with the railway bank, even the temples of leisure stood deserted.

By half-past six the last cars from the multi-storey parks trundled towards Clearwater and Mount Pleasant. Commuter footsteps faded from the bubble-gum pink of the shopping precinct tiles. Great Western Street was silent but shoplit, as if a neutron bomb had wiped it clean of life.

'What kept you?' Hoskins asked, as the Sierra pulled in by the station kerb.

Jack Chance, red and self-confident under the dark hair, was unabashed.

'Some of us been working this afternoon, Sam. Had a

55

visit from Mr Draycott, driver of the pharmacy van. A detail he forgot to tell us at first.'

'Oh, yes?' said Hoskins sceptically as Chance pulled out across Atlantic Wharf, heading for Balance Street river bridge and the dockland Peninsula. 'If I was running the inquiry, I wouldn't be too sure that the lovely Mr Draycott wasn't part of his own hi-jack.'

Chance pulled a face as they rumbled over the iron arch of the bridge, the dark river rippling with bronze street-light.

'He's not got form, Sam. Nothing that Criminal Records computer knows about. A life of charity walks and sponsored runs, he told Clitheroe's DIs. And what he remembers isn't what a put-up remembers. It's their voices.'

The road dipped down between high pavements, under the Victorian plate-iron grey of the railway bridge, the heads of its rivets neat as embroidery. This was the beginning of Dyce Street, the spinal column of dockland Peninsula.

'What about their voices?'

'They weren't ordinary. Not exactly private school but not talking like yobs.'

Hoskins stared at the narrow Victorian terraces running off to either side, dockers' houses with their corner-pubs.

'Yobs and private schools talk much the same nowadays, my son. And I don't like witnesses that have second thoughts.'

Dyce Street lay ahead of them, the pier-head at its end a mile away.

'Anyway,' Chance said, 'Alan Pargiter went out to the Hope and Anchor at Mordaunt village after that. Had a quiet word with Mrs Preece, the landlady. Asked her what she remembered about the voice of the one who tried to buy drink off her. She said he was definitely not common.'

Hoskins grunted at it all. 'McPhail run down and Cross shot dead! A vanload of drugs hi-jacked! Gunfire on the motorway! But at least he's not common! If that's the best Division can do, they might as well pack up the whole thing.'

Chance shrugged and slowed down at a pedestrian crossing for an overweight young woman with three children in tow.

'Face it, Sam. There's not much else. If we could find the Saab, that'd be something. They'd leave traces all over it, a bunch like this.'

Hoskins jerked a thumb at the blank concrete of the

railway wall down one side of Dyce Street. From the miles of brick sheds and corrugated workshops beyond rose an Armageddon of wrecked car bodies in the Western Reclaim scrapyard.

'That car's long gone, Jack. Probably been through the crusher by now. Or else down the bottom of the Railway Dock.'

'All right,' said Chance reasonably. 'But, if Draycott's bent, where's the point in coming back and telling us that they hadn't got voices like a gang of tearaways?'

'Nuisance value, my son. With what Clitheroe's got now, their voices won't take him very far. Still, we'll let ACC Crime and his bum-boys sort out motorway hi-jacks. Our undivided attention goes to Billy Catte. Girls missing their school hockey has to be stopped before the whole country goes to ruin.'

Jack Chance gave up. At the traffic-lights short of the pier-head he turned right into the decaying grandeur of Martello Square. He made for the multi-storey car park above the deep tombs of the Canton Graving Dock. A uniformed attendant was warming himself in the ticket-box by the entrance. Chance stuck his head out of the driver's window.

'Look after us, will you, Freddie?'

The old man turned and came out.

'Right, Mr Chance. You park there. Just there, where it says disabled. You'll be all right there. No sense leaving it on the other floors. You wouldn't have wheels on the motor by the time you got back, nor anything inside that was worth taking.'

Chance parked the car and got out.

'Thought you was supposed to guard the limos here, Freddie.'

'Yes,' said the old man sardonically. 'Archie Hammet thought that as well. He's still off sick after four weeks. Went upstairs to ask several young gentlemen what they thought they was doing to a punter's car. They showed him with the toes of their boots. Not me. First sign of trouble, I lock myself in the ticket office. Armoured glass they put in it now. Then I dial three nines and wait for you lot.'

'That's nice, Freddie,' Chance said, patting the old man on the shoulder. 'See you in a bit.'

In step with Hoskins, he crossed Martello Square, past the row of dockland shops, now occupied by a ship's chandler, a pin-ball machine manufacturer and a wholesaler of fire extinguishers. Hoskins and Chance walked through the cold evening wind from the pier-head railings, past the columns and the friezes picked out in lilac and gold. The cars of the Realito's patrons lined the road on both sides, as well as the streets leading off it. A shimmering night tide was flooding the dredged channel already, lapping the flanks of mud in the sodium glow of the street-lights. Several tugs had manoeuvred the first outward-bound container ship to the sea-lock moorings.

The Realito Club stood opposite the banking halls and Edwardian grandeur of Dyce Street Chambers. It was a disused chapel of the Baptist Dockland Mission. Barley-twist pillars and doorway arch had been repainted in discothèque blue and white and orange. Either side of the door, a chromium-framed case presented photographs of showgirls, the faces of painted dolls, whose department store underwear was the Realito's usual costume. Above the door, a simple but effective pattern of plain light-bulbs flashed on and off, spelling out the message: TOTTY-BOXING – NIGHTLY 7.30 & 10.

From the parked cars, groups of young men in business suits, laughing and hallooing, edged towards the entrance between the other vehicles. Sometimes it was a man and woman alone, sometimes the middle-management. Aggressive young commission reps and account managers from Hawks Hill or Clearwater were the Realito's true friends. These were the flat vowels of London suburbia, exiled two hundred miles to Canton where commercial rents were cheaper. The entertainments of shabby dockland were perversely chic to them. A colour supplement had devoted two Sunday pages to Dyce Street the year before.

'Enough to make the old breathalyser blush,' Chance said wistfully, staring at the new arrivals.

Hoskins glared at the scene. 'All the little ladies out Lantern Hill and Taylors Town. Keeping it warm in the oven for young Mr Successful. Story about a sales conference and a late train from Paddington. Or a client to sell a policy to on the way home. Wallace Dudden says Billy Catte's early show down here gets more punters than ten o'clock.'

'Yes,' Chance said. 'Then old Dudden's the sort who'd

know. He's been itching for a turn on the dirty squad. Moaned like the devil when they moved him to Traffic Division instead.'

Hoskins bought two tickets from the girl in a crimson pill-box hat and matador jacket whose pay-box was just inside the arch. A stone-face tore the tickets and pushed open a velvet-hung door. The Realito burst on Hoskins like a thunderstorm. The thump and blast of Blitzkrieg punished the amplifiers with the group's latest single, 'This Side Up'.

> Ah wanna be on the side of the winnin'
> Where men are men and women are women,
> Where pigs don't fly nor flies go swimmin'
> And tits are birds and the force is risen,
> And he is hers and she is his'n . . .
> This side up is my true heaven . . .
> Ah wanna be . . . !

Like fairground whirlibirds, the patches of coloured light circled the domed roof of the darkened auditorium through the din. The gallery of the old chapel had been retained, the aisles beneath it turned into bars and the gallery itself occupied by the lamps and consoles of the lighting crew. At the centre was the spot-lit boxing-ring, raised a couple of feet above the floor. The floor had been stepped towards the ring with benches running along each level. But as Blitzkrieg bellowed its determination to be on the side of the winning, most of those who had crowded into the Realito Club preferred to stand for a better view. Hoskins put his mouth close to Chance's ear.

'You think the Health and Safety Executive might like a look at this merry little fire-trap?'

Chance shrugged. Jackets of executive suits were being taken off in the heat and ties pulled loose. The flat Thatcherite vowels now hurtled about like hunting calls. Shards of thin metal rattled underfoot as the cans of lager and special brew were torn open by thirsty workers. There were long queues at the bars before the contest began. Hoskins saw Billy Catte, the local Caesar with his dark pug features and broken nose. He was sitting on a bench at the front with a girl either side of him. Each was dressed in a dark fur coat which fell open to reveal legs bare to mid-thigh. Billy Catte's schoolgirl family in the silky fur of grown women. He was cuddling them, one arm each, and talking across the larger girl to a man beyond her. This elder girl was in her teens, the other was less than ten. They pressed against him as Billy Catte grinned and gaped at the man he had spoken to.

'The elder one's his step-daughter, Emma,' Hoskins said for Chance's benefit. 'I couldn't tell you who the young one belongs to. Emma's little friend, I daresay, or Billy Catte's fancy.'

A blonde woman in a black track-suit, trailing a microphone lead, appeared in the ring. Blitzkrieg faded. The amplifier whanged and screeched. The blonde shook her hair back and grinned over the ropes at the audience.

'My!' she cried at them through the microphone. 'Ain't she cute! And ain't she mean! A big welcome for Annie Fanny!'

There was applause and a rhythmic hooting from the young executives. Hoskins saw her in the ring, a girl with silky fair hair swirling on her shoulders, a strong face and rather heavy-lidded eyes. She was wearing a vest that left her arms and shoulders bare and a pair of diminutive red boxer shorts with a white stripe.

A thump of music resumed in the background. Annie toured the ring, jerking and bumping her hips at the onlookers, rolling her shoulders, arms held up with fists clenched. The waistcoated account managers and commission reps pulled their ties looser, clapping and yelping. Annie bent over and waggled her behind at them. The blonde compère was back.

'And we have a challenger! Lovely Lizzie. Look at her and tell me, ain't she finger-licking good?'

The taller of the two, Lizzie, showed a hard-featured face with a mane of carefully styled auburn ringlets, her arms and shoulders bare, the boxing shorts blue for distinction. She raised a fist and held it high with rhythmic jerks of aggression. Then, along the front benches, she performed the same convulsive hip gyrations in the faces of the happy customers. Billy Catte's hand moved appreciatively as she passed.

'Oh, my!' cried the blonde compère again, as the two girls stood close in a rumba rhythm. 'Let's hear from the Lizzie-lovers out there!'

There was a roaring and hooting.

'And now the friends of Annie Fanny!'

Hoskins and Chance shouldered forward a little. No one cared about them.

'And now, which of you gentlemen is going to come out here and help these little ladies lace-up?'

There was elbowing and shoving. A young executive in sleek-backed waistcoat and a roll of flab over his trouser-waist won the race. He stood there, the two girls either side, each gyrating as if to rub against him, dragon-breathing silently at her rival. The boxing gloves looked large to Hoskins, large and amply padded to avoid real damage. A man who might almost have been Billy Catte's look-alike entered the ring as referee.

'Five rounds of sixty seconds each!' squealed the blonde compère, jumping clear.

A bell rang. Annie and Lizzie approached, prancing up and down in imitation of footwork. They began to slap one another inexpertly about the head and face with their padded gloves. No attempt was made to match their size, Lizzie being several inches the taller. Using this advantage, she cuffed her opponent vigorously. Annie emitted several gasps, then a cry, and tried to cover her head with her hand.

'And she is being hurt!' squealed the blonde excitedly through the microphone. 'Annie Fanny is really feeling this!'

An Indian whooping of partisan excitement broke out somewhere in the audience. With her forearms wrapped round her head, Annie began to lash out with her feet. She landed a deft kick to Lizzie's knee, which sent the larger girl hobbling back towards her own corner. The smaller blonde stampeded after her and aimed a second savage kick at the seat of the blue boxer shorts. Lizzie plunged forward on to the ropes and slid down, features contorted in an anguish so improbable that it must have been rehearsed. Billy Catte and his two juvenile companions were hugging one another as if in triumph. They bowed backwards and forwards on their seats, cooing and crowing. A bell rang for the end of the round.

'And in a moment,' cried the blonde, 'Lizzie is going to have to come out again and take some more – a whole lot more! And she is hurting already! I mean – look at her! – Lizzie is hurting!'

Lizzie obligingly put on the same clenched grimace.

'Already,' breathed the blonde, 'already Lizzie is hurting so she can't hardly stand nor sit. And that is one little lady who is going to have to push her bicycle home tonight. Four more rounds – and Annie Fanny is going to give her hell. Meaning – give her hell!'

They came out again, slapping and kicking. Lizzie tore at the laces of her right-hand glove with her teeth. Holding it between her thighs, she managed to wrench it off. Then she went at Annie with her nails. The crowd, women as well as men, began to jump up and down with inexpressible excitement.

'And now it's Annie that's in trouble!' squealed the compère. 'I mean, is this trouble – or is this trouble?'

But the excitement seemed to be over. Exhausted by the performance, the two contestants spent the remaining rounds in cartwheeling punches that landed without effect.

After Annie and Lizzie there was a grudge match between Viv and Claire. No gloves were worn and far more time was spent on the floor of the ring, tearing at one another. Hoskins supposed that this, too, had been rehearsed. Despite the best that Billy Catte could offer, the audience was losing interest by the time the interval came.

'And now,' breathed the voice from the amplifiers, 'during the interval of every programme at the Realito we have our amateur spot. We make no charge for this and everyone is welcome to stay and watch. This evening, by courtesy of an old friend of young people's organisations in the city, Billy Catte, we present a team feature by Young Blood, starring Mr Cat's Kittens. These plucky little ladies have boxed their way to fame and fortune on behalf of Canton's good causes. Spina bifida and the baby unit, as well as Under the Sun Famine Relief, Childline and Kids-for-Kids. During the contest two other lovely little handfuls will be coming round to get their fingers in your trouser pockets on behalf of the Children in Need appeal. You won't mind a bit – that's a promise! And now – Amateur Spot. Welcome, please, our first two spunky young contenders, Nicola Druce and Trisha Dearlove.'

The audience was silent for a moment, hardly able to believe its good fortune. A pair of meagre-fleshed adolescent girls in bikinis bobbed up in the ring, hip-grinding and shoulder-writhing. There was a storm of applause.

Chance put his mouth to Hoskins' ear. 'You could do

him for this, Sam! One's not more than about fourteen.'

'Not a hope, Jack. His brief'll say it's just like hockey and netball.'

Chance shook his head. With gloves on, Nicola and Trisha began to pat and slap at one another. In no time at all Nicola had the better of the younger girl. How it happened Hoskins could not quite see. Somehow, Nicola got the fingers of one glove in the waistband of the other girl's bikini and wrenched the garment away.

'Bloody hell!' Chance said. The audience gasped. While Nicola continued the attack, Trisha protected her head with one hand, the other shielding her decency. Recovering its wits, the audience stamped and shouted. Trisha was running round the ring with Nicola in pursuit. The referee made one or two vague gestures, not trying too hard to stop the contest.

The final display was a team event, in which two groups of four bikini'd kittens made a mass attack on one another. It ended in a scrimmage, a playful confusion of interwoven bodies, hips and buttocks sometimes clad and sometimes almost bare. The compère brought the hour to an end among a storm of appreciation from the fans. As they turned away to the bar or the exit, Blitzkrieg homed in on them like a dive-bomber squadron with its performance of 'This Side Up'.

> Ah wanna be on the side of the winnin'
> Where men are men and women are women . . .

'We could nick him now,' Chance said hopefully.

'No,' said Hoskins quietly. 'When I give a tug on the line, I want to feel Billy Catte hooked tight. I can't see this lot as being more than rubbish to part the punters from their wages.'

They followed the duck-trail of reps and junior managers into the street. There was an edge of ice in the wind from the half-covered mudflats.

Two young men and their girls stood to one side of the door on the uneven paving. They bore silent witness, like evangelists at a race-meeting, holding between them a square of white card nailed to a wooden lath. As so often with such enthusiasts, they had failed to realise that it was the thickness of lettering rather than its height which made it

legible. Hoskins peered at the Totty-Boxing protest banner.
THIS DEGRADES WOMEN, it said.

Chance nodded in their direction. 'There's some in the Division would have them for obstruction,' he said.

Hoskins shook his head. 'Not unless you can nick people for stating the bleeding obvious. Still, I reckon the next time I'm on the pavement with several smelly skinheads trying to boot my face in, or I'm dancing about so as not to have my appendages kicked up past my Adam's apple by a couple of drunken yobs, I might try waving a little sign saying "This degrades Samuel Hoskins". Not that I'd count on our friends over there hurrying to the rescue.'

'Course not,' said Chance triumphantly. 'I mean, in their book, you're a Sado-Fascist Pig, aren't you? I got called that once in a set-to. Some prat from the government was getting free egg down his suit outside the students' union. I was given the general message, along with a dollop of spit down the tunic. Uniformed branch in those days. That's what you are in their book, Sam. A Sado-Fascist Pig.'

'I try,' said Hoskins modestly. 'I try.'

He looked about him. Billy Catte was with his younger girl and a woman of thirty-five or forty. She was black-haired and the pancake make-up gave a dark unhealthy look to her eyes. But her figure was one that most eighteen-year-olds might have envied. It was on display just then in black stocking-tights and velvet briefs with a coatee top. Billy Catte lumbered off with one arm round the woman and the other round the girl.

'Good thing Mrs Catte's not here to see,' said Hoskins thoughtfully. 'She's usually the one in the black tights and not much else. You could count on a real bit of Totty-Boxing out here, with Billy Catte in the middle.'

He and Chance walked at a distance behind the three of them. Billy Catte's right hand insinuated itself under the waistband and into the seat of the dark-haired woman's tights. It could be seen, moving slowly and reassuringly.

'If he does the same with his other hand, I suppose I could have him,' Hoskins said thoughtfully. 'Unlawful touching up.'

They followed the trio round the pier-head corner to the decaying grandeur of Dyce Esplanade. The tall Victorian houses, looking out across the concreted remains of communal gardens, had a view of the tidal channels beyond the docks, a distant glimpse of ocean past the headland of Harbour Bar and Lantern Hill. A hundred years before, the houses had been built for the managers and senior clerks of the dry-docks, the shipping lines and the tug-boat fleets, whose offices stood behind the esplanade in Martello Square.

Billy Catte escorted his two companions into a house at the far end of the esplanade. Its windows were uncurtained and lit in the cold January night, the front door standing wide with invitation. A straggle of guests, the courtiers of Dyce Street's 'entertainment king', was making its way along the low sea-wall of the waterside promenade, the tide withdrawn far out across the muddy foreshore. From Billy Catte's decaying mansion, the thump and snarl of the Hangman replaced the tornado of Blitzkrieg.

> If there's a bomber in the bed,
> Then we'll do it on the floor.
> So don't stand beneath the ceiling,
> When we do it on the floor . . .

'Do It On The Floor' was regarded by critical opinion as marking a slapstick and more benevolent phase in the cult of the Hangman's Children.

The guests, with a sprinkling of Mr Cat's Kittens, wedged their way through the open door. There were shouts and laughter. The woman in the black tights crossed a lighted window, smiling and holding a leather switch in her hand.

'Charming,' murmured Chance from the shadows of the esplanade. 'Real House and Garden stuff.'

'Waste of time standing out here any longer,' Hoskins said glumly. 'I'm going back to write this lot up, for all the good it's likely to do.'

# Chapter Eight

It was not until the next evening that Hoskins finished writing it up. He put aside the pages, ready for delivery to Clitheroe as ACC Crime. Then he looked at his watch. It was after midnight. Time to check the evening delivery of tapes from the pirate radio *Hit-Back Show*. Despite official alarm at their encouragement to public violence, the youthful voices of the show sounded to Hoskins like schoolboy jokers. The cruel humour of the playground wag. Give them quarter of an hour. After that, with five hours overtime under his belt, he was off to bed. No two ways.

The fluorescent strip in its metal shield cast a tropical glare on the white distemper of the office wall and the grey metal slats of the window blinds. Hoskins rested his face between his hands, yawned, and drained his coffee cup. Then he pressed the play button of the cassette recorder.

'Have you ever come back from holiday?' asked a friendly voice. 'Had a good time? Landed at the airport late and feeling tired? Ever had trouble with the Customs there? Ever been harassed? Ever been snarled at and humiliated by a rat-face in a uniform? Wanted to do something about it? And the worst thing, perhaps, was having to stand there and take it. But not any more! Thanks to the *Hit-Back Show*, you can do something about it now. We give *you* the chance to even the score with *them*. In a moment we'll describe some of your legal rights. How to complain. How to make trouble for the people who've made trouble for you.'

Hoskins growled quietly to himself. The solving of real crime had been given to others. His own career sank to the level of public nuisances like Billy Catte and the *Hit-Back Show*. It could be worse, he supposed. Dressed up in blue serge and the tall hat of the friendly bobby. Holding up the impatient commuter traffic while mums and prams crossed safely over Clearwater Avenue from William Forster Infant School. He refilled the coffee cup from his flask and paid attention to the tapes once more.

'But first,' the voice was saying, 'who are the people you're dealing with? Names and addresses coming up. They know your name. Why shouldn't you know theirs? Thanks to a sympathetic source at Canton Airport, we'll give you a list of the so-called Waterguard officers on Customs Duty there. Names and addresses, details of families. They can find out these things about you. Why shouldn't you know the same about them? Perhaps you just want to complain. You need a name for that. Perhaps you've had a hard time and you want to go looking. Your choice. Either way, the *Hit-Back Show* is here to help you.'

'Bloody hell!' said Hoskins wearily.

'And pictures,' the voice said reassuringly. 'Their cameras have you under surveillance. So why shouldn't you have snapshots of them? For those of you who'll be looking to even the score, we're putting our photos of them on public view. But, first, who are they? The Customs staff at Canton Airport is quite small. Only ten. Raymond Allen, the senior man, lives at Eighteen Pontarlan Drive, Ocean Beach. He has a wife, Denise, and a daughter of eighteen, Alison, studying at University College but living at home. His car is a yellow Datsun, registration number B249 RHS. His telephone number is Ocean Beach 348616. Want something to do after this broadcast? Why not telephone Mr Allen, or his wife Denise, or young Alison, and have a chat? Better still, why not go round and see them?'

'Mad,' Hoskins said helplessly.

'The senior woman officer at present is a Mrs Scott, Flat Six, Wexford Flight, Lantern Hill. Though you wouldn't kick Scott out of bed, she'll never win the Miss World Contest. Scott is twenty-nine years old, divorced and lives with a man who has a small-scale criminal record in the United States. How about that, all you Commissioners of Customs and Excise? Did you know about Mr Vanning's little secret? Did you know that this small-time crook was bedding your cuddly Scott? Scott has a child, whom she takes to school most mornings at Shackleton Primary, driving a red Volkswagen Polo RLT 657W. If you've had trouble with Customs at Canton Airport and you'd like to talk with Mrs Scott when the show is over, her telephone number is Lantern Hill 446690.'

A knock at the door. Hoskins switched off the tape. It was Chance.

'No joy from the DTI direction-finder, Sam. Wallace Dudden reckons these jokers must have recognised the van by now. You finished with those tapes?'

Hoskins waved him to a seat.

'For what good it'll do. Half the time I reckon it's bloody silly. The other half, I keep thinking it could all turn nasty. It's Customs tonight. Names, addresses, car numbers, telephones, wives and kids. Hundred to one it won't go further than spite like this. But if a punter with a grudge tries to burn a house down one night, or snatch a child, or attack a wife, you tell me what to do. Do we have to put a twenty-four-hour guard on every tax inspector, magistrate, Customs officer, programme maker at CNT? There's no end to it.'

Chance yawned and rubbed his eyes.

'Could catch the buggers that're broadcasting, Sam. That's what it's about.'

Hoskins nodded. He pressed the cassette button again.

'So from now on,' said the friendly voice, 'we'll put up our own surveillance photographs of names mentioned on this programme. After all, we don't want the wrong ones being visited. When this broadcast is over, you'll find pictures of Raymond Allen, his wife and daughter, and Pippa Scott posted on the side wall of the Longwall Circle Holiday Inn, facing the interchange.'

Hoskins switched off the machine and got up.

'Coat on, Jack. These nutters could be bluffing about putting pictures of people on walls. Take a look down Longwall Circle. See what you can find.'

'Me?' Chance asked suspiciously. 'Alone?'

Hoskins stood up.

'You alone, my son,' he said philosophically. 'I've got the Ripper at ten o'clock tomorrow morning. And very likely a to-and-fro with the stipendiary magistrate in the afternoon, telling me why I can't have a warrant for Billy Catte. Just this minute, I'm going to bed.'

In a full moon from Hawks Hill, the car park tarmac glittered with early frost as Hoskins went down and unlocked the Vauxhall Cavalier. What he had in mind now was disaster. Nothing short of it. And he did not care.

The empty Mall stretched ahead of him, its Memorial Gardens dark as shrubbery, City Hall in the moonlight, the custard-yellow buses marooned along the kerbs of King Edward Square. He turned west by the toy castle, 'The Keep', built by Giles Gilbert Scott for the first Lord Dyce, with its prettily painted Florentine watch-tower and spiky baronial turrets.

He followed the road west and, once clear of the city, he turned up the long incline of Lantern Hill which brought him at last to the headland, looking down across the wide harbour approach to the arc-lit dockland map of Peninsula a mile or two away. Hoskins parked the car by the tall iron railings which edged the road.

He walked quietly round the corner, into Arran Street, and pressed the illuminated bell-button. Standing on the uneven pavement he could hear across the water the murmur and sub-dued reverberation of dynamo and generator, the harsh breath of molten slag, as the wharves of Prince of Wales Dock and the rolling mills of Atlantic Factors worked the night-shift.

A light came on in the hall behind the bubbled-glass strips of the door. At least she had not been in bed. The chain rattled and the door opened on its length by a few inches. He saw no more of her than the firm jaw and the slight wilfulness in the line of the mouth, the blue eyes under the long parted fringe of her plain crop.

'I just thought it might be a good idea,' he said quietly.

Lesley pushed the door and undid the chain.

'Ten minutes more and I should have been in bed.'

'Yes,' Hoskins said thoughtfully, putting his arms round her as the door closed.

'Have you eaten?'

'Canteen supper. Stays with me for days.'

She went through to the back room and turned the light off. On the stairs, Hoskins admired the suggestive movement of her hips in the black trousers, the agile length of the thighs. All the same, it was probably a mistake. Worse even than the previous afternoon.

He sat on the edge of the bed, unlacing his shoes, and watched appreciatively. The sweater came off over her head and he supposed that it was only full womanhood which gave that beauty of sleek pallor to her shoulders and back. Jack Chance's Julie would be knobbly by comparison. The black trousers came down. A hint of pale thighs and taut hips through the honeyed nylon haze of tights, the firm swell of her bottom as she turned to fold the black trousers on a chair. Lesley paused, half-way through peeling off the tights, shaking the fringe clear of her eyes.

'Come on!' she said sharply. 'It was your idea!'

Lying in the warmth of the bed afterwards, the pink curtains turning black as the moon went behind a cloud, Hoskins thought that it had been a good idea after all.

'Perhaps surprises are best,' Lesley said quietly. She turned over with her back to him as if to sleep. Hoskins stroked her shoulders, the inward curve of her back, and patted her behind.

'Does this mean what I think it means?' Lesley inquired patiently.

Hoskins chuckled.

'You never know,' he said quietly. 'You never know.'

They slept soundly until the phone by the bed emitted a soft treble purr just after eight o'clock. Lesley picked it up, listened, and handed it to him without speaking.

'Sam?' It was Jack Chance. 'You there, Sam?'

'Yes. Why?'

'I'm off watch in a minute. There was photographs down Longwall Circle, copies on your desk. And you've got your conference with the Ripper at twelve, instead of ten. He phoned in something about him seeing the stipendiary before you do.'

'You woke me up now to tell me all this?'

'No,' said Chance. 'There's also been a call from your favourite pair of ears, Jimmy Riddle. Won't say a word to anyone else. Wants to see you. Soon as. Usual place.'

'I'll try.'

'Thing is,' Chance said, 'I'll watch your back for you if it's in the next hour or so. After that, I'm definitely off home for kip. No way am I waiting until after your Ripper appointment.'

Hoskins raised himself on his elbow.

'When Jimmy rings back, tell him I'll be there at ten. And don't call him Jimmy Riddle. He gets offended and goes dumb on me.'

'Right-o,' Chance said. 'On socks, then.'

Hoskins put the phone down. Lesley's head appeared through the spreading neck-hole of the sweater.

'Jimmy Riddle?'

'Course he's not. Just young Master Chance making free with people's names. Trouble with young Jack. Gets up too many noses. He's going to come unstuck one day.'

'So this man's not Jimmy Riddle?'

'He's a pair of ears.' Hoskins drew on the second sock and gazed appalled at his sleep-crumpled mirror image. 'An informant. Grass. Snout. And if you don't know his real name, you can't come to harm. Incidentally, that wasn't a bad bit of roly-poly. Was it?'

Naked but for the sweater, Lesley stared at him.

'You are a pig, Sam Hoskins!'

'A Sado-Fascist Pig, according to young Chance. Not an easy reputation to live up to.'

There was no resistance when he pulled her on his knee. Hoskins felt a lift of the spirits. It had been all right, after all.

# Chapter Nine

Hoskins went home to shave. It was too soon to suggest leaving a spare razor at Arran Street. Too much like moving in. Opening his door, he sensed the quietness of rooms unslept in and unvisited. On the kitchen portable, Coastal Radio was just winding up its nine o'clock news. Last of all came the times of high tide, morning and evening, for Canton Dock, Ocean Beach, Sandbar, and as far down the western coast as Minavon and the Burrows. He buttoned himself into a clean shirt.

Five minutes later, Hoskins turned the Vauxhall Cavalier into the refurbished Edwardian elegance of Great Western Street. He drove down to the wide commercial square of Atlantic Wharf, between the Paris Hotel and the elegant window-displays of the Royal Peninsular Emporium.

The railway bank hid Peninsula dockland from Atlantic Wharf. But on a fine January morning, the bare branches of embankment trees ran like plaster-cracks across the Arctic blue of a windless sky. In its chill marine brilliance, the light of an invisible winter ocean danced and shimmered.

Hoskins parked opposite the Emporium, outside the chic gowns and lingerie of Madame Jolly Modes. There was no competition between the two establishments. Like so much else in Canton, Madame Jolly and the Emporium were both playthings of Councillor Carmel Cooney.

By half-past nine the buses had deposited their rush-hour passengers at the ocean-liner shapes of the insurance offices on King Edward Square. The hurry was over and the town was briefly quiet again. Hoskins' progress towards the newspaper reading-room in Navarino Street was accompanied only by the light resonant slap of other footfalls on the gum-pink tiles of the Great Western shopping precinct, where the side turnings had been blocked off from traffic.

Navarino Street was not one of these. It was a survival of Canton wholesale imports within a stone's throw of the shopping centre. The narrow street was clogged by lorries unloading, pavements broken and uneven from the weight of tall wheels. Brick warehouses rose high on each side, display-windows whitewashed over. Stock-control managers were checking rolls of cloth wrapped in brown paper and machine-tool parts that might equally well have come from a steam-engine or a spacecraft. No casual customer ever entered these premises. They were places of double-locks and window-mesh, men in thick-knit sweaters with Alsatian dogs. Cards in window-corners promised 'Trade only'.

At the far end of the street, Canton City Council had its commercial library and newspaper reading-room. Users of the main lending library and reference section were not to be disturbed by the old men who sought refuge among the tall reading-stands with the day's papers clipped to them. Turned out until evening by the Salvation Army hostel in Dyce Street, or by unsympathetic daughters and daughters-in-law from Barrier or Mount Pleasant, the mackintoshed refugees shifted and snuffled their way through the day's news.

Chance had parked on the opposite side of the street, in the lee of an articulated lorry at the bonded whisky warehouse. The plain brick front and the barred windows concealed the Customs and Excise surveillance. There was usually a space outside it. Hoskins put his head down to the window of the car.

'Is he in there?'

Chance shook his head.

'Couldn't tell you, Sam. I'm watching your back for you, that's all. There hasn't been any other face we know. I reckon you're clear.'

'Right,' Hoskins said. 'Give me ten minutes. Then come in. Just in case there's anything needs a second pair of ears.'

Chance unfolded that morning's *Western World* and yawned as he turned to the sports page.

'Okey-doke,' he said.

The disinfected odours of the newspaper library reminded Hoskins of prison interviews. It was as if an unwashed stench had become ingrained like airborne grime in the grey Victorian stone. As a matter of council policy there was nowhere to sit down. In the main hall, with its mottled grey floor and tall frosted glass, the reading-stands ran in three rows down its length. The occupants leant forward on them, as if scanning the papers short-sightedly. Each of the wide wooden frames bore its familiar plaque: PLEASE VACATE THIS STAND WITHIN FIVE MINUTES UPON REQUEST BY ANOTHER READER.

Hoskins walked quickly down the length of the room

and past the counter at the far end. There was not a face that he knew. Beyond this, a short corridor led to an inner room, also lit by the frosted glass of its high windows. This was where the commercial papers were kept. Its tall stands carried *Lloyds Shipping Register*, *The Farmer and Stockbreeder*, *The Steel Trades Journal*, *Canton Market Listings* and their kind. As if by common understanding, the elderly refugees kept clear of this and the room was usually empty.

'Well now, Mr Liddell,' Hoskins said quietly. 'How're we keeping this long time?'

Jimmy Liddell turned with a smile. He was a tall thin man, the downward sweep of grey hair on either side of his head giving him the air of an amiable water-buffalo. Though his suede coat shone patchily with wear and his blunt shoes were white with damp, he bore himself like an officer and a gentleman temporarily out of funds through no fault of his own. He smiled again at Hoskins and took his glasses off.

'I'm not one to complain, Mr Hoskins. Never do that. How's yourself?'

'Bit tired, Jimmy, to tell you the truth. So's Mr Chance. Been on nights for a while.'

Jimmy Liddell rested an elbow on the edge of his reading-stand and turned crookedly towards Hoskins again.

'Knackering, that must be, Mr Hoskins.'

'Right,' said Hoskins quietly. 'So what've we got this morning, Jimmy?'

Liddell scratched his forehead, as if he might have forgotten.

'Word is, Mr Hoskins, that you've got a strong interest in Billy Catte just now. Worth anything, would it be? I mean, a bit of gen about Mr Catte?'

'Might be, Jimmy. Try me.'

Liddell hunched forward towards the Chief Inspector as if they might even now be overheard.

'Billy Catte had his motor stolen. That's what, Mr Hoskins.'

'Just that?' Hoskins asked. 'Just that?'

Jimmy Liddell hunched forward a little more.

'Had his motor stolen, Mr Hoskins. Had you heard that? Course you hadn't. That was eight thousand quid on wheels stolen from him and never raised a squeak to the law nor to anyone else. That's what I'm on about.'

Hoskins felt his heart beat a little faster.

'This motor of his, Jimmy. Wouldn't happen to be a maroon Saab, by any chance?'

But Liddell shook his head. 'Nissan Bluebird, Mr Hoskins. That's what I heard. Thing is, though, it happened a week ago. He hasn't seen it since. And he's refusing to say anything about it.'

'And what else, Jimmy?'

'What else, Mr Hoskins?'

'Yes, Jimmy. What else about him? All of a sudden, out of the blue, you pop up with a story about Billy Catte's Nissan being stolen. Not connected to anything. What makes it so important all of a sudden? Why should I pay you for telling me that Billy Catte's motor has gone missing? Who cares?'

Liddell pulled himself upright, defensively.

'You're putting salt on his tail, Mr Hoskins. That's what. That's the story round the manor. Him and his amusement arcades.'

'Then tell me something else about him, Jimmy.'

Liddell screwed up his face, a pantomime of honest recollection.

'He's got that German bit he married a few years back. They reckon he has parties in his house where things go on you wouldn't see in a Port Said knocking-shop.'

'Anything illegal, Jimmy?'

'Play fair, Mr Hoskins. It's only what I hear. And there's some of the girls in the arcade and the Totty-Boxing that's a bit on the young side. Whether he likes that or whether it's just for the customers, I couldn't say. What else can I tell you?'

Hoskins hitched his elbow on to the reading-stand.

'Since we're here, Jimmy, let's try and see how we go. I don't see how you've earned your lunch-money so far. For instance, what's the reckoning in your part of the house about the hi-jack and the shooting?'

Jimmy Liddell sucked his teeth and shook his head.

'Well out of order, that was, Mr Hoskins. There's not a face I've spoken to that thinks otherwise. Even some of them that done a stretch inside. Whoever did that to Mr McPhail and Mr Cross ought to be put down like animals. That's what's said.'

'Anyone suggesting who might have done it?'

'Freelance, Mr Hoskins. Bloody young hooligans with

no sense. I mean, all they need do is carry baseball bats when they stopped that van. Where's the sense in shooters? Couldn't fire 'em on the motorway without being noticed. And that business with Mr McPhail and Mr Cross, that was wicked.'

'What about the guns?'

Liddell explored his ear with a forefinger.

'There was a story about a year ago. A few old army revolvers, surplus to Irish requirements now they get automatic weapons from Libya. Done up and sold off by a bloke from the Dublin ferry. Barrels cut short to fit a pocket. Sonny Hassan was carrying one when you met him last year. An Eley four-five-five. No one in their senses would touch it. For a start, you have to file down most ammo to fit it. Reckoning is, each time you fire it, you've got a good chance of blowing your own hand off. That's the sort you're dealing with, Mr Hoskins. Bloody menace to everyone.'

Hoskins sighed. 'All right, Jimmy. And what about this pirate radio lark, the *Hit-Back Show*? Any murmurs on that?'

Liddell shook his head and grinned.

'Waste of time for you, Mr Hoskins. Everyone enjoys it that listens to it. I mean, on the usual television nowadays you get some po-faced git of a newsreader reading out names and addresses of people that's failed the breathalyser. Making bother for 'em. Trying to punish 'em a second time, sort of thing. Then whoever reads it goes out the car park after the programme and gets a kick up the arse. Long overdue, that's the reckoning. People're bloody fed up with television acting like judge and jury. Moaning if someone gets off light in court. Wanting the judge sacked if a bloke don't get life for being indecent. It's the judge knows the facts, not them. They're not allowed to. Who the fuck do they think they are? Bunch of sanctimonious prats. What I've heard, there ought to be more arse-kicking round the BBC and Coastal Network.'

'It was a broken wrist, not a kick up the arse,' Hoskins said patiently. 'And the producer's house was firebombed.'

'Ah,' said Liddell dismissively. 'People like the *Hit-Back Show*. Not that they want broken bones. But they like to think of all these mean-streaks in tax offices and places, sweating on getting a real hiding the moment they step out in the dark. Bit of a laugh, that's all. Word is, there's quite a following for this pirate stuff. Sort of cult, you might say.'

Hoskins scratched his chin. 'And that's all the morning news?'

Liddell looked down at his ash-coloured suede shoes. He scraped off a little street mud from one with the aid of the other.

'There's something else a bit naughty, Mr Hoskins. No offence intended. Something rather iffy with your lot. You remember when several of the chaps was caught burgling Orient Video? Nicked while actually loading up a van at the back of the building?'

'I remember,' Hoskins said. 'What about it?'

Liddell had another go at the mud on his shoe and watched it fall to the floor.

'Come to court last week. Sammy and Phil pleaded guilty. Only what they couldn't understand is why they was only charged with nicking eight videos, when they reckon they was found with about fifteen. I mean, they ain't objecting and they ain't saying nothing, seeing they got off easier. But there's half a dozen machines that Orient Video had stolen and the insurance paid 'em for but what your lot never mentioned finding. No offence, Mr Hoskins. It's only what I hear. Course, Sammy and Phil reckon some of your lot must have had new videos for Christmas.'

Hoskins felt his face tighten with fatalistic anger. 'I'll see, Jimmy.'

'I'm not one to make trouble, Mr Hoskins, you know that. But there's half a dozen of those machines that was in the van when Sammy and Phil was nabbed and what ain't anywhere now. Supposing you believe Sammy and Phil.'

Hoskins sighed again. He took a banknote from his pocket, folded it, and pressed it into Liddell's hand.

'I can't say you've earned your luncheon-vouchers today, Jimmy. Look on this as an investment. Don't expect another till it pays a dividend.'

Liddell resumed an upright dignity.

'Billy Catte's car, Mr Hoskins. That's worth something. You know it – and I know it.'

'We'll see, Jimmy. If it is, you'll hear all about it.'

Liddell's eyes moved, as if in proof of sudden recollection.

'Billy Catte's state of health any use to you?'

'He's waiting on a hip-replacement, Jimmy. I know that already.'

But there was no mistaking the pleasure in Liddell's face now. He pushed the flop of grey hair back from his forehead.

'Then you don't know, Mr Hoskins?'

'About what?'

'The rubber room. He was that far gone about a year ago. They had him in the rubber room, down the funny farm. Touch of the old psychiatrics. That private loony-bin up the valley. Roselands. Catte come back and let on how he'd been in Germany where his wife come from. He never was. I know someone used to take out fresh fruit and chocolates for him twice a week. See? You didn't know, did you, Mr Hoskins?'

'No,' Hoskins admitted thoughtfully, 'I didn't. Not allowed to pry into medical records.'

'Ought to be worth a bit,' Liddell said. He stood there stooping with his belted coat open and the hair flopping to either side of his head, the image of a race-course punter on a bad day. Hoskins took out his wallet again. Liddell flexed his fingers.

'Make it last a bit, Jimmy,' Hoskins said. 'Sip it. Don't gulp it.'

He stopped at the sound of footsteps in the passageway connecting the two rooms.

'Hello, Jimmy Riddle,' said Jack Chance cheerfully.

'You got no call to use that sort of name, Mr Chance,' Liddell said quietly. 'I never done nothing to you.'

Hoskins put a hand on the old man's shoulder.

'That's true, Jimmy. You'll have to excuse Mr Chance. He can be a thoughtless young clown at times. You stay here and we'll go out one by one.'

'I'll keep you posted on that business of the motor, Mr Hoskins.'

'Do that, Jimmy.'

A few minutes later, by the parked car, Chance said, 'Well? What's Jimmy Riddle got to say?'

'Not much to you, I shouldn't think. Seems Billy Catte had his car stolen and never reported it. Seems he was under psychiatric treatment out Roselands a year ago. Apart from that, there's several Eley four-five-five revolvers floating round in a dangerous state, thanks to some merchant from

78

armalites and semtex. And the public likes the *Hit-Back Show* and the idea of BBC staff being beaten up in the car park. And I'm now going back to see the Ripper.'

When Chance had driven off, Hoskins walked slowly to Atlantic Wharf. He sat in the car and gazed thoughtfully at the window of Madame Jolly Modes. An almond-eyed and tan-skin girl with a bee-hive of dark hair and a sharp young profile was arranging the window-display of lingerie. Hoskins tried to imagine some of it on Lesley. In a casual movement the girl caught his eye. Hoskins let in the clutch, circled Atlantic Wharf, and drove bacck towards City Hall and the Mall. Too much of Madame Jolly might keep a man awake at nights.

# Chapter Ten

'This one has to be by the rules, Sam,' Superintendent Ripley said.

They sat either side of Ripley's desk. Beyond the steel-framed window, the same cold Atlantic sky shed its brilliance on the leafless trees and sheltered gardens of Hawks Hill on the opposite ridge.

'I'm passing on the information,' Hoskins said calmly. 'For what it's worth.'

A sheet of paper, hastily turned over, concealed most of the brochure in the Ripper's in-tray. Hoskins could just catch the words, 'Littlehampton . . . Golden Acres Condominium Development.'

Ripley stood up. From the motorpool below his window the engine of a squad car coughed and failed. It erupted a second time, sustained a bronchial aria, and then settled into long silence. The Superintendent turned towards Hoskins, an expression of concern weighing upon him.

'I don't suggest that Catte and his unsavoury little empire are unimportant, Sam. Mr Clitheroe thinks they're important enough for you and Jack Chance to be put on them full-time. But we can't start digging into his medical records.' He smiled helplessly at the outlandishness of the thought. 'God's truth, Sam! Can you imagine the snappy piece of investigative journalism on Coastal TV when they discovered that the police were ferreting through confidential medical files? What was Catte supposed to have had wrong, by the way?'

Hoskins pulled a face. 'My informant didn't say. Psychiatric diagnosis wouldn't be his long suit.'

Ripley sat down again, mid-way between the old-fashioned cylindrical ruler and the silver-framed photograph.

'By the book, then, Sam. See what mileage we can get out of Melanie Paget and the others playing truant. Ear to the ground for any other complaints about Catte's arcade. Totty-Boxing down the Realito Club might just constitute keeping a disorderly house or indecent display. See if there isn't something under fire regulations as well. As for the stolen car that wasn't reported, you'd better leave well alone for the moment. We've only your informant's word that it was taken. Perhaps it turned up of its own accord.'

Cold winter sun caught fire against the picture-window of a 1930s gabled villa on Hawks Hill, as if an imprisoned commodity broker or consultant surgeon might be heliographing a message to the world. Hoskins stared at it with detachment.

'In other words,' he said calmly, 'the great gang-busting inquiry is about to come to pieces in our hands. Little girls playing truant and old ladies complaining about the noise down the Realito! Real first division stuff. Billy Catte's likely to bust his other hip laughing at us!'

The Ripper shook his head. 'Sit down, Sam. Let me make you a proposition.'

'Early retirement, I should think.'

But Hoskins sat down. Ripley picked up his cylindrical ruler by its ends, slid his fists to the centre and put the ruler down again. He looked unaccountably pleased with himself.

'What's your opinion of Catte, Sam? As an individual.'

Hoskins thought for a moment.

'Hard nosed,' he said presently. 'Crooked as they come. Probably degenerate. No scruples nor conscience. And quite possibly psychopathic. I don't doubt he exploits his girls as a work-force. I don't think he'd have many qualms about getting his hands up their skirts either. There was a smuggled porno-paperback on his desk about girls in reform schools.'

Ripley nodded, almost smiling in his eagerness at Hoskins' catalogue of vices.

'Might tell you something about his character, Sam. That and the Totty-Boxing.'

Hoskins stared at him.

'I don't need telling about his character, Max. I've had it over me by the bucketful. And I can't arrest him for reading a paperback about girls in reformatories!'

The Ripper gave a gentle smile.

'You're out of touch with modern thought, Sam. Mr Clitheroe was saying, and I'm bound to agree, that we need to mobilise our allies in this city. You think Catte might benefit from a raid by social services? See what they can dig up for us?'

'I don't believe I'm hearing this, Max. Social services?'

Ripley shook his head with the expression of a man asking a fair hearing.

'They've got certain real powers now, Sam. And they're not answerable to press or media. I mention this because there's a ripple of interest in their office about Catte's two daughters. One's fifteen and the other ten. In point of fact, they're his step-daughters. The younger was born in Germany to Sonja Catte during her first marriage there. Sonja Franz, as she was, married Catte the same year and came to England. I gather a social services hit-squad wants both girls in hospital for examination. Seems the younger one has been showing inappropriate sexual knowledge in the playground. That sort of thing.'

'Inappropriate?' Hoskins snorted at the absurdity of it.

'Could be our way in, Sam,' said the Ripper simply. 'I've no complaints about your investigation. But I have to tell you, the news from the lawyers and the stipendiary isn't encouraging. As it stands, you won't get a warrant to arrest Billy Catte — much less to search his premises. You need allies.'

Hoskins looked up and confronted the vast window-rows of the Mount Pleasant tower-blocks dominating the northern skyline.

'Not sure, Max. Gerald Foster reckons that a lot of this child abuse panic is being pumped up in the social services because of frustrated ambitions. Promotion blockages, among other things. That and ladies who'd do anything to show what a rotten lot men are.'

Ripley's amiability faded. He pursed his lips thoughtfully.

'I wouldn't recommend you airing opinions of that sort outside this room, Sam. Not unless you have some other line of employment open.'

Hoskins paused. Then he spread out his hands.

'Max, these people don't even issue statistics, just estimates. Can you imagine what the response would be if we went round estimating how many cars were nicked or if someone was murdered or not? Up go the estimates, next thing they're demanding more money and more senior posts. Jobs for the boys and girls. All I'm saying is let's not get into bed with that lot just as they're found out.'

The Ripper looked at him quietly.

'No one's asking you to rely on them, Sam. I want them to begin their investigation of the family circumstances of Emma

Catte, *née* Franz. I want the pressure stepped up on Billy Catte in every way known to man. And I want us to watch carefully as he starts to come apart at the seams.'

Hoskins shook his head, as if clearing it.

'Max,' he said, 'there's something someone's not telling me. Catte is a grimy-fingered arcade proprietor down the Beach with some unpleasant personal habits. I'll be singing and dancing all the way to the car park the day he's banged up. But why this sudden promotion of Billy Catte to the big league?'

Ripley took out an undernourished folder from his desk drawer.

'Mr Clitheroe thinks our friend Catte is up to no good. Probably being used to import porn videos and such, possibly worse than that.'

'Worse?' Hoskins screwed up his face in disbelief. 'Warehouses of cocaine? You could sell him chalk dust and he wouldn't know the difference.'

The Ripper frowned. 'Mr Clitheroe's speciality is arms shipments for the boyos, Sam, not cocaine. Short haul from here to Dublin and Rosslare. That foreign paperback Catte was reading, by the way. You recall the title?'

Hoskins closed his eyes. 'Not off-hand. I think I've got a note somewhere.'

The Ripper nodded approval. 'Get on to Customs and Excise, Sam. See if it's on their Stop-List of titles.'

Outside in the corridor, Chance was disappearing towards the lift in his driving-coat.

'Jack!'

Chance turned round but made no effort to come back. Hoskins walked up to him.

'I'm off watch, Sam.'

'Too right, my son. And you'll be back tonight. First thing, get on to Customs and Excise. See if there's a book on their Stop-List called *Elaine Cox, A Well-Reared Tomboy.*'

Chance snorted with laughter.

'Having readings in the briefing-room are we?'

'Could be major-league crime, Jack. Mr Ripley wants a result. I can't trust myself to make the call.'

'Poor old sod,' Chance said sympathetically. 'He probably wants something a bit fruity for Mrs Ripper to read to him in bed, while feeding him spinach with the other hand. Hair-curlers, mugs of Ovaltine and choppers grinning in the glass. Enough to get anyone wild with lust.'

Before Hoskins could reply Chance turned round and sauntered off to the lift again, whistling and ostentatiously practising his limp-wristed walk.

# Chapter Eleven

It was the following evening when Hoskins and Chance were next on watch together. After the late canteen-break, they walked down the stairs to the motorpool and the Sierra. Chance started the car and turned out on to the Mall.

'She's got this notion,' he said quietly. 'Over a grassy bank. Open air. No clothes on. I could fancy getting some of that.'

'What you'd get this time of year, my son, is hypothermia,' said Hoskins bleakly. 'And the only grassy bank round here is in the countryside park. You could reckon on a dozen families of happy campers cheering you on, followed by an internal disciplinary inquiry and a boot out of the police force. Take Great Western Street and Balance Street bridge. I want a look at Billy Catte's boxing fans coming out. See if there's a face or two we might know.'

Before Chance had cleared the Mall and crossed King Edward Square, a neat female voice spluttered through the car radio static.

'Bravo control to Bravo Four, DCI Hoskins.'

Hoskins recognised the gentle diffident tone. It was reserved for bad news.

'Bravo Four, DCI Hoskins. Go ahead, please.'

There was a pause and then the same cool, starched voice.

'Suspect vehicle C8 sighted in the approach to Longwall Circle by Delta Five, believed to be still in area, possibly parked. Proceed to Market Cross intersection and rendez-vous with DCI Nicholls in Tango One on West-Wing Car Park high-level in five minutes.'

'Understood, control. Listening and out.'

He put back the microphone and turned to Chance, his face tense with vindictive satisfaction.

'Step on it, Jack. C8. Target reference for Billy Catte's limo. The one that he never reported stolen. White Nissan Bluebird. D4250 AJT. Four-door model. Let's see who's driving it now.'

Chance swung the Sierra from King Edward Square into the eastern length of Longwall. Neon and sodium glared above the Victorian store fronts, the street now clear of shoppers and their cars at half-past eleven.

Two drunks from a side-street pub began their leisurely progress across the shoplit street towards the Longwall Metro-rail entrance. Chance pressed the switch and hounded them aside with the hee-haw of the twin-tones and the diffused reflections of flashing blue. The tyres of the Sierra drummed and hissed down the open avenue, window-displays of petri-fied wax dummies flicking past like frames of a badly pro-jected movie.

'Bravo control to Bravo Four. Message from Superin-tendent Watts. Please take up position as instructed and await DCI Nicholls in Romeo One. Romeo One now despatched.'

'Romeo One?' said Chance incredulously. 'Whatever hap-pened to Tango One?'

'Wouldn't start,' Hoskins suggested glumly. 'Another motorpool casualty. Though last time the problem was Wallace Dudden. Took short. Gone off with the keys in his pocket. People going round banging on all the bog doors in the building trying to raise him. Meantime the city burns and the looters chuckle. Turn the hooter off, Jack. No sense announcing our arrival.'

The far end of Longwall, wrought-iron Victorian shopping arcades, had been levelled by German bombers in 1941. Longwall Circle had risen in the 1950s, a double curve of chain-stores in the grey cement rendering of Stalinist cityscape.

Chance slowed down, turning off the siren and the revolv-ing light. The road branched round either side of the central lawn and monument, a Henry Moore mother and child. A four-lane underpass, joining Canton centre to the ring-road, ran through twin tunnels beneath the shops. It surfaced in the urban motorway interchange of Market Cross at the far exit of Longwall Circle.

They came round the circle, following the traffic lanes towards the Market Cross exit which ran slightly uphill. A steel security fence prevented the agile from trying to cross the four-lane traffic on foot. In addition to the network of pedestrian tunnels under the Market Cross interchange, a white concrete-walled bridge spanned the Circle exit from the Holiday Inn to the Coastal Insurance building. A brave experiment of the 1950s, it was reached by escalators in white towers, rising from either pavement.

Two lanes rumbled up towards the crossing and two lanes

whined down from it. In the earth below, four lanes of traffic shook the shop foundations from the Longwall underpass. Through the earlier darkness of rush-hour and late-night shopping, the emerging cars and buses rose like a double chain of rubies beyond the interchange, mile upon mile of rear lights dwindling towards semi-detached Clearwater and high-rise Peninsula. But by this time of night it was vast and deserted as an empty skating rink.

Chance turned off on the approach to West-Wing Car Park, adjoining the Holiday Inn. Here and there a car stood dark and abandoned. The fifth level, open to the sky of the January night, was empty. Across the grey parapet of its concrete wall there was a wide view of Longwall Circle. With Nicholls in command up here and mobile units at the main exits, the territory would be under control.

A chaos of radio chatter began to confirm Hoskins' gloomier predictions.

'Delta Three to control. Suspect vehicle heading towards Longwall Circle from Churchill Avenue South. About three minutes ago. Delta Three now parked and observing this exit.'

'Charlie Six to control. He's not come out on Park Drive North and we can't see him in the Circle.'

'Charlie Two to control. Not on Market Cross West, boss. We're bang on the intersection.'

'Foxtrot One to control. No traffic on Longwall East exit for the past four minutes.'

As the points of the compass were ticked off, the airwaves went quiet. Someone whose finger had forgotten the transmission button and whose mouth was too close to the microphone said softly, 'The bugger's vanished . . . '

'Still in there somewhere . . . '

'Bloody brilliant deduction,' Chance said quietly. 'Where the hell's Tom Nicholls?'

Hoskins opened the door and walked across to the waist-high concrete parapet of the car park. Far below them, Longwall Circle remained empty.

'Control to all units,' Hoskins turned back again as the crisp voice summoned him. 'Lewis and Jones department store. Security patrol reports one suspect on foot in black balaclava mask, sighted by Market Lane loading-bay. Charlie Six and Foxtrot One respond to call. Charlie Two remain to cover Market Cross intersection.'

The end of the message coincided with the shrill metallic chatter of an alarm-bell, somewhere beyond the soaring concrete shaft of the Holiday Inn. Chance started the car.

'Leave it, Jack,' said Hoskins sharply. 'I'm staying here till Tom Nicholls shows up. If we go now, no one's left with a view of the Circle. You can't see into it properly from the Market Cross intersection.'

The alarm clattered on, urging him into action. Hoskins ignored it. Charlie Six and Foxtrot One swept round the Circle and disappeared towards Churchill Avenue South. Half a minute passed. Then a white car with a long sloping back eased out of a side-lane on the turning past which the two police Rovers had vanished.

'Nissan Bluebird,' Chance said knowledgably.

Hoskins reached for the microphone as the Nissan cruised towards the northern exit and Park Drive.

'Stay put, Jack. You won't catch him from here.' He drew the microphone closer. 'Bravo Four to control. White Nissan Bluebird entering Longwall Circle from Churchill Avenue South. Believed proceeding to Park Drive North. Block Park Drive and all approaches to the Circle on that side. Repeat, block Park Drive and all approaches to Longwall Circle from the north . . . '

'Sam!' Chance was pointing vigorously. 'They're not going! Look!'

The Nissan Bluebird had pulled up twenty yards or so along the Park Drive exit from the great open circle of the shopping-centre. Hoskins could just see that two passengers had got out. The driver pulled forward a little. Then the car went violently into reverse. It jumped the pavement. The rear of the vehicle vanished at speed into an alcove formed by the side-entrance of Boots the Chemists. The accelerating roar of the car engine drowned the crash as it burst open the glass swing-doors of the Audio-Visual Department. Like a peal of bells joining a celebration from another steeple, the second alarm went off.

'Bravo Four to control. White Nissan Bluebird backed through the doors of Boots' side-entrance in Park Lane North. Robbery in progress by three suspects. Proceeding to investigate. Inform, DCI Nicholls.'

Chance threw the Ford Sierra down the curves of the car park levels like a mat down a helter-skelter. Hoskins pushed a plastic security-card into the slot to raise the barrier.

'C'mon, you dozy bugger,' he said to the lumbering machinery as the pole was hoisted aloft.

They bumped over the ramp and down the incline on to Market Cross intersection. Chance braked sharply to avoid Romeo One with DCI Nicholls aboard which had just arrived and was trying to turn back on its tracks. Hoskins gestured helplessly, in time to see Nicholls being borne up the slope and into the car park.

'Bravo Four to control! Why is Mr Nicholls going up to the car park?'

'Control to Bravo Four. Tactical Support Unit despatched. DCI Nicholls to command from West-Wing high-level.'

Hoskins put the microphone down.

'Guns!' he said with quiet exasperation. 'They're sending guns again. Bloody Clitheroe! Fixation about the Dublin ferry. Canton infested by the boyos with bottles of Guinness and rocket-launchers. Get in plenty of practice before they come! Someone's going to be killed in the end.'

'It's McPhail and Cross,' said Chance, disagreeing gently. 'That's Clitheroe's hang-up at present.'

They came out on to Longwall Circle. Hoskins saw the white shape of the Nissan in the shadow of Boots' entrance. The headlights of the stolen car came on again. The tyres spun and scuffed grit. Chance skidded the Sierra on the first curve, recovered on the straight, and skidded again. As they raced for the next corner, Hoskins saw the Nissan jolt and bounce.

'Control to Bravo Four. Observe suspect vehicle but do not approach. Repeat, do not approach. Tactical Support Unit will be there in two minutes.'

'It's too late for that,' Hoskins said. 'We've already approached. They must have seen us. We're on Longwall Circle passing Longwall East.'

'Maintain circuit, Bravo Four. Do not turn on to Park Drive North. Repeat, do not turn on to Park Drive North.'

'Bravo Four. Understood.' He watched as they passed the turning. 'Jack, I swear those three dumbos have got the Nissan stuck in the entrance. Easy to bust the swing-doors inwards. But you can't pull 'em outwards when they're locked. Like a thumb in a bottle. Go round again.'

Chance accelerated, turning more smoothly past the long

quadrants of brightly lit department store windows.

'This time,' Hoskins said, 'turn into Park Drive.'

Chance gave a sigh. They rounded the corner of Boots as three doors of the Nissan were thrown open and the occupants scrambled out. Chance flicked on the blue flashing light and siren to join the cacophony of the department store alarm. There was no gunfire nor resistance. Two hooded figures sprinted down access lanes on either side, the third down the main sweep of Park Drive.

'That one!' Hoskins shouted, pointing at the third sprinter. 'We'll take him. No sense two of us trying to follow three. Get that one and make him talk.'

Chance accelerated again and passed the hooded runner, driving up on to the pavement to block his escape. The fugitive hesitated and doubled back, disappearing into a narrow turning. Chance began to reverse.

'Watch it, Jack! This is one-way traffic!'

Hoskins, on the nearside, jumped out as they reached the alley down which the youthful thief had vanished. It led past the blank side-wall of the first of the tall Victorian houses on Park Drive. Somewhere in the darkness behind the houses was a rear access lane. Hoskins saw the shape of the man ahead, arms pumping and legs flying as he raced for the nearer footbridge. It was a metal walkway over the Metro-rail behind the Park Drive houses. Less than half Hoskins' age, the runner glided up the open tread of metal steps and down the far side. Chance was somewhere behind. Hoskins, a needle sharpness in his belly, lungs scorched by cold air as if drowning in caustic, lumbered up the metal slats. The thin steel of the bridge shook under the failing bulk of his legs. He saw the man ahead turn a corner and disappear.

'That's it, Jack!' Chance found him bending with palms on thighs. 'One – nil to the away side. Back to the car and radio in.'

Like members of a beaten team trailing over the turf of Lambs Acre to the changing-rooms, he and Chance made their way towards the abandoned cars. In the darkness of the lane by the side of the houses a voice shouted:

'Stop! Armed police! Stand where you are! Now, put your hands on your heads and kneel. Then stretch your arms out in front and lie down slowly on your faces! Legs apart! Do it!'

'Don't be fucking daft,' Chance said wearily. 'It's us.'

'Do it!'

'Do it, Jack,' Hoskins said. 'No sense getting shot.'

Presently a dark figure stood over them.

'In my breast pocket,' Hoskins said breathlessly. 'Warrant-card. Hoskins, DCI, "A" Division, Canton CID.'

A moment later he was standing up and the apologies began. Hoskins glared at the black-clad figure in the baseball cap.

'Two bloody pins, my son,' he said furiously. 'I'd have you for impersonating a police officer. Just look at the state of this bloody suit!'

Under the low peak of the cap, the blank eyes and the regulation bandit-moustache remained impassive.

'You want to be glad we're here, boss. There's a gun in that car. If they'd stopped to pick it up, I reckon you'd both be dead by now.'

# Chapter Twelve

January ended on the following afternoon with divisional briefings.

'Right people! Settle down!' Ripley brought the CID detail to order with a monotonous bray, like a muezzin calling the faithful to prayer. Large bottoms shifted their cramped cheeks on the little wooden chairs which Home Office allocation judged adequate for the physique of its employees. The January weather had turned milder but damp with a gentle Atlantic breeze, which Coastal Radio insisted was coming all the way from the Azores. In consequence the fading light of late afternoon glowed the colour of a maiden's blush through windows fogged by moisture. Rain-beaded anoraks and plastic bike-gear lay on the tables at the back.

'Right!' said the Ripper again, triumphant in the general calm. 'First let me say that no one is handing out blame for any of last night's events in Longwall Circle. But there won't be any medals either. We are here this afternoon to see what, if anything, can be learnt from the shortcomings of our operation. When I say shortcomings, I balance them against the frustrating of armed robbery. Though the thieves managed to load three thousand pounds value of video equipment in the stolen Nissan, they fled empty-handed. But we were wrong-footed by a simple tactic. One member of the gang hitting a Lewis and Jones alarm-bell very hard with a hammer to set it off. Our cars converged on Lewis and Jones, while the actual robbery was attempted half a mile away on the far side of Longwall Circle. That mustn't happen again. Now it seems to me . . . '

The door opened. It was Clitheroe, ACC Crime. He gave Ripley a wan apologetic smile.

'Mr Hoskins? If you can spare him.'

Hoskins felt like a boy rescued from class by the news of a family bereavement. He got up and pushed past the large trousered knees in his row. Clitheroe led the way to the floor above, where visitors stepped suddenly on to a carpeted level of brown and murky yellow. It was quieter here. Money had been spent upon luxuries. Clitheroe opened a door that led directly into his office, by-passing his secretary. Carpets again. Photographs on a shelf behind the desk, showing rows of uniformed officers, posing on benches like cricket teams.

'Sit down, Sam,' Clitheroe said. 'Not too early for you, is it?'

Sherry so dry that it looked and tasted like lighter fuel sloshed into two glasses from Clitheroe's cupboard. Hoskins had a wild notion that he was about to be promoted. He dismissed the idea and watched Clitheroe pour. The neat face with its dark Edwardian-poisoner moustache was intent on the task. The charcoal-grey suit was set off by a shirt of thin white and red stripes with a plain white collar and cuffs with gold links. There was a hint of scarlet braces. Clitheroe looked like a man who had been tailored by some costumier of the banking world or the entertainment industry.

Hoskins took the glass with a murmur, uneasy at the hospitality of a man he had never liked.

'Sam,' Clitheroe raised his glass and Hoskins did the same, 'here's to a successful outcome. You've got Billy Catte. Lock, stock and barrel.'

Hoskins put the glass down, his lips shrivelling from the dryness of the sherry.

'Got him?'

'Mr Catte has been upgraded. From now on he is a target rather than a nuisance. I'm telling you in detail what Max Ripley is giving to the others in outline. When those villains did a bunk last night, they forgot the glove compartment. Area Forensic had a preliminary look at the car and the gun this morning. It's an Eley four-five-five service revolver with a couple of inches sawn off the barrel. Several rounds of forty-five ammo with the cartridge bases filed to fit. It's the gun and the sort of bullets that killed Terry Cross. The murder case stays with me. But Billy Catte is down to you, Sam. This is no place for vanity. You've put in more time on him than I ever could. He stays with you.'

Hoskins put his unfinished glass on the desk.

'He was with me – Jack Chance and I were questioning him – when Cross and McPhail were killed.'

Clitheroe nodded. 'Exactly, Sam. But this thing is bigger than Billy Catte now. It's a bit too convenient to have had his car stolen like that by a man who owned the murder gun. We need to think in terms of who might have had access to Mr Catte's vehicle. Alibi or not, this could end up with him being accessory to murder of two police officers. He's got two sons, eighteen and sixteen, and some very unsavoury associates.'

'Anything known?' Hoskins asked.

Clitheroe shook his head. 'Not by CRO. The elder son, Steven, fancies himself. Known as "Tom" Catte for self-evident reasons. The younger, Kevin, remains an unknown quantity. I'd pull them both in and put them through the wringer now, if I could find them. And if I could hold off the family brief long enough. Claude Roberts. A friend of yours, I think?'

Hoskins looked up. There was no misting on the sixth-floor windows. That was another thing, air conditioning.

'I've known Claude Roberts twenty years,' he said evasively.

Clitheroe's mouth went a little tighter.

'The gun that killed Terry Cross is found in Billy Catte's car during a robbery. The man is a sexual degenerate. An animal that copulates like a dog and treats the world accordingly. That committal to private psychiatric care last year was to forestall a complaint by a girl in his club. So my informant assures me. I want him shaken down. And his sons. But you stick with Billy Catte, Sam. Leave his tearaways to me.'

'I could get him under the Gaming Act,' Hoskins said. 'And probably the Children and Young Persons Act. That's about all at present. And I'm still his alibi.'

Clitheroe gave him the thin poisoner-smile.

'You'll do better than that, Sam. Maxwell Ripley told you, I understand. Social services are convinced that the two step-daughters are being abused, almost certainly by Catte himself. Their people could help us to get the spade under him. Catte is a man who could be tipped quite easily by the right sort of stress. He won't know if we're after him for complicity in armed robbery and murder, for statutory rape, gaming and corruption of public morals. Or the whole lot. Step up the pressure and he'll split wide open. That's the suggestion.'

'Just like that?'

Clitheroe's smile was quick as a light going on and off.

'Work with the welfare people, Sam, but don't let them know more than they need. It's a tall order. The feeling in our higher echelons is that you are one of the few people who might do it justice. Catte and the rest of his entourage need flushing out. Sonja Catte and the younger girl, Claudia, come back from Germany the day after tomorrow, according to my information. That's the signal for action.'

Hoskins tried to decide whether Clitheroe had an inscrutable master-plan for the detection of murder and the destruction of Billy Catte's empire, or whether it was bluff of an office-holder with too much to lose by unsolved police murders. He guessed it was bluff.

'I'd rather have the ground well laid,' he said simply.

Clitheroe gave him the poisoner-smile again.

'We can't stop the social services, Sam. When they go, we have to follow. Armed robbery, complicity in the murder of two police officers, incest and statutory rape. That's the pot of gold at the end of the rainbow. And if he tries to do a bunk, nick him for speeding as well. You've got a couple of days before the caring professions hit him where he lives. You might even have Billy Catte tucked up by then.'

'Supposing the bed fits him,' Hoskins said.

Clitheroe looked at him, prepared to quell defiance.

'Whether it does or not, Sam, you're about to make a start on the process. There's no point pulling in Catte on a warrant to begin with. He'd act dumb and insist on his brief being fetched. So we're opening the game with kid-gloves, before he knows what else is coming his way. Mr Ripley has spoken to your friend, Claude Roberts. We had confirmation from Mr Roberts just before I fetched you from the briefing. Billy Catte is to be interviewed, by arrangement, in Claude Roberts' office tomorrow morning at ten. On the subject of his stolen car. Handle it well, and you could be half-way home.'

# TWO

# Mr Cat

# Chapter Thirteen

The escalator of the Royal Peninsular Emporium carried Hoskins upwards from the roast coffee and cooked meat odours of the Food Hall on the ground floor. He rose through the candy sweetness of Perfumery, the ammonia smell of Gents Suiting, to the clatter of tables being laid for lunch in the Marina Suite on the top floor. At one side was a door with the figure of a spreadeagled man upon it. Hoskins went in, ran warm water and washed his hands. As he drew the comb through his hair, the new ceramic tiles that had the tone and sheen of toffee were reflected in the wide mirror. The place was windowless and airless, except for the hum of fan-driven warmth. It was as remote from the world as being down in a submarine.

Even this enclave of warm pipes and disinfectant-perfumed porcelain was not immune from the public address system. Hoskins was treated to the rippling and clonking of a club piano in the Marina Suite, stringing together tunes of a middle-aged past, words remembered as soon as he heard the notes. While water swept and gurgled, the shimmering chords assured him that when he was in love, the whole world sang a melody. But during his passion for Lesley Wiles, the world had behaved in much its usual way. It had punched and spat, fled with armfuls of stolen goods and demanded to see its brief when taken into custody. It had sung him no melodies.

Washed and combed, he braced himself for Claude Roberts. The door swung to stillness behind him as he went down the escalator and out to Atlantic Wharf.

Chance was sitting at the wheel of the Sierra.

'Five to ten, Jack. Let's keep our appointment.'

They walked in step towards Prince's Passage, a covered Edwardian mall of shops cutting the corner from Balance Street to Great Western Street along the rear of the Emporium. Bijou shops and the Emporium windows ran on opposite sides of the arcade. At the higher level, under the pitched glass roof and hanging lamps, a wrought-iron gallery gave access to some of Canton's more expensive and exclusive offices. Accountants and solicitors, graphic design and barristers chambers competed for space behind the Venetian windows and fairy mouldings. The arcade was still and sunlit, its iron pillars freshly painted in leather-red and cream.

Hoskins led the way up the stairs to the gallery. He pushed open the door of Pollard Roberts and Son, Solicitors and Commissioners for Oaths.

'DCI Hoskins and Sergeant Chance to see Mr Claude Roberts in the matter of William Catte,' he said to the receptionist. She disappeared and came back smiling, leading them to a finely panelled door that promised a drawing-room of piano and aspidistra. It opened upon a sunny office with a desk the size of a double-bed. Billy Catte sat like a scowling child in a wooden carving chair. Two silk-seated dining chairs had been put for Hoskins and Chance.

Claude Roberts rose from behind his desk and held his hand out to Hoskins with the air of one who had done it a hundred times in the past. Tall, spruce and white-haired, he was still 'Mr Claude' in his father's practice. His thin face was pink from the razor and his hair springy from a stiff brush. He had an air of the senior squash court and the Turkish baths on Victoria quay. Black jacket and grey tie were brightened by a button-hole carnation.

'Mr Hoskins . . . Mr Chance . . . ' he waved them to seats and pressed his intercom. 'Linda, ask Nicola to serve us coffee when she has a moment. Four cups.'

He sat down and smiled around him.

'I spoke to Superintendent Ripley, Mr Hoskins, and conveyed my client's willingness to co-operate in your investigation. The matter of the stolen car. At the same time, I thought it only fair to add that you and Mr Chance had paid Mr Catte a visit the other week of a less than friendly kind. Without prejudice to that matter, I suggested our present business should be transacted here. One thing we can all agree on. Mr Catte wasn't anywhere near Longwall Circle at the time of the attempted robbery. So Mr Ripley had no objection to my request. Mr Catte naturally wants to assist the police in any way that he can. I hope the arrangements meet with your satisfaction.'

Hoskins shifted his bulk a little. 'What all this won't do, Mr Roberts, is inspire my confidence in your client. I've been checking stolen cars for twenty years. This is the first time that a victim has refused to talk to me without his solicitor being present.'

Claude Roberts touched his fingers together under his chin.

'Tell me, Mr Hoskins, how many of these previous victims had received a visit from you a week earlier when you had threatened to put them in prison for two years for something of which they had not been found guilty?'

'That's not the point.'

'How many, Mr Hoskins? Could you give the names of ten? Or two? Or none at all?'

Roberts had positioned himself with the window behind him so that, as the sun brightened, Hoskins saw only a dark outline. He glared at the silhouette.

'This isn't a court,' he said sharply, 'nor a cross-examination.'

Roberts' voice was as silky and silver as his tie.

'It may very soon be both, Mr Hoskins, if I have reason to think that my client is being treated improperly by the police. Now, if you please, we will have your questions.'

But just then there was a tap at the door. Chance's eyes followed the tall lithe figure in the short woollen dress as she set down the tray and distributed cups of coffee.

'Thank you, Nicola,' said Roberts demurely, watching the door close. 'Now, Mr Hoskins, if you please.'

Hoskins looked at his notepad.

'Nissan Bluebird, white, registration D4250 AJT. That your car, Mr Catte?'

'Got the registration documents here.'

'And when did you last see the vehicle?'

'Week ago Friday. Half-past four in the afternoon.'

Hoskins frowned to himself, suspecting the precision of the answer.

'And since then?'

'Since then I been driving the Montego.'

Hoskins looked up from his notes.

'I daresay you have. What about the Nissan Bluebird since then?'

Catte, pug-nosed and creased, stared up at him.

'You tell me,' he said.

Hoskins sighed.

'When did you know that the Nissan was stolen?'

'I didn't,' Catte said. 'Not until I was woke up and told the night before last, by two of your lot that came busting into the house. I got a complaint in about that.'

'The car was in your possession until the day of the attempted robbery at Boots, on Longwall Circle?'

'I never said that.'

'When did you lose possession of it?'

'Can't say. Mrs Catte had it last, that Friday afternoon. She drove to Canton airport. Left it in the long-stay car park. Then she and little Claudia flew to Munich to see her family for a couple of weeks. Next thing, two of your lot bust in night before last. Near enough kicked the door down. Start shouting the odds about me using my car to rob Boots the Chemists. I didn't know what the hell they was on about. All I knew, it was parked out Canton airport for when she and the nipper comes back. Which they do today.'

The case clock upon Claude Roberts' wall chimed eleven in rich tones. Hoskins tried again.

'And how do you suppose it went missing from secure parking at the airport?'

Claude Roberts intervened as the tones of the clock died.

'Mr Hoskins. My client will not answer that question. If he knew the answer he would no doubt be drawing a salary as Detective Chief Inspector. How his car was stolen is for you to find out, not him.'

'Then how many ignition keys were there?'

'Three . . .' Catte creased his brow deeply with thought under the clustering of dark hair-oiled curls. 'Two . . . I think there was three and one got lost. Any case, she took 'em both with her.'

'So no one could collect the car?'

'They wouldn't want to collect it, would they?' Catte assumed the exasperation of bewildered honesty. 'It was left there ready for her to drive home when she come back.'

'Suppose the Montego had broken down while Mrs Catte was away?'

'But it bloody didn't break down, did it?' said Catte furiously.

Claude Roberts raised his hand for peace.

'Mr Hoskins, my client is not going to answer any further questions of this nature. What might have happened but didn't is irrelevant. And events beyond his knowledge are being used by you as a provocation.'

'Wait a minute!' said Hoskins, with the first sign of heat. 'His car went missing. I suggest he can explain that. At least he can account for the ignition keys and who might have had access to it.'

Roberts shrugged. 'All right. But he's answered that. Three keys. One lost some time ago. The other two in Mrs Catte's possession.'

Hoskins persisted, wide eyes deceptively gentle behind the tinted glasses.

'Access to the car, Mr Catte. Two sons and two step-daughters, I think?'

Catte was half-way out of his chair before Roberts urged him back.

'You are well out of order, Hoskins! Bloody well out of order! My kids aren't nothing to you! Nothing!'

'I'm not accusing anyone, Mr Catte. I need to eliminate possibilities. Forensic also needs to eliminate fingerprints that might legitimately be found in the Nissan.'

Claude Roberts added his soothing influence, the voice sleek and assuring.

'So long as that's the extent of it, Mr Hoskins.'

'We'll discount the two girls,' Hoskins said gently. 'The two boys drive the car, do they? Steven and Kevin?'

'Kevin's sixteen,' Catte said gloomily. 'He's too young to drive at all.'

'And Steven?'

'Not that I know. I've never said he could use the Nissan, nor's Mrs Catte. He's a good boy. Does as he's told.'

Hoskins nodded, as if accepting this.

'The two girls are at school, of course . . . '

'Mr Hoskins!' It was Claude Roberts again. 'Whether the girls are at school or not can have nothing – absolutely nothing – to do with this inquiry.'

'Just thinking aloud,' Hoskins said with a brief, apologetic smile. 'What about Steven and Kevin?'

'This is out of order!' Catte said furiously.

Hoskins shook his head.

'Not really, Mr Catte. I need to know that neither of them collected the Nissan from the airport car park for some purpose or other. Perhaps I could ask them about it.'

'Like hell you could,' Catte said grimly. 'You'd have to find 'em first.'

'Not at school, then?'

The weight of Billy Catte's skull pressed the lines of his forehead scowl deeper.

'For what it matters to you, they're not.'

'Do you know where they are?'

Billy Catte brightened up at this. He looked up at the ceiling as if he might grin.

'Not exactly. No.'

'And what does that mean?'

'It means,' Catte said, 'that they're travelling the world on those rail-passes for young people. Seeing Europe. Could be in Munich now for all I know. They're good boys, both of 'em. They sent me some lovely postcards.'

He lowered his gaze and stared straight into Hoskins' eyes, defying the Chief Inspector to disprove the falsehood. There was a silence, while Hoskins pretended to look at his notes.

'Anything else?' Claude Roberts inquired innocently.

'Yes,' said Hoskins to Catte. 'When did you last own a gun?'

'Wait!' Roberts said. Hoskins turned back to him.

'A loaded gun was found in the glove compartment of the Nissan Bluebird.'

Roberts nodded to Catte.

'I never owned a gun,' Catte said sourly. 'Why should I?'

'You were fined in 1978 for illegal possession of a firearm.'

'That! That bloody thing? My brother came back with that from Germany in 1946. Old broken Luger as a souvenir. He died in 1976 and it was in a box of his odds and ends. I was trying to get rid of it to an antiques merchant.'

'It was found to be in working order.'

'Well I wouldn't know, would I?' Catte said. 'I never used a gun and I wouldn't know if it worked or not.'

'And since then?'

'Nothing.'

There was a pause. Hoskins flipped over a page.

'Your movements on Wednesday the fifth of January. What were they?'

Roberts was back again. 'What has this to do— '

'The gun that was in the Nissan Bluebird is identical to that used in the killing of two police officers in Mordaunt Lane that afternoon.'

Catte waved Claude Roberts aside.

'I don't mind answering that, Hoskins. You know where

I was that afternoon. I was being asked a lot of bloody silly questions by you and your boyfriend here when those two poor devils got topped.'

'The morning?' Hoskins persisted doggedly.

'Mrs Catte drove me and the little girl to the school about nine. Dropped her off and drove me to Rundle Street. I was there after that.'

'Can anyone verify that, if necessary?'

'Not more than about twenty people,' Catte said with bitter satisfaction. 'And I went and spoke to her form teacher about her being away when Mrs Catte went to Germany. She wanted to take the nipper with her to see the family.'

There was a pause and Claude Roberts cleared his throat a little.

'Mr Hoskins, this has gone beyond what I would normally allow. My client's car was stolen and you were to investigate that. We are now in the territory of armed robbery and the murders of two police officers. My client and I are both concerned to see such criminals brought to justice. You have therefore enjoyed considerable latitude. But Mr Catte has now told you all about the theft of his car that you can reasonably want to know. There will be no more questions this morning. Or, if there are, my client will withhold answers to them on my instructions.'

Hoskins flipped his notepad shut. Argument would get him nowhere. Chance was looking sideways through the net curtains, watching a girl with a mane of tiny red curls who was dressing a dummy in the Emporium's rear window.

'Perhaps,' said Roberts suavely, 'we might have an agreed aide-mémoire of our discussion. If you would leave me to draught one, I shall submit it for general approval.'

Five minutes later, Hoskins and Chance stood in the outer office, its pale carpet soft as snow. Roberts walked out to the open gallery with Catte and then returned.

'Thought you were going to go soft on me for a moment, Claude,' said Hoskins cheerfully, as he and Roberts met in the doorway. 'Never known you be that nice before.'

Roberts chuckled and touched his tie.

'You know how it is, Sam. One gets mellow. Still, you've got a real bugger with this new lot. Who in hell would try doing Boots with Canton "A" Division on alarm-call half a mile away? Unless they were too stoned to care.'

'Dunno, Claude. One of 'em gave me a run for my money. If he moves with that kind of style when he's stoned, I'd hate to meet him sober.'

Roberts shook his head. 'Your young friend,' his eyes indicated Chance as he lowered his voice. 'You might tell him how difficult it is for us poor hacks to keep good staff. Doesn't help when a young lady brings the coffee in and the visitors try to wish away every stitch she's wearing.'

'That's young Mr Chance,' said Hoskins philosophically. 'Mr Clitheroe's going to give him the option of chemical control or the chop, on my advice.'

Claude Roberts chuckled. 'See you in clink, Sam.'

'Take care, Claude.'

As they walked back together to the car, Chance said quietly, 'You want to make up your mind whose side you're on, Sam. He's the nastiest of the lot in court.'

Hoskins chuckled. 'Old Claude Roberts? He's all right. I've known him since he defended his first careless driving. Not a bad old stick. Some of us were born in this town, Jack. And likely to die here. No point snarling at people all the time just because they happen to be in the rival concern.'

'You know he started three inquiries under the police complaints procedure a year or two back?'

'That's right. Every one of them justified.'

'Justified?' Words failed Jack Chance. The two men walked in silence towards the open street. Hoskins saw the day brighten in the chill blue sky above the docks and felt unaccountably cheerful.

'Park us round the corner for twenty minutes,' he said hopefully. 'I've got a date with our friend Jimmy Riddle. I'm beginning to get a taste for Tom Catte and his younger brother. Jimmy might just have something to say about 'em.'

'How's that then, Sam?'

'Doing the grand tour of Europe on a rail-card. Postcards from Munich or wherever. All a bit too easy, my son. Bring some pretty cards home on a previous visit. Write them out and give 'em to young Claudia or whoever to post at regular intervals while she's there. Meantime, nick the car from the airport with a spare ignition key and rob the city blind. Not an alibi that would stand close examination. But good enough to brush off a casual inquiry.'

'So where's that leave Terry Cross, Bob McPhail, and the pharmacy van?'

'In Mr Clitheroe's hot little hands,' said Hoskins unhelpfully.

# Chapter Fourteen

Half an hour later, Hoskins sat with Jimmy Liddell in the front seats of the Sierra. They were parked in River Street, a side-turning between Atlantic Wharf and Balance Street bridge.

'Other people knew that Nissan was pinched,' Liddell said, 'even if Mr Catte never did. It was seen round the Peninsula with a strange face at the wheel.'

'He thought it was still parked out the airport, Jimmy. He says so.'

Liddell sniffed. 'Anyone down the Peninsula knows security out the airport car park is a joke. They give 'em a ticket and tell 'em not to leave it in the car. But half the charter flights is more scared of losing car park tickets in Tenerife than having the car nicked. They hide it under the mirror or somewhere. You go out there, choose a limo, bounce the door and find a ticket. Give the engine a taste of hot whisker and off. Half the punters don't put the steering-lock on. And you got two weeks before the owner even gets back and finds it missing. Compliments of the airport management. Billy Catte ain't daft.'

'He says he didn't know, Jimmy. I can't prove he did. His missus was in Germany a few weeks. She left the car. He certainly wasn't in it when they rammed Boots the Chemists. About fifty people saw him in the Realito at the time. Sorry, my son, but this is wasting a busy morning for me.'

Liddell sighed. He took out a menthol inhaler, inserted it in his nostril and breathed deeply. He removed it, screwed the cap on and turned to Hoskins.

'How about him feeling up his step-daughter? You in the market for that?'

Hoskins clucked his tongue.

'Thing is, Jimmy, I could probably tell you more than you can tell me.'

'There must be something, Mr Hoskins. Play fair.'

Hoskins watched two shaven heads rolling empty steel beer-barrels from the rear service doors of the Black Velvet Casino Club. The pressurised casks stood in rows on the cracked and stained paving, awaiting the brewers' lorry.

'Tom Catte and his younger brother,' he said casually. 'Anything on them?'

Liddell made a mouth.

'They reckon Tom Catte fancies himself. But he keeps his own company. The other boy's only old enough to be practising as a football hooligan. Mind you, Tom Catte's got a bit of class. Not like his dad. Bishop Hoadley's High School. I think he got A-levels or something.'

Hoskins sighed.

'This is doing me no good at all, Jimmy. I need to know where they are and what they're up to. Times. Places. Events. See what you can do.'

Jimmy Liddell shook his head, the water-buffalo flop of hair stirring.

'You're behind the times, Mr Hoskins. There's a new generation that don't talk much and don't mix much. You heard it on the news this morning about the *Hit-Back* lot? Inspectors nearly catch 'em. So those lunatics drop a concrete block through the car roof from half a dozen storeys up a tower-block. Would have killed anyone in that motor. And another down the stair-well.'

Hoskins nodded at the prismatic shell-colours on the Philharmonic Importers' accordions.

'I heard, Jimmy. The two chaps from the detection car managed to do a runner on foot. I'm not sure they'll be going back.'

Liddell shook his head.

'Concrete blocks, Mr Hoskins! And the *Hit-Back* mob got university degrees or something. Not like the old days. You knew who was doing what and wnere. There was buying and selling. Not many secrets then. It's all different now. White-collar con-tricks. Robberies by tearaways that no one wants to know.'

'The crimes they are a-changing, Jimmy,' Hoskins said philosophically. 'And I'd still like to hear about Mr Catte's boys. Or even the *Hit-Back* mob. Find out where that's going to be tonight – or any night – and tell me in good time. Not my case any more but someone else might feel really grateful.'

'You want me to get my head bashed in, Mr Hoskins, for a tenner from the police fund?'

Liddell opened the car door, moving with significant slowness.

'All right, Jimmy.' Hoskins handed over a banknote. 'But make it last. Next time, you owe me.'

'Try to oblige, Mr Hoskins.'

Hoskins found Chance on the corner of Atlantic Wharf, where Madame Jolly and her modes occupied one café-pavilion end of the Paris Hotel. Chance was gazing at the girl with her long levantine nose and tight-lidded almond eyes, the narrow waist and the tight swagger of her rump as she walked.

'How d'you reckon a girl like her owns that shop, Sam?'

'Mr Cooney owns it, Jack, and her as well. Come on. Take me out the Beach. I want lunch before I get Forensic on the Nissan from Charlie Blades.'

Half an hour later Chance turned the car on to Bay Drive. Even before the sea came into sight, the sky above the promenade rails shimmered with cold brilliance, veiled by frosty mist that might have been a heat haze.

'Take me up to the top, Jack, by Alexandra Gardens. Drop me off there and pick me up at three from Area Forensic. Right?'

'Okey-doke,' said Chance cheerfully. 'I'll see if Julie can take a long lunch-hour. They gave her a room over the shop. Health and Safety at Work laws. She can cook on the boiling ring. Managed spaghetti bolognese the other day.'

Hoskins grunted. At low water the winter sea left a vast silence over its corrugated expanse of wet sand. The tide glittered beyond a glare of molten silver on the exposed mud-flanks of outfall channels. Against bright ocean sky, a few silhouettes of elderly promenaders moved with walking-sticks and dogs.

Chance left him by the gardens. The way to the promenade led down alleys between hotels and cafés. Hoskins caught the tang of shell-crusted sand, the fish-odour of uncovered rock, a sharpness of warm vinegar from the snack-bars. The tide sparkled at the foot of the deep steps. From open doors at the rear of hotels came a clash of cutlery and a shouting of orders. But the raised patios were empty and the coloured bulbs were dead. He passed the Pavilion Theatre. Its pantomime season was over and renovations for summer variety had begun. Emergency doors stood open allowing rare sunlight on the dark plush of the seats. There was a smell of fresh paint and a glimpse of ladders.

To Hoskins, born and raised in Ocean Beach, the smell of wet paint and the sight of ladders was a better guarantee of spring than any amount of flowers or birdsong. Posters from the information office spoke of Ocean Beach as Queen of the Atlantic Coast. At this time of year he thought of it as an old Bay Drive tart with her make-up off, revamping a pair of stockings.

Lesley was there first, at a table behind the window of Nono's. The fringe of her fair pudding-basin crop and the slight wilfulness of her mouth made her seem like a prim little girl on her way to a ballet class. Hoskins slid into the other side of the booth, the promenade and distant glitter of tide still looking summer-warm through the plate-glass. Their hands met under the table.

'Sorry to be late,' he said. 'I didn't want Jack Chance dropping me off outside here, so I walked down from Alexandra Gardens.'

'Where is he now?' Her hand remained busy with his.

'Gone to see love's young dream. Julie. Little-girl sort of girl. Works in a shop in town. Long blonde hair. Spray-on jeans. Legs like malnutrition.'

'Not your type?'

'You're my type,' he said firmly. 'I was thinking about the summer. We could hire a place down Minavon or the Burrows for a week. Open beaches. Atlantic breakers. Free and easy. Nude bathing by moonlight. Do as we like.'

Lesley sighed and gripped his hand tighter.

'Miles of gruesome families in nasty little slums on wheels,' she said gently. 'And what rolls in on the beaches is mostly Canton, carried forty miles on a westerly current. We can do as we like anywhere.'

'True,' Hoskins took a menu from the waiter. 'Try the lasagne verde and the mozzarella salad.'

'All right.'

'And the Valpolicella.' He turned to the waiter. 'Ask Freddie if he's got the lunchtime *Canton Globe*, will you? Tell him Mr Hoskins would like a peep.'

Lesley moved his knee with her own.

'What do we need a peep at?'

He returned the pressure.

'Last night's capers. Pirate radio *Hit-Back Show*. Tried to assassinate a couple of DTI inspectors who got too close. On the news this morning.'

The waiter returned with the lunchtime edition.

'Hell's teeth,' Hoskins said. 'Trust Gerald Foster. Right across the front-page. Pirate Radio Murder Attempt. Mob Attack Mount Pleasant Investigators.'

Lesley craned forward, trying to read it as well.

'Murder attempt?'

'About eleven last night. Department of Trade Investigators. Their job is to track down pirate radio. They thought they'd located the *Hit-Back* lot. A nasty bunch and difficult to pin down because they only broadcast for about ten minutes and keep on the move. They traced them to one of the high-rise blocks on Mount Pleasant estates. About twenty storeys up. They have two DTI inspectors in each car. One driving and one working the direction finder.'

'What happened to them?'

'They went into the lobby of the flats. Lifts not working. Up the stairs instead. Two floors up, someone starts dropping twelve-inch concrete slabs from the top. Certain death if one hits you on the head. The DTI pair legged it to the car. Someone else from the top floor had lobbed a concrete facing-slab through the car roof. Anyone in the car when that hit it would have been killed outright. So they ran for it with a mob at their heels. Not the *Hit-Back* lot. Just citizens of Mount Pleasant tower-blocks that hate snoopers.'

'It's unbelievable,' she said.

'Not if you've done time up the Mount Pleasant estates. Cosy as a nuclear winter. Anyway, Gerald Foster says here that these chaps' union is telling its members not to confront these maniacs without adequate police escort. Trouble is, it would take about two dozen of us in those tower-blocks. It's not on.'

The waiter poured Valpolicella and brought lasagne.

'So what happens?' she asked.

'Stop looking for the *Hit-Back* mob and concentrate on pirate disc-jockeys. They're nicer people. You catch them and they put their hands up. Take 'em to court and fine 'em. And then they start all over again somewhere else.'

'But how?'

'Biscuit-tin transmitters,' Hoskins said. 'Small as that. Cost

112

a couple of hundred quid to assemble. Of course, disc-jockeys need all the equipment for playing music as well. They make money by advertising what the networks won't take. Someone's hairdressing salon or someone else's massage parlour. But *Hit-Back* is just one bloke talking. They can almost take their gear by bus. Worse still, a lot of people like them. With the BBC and the rest being sanctimonious and goody-goody, there's a market for the other point of view.'

At ten to two he left her and walked up Clifton Hill. The incoming tide drove a piercing wind past the little hotels, ice cream parlour and filling-station. Area Forensic was a two-storey building at the top of the hill, behind Ocean Beach headquarters. Dr Blades, his face prematurely lined after the removal of a malignant stomach, emerged from a room behind the cubby-hole reception window. He had personified Area Forensic for as long as Hoskins could remember.

'Hello, Charlie,' Hoskins said brightly. 'How's life on the Riviera, then?'

'Keeping busy, Sam. Just busy. Not seeing as much home life as I'd fancy. Come on up the rumpus-room and see what we've got.'

He led the way up the concrete stairs to his office.

'Your young lady still keeping you busy, is she, Charlie?'

Blades paused and lowered his voice.

'Open University. English and sociology. Poncing rubbish. If they want to make the world happier, they'd have classes in belly-dancing and striptease.'

He pushed open his door. A sunlit panorama of Ocean Beach, the Cakewalk and the New Pier, Ocean Park funfair and the tiled Art Deco of cinemas and department stores seemed to swim at them through the wide window.

'More or less what Billy Catte was saying, Charlie.'

Blades sat down behind his desk and his worried face tightened, as if at a twinge from the phantom stomach.

'Yes,' he said grimly. 'I was just coming to Mr Catte.'

Hoskins took the other chair and gestured at a folder.

'What've we got there then, Charlie?'

'Not much joy for you, Sam. Not if you want Billy Catte. There's prints on the steering wheel of the Nissan. Mrs Catte's not available. But they're identical to those on the hand-mirror from her bedroom that was supplied. Superimposed on them, there's gloved fingers of whoever drove the car last.'

'And Billy Catte?'

'We've got his prints from his firearms offence. He's on the passenger doors, not the driver's door. This was his wife's car. Prints that look like the two girls. Mrs Catte drove the Nissan. Billy Catte and the girls sometimes rode in it. And that's its family history.'

Hoskins looked out at the glittering sea.

'We checked on Mrs Catte. She flew from Canton to Munich with the younger daughter, as he said. Due back tonight. I might put her through the wringer but I don't see much in that. Which means there's not much there for us.'

Blades turned a page in the folder.

'Not on Billy Catte. Still, the Eley four-five-five in the glove compartment fired the two bullets that killed Terry Cross. No doubt of it. There were bullets in three chambers, all of them forty-five ammo with the bases of the cartridges filed to fit. Once again, no prints.'

'And no connection with Catte or his associates?'

'Not that I can see, Sam. One thing, though. This is not a gun that a professional villain would touch, let alone use.'

'As likely to blow your hand off as fire the bullet, I gather.'

'As likely to blow your face off, Sam. And with the barrel cut short and the wrong-sized bullets it wouldn't be accurate within three feet at a distance of twelve feet. The only reason Terry Cross was killed, according to the post-mortem, was that one bullet was fired from three feet and the other from about eighteen inches. Not professionals, Sam. And, therefore, much worse.'

'Not much cause for celebration there, Charlie.'

'No,' said Blades. 'Still, the electron-beam got clever with bits of thread. Nylon car seats pull out threads from worsted suiting. Coarse threads, like a cat's whisker. There was a white thread on the Nissan driver's seat. Same thread on the seat of the Ford Transit that was hi-jacked for its drugs. Both from a grey jacket made in Portugal and sold in Marks and Spencer stores.'

'That's more like it, Charlie.'

'Is it, Sam? They sell thousands of them. Still, you can reckon that at least one of the Ford Transit hi-jack was there when they tried to go late-night shopping at Boots. And whoever killed Terry Cross was there. But not Billy Catte.

This is something you are never going to nail on him.'

Hoskins nodded. 'I can't get Billy Catte for shooting Cross or McPhail. I was with him when it happened. He's watertight for when the pharmacy van was hi-jacked. Still, what we might nail on Billy Catte is going to be a bit more permanent than three years for ramming the side-entrance of Boots. In fact, if I'm right, he could be facing ten or fifteen years for statutory and aggravated rape.'

Blades let out a quiet whistle.

'Billy Catte wouldn't last five years, let alone ten or fifteen.'

Hoskins pushed his chair back.

'Exactly, Charlie. When he figures that, I'll get somewhere. He didn't ram Boots, or shoot Terry Cross, or rob a pharmacy van. You think he doesn't know who did? Before I've finished, Mr Catte is going to beg me to listen.'

# Chapter Fifteen

Two evenings later Hoskins went in the first car with Swinton, the strong-arm of the social services team. Chance followed, driving the Sierra with Mrs Wardle, the team leader, and Claire Cawte, a social work probationer. Light flurries of snow hung in the lamp-haloes of King Edward Square, a pale frosted glare falling on the stucco twiddlings and domes of City Hall. The tall Viennese finger of the clock-tower showed half-past ten.

Swinton drove. He was a youngish man with an aureole of untidy fair hair. His beard seemed intended to convey wisdom and sympathy. His eyes swivelled from side to side of the road, as if alert for ambush. There was a light moisture of perspiration on his smooth forehead.

'It's not an ideal solution,' he said, exhaling spearmint at Hoskins. 'I mean, you're in at the deep end. We'd normally have you in on the case conference before serving a care order like this. But, I mean, we had the conference this morning and you were out at Ocean Beach. No way we could postpone action. No way at all. We've got to be looking at a situation where the younger girl – the ten-year-old – is being sexually abused. No question. This business in the playground. You know, "Let's play I'm walking down the street and you rape me." You don't get that without emotional abuse at least. And that's the tip of the ice berg. The school doctor's report is horrendous. Indications that she is no longer *virgo intacta*, was how it was put to me. We couldn't get a magistrate to sign the care order in time, otherwise we'd have taken her straight from school. What's it now? Half-ten? Better late than never.'

He chuckled self-consciously and pulled his beard with his left hand. The iron joints of Balance Street bridge rumbled under their tyres as they crossed the dark tide of the Town River and switchbacked under the railway span into Dyce Street.

'Straight on down here,' Hoskins said. 'I'm not taking this ride as an apprentice social worker, Mr Swinton. Billy Catte is a convicted criminal of violent habits. I'm here to see you execute your care order and prevent grievous bodily harm.

That's all. Case conferences would be a waste of time.'

'Oh, sure,' said the young man hastily. 'But, I mean, you'd be looking to do Catte for rape and incest, I imagine. If what I suspect is right. Claudia the ten-year-old is pretty certain. The fifteen-year-old, Emma, seems blatant.'

'Stop at the pedestrian crossing,' Hoskins said. 'There's someone trying to cross. You don't want to be nicked for careless driving half-way there.'

Swinton braked and turned a lop-sided grin at what he took to be police humour. Another cloud of spearmint enveloped Hoskins. Swinton began again.

'If Catte obstructs us to an extent we can't remove the children from the house, then it's down to you and Mr Chance. I checked the code of practice.'

Hoskins yawned and nodded. They turned off Dyce Street to Martello Square and the deep tombs of the graving docks. Billy Catte's house blazed light. There was a din of amplified music. The evening guests had gone and Mr Catte was putting his feet up.

Swinton stopped the car outside the house, across the road from the little esplanade. Hoskins got out. A dark squall of razoring wind across the mudflats clapped at his ear with a clout of ice. There was a distant hiss like snow among the reeds. Chance parked the Sierra immediately behind and the two women got out. Claire Cawte had a painted-puppet look. Mrs Wardle was the trained professional. Her dark hair had been cropped to a helmet, leaving shadowy stubble on her lower nape. Under the grey make-up of their lids, Hoskins noticed, her eyes had a curiously dull and immobile stare.

'When you're ready,' he said, 'DS Chance and I will be here. You may find Billy Catte's sons by his first marriage. The elder one known for obvious reasons as Tom. I shouldn't try taking them into care. Not unless you want to get abused yourselves on the way back to the infirmary.'

'Right,' said Swinton uneasily. 'We'll make a start. Call you if necessary.'

Hoskins sat with Chance in the Sierra, the fan blowing the last warmth from a cooling engine. He felt an unexpected shift of sympathy towards Billy Catte. The force that was now to break him was formidable in its power. A policeman could not have done it. The criminal law required evidence beyond reasonable doubt. But social services operated under a civil law, which required only a balance of probabilities. Billy Catte as a criminal had rights enshrined in law. Billy Catte under siege by the social services had no rights whatsoever.

A confusion of ill-temper began in the brightly lit doorway of the house. Swinton and the two women were standing just inside. Swinton had prudently left the door open as a line of retreat. Hoskins glimpsed Billy Catte, the tight dark curls and the furrowed brow that suggested the skull's oppressive weight. In high-necked sweater and slacks he was barrel-chested and muscular.

'If you'd let me explain, Mr Catte, it'll be easier all round,' Swinton was saying loudly. 'Claudia was examined by her school doctor after complaints about her conduct in the playground.'

'What complaints?' shouted Catte contemptuously. Swinton was not deflected. Though Catte continued to snap, Swinton talked him down in a loud monotone.

'Dr Varney found evidence consistent with physical sexual abuse of your daughter. He informed the paediatrics and social services departments.'

'Well he never informed me! What the fuck does he think? I've got no right to know or something?'

'He was of the opinion that you might know already, Mr Catte.'

'And what's that supposed to mean?'

'If we could just get on, Mr Catte . . . '

'Lis'n, you little pig-face! What is that supposed to mean? Before I do something very original to you! What is that— '

'It means, Mr Catte, that I have here two interim place of safety orders, signed by a magistrate. It is my duty to deliver them to you, which I now do. They authorise the social services department to take Claudia and your stepdaughter Emma into care for a period of twenty-eight days. The initial purpose is to remove them to the children's wing of the infirmary, where they will be examined by specialists to determine whether either or both may have suffered sexual abuse. If you're innocent, you've got no reason to object.'

'No reason to object? You're an idiot as well as a bender, are you? You come here, almost midnight, and tell me you're taking my girls to be sexually examined! And if I don't like 'em treated that way, I must be screwing 'em!'

'If you've nothing to hide—' Mrs Wardle began. Billy Catte was ready for her as well.

'No festering old whore like you is taking them anywhere. If I so much as think a finger's been laid on my little girl, I'll have her examined properly. She'll go private and be treated with respect. Not pawed over in some National Health Service dog-house like the infirmary. So you and your boyfriend get out of this house before you're put out, head-first and arse-up!'

'Your parental rights, Mr Catte, are removed from you by the care orders . . . '

This provoked a chaos of shouting and screaming, a struggle in the doorway. Hoskins caught fragments of shrill exchanges. Swinton was shouting, 'We're not leaving here without them, Mr Catte. You're only making it more difficult!'

'No bloody pouf like you is getting near my kids . . . '

Swinton was trying to push in while Catte shouldered him back to the garden path.

'If we don't take them, Mr Catte, the police will. By force if necessary.'

Then Hoskins saw what Swinton was struggling towards. Mrs Wardle and her probationer had cornered Emma Catte and were wrestling with the girl.

'Get your hands off! Get your fucking hands off me!'

There was shrill despair and fear in the voice, as well as sharp anger.

'Stop that and do as you're told,' Mrs Wardle shouted, 'unless you'd rather see your dad in prison.'

'I'll kill you first, you bloody old cow.'

Hoskins watched the alternate tragedy and farce of the child-taking. Chance was uneasy.

'You think we ought to go in there, Sam? Before someone gets hurt?'

Hoskins looked again and then shook his head.

'Don't think so, Jack. Our three look as though they're doing all right. Swinton's a lot younger and fitter than I am. I'm staying here.'

Suddenly, through the scrimmage, a figure burst out and ran towards the pavement. Hoskins saw a shoulder-length of wispy blonde hair and a rather frail body. Emma Catte, he supposed. As he got out to block her escape, it surprised him that so slight a girl had fought two grown women for so long.

Emma Catte saw him and hesitated. In that moment, Mrs Wardle pounced from behind, seizing her by the shoulders in the manner of a woman hauling back a child from the kerb. Emma saw the two policemen and the fight went out of her. She began to shiver from the upset and the cold. Swinton was pursuing Billy Catte into the house, racing to reach the younger girl first.

'Put this one in our car,' Hoskins said aside to Mrs Wardle. 'Heater's on.'

Mrs Wardle and Claire Cawte sat either side of her in the back of the car with the doors locked. Swinton was coming down the path.

'We've got a problem,' he said loudly. 'No sign of Sonja Catte, the mother, nor the younger girl, Claudia, nor the two sons. They could all be together somewhere.'

The edge of ice in the wind seeped through Hoskins' coat. 'What's the form, then?'

Swinton breathed into his hands and did a little dance.

'If any of the kids are out when we come calling, we watch the house for them to come back and take them away then.'

Hoskins looked back wistfully at the heated car.

'You might have to wait a bloody long time. Once Mrs Catte gets word of this lot, I don't suppose she'll be coming back from her evening out.'

At that moment the door of the house slammed and Billy Catte came down the path in a driving-jacket. To Hoskins' surprise he ignored them and turned aside, down Dyce Esplanade, towards Martello Square.

'Where's he going?' Swinton asked.

'To a call-box to call his missus,' Hoskins said. 'He thinks his phone might be tapped, I suppose.'

Between the beard and the halo of hair Swinton's face was taut with anger.

'Contempt of court. If he warns them off, it's contempt of a court order.'

Hoskins nodded. 'You'd better go and tell him. I can't.'

'Why not?'

'Mr Catte's free to come and go. He's not charged with any crime. Free to use the telephone. I'm here to see the orders served and to prevent violence. I'm not here to arbitrate over civil law. Your lot chose to operate under civil law because you don't need the same degree of proof. You can't have it both ways.'

'Stop him!'

'He could have me for wrongful arrest and unlawful imprisonment, Mr Swinton.'

'All right. Get them to put out a bulletin to have him picked up.'

'They wouldn't, Mr Swinton. You can't arrest him without reason. What's he charged with? Walking down the street with intent to use a phone-box?'

Swinton glared at him and set off down the pavement. He caught Billy Catte just before the corner of Dyce Esplanade and Martello Square, where the deep concrete berths of the graving docks lay waterless and echoing behind their entrance gates. Swinton said something and Catte ignored him.

Then Swinton said loudly, 'You warn them off and I'll have you! I'll have you for contempt of court! That's prison!'

In his irritation he took Billy Catte by the left arm. Catte turned and bowed his head deftly, butting Swinton hard, full in the face. The young man stepped back, hands over his eyes and nose. Catte pushed him hard, watched him stagger against the wall and slither down to sit on the pavement, hands still over his face. Then Billy Catte walked on round the corner and disappeared.

'Mr Swinton's having an exciting evening,' said Chance quietly at Hoskins' elbow. 'Isn't he having an exciting time?'

Hoskins sighed.

'Better go and get the stupid young prat on his feet,' he said wearily. 'If he'd had his way, Jack, that could be you or me sitting there with tomato sauce streaming from the nose. And him standing here watching. And a complaint for assaulting a civilian on the Ripper's desk tomorrow.'

They led Swinton back, while he sniffed and dabbed at his nostrils.

'That's not too bad,' Hoskins said encouragingly. 'I used to get worse than that every week down the boxing club when I was a nipper. All right to drive the car, then? We'll take the ladies back in ours. See you back at Division if you want us again tonight.'

As he slid into the front passenger seat of the Sierra,

# Chapter Sixteen

Jack Chance was waiting at the wheel of the motorpool Sierra. Hoskins closed the door behind him and came down the frost-rimmed steps of Lambs Chambers. Eight o'clock, a cold yellow sun struggling through sea-pearl mist. The paving was splashed and stained by last night's customers from the shabby pub on the far side of St Vincent Street.

Chance leant across to open the car door from inside.

'Morning, Sam. Not up to driving today?'

'Car's in dock,' Hoskins said gruffly. 'Surprised it works at all with the hours it does when Division transport is on the ramp.'

Chance brushed back the flap of black hair from his full red face and slid the Sierra into gear. He turned out of St Vincent Street, across the Town River, frost sparkling on the mud-flanks at low water. The pale fire of the misty sun made an impressionist masterpiece of The Keep and its Victorian Gothic. Jack Chance hummed a little and then began to croon to himself.

> I want some red roses for a blue lady,
> Send them to her Mr Florist, please . . .

'For God's sake!' said Hoskins irritably.

'All right,' Chance said amiably. 'So what about Mrs Thatcher, George Bush, and the Pope? Got it off Stan McArthur in the Welsh Harp last night.'

'What about them?'

Chance pulled out round a bus.

'Well, she's at home in Ten Downing Street. All right? And this flunkey comes in and says that there's George Bush and the Pope outside. Which one does she want to see. So she says . . . '

'The Pope because I'll only have to kiss his hand.'

The smaller shops at the eastern end of Longwall heralded the civic centre and the sweep of the Mall past City Hall.

'Fair enough,' said Chance gamely. 'So what about this? Wallace Dudden's being made up to inspector.'

'As a joke . . . '

122

'Nope,' Chance said confidently. 'If you hadn't been on rest-day, you'd have heard the whisper last night. It's official today.'

'If I hadn't been on rest-day, my son, I'd be about oven-ready for the crematorium now. I'd been on my bloody pins fourteen hours before we got shot of Swinton and his friends. Wallace Dudden? Should have the criminal underworld giggling with relief. When's the celebration?'

'Down the Harp tonight. Eight o'clock. Upstairs room. He's hoping they'll give him a turn in charge of vice now that Dawson's had the nudge.'

'I'll bet!' said Hoskins sardonically.

They were passing the painted Florentine watch-tower of Lord Dyce's toy castle, when the car radio bleeped and Hoskins heard his own call-sign.

'Control to Bravo Four. Report position, Bravo Four.'

Hoskins put the microphone to his mouth.

'Bravo Four to control, DCI Hoskins. We're heading east on Longwall, level with the watch-tower. In lane for the Mall turning.'

There was a pause and then another bleep.

'Control to Bravo Four. Message for DCI Hoskins. Please proceed direct to Canton Royal Infirmary. Man seen behaving suspiciously in the grounds.'

'Bravo Four. DCI Hoskins to control. Message understood.'

'Behaving suspiciously?' Chance looked at the traffic blocking his change of lane. 'Probably trying to jump the waiting-list for gall-bladders.'

'That girl of Catte's!' said Hoskins furiously. 'I'd lay odds she's part of it! Give 'em a blast on the hooter, Jack.'

Chance switched on the twin-tones and the early office-bound commuter cars edged grudgingly aside. With head-lights on full beam, he picked up speed towards Longwall Circle, the grey unlit window fronts of department stores deserted at half-past eight. With the opening of a new main hospital at the Crest, Canton Royal Infirmary had reverted to its Victorian role of workhouse, a last-stop for geriatrics and a temporary paediatric reception block that had long since become permanent.

Chance swung north on to Park Drive, the prosperous uphill curve of pillared town-housing, pieced out by parades of hair salons and Italian or Oriental restaurants.

They turned into Henley Road. Across the far end stood the college gate-tower and arch of the infirmary, built of rough-faced stone. The Sierra bumped gently over the archway ramp and entered the yard with its central lawn. There was no one at the main entrance of the building with its wide shallow steps and double-doors.

Hoskins went up the steps and into the overheated disinfectant stench of the vaulted concourse. The first sign of something amiss was the unmanned inquiry desk. The glassed-in office had a grey monitor screen angled towards the door. The liquid crystal display was flashing its message to the empty room. STAFF UNDER ATTACK IN EXTENSION BLOCK.

He walked on and turned into the main corridor. A uniformed security guard, his grey head uncapped, sat splay-legged on a metal chair, staring at the ceiling. A white-coated house-doctor turned the man's face gently, this way and that, inspecting the damage.

Hoskins flourished the misty green plastic of his warrant-card.

'DCI Hoskins and DS Chance. Where's the trouble?'

The doctor looked up briefly.

'Somewhere down there. Down the corridor that joins the two buildings. The staircase is facing you as you come out of it. A man came in, attacked the security guard and rushed off that way.'

Hoskins paused. 'Thick-set, dark wavy hair, middle-aged, broken nose?'

'Catte,' said the security guard indistinctly. 'Looking for Emma Catte.'

Hoskins walked briskly with Chance beside him, down the heat-deadened corridor and into the concrete passageway that led across a delivery yard between the buildings. The three-level extension was built round an airy staircase-well. Wide open-tread stairs went round three walls with an access landing for each floor on the fourth side. These flights and the lobby below were lit by a frosted skylight.

'Sorry, no way through there!'

It was a tall young doctor with tousled hair behind them, his white coat unbuttoned as a sign of rank. Hoskins turned.

'DCI Hoskins, DS Chance, Canton CID. We've got a call about an intruder on the premises. What's happened?'

The young man managed to look relieved and nervous at the same time.

'He's got one of the female staff on the top landing. Dr Underwood. Either he gets his daughter back or else he'll throw Underwood over the rail. It's not even her case. He came straight in, laid out the security guard with something like a chair-leg and grabbed the first person he could handle.'

Hoskins peered through the porthole window of the heavy doors, trying to get a view of Billy Catte high above.

'Don't let him see you,' the young man said quickly. 'We think he's got a record of mental illness.'

'He has,' Hoskins said coldly. 'He also has a record of actual bodily harm and firearms offences, among other things.'

Through the porthole window Hoskins saw several people at the foot of the stairs. With gloom and frustration, he took in the scene. Billy Catte was on the highest access landing, about twenty-five feet above. He was holding a woman with her back against him by turning her wrists up between her shoulder-blades. White-coated and untidily ginger-haired, she seemed as puny as a child in Catte's grip. Like a presidential leader on his balcony, he addressed a doctor and three hospital administrators below. Billy Catte's face was reddening as if for tears. His raised voice was almost a scream.

'My girl was took into this dog-house night before last. I want to see her. I know what my rights are.'

The hand that was not holding the young woman's wrists now grabbed her by the cropped curls of her ginger hair. He forced her against the thin steel of the black-painted stair-rail, bending her forwards and holding her head out by the ginger curls clenched in his fist. It was a registrar, balding and spectacled, who answered him.

'Your daughter is no longer here, Mr Catte.'

'Then fetch her back! Why isn't she here? Why?'

'Emma was transferred to an assessment unit last night, after she was examined. Be reasonable and you can visit her there.'

Catte paused, as if at the wickedness of it.

'Examined? I know what that means! Which one of you did it? I want the bastard that did those filthy things to my girl! Who was it?'

They stared up in silence from the sunlit floor of marble tiling. Billy Catte's lined and squash-nosed face betrayed a sudden tremor. The ginger-curled woman stared out into space like a gargoyle-spout on a church. Her face was expressionless, as if she had no thought in her mind. Then her mouth tightened in pain as Billy Catte took a firmer grip of her curls. A plastic pen slid from her top pocket and bounced on the marble tiles below.

'It was this little slag!' There was a savage triumph of discovery in his voice. 'Wasn't it? It was this dirty little sow! Wasn't it?'

'No, Mr Catte. She has nothing to do with your daughter's case.'

'Don't give me that! I know it was her! It's in your face!'

For the first time the young woman cried out as he twisted her wrists higher. Below him the doctor and administrators stared up at his rage. No one answered him.

Hoskins drew back from the window and turned to Chance.

'We've got to believe he means what he says, Jack. Get to the car. I want back-up from Division. No uniforms. If necessary leave their hats off and put on civvy overcoats. We'll need a dozen, three carloads, to cover the entrances. And I want fire services with a jump-sheet, if they've still got one. Tell 'em all that. Then get back here quick as you can.'

Chance went off down the tiled corridor at a lumbering run. Hoskins turned to the young doctor.

'How many ways off that staircase landing?'

'There's a door on each landing, leading to the corridors of the extension. There's lifts and stairs at the far end of those. Otherwise he'd have to come down these main stairs to the lobby that you're looking at now.'

Chance returned presently with Micky Finn, ex-CID sergeant and senior man of the hospital security watch. The thickness of his glasses gave him a pop-eyed and accusing stare.

'Right, Micky, what's the score on this lot, then?'

'We want to try and take him from above, Sam. He's shoved the chair-leg or whatever it is through the handles of the double-door on his level. And he's hung something over the little window in it, so we can't see him up there. Means busting the door open. We could grab him in two seconds then.'

'During which time he heaves her over the rail.'

Finn shook his head. 'You won't need fire services, Sam.

We've got jump-sheets here. Have to with psycho-geriatric. No need to wait for back-up. Co-ordinate it on the walkie-talkie. Hospital rescue team rushes in down here and stretches the canvas. Five seconds after that, we ram the door open up there. He'll see the game's up with a jump-sheet to break her fall. Message from psychiatric is do it fast. He's in the state that he could flip any minute and throw her down.'

'There's three carloads of back-up on the way,' Chance said.

At that moment, as if on cue, the hee-haw of an emergency siren sang high and clear somewhere on the road from Longwall Circle. It rose and fell for several seconds before it ended abruptly.

'Stupid sods!' said Chance furiously. 'I told them, no warning of approach or arrival. Some lucky patrolman is going to find himself out of his nice comfy limo and back directing traffic in a pointed hat and white gloves.'

Before Hoskins could reply the doors opened. The doctor and the administrators came out, as Billy Catte shouted after them. Then the doors swung to again. It was the balding registrar who explained.

'If he sees or hears anyone, he'll kill young Underwood. So he says. If his daughter isn't standing at the foot of those stairs five minutes from now, he'll throw Dr Underwood to her death. So he says. And if we try to prevent his daughter leaving for the place he tells her to, he'll still take Mrs Underwood's life. If we do as he wants, and when he hears from his daughter that she's at the place he's chosen, he'll give himself up and let his prisoner go.'

'But you haven't got his daughter here,' Hoskins said.

Before there was time for a reply, several white-tunic'd hospital orderlies began carrying a long roll of canvas towards the door. Hoskins heard the distant shout of Billy Catte.

'Four minutes, you bastards!'

'If your lot get here in time, well and good, Sam,' Micky Finn said quietly. 'But they can't show themselves and they won't be able to do much different to what I'm planning. Except they might do it too late. Three and a half minutes, if he means what he says. Come on. I've got the others upstairs.'

Hoskins looked round for Chance.

'Stay put here, Jack, and keep me posted. If this gets nasty, I'm not waiting for Tom Nicholls or whoever it may be to get his head out from under his armpit and come after us.'

He panted beside Finn as they jogged into the yard. Circling the extension, they rode the lift to the second-floor corridor. Wards and day-rooms led off to either side. At the far end Finn's three-man security team had loaded a hospital trolley with orthopaedic weights as a makeshift ram. The porthole window in the double-door was blacked out by whatever Catte had hung over it.

'About a minute, Micky,' Hoskins said glancing at his watch. 'And somewhen you must tell me how the hell this mess came about.'

Finn shrugged.

'No one had any warning. He got here first thing, screaming that he wanted his daughter. Argument with Proctor on the door. Chinned him. Burst into the extension. Face-to-facer with Dr Underwood. Choice language. Grabs her. Strength of a bloody maniac. Drags her up the stairs. Help arrives to find that he's wedged these doors and he's threatening to throw her over the rail unless given what he wants. Simple as that. Hang on a jiffy.'

Finn flicked the walkie-talkie switch and talked to the registrar in the corridor below. Then he was back.

'That's it, Sam. Still no sign of your lot. The reckoning is that he's a psycho and that we'll deal with him as such. No offence to Division. There's six of 'em with the canvas jump-sheet now. On the dot, they go in and stretch it, so he'll see there's no point throwing her over the rail. If he still throws her, it might shock her but it won't kill her. Five seconds after, while he's still dithering, we go through this door and grab him. The buildings officer reckons that either we'll break whatever he's jammed the door-handles with or, if it holds, it ought to wrench off at least one handle with the force of the impact. They're only held by four quarter-inch screws.'

'About twenty seconds, chief,' said one of the security team.

'Wait for my word, then.'

Hoskins stood back and heard Chance on his handset.

'Sam? I can't see much from here. He's holding her back from the rail now. I'm going in with the rescue squad. Keep you posted.'

'All right, Jack. Watch yourself. I don't think he's got a

gun or he'd have waved it. But don't take chances. He could still be carrying something.'

There was silence everywhere, unbroken even by a car siren. The upper corridor was lit only by its ceiling bowls now that Catte had covered the round window in the double-door. On the walkie-talkie a voice below counted:

'Four . . . three . . . two . . . one . . . Now!'

Hoskins caught the distant scuffle of feet and a far-off thundering noise which he supposed was the stretching of the canvas jump-sheet. No one moved in the corridor above. Finn counted and the security team crouched at the laden trolley, well back from the doors for a good run.

'Two . . . one . . . '

'Sam!'

It was Chance on the handset.

'Stop them, Sam! He's tied her back to the door-handles by the tunic sleeves. You could rip her arms out of her shoulder-sockets.'

Hoskins jumped at the trolley, dragging back, thrusting aside to drive off Finn's team. Tunic sleeves. Nylon. Strong enough to moor a battleship. Strong enough to wrench arms like a strappado. The trolley slewed but hit the door with a jarring impact, sufficient to shake the covering from the round window. He heard a wild rising cry, like an arpeggio of pain.

'And he's gone!' Chance shouted from the walkie-talkie. 'The bugger's gone, Sam! He must have tied her so he could move about.'

Finn, white-faced at the realisation of what had almost happened, turned from the little window.

'He's not there, Sam. And this door's got to be opened from the other side. He can't have gone down to ground level. They'd have seen him. He must have crouched down and edged round the walls out of their line of sight and gone through the second-level door underneath us. Means going back to the far end.'

'He'll make for outdoors, Micky. Tell your lot to close the entrances.'

Hoskins ran back the length of the corridor to the further exit. The lift was on the ground floor. He took the stairs and met Sergeant McArthur coming up, blue uniform trousers protruding from under a fawn raincoat.

'What's the form, boss?'

'Billy Catte is the form, Stan,' said Hoskins breathlessly. 'On the run, somewhere down there. I want him.'

McArthur kept pace beside him.

'No one said, boss. Just get here. Nothing about Catte. Our team doesn't even know what he looks like. Mr Dudden just said get here. Report to you.'

'Mr Dudden?'

'Yes, boss. He's team leader.'

Hoskins felt his heart sink. The lower corridor was empty. He raced to the end and came out at the foot of the stairs which Catte had occupied. Still no sign. Several lightly disguised members of Dudden's team were walking about the further lobby at the end of the concrete passage connecting the two buildings. Hoskins made towards them. Half-way along the passage he saw Catte through the glass, sprinting across the delivery yard between the main building and the extension, making for the lawn and the gate by a side-route.

Drawing a deep breath Hoskins began to run again. In the lobby he shouted at Burden and Driscoll to follow him. Billy Catte was far off the main entrance of the building now, running for the corner of the grounds. But Dudden, as well as Parker and Anstey, were in his way.

'Head him off!' Hoskins shouted. 'Stop him!'

Hoskins skirted the three patrol cars and fire tender which had converged at the hospital steps like wasps at a pool of jam. He joined in the general pursuit across the wet winter grass. But short of being nature's wing three-quarter, Catte had no chance of dodging the further line of men.

At that moment, with commendable initiative, an unmarked car drew forward from the side of the hospital. It bumped and churned across the lawn, ripping grass and smearing mud, slewing a little but recovering with the skill of a stock-race driver. The direction of the car would cut off Catte's escape in a few seconds. Seeing this, he slowed down, apparently ready to give up. The car slithered beside him. The passenger door swung open. Billy Catte stumbled and hauled himself in. His door swung back and then slammed as mud and grass flew from accelerating tyres. With a jerk and a grinding of gears, the car shot forward again between the two groups of policemen.

PC Aspinwall, at the main gate, jumped clear as Billy

Catte's rescuer gathered speed, vanishing down Henley Road and into the traffic of Park Drive. At the main entrance of the building Hoskins could hear the wild competitive keening of the squad car engines in reverse. On the morning's present form they might just manage a three-car collision in the hospital entrance arch.

He stood at the centre of the lawn, unable to find words. It was Chance who met him first. Hoskins was scraping mud from his shoe against the hospital steps.

'Will you look at this bloody mess!' he said with quiet bitterness. 'Lawn like a ploughed field! Hostage-taking! Actual bodily harm! Suspect evades fourteen CID officers and the security staff! And it doesn't even happen in Chicago or Miami. Just our local geriatric hospital. I want someone's knackers for this fiasco, my son! Stuffed and mounted for the hat-badge on ceremonial occasions!'

'Yes,' said Chance impassively. 'Well, the feeling seems to be mutual. Wallace Dudden and Stan McArthur reckon that it's going to be old Clitheroe that gets yours for his office wall.'

# Chapter Seventeen

'Keystone Cops,' said Ripley thoughtfully. 'That's what we have to avoid. Bound to seem like that to anyone who wasn't there.'

'It was like that!' Hoskins said, the memory of the morning tightening his throat. 'Except for the car at the end. I'd like a word with whoever was driving it. Probably one of Mr Catte's two sons. They've got to be number one, Max. He's not likely to find some hired hand who loves him that well. Not well enough to risk ten years' gaol for hostage-taking and attempted murder. Family loyalty. That's what's at the bottom of this bloody lot.'

Ripley nodded and sat down behind his desk. He fondled the cylindrical ruler and stared at the ancient photograph of his wife and child.

'Not to mention the social services' angle, Sam. One of her step-brothers, as easily as Billy Catte, might be responsible for Emma's sexual experiences.'

Hoskins took the other chair as Ripley waved his hand towards it.

'I'd thought of that, Max. What interests me more is Catte and his sons being hip-deep in armed robbery and the deaths of two policemen.'

'And Emma?'

'Her too, for all I know. That could be the reason they want her back before she starts giving us answers. She won't even talk to the doctors as yet.'

The Ripper's grey moustache moved in a soft reassuring smile against the port-wine flush of his cheeks.

'First things first, Sam. No one's going to blame you for what happened at the infirmary. You were pitched in with Jack Chance. Impossible situation for two men alone and hospital security in arse-order. I suppose it might be argued that you should have waited for back-up before going for Catte.'

'There was plenty of back-up, Max. All in the wrong place. No one briefed them. As for Catte, he's a known psycho. Medical opinion was that he'd boil over any minute and chuck that girl down three floors. If I'd waited for back-up and he'd killed her meantime, I'd be putting my papers in now.'

Ripley smiled. 'Just how I phrased it to ACC Crime. Better to have Dr Underwood alive than Catte in custody. To be fair to old Clitheroe, he went along with that.'

'I'll have the report typed up this evening,' Hoskins said.

Ripley smiled as if his mind were elsewhere. Hoskins got up to leave. It was just five o'clock. Time to reclaim his Vauxhall Cavalier, which had spent its day expensively on a garage ramp.

News of the infirmary 'incident' was too late for that evening's *Canton Globe*. The teatime bulletin of Coastal Radio News laid the drama blandly to rest as Hoskins drove the Cavalier from St Vincent Street Motors and found a space in the new underground bunker of the headquarters car park.

'Police were called to Canton Royal Infirmary this morning when a former psychiatric patient attempted to hold a junior doctor hostage. The doctor was released unharmed before police could arrest the man, who ran off through the grounds. A hospital spokesman said that there had been slight damage to one of the staircase doors and that the incident was now closed. The doctor had not at any time been in real danger. This afternoon the Area Health Authority refuted suggestions that security had been lax at the hospital or that there had been any delay in informing the police of the intruder's presence.'

Hoskins turned off the radio and went up to his office. Chance tapped at the door. His anorak hung open and he was pulling on his gloves.

'You coming down the Harp for old Wallace Dudden's piss-up, Sam?'

'Later,' Hoskins said. 'I'm looking in later on. Any news on Catte so far?'

Chance shook his head.

'Burden and Drew watching his house. Hollister and Sid Allen staking out the Rundle Street arcade in an unmarked car. Still, he's too fly to go straight home or to work, isn't he? He'll turn up in time. All the cars and foot patrols have got his picture.'

'Anyone recognise the face that was driving the getaway car this morning?'

Chance shook his head again.

'Youngish. Could have been one of his sons. "Tom" Catte's

about eighteen. No form. A-level student or something. Still, he might feel bad about having his step-sister took away by the likes of Swinton.'

'No doubt,' said Hoskins sourly. 'Worried what she might say about their family parties and their armed robbery frolics, perhaps.'

Chance waved and withdrew. Then his head reappeared round the door.

'By the way, Sam. There's a whisper from one of the police surgeons. Chalmers. So Stan McArthur says. They gave Emma a valium injection to stop her struggling. Then they had a look at her naughty bits, McArthur says. Seems Miss Catte's been a very lively young lady with someone or other. More ways than one. And she even said one or two things that Billy Catte might find embarrassing.'

Hoskins stared at him. 'While she was doped? Admissions made under the influence of drugs? Try imagining what Claude Roberts would do to that in court!'

'They won't give him the chance, Sam,' said Chance coolly. 'Swinton and his mob reckon they play by different rules. I'd say your mate Claude Roberts could get shafted on this one.'

At eight o'clock Hoskins went down the stairs. In driving-coat and gloves he ignored the Vauxhall Cavalier and walked out into the Mall. Passing the bare branches of the cherry trees in the Memorial Gardens, he brooded on the new species of law. A rising generation of vested interests had rigged the rules against open justice and equal rights. Anonymous defendants and uncorroborated evidence were to be the order of the day. Under the new regime, a sweaty-faced and ear-ringed prat like Swinton might shaft Claude Roberts or Jack Cam with their night-school legal training and their wits sharp as a dockland pimp's trouser-crease. The old order was changing. That change gave Hoskins no comfort at all.

Shadows of the tree branches blown in a light Atlantic squall patterned the shifting lamplight on the sleek wet tarmac of the Mall. To the few other pedestrians, coat collars turned up and shoulders hunched, the windy night and the spattering rain were no more than inconveniences. But Hoskins had lived all his life on this western coast. In the fitful wind and the slap of rain he felt the first promise of spring.

Before the domes and flying chariots of City Hall, Rossiter

Road turned east off the Mall. It was an avenue of gabled Victorian villas. On its first corner stood the Welsh Harp, a mock-Tudor pub of bar-snacks and middle-class pretensions. A few minutes' walk from the headquarters building, it had long ago been colonised by CID and uniformed sections. Hoskins pushed open the door. He stepped into a buzz of conversation and a smoke-tinted air of the carpeted saloon bar. Stan McArthur was talking to the landlord across the polished mahogany of the bar, ordering beer in quantity. He turned as the door opened.

'Hello, boss. We're in the upstairs room.'

Hoskins nodded. He crossed the bar to the door that led to the toilets and climbed the stairs the other side of it. There was a tidal surge of talk from the doorway ahead. They were all there from the sergeants' room: Dudden himself and Jack Chance, Driscoll and Pargiter, Strachey and Tappin, as well as several from the other watch. Burden and a dozen of the younger DCs were there. From the senior ranks, Ripley and Nicholls were having a quiet, serious conversation in the corner. A girl whom Hoskins knew by sight was setting up a makeshift bar at one end. Someone drew the curtains, shutting out the spattering raindrops and the diffused orange glow of street-lamps in the leaded lights of the Tudor windows.

'That it for the night, Sam?' Chance asked at Hoskins' elbow.

'Seems so, Jack. No sign of Catte at Dyce Terrace or the Rundle Street arcade. Someone must be putting him up tonight. I reckon tomorrow has to be search-warrant day. Turn over the house and see what comes up.'

'Come on,' said Dudden jovially, the mouth falling open in a smile. 'Clench a fist round this, Sam. Pint of Jupps Special Brew. All right?'

'Oh,' said Hoskins, as if pleasantly surprised. 'Cheers, Wally. And congratulations. I'm just here for a minute. Got a date later on.'

'Lantern Hill?' Chance inquired innocently.

'For what it matters to you, Jack.'

Chance drew in another inch of beer and then lowered his glass.

'We're going to my place tonight. Julie's picking me up at eleven, when this lot's done. More subtle that way. But I reckon it's definitely got to be leg-over this time.'

Hoskins gazed at him. 'Your love life, my son, is about as subtle as a traffic accident.'

From the far end of the room the tribal songs of the occasion had begun, courtesy of John Brown's Body. Even Ripley was mouthing the words, frowning intently as if it had been a hymn at a funeral.

A naughty inspector went to jump right up his sergeant's
  back . . .
And his chief inspector jumped right up this naughty
  inspector's back . . .
Then the superintendent jumped right up the chief
  inspector's back . . .
And the old commander jumped right up his
  superintendent's back . . .

'Here we go,' Chance shouted in Hoskins' ear above the din. 'Look at old Dudden's face! Colour of raw beef! He'll have a seizure one day!'

We prefer to call it leap-frog,
How we all love playing leap-frog . . .

Hoskins glanced at his watch, marking time until nine o'clock. The faces grew redder and the air thicker. Wallace Dudden, with his scant curls and large face, was telling a joke above the din, involving his sworn adversary, Eve Ricard, Chair of the City Council Women's Committee, on her first night in a harem. He guffawed at what was coming next.

'Anyway, Eve Ricard says . . . She says, "I'm not going to choose the trousers. I'm wearing the veil. After all," she says, "it's my face that all the viewers know me by . . . "'

'Someone's going to have to see him home,' Chance said warily.

A chair fell over. Hoskins saw Ripley look about him with concern. At nine o'clock he shook Dudden's hand, congratulated him again, apologised, and left. The drive to Lantern Hill seemed like the silence of outer space after Dudden's celebration. An hour later he sat in bed with Lesley, their toes touching and the local news from CNT flickering on the screen of the portable television.

The newsreader was one of a look-alike breed favoured

by the network. She had the required unisex crop and nasal classless voice. CNT news was structured to contain scolding of anti-social behaviour, a heart-warming story and a joke to end with. A list of drunk-driving cases and sexual offences was recited. During this, the reader's face assumed a pained expression, like an infant teacher first sensing a repellent odour in the classroom.

There was nothing about the 'infirmary incident'. It had already passed into history. Hoskins yawned and stroked Lesley's thigh.

'They might take the bolt out of her neck before they put her in front of the camera.'

As he reached for the remote control the voice said something about *Coastline* after the break. A studio discussion on the growing crisis in social provision whose participants included . . . He heard the name Councillor Carmel Cooney and drew his hand away from the control.

Lesley nudged him impatiently. 'What's the matter?'

Hoskins kissed her on the cheek. 'Sorry, pet. This I must see. Professional interest. Biggest villain in Canton talking about welfare. More than meets the eye.'

Like alphabetical fish, the letters of *Coastline* swirled round the screen and came to rest. There were four contributors sitting at a horse-shoe table with a grey-haired but young-faced compère at the centre. A studio audience rose in tiers on the far side. A first question was asked and answered in the manner Hoskins could have predicted. The estimated incidence of child abuse was increasing at a rate scarcely known in the annals of crime. It would increase still more, the estimated figures for next year having been already announced. Known cases were merely the tip of an ice berg. It was an accepted fact that at least ten or fifteen per cent of all children were abused. More resources must be found. More appointments must be made.

There was no dissent. Carmel Cooney was shown listening. Even sitting down he still had the look of a tadpole that walked on its tail. The expensive grey suiting was too tight, giving his paunch the shape of an inflated rubber ball. The large head with its melon-smile seemed too big for his body. Despite his ownership of Mount Carmel Ground Rents and the Royal Peninsular Emporium, Canton Coastal Construction and the Blue Moon Club, he looked to Hoskins what he had always been – a fifty-year-old razor-boy made good. Councillor Cooney of Hawks Hill. He waited his turn.

When it came, he began with a deceptive flash of the melon-smile. Hoskins recognised it from experience as the tightening of Cooney's anger.

'I'm going to begin,' he said quietly, 'by doing something that's never been done on these shows before. I'm not going to bleat about how someone else ought to give us more money for these things. I'm an ordinary man, not an expert. Not social services nor none of that. It's time us ordinary people took matters into our own hands. So I'm offering you good people – you sitting at home and watching – one hundred thousand pounds of my own money. I'm offering it towards a clinic where kiddies can be taken without fear of being diagnosed as abused when they never have been. Where they won't be dragged frightened and screaming from their mums on evidence that a court of law would laugh at and that would disgust any fair-minded person.'

The Director of Social Services, with his youthful but concerned look, began to speak in competition.

'You just listen a minute,' Cooney said softly. 'Our friends out there want to hear this, if you don't. And they won't thank you for interrupting. Now, the good and decent people of this city raised money for the Enid Cooney Surgical Ward for sick children out the Crest. Those good people and kind hearts never raised it to have this kind of carry on. Children snatched from their parents and taken to hospital by force. Having things done to 'em that I wouldn't even name on this programme. Done by so-called experts that's supposed to be protecting 'em!'

The fresh-faced grey-haired compère watched eagerly, sensing news being made on his show. Cooney was back in his stride.

'Of course a man that does anything dirty to a kiddy should be locked up and the key thrown away. But social services don't want a trial. They don't have proper evidence any more! Just watch how a little girl plays with a dolly. One way her dad's innocent and another he's guilty. They reckon they can tell. Who says they can tell? Only them that's got most money and jobs to gain from it. Now, then . . . No! You had your go, my friend. I'm going to finish what I got to say. You bloody listen to me for a change. So-called evidence that'd be laughed out of court in any fair-minded trial. But we got powers given to social services so they can get round the criminal law. Oh, yes we have, my friend! Oh, yes we have! And the result is public officials that gets paid from our money – your money and my money – and that wouldn't last five minutes in a proper job where they had to be publicly accountable.'

'And yet children must be protected,' said the compère wonderingly. Cooney was across the table, wagging a finger in his face. A hostile murmuring that had begun among the studio audience was briefly stilled.

'You want to protect kiddies, put a stop to some of this teaching in schools. Telling 'em that poufs and lessies is just as good as being anything else. You don't tell me that teaching 'em poison like that don't lay 'em wide open to being abused. Get the pouftahs out of the education service. That's what I say. And get 'em out of the social services, too. Taking children into care? Wouldn't they just like to! Kick 'em out, is what I say. And it's what all the decent people in this city say as well.'

There was uproar in the studio. Half the audience clapped and the rest began to shout and chant. Cooney put his face to the microphone and talked them down.

'And I tell you this, my friends. If there's people in this city been wronged . . . And if they want to march on the social services office or the infirmary and make their lawful protest . . . I'll lead 'em. That's a promise. And if the people of this city wants a proper clinic for sick kiddies that's free for everyone and where the poor sick little ones are guaranteed not to have these horrible things done to 'em, I'll lead a public subscription and I'll put up that first one hundred thousand pounds out of my own pocket. Not to mention five thousand I'm giving to FACT. What's FACT? Families Against Child-Takers. Make the truth known. And believe me we shall! Remember that name. FACT. For the sake of the kiddies. And if our Director of Social Services cares so much about children as he and his department reckons, let's hear how much he'll give to help them out of his own pocket.'

The concerned youthful Director thought it preposterous. 'That's not the way to deal . . . '

'Come on!' said Cooney triumphantly. 'You got a nice

fat salary. You take home three, four times as much as most of the good people watching this show. And they gave from their hearts to open that kiddies' ward two years ago. So how much'll you give? I think they'd like to hear.'

'I don't consider . . .'

'Would you give one penny piece?'

'Money isn't . . .'

'You wouldn't, would you? You don't really care enough to give one penny piece. It's the good-hearted people of this city that'll solve their own problems, not the so-called experts that come here for well-paid jobs and never cared a toss about the place until they was paid a salary. I reckon this city can do without expertise like that. And if it does, my friend, you come to me and I'll find you a job. Out the Blue Moon Club, tearing tickets.'

Even the studio audience was silent now, fascinated or appalled. Cooney sat back, arms folded and satisfied. The compère could scarcely contain his excitement at having scooped such an outburst. The camera moved tactfully away from the Director of Social Services.

'Perhaps,' said the compère to the forest of raised hands, 'we could broaden the discussion a little. The gentleman in the back row, trying to say something. Gentleman in the canary-yellow sweater. Yes?'

Hoskins stared in awe. Cooney's had been a bravura performance, argument used like a knuckle-duster, insults pat as a flick-knife. The moral authority of the Director of Social Services had been publicly ambushed by a municipal gangster. Hoskins was uneasily aware that he had enjoyed what he saw. Perhaps it was not all one-way. Perhaps the counter-revolution had begun. He might have underestimated Claude Roberts, Jack Cam and their breed. Night-school Canton, its courtroom voice edged by Saturday-night Peninsula, was not to be worsted by the products of new universities and new social science. With a bit of luck, it might still be Swinton and his kind that got shafted after all.

# Chapter Eighteen

Hoskins woke beside Lesley the next morning, the pale light of nine o'clock flushing the pink curtains. They lay sleepily for a while. His hands moved on the warm smoothness of her back and hips, Cooney's performance echoing in his mind. Presently they drew apart. He stretched as he watched her go out through the doorway and down the stairs. A moment later, he swung himself upright and leant to search for his socks. Somewhere below him a phone began to ring. Even before Lesley called out, he guessed it was Jack Chance.

'Sam?' Chance's voice was bright with anticipation. 'I'm still home. Gerald Foster couldn't get an answer from you so he called me. Seems we might have heard from Billy Catte again. A dress van was hit about half an hour ago. Atlantic Wharf. Outside Madame Jolly Modes. There was a reporter down there in minutes and Gerald's been for a look himself.'

Either he or Chance had got it wrong, Hoskins thought.

'Madame Jolly Modes? What's he want with a load of LBDs?'

'LBDs?'

'Little Black Dresses, my son. What every new little girl buys for her party. Backbone of the trade. Even suppose it was Billy Catte or the hi-jack merchants, what's the point? What's more, it's Cooney's empire, Madame Jolly Modes. Some tart of his. Billy Catte's not going to add Mel Cooney to his list of problems. He's not that daft.'

'Cash,' said Chance simply. 'Normally on Friday morning, Gerald Foster says, they do a run. They start out the Beach. Pick up Cooney's money at the Blue Moon Club and the Winter Garden before the weekend. Then drive into Canton and collect from the Modes and the Emporium. Then off to the bank. If you believe Gerald Foster, it was different today. The van was collecting dresses that hadn't shifted in the spring sale – and delivering new stock from Cooney's warehouse. They picked up cash but only from the Modes itself. About a grand and a half, Gerald reckons. Any other Friday, Madame Jolly was likely to be the last stop before the bank. Tens of thousands of pounds on board the van by then.

Reckoning is, about fifty thousand quid leaves in a good week and forty thousand gets banked. The rest goes into Cooney's Christmas stocking.'

'Who's covering all this for us?'

'You among others,' Chance said. 'Seeing you got an interest in Catte.'

'I'm going over his place down Dyce Esplanade this afternoon,' Hoskins said blandly. 'Any visit to Jolly Modes will be strictly "hello" and "goodbye". Did you catch Cooney on the box last night?'

'Busy,' said Chance happily, 'hardly allowed a wink of sleep. The sexual harassment I been suffering is no one's business.'

There was a girl's laughter in the background and the impact of a pillow.

'You'll hurt yourself, my son, the way you're going,' Hoskins said grimly.

Driving through the city he noticed a placard for the lunch-time edition of the *Canton Evening Globe*, outside a jelly-baby and skin-mag newsagents in Orient Road. COUNCILLOR'S TV 'SLANDER' FURY: ONE-DAY STRIKE CALL. Cooney had made his point. Hoskins followed a slow procession of cars down Great Western Street, along the Edwardian art nouveau of the old family department store fronts. On Atlantic Wharf the drama of armed robbery was over and forgotten. In what had been the end pavilion of the Paris Hotel with its pumpkin roof and cupola blinds, Madame Jolly Modes was doing business as usual. A blue Renault Traffic van, tall and narrow, was being drawn up the ramp of a breakdown truck, the evidence taken away for forensic examination.

Hoskins pulled up behind it and saw Stan McArthur watching the pick-up.

'Anything for Jack or me, Stan? A touch of Billy Catte, perhaps?'

McArthur shook his head.

'Not that anyone knows as yet, boss. Mr Nicholls was here about twenty minutes but he and Mr Pargiter gone back to Division. Could have been an inside job, come to that. Her and a boyfriend might have set it up.'

He jerked his head at the elegant little shop where the wax mannequins in the windows wore expensive fashions from deep-piled mink coats to black suspender-belt outfits that seemed to Hoskins as antique as a Victorian harness. Cooney's girl was scouring the carpet of a bow-fronted window-space. Braced on all fours, she worked the brush busily in a tight circling movement. The dark gold profile with its sharp nose and weaker chin was directed downwards. The waist was hollowed down while the hips swelled and quivered with the energy of her contortions.

'Enough to have Jack Chance clawing at the glass,' Hoskins said. 'No, Stan. Cooney must have set her up there. She knows the sort of spanking he'd hand out if she was to try crossing him in public. What happened exactly?'

McArthur shrugged. 'Nothing very original. Driver and his mate both employed by Cooney for a couple of years. Unloaded the gowns from the back of the van. Wheeled them on a rail into the shop. Changed 'em over. Wheeled the old ones back out. Went in again for the takings. They reckon they closed the back of the van. Mr Nicholls thinks they're just saying it. Covering their backs against Cooney and his insurers. Even if the van doors were closed, they weren't locked.'

Hoskins gazed across at the rain-dripping window-arches of the Royal Peninsular Emporium.

'Don't tell me, Stan. They got back in the van with the cash-box and a face with a gun popped out from among the dresses.'

'Two faces,' said McArthur pedantically. 'Rubber masks, gloves and shooters. Driver and his mate had to sit back-to-back in the rear of the van, wrists tied to each other. The two masks stepped out with the cash and just walked off among the shops. No one noticed anything. Not even Madame Jolly herself.'

'Nothing?'

'Well,' McArthur said, 'after a bit she realised the van was still parked there and she went out. Found these two grinding and wrestling among the off-the-shoulder evening wear.'

'Anything on the gunmen?'

'Tall. One of 'em on the young side, they reckon. Not much to see otherwise except the backs of their heads. Dark hair in both cases. Pretty useless, boss. I don't like the smell of the driver and his mate. Nor the assistant in the shop neither. Got a distinct aroma of put-up.'

Hoskins sighed. 'I'll keep an eye open for any connection between Billy Catte and this caper. I'm going down his place on Dyce Esplanade presently. Give the old drum a spin. He's not been back there since the set-to out the infirmary, of course. Missing person, in fact. If this lot's down to him, there'll be a sign somewhere.'

McArthur shook his head as the winch on the pick-up revved faster.

'I reckon you might come in second there, Mr Hoskins. According to what Mr Nicholls said, it's Forensic got priority down Dyce Esplanade, after this. They were starting to get 'em down to Catte's place half an hour ago. Before there's another robbery where someone gets so excited the gun goes off.'

Hoskins returned to the Vauxhall Cavalier and made a circuit of Atlantic Wharf. He drove back in slow traffic towards the intersection where Great Western Street crossed Longwall and entered King Edward Square. The doors of City Hall stood within a *porte-cochère*, built to suggest the colonnade of a modest opera house or a Parisian mansion. A group of men and women waited beside it, like a coach party expecting their bus. Hoskins saw one or two home-made placards on sticks. The lettering was amateurish but the word FACT was clear. A long banner held by two women at either side announced FAMILIES AGAINST CHILD-TAKERS. Councillor Cooney was already getting value for money.

An hour later, with Chance driving the motorpool Sierra, Hoskins was on his way to Dyce Esplanade. A mist like thin steam hung over the estuary reeds and dockland mudflats at low water. The little dockside promenade of Dyce Esplanade was bleak as a winter graveyard.

Two cars and a police Transit had parked outside Billy Catte's large end-of-terrace house. Hoskins went through the open door and met Charlie Blades cantering down the stairs. Blades was whistling like an errand boy.

'Morning, Sam. You and young Mr Chance jumped the gun, I'm afraid. Got a little bit of the clever stuff to finish before we let you loose.'

'That's nice, Charlie,' said Hoskins equably. 'Anything that might make me happier?'

Blades drew his lined saturnine face into a mask of distaste.

'Nah,' he said contemptuously. 'Bits and pieces from rude

144

parties – girls from the Realito Club, I'd say. Brought here to amuse the boss and his friends. Sheets on the beds didn't get washed much – or got used a lot, according to how you reckon it. Half-finished bottles of booze everywhere. Cigarette burns on the dining-room carpet from trodden-out dog-ends. How they never set light to the place, I don't know. There's a dead mouse down the side of the sofa and a johnny behind one of the arm-chairs in the corner of the living-room. Real Homes-and-Gardens stuff, this is. Right little slaughter-house.'

'Nothing in the way of firearms?'

'Nope,' Blades said. 'But come and have a look at this before I get busy again.'

He led the way back up the stairs to the landing, whose arched window overlooked the misty mudflats of low-water dockland. A matching archway led into the master bedroom. There were pink-quilted cushions and fan-backed basket-chairs, as well as a mirrored ceiling above the bed.

'If he was having this much fun,' Hoskins said thoughtfully, 'I wonder what made him such a miserable old swine?'

Blades waved him to silence and opened the double-doors of a built-in wardrobe. Whatever clothes had hung there were now on their way to Area Forensic at Ocean Beach. Blades slid aside what appeared to be another door at the back of the wardrobe. Hoskins found himself staring at a grey twilit impression of a large bathroom.

'Hang on,' Blades said.

He went out. Presently, the bathroom sprang brightly into view as if Hoskins were standing in a doorway looking into it. It was the first time he had seen a two-way mirror of such size, almost floor to ceiling and the dimensions of an internal door. Blades returned. He reached up, pulled a cord, and produced a purring of warm draught from above them.

'He'd even put a warm-air flow this side, Sam, so's it shouldn't get steamed up.'

'Who was the great centre of attraction then, Charlie? Mrs Catte? Step-daughter? Ladies popping in for a party and a bath?'

Blades chuckled. 'That's down to you, Sam. However, there's a couple of grateful postcards from German au pairs. Greta and Gaby. I suppose Mrs Catte had a regular supply of willing workers from home.'

145

'Certainly can't ask her now, Charlie. The only member of the family that hasn't scarpered seems to be young Emma. And social services won't part with her until they've finished their so-called disclosure sessions. The only bit of disclosure I overheard was when she told their care-officer to piss off.'

'Not much sense wasting time with her, Sam. And I have to tell you this doesn't smell to me like the house of whoever knocked off Madame Jolly Modes this morning. This bloke couldn't organise himself well enough. Floor-shows for the punters, Samuel, that's what this is all about. And the staff did a lot of overtime back here. As a stick-up artist, I reckon there's only one thing Billy Catte ever stuck up anywhere.'

They walked back downstairs to the hall.

'You catch Carmel Cooney on the telly last night, Charlie?'

'Nope,' said Blades. 'Caught him in the *Globe* at lunch, though.'

'How's that, then?'

'They reckon he broke all the rules. He's being banned from BBC and Coastal Network broadcasts.'

'There was one or two home truths among all the aggravation,' Hoskins said. 'How can they ban him?'

'Producers just won't pick him for their shows.'

'He'll start his own television station.'

'Government won't allow, Sam.'

'Then he'll start his own government,' Hoskins said philosophically.

Blades and his team left. As the afternoon wore on, the CID search produced only further evidence of Billy Catte's private life. *Pearls of the Orient, Days at Florville* and other classics of the kind that Hoskins had noticed at Mr Cat's Prize Bingo seemed to be the staple of bedside reading. *Villa Rosa* and *Belle Sauvage* were among the 'Erotic Video Classics' awaiting attention from Mr Catte's home entertainment system.

The search upstairs ended while Jack Chance and the others were still rummaging below. Hoskins went down and found his sergeant.

'Same old rubbish,' Chance said. 'JVC video camera-case. But no camera.'

'Nothing that connects with armed robbery?'

Chance shook his head. At that moment there was laughter from another room. He peered through the crack in the open door.

'Idle buggers!' he said. 'Looks like they got Billy Catte's home movies on the box.'

Hoskins joined him, squinting into the room. The bright toy world of the television screen reflected images of Billy Catte's peach-furnished bathroom. There was a rumble of amusement from the team, perched on chairs and window-sills as two video'd figures in a wet embrace splashed out of the bath and began to grapple on the floor.

'Wash behind your ears, you dirty devil!' Sergeant Tappin called to the figure on the screen. There was another rumble of laughter. Chance frowned.

'Don't want that one to go missing,' he said grimly. 'Could easy travel out of here in someone's pocket and off to Wallace Dudden's private video-hire.'

Hoskins moved into the doorway. The screen went blank. Presently there was a flutter of light. The bathroom image was replaced by moving traffic seen from the window of a parked car. The camera panned to a long pavement angle. Hoskins saw an unlit neon sign for the Brasserie Magenta at one side of the main Paris Hotel entrance. It was a cloudy day on Atlantic Wharf. Then the sky spun as if the camera had abruptly turned away. It came to rest on the rear view of a white van. The van was stationary and its door open. A man in a motorcycle helmet and padded leatherwear crossed the pavement towards a shop front. Hoskins caught the sign. Madame Jolly Modes. There was a flash, a loss of picture, a flutter of light. Another girl stood naked, as if in a doorway. She turned and walked off, revealing as she did so the peach tiling of the bathroom wall. The tape jumped again. A man was walking back from the shop towards the van, carrying an attaché case. The picture flicked and they were back with the girl pulling on her under-clothes.

Sergeant Tappin turned and saw Hoskins.

'Something here, boss. Must have filmed the Modes at least a week ago.'

'Wind it back,' Hoskins said. 'That's evidence. Not in-flight entertainment.'

Tappin shrugged. 'About all there is, boss. Someone's took the rest. There's empty boxes that a dozen tapes must have been in, but the tapes are gone.'

Hoskins turned away. The last daylight was pale bronze

above the gathering flood-tide that swirled in from the head-land of Lantern Hill with the jetty and foreshore of Harbour Bar at its foot. He looked at his watch.

'Don't get too comfortable,' he said to the men on the chair-arms. 'I'll be back in an hour. I want this lot finished tonight.'

They shifted lethargically like reluctant schoolchildren.

'You want the tape, Sam?' Chance asked.

'You bet I do, my son. Wouldn't trust this lot with it. Hang on here for a bit. I'll be back as soon as I can. Need a word or two with Charlie Blades.'

He drove to the headquarters building in the February rush-hour. With the tape locked away, he noted time and details in his diary. The phone rang.

'Sam? Gerald Foster. What's the score on searching Billy Catte's place?'

'Nil – nil at the moment, Gerald.'

'Come on, Sam! Catte and his daughter are also at the centre of this child-abuse rumpus. He is going to be news.'

'Not if social services can help it,' Hoskins said. 'Anyway, I've just come back from Dyce Esplanade and there is definitely no comment yet.'

'Look,' Foster said reasonably, 'there's hell broke loose with Cooney and his lawyer, Jack Cam. They're acting for this FACT organisation. Cam's going to contest about twenty place of safety orders for children taken off their parents by social services. And he's ready to brief Toby Raven QC for the High Court, with Carmel Cooney's money. Did you know this?'

'Had a busy day, Gerald. No, I didn't know it. Doesn't surprise me.'

'Right,' Foster said. 'My problem is this. I'm getting whispers about Emma Catte. Billy Catte was the face at the infirmary who held a doctor hostage. We know that. But there's a charge of criminal assault pending against hospital staff. Jack Cam and FACT are alleging that some of 'em held Emma Catte down for examination against her will. And they're bringing charges against someone else who injected her with valium to stop her struggling while they had a look. If this is true, it is going to be very heavy stuff in this city. Have you heard anything, Sam, about a charge being brought?'

'No I haven't, Gerald. And it won't do you any good. You

can't use it. You can't print it without identifying her. She's fifteen. She gets anonymity, whether she likes it or not.'

'It's not her that'll be named,' Foster said. 'It's the others that'll hit the headlines. I don't even need that yet. If there's twenty cases going before the High Court in one go, I've got enough to be going on with.'

The first night-blue of the sky had gathered behind the window-lit office buildings of the Mall below him.

'I don't know anything about it, Gerald,' Hoskins said. 'Not sure I could tell you if I did. My case is Billy Catte. That's all.'

'You've been turning over Billy Catte's since this morning, Sam. I've had a trenchcoat on the esplanade. Keeps phoning to tell me how cold it is there. So what's Billy Catte? He's got you in person as his alibi over killing Bob McPhail and Terry Cross. Was he on the rob from Madame Jolly this morning?'

Hoskins sighed. 'Don't know, Gerald. He's got to be at the centre of it all. Him and family. Wife, daughters, sons. Just now, Emma is the only one of them to be found.'

Foster chuckled. 'Watch yourself with Emma Catte, Sam. She's got a brief acting for her now.'

'That'd take Billy Catte to authorise.'

'No it wouldn't, Sam. Emma Catte is pressing charges of assault. She is also one of the twenty kids for whom place of safety orders are being contested. For both actions her lawyer is being instructed by the mother in Germany and financed by the good Carmel Cooney. And in both cases Emma Catte's lawyer is going to be Jack Cam. A man with as much compassion and warmth as an alligator that's had its larder robbed.'

Foster rang off and Hoskins dialled Area Forensic.

'Dr Blades, please. Charlie? Sam. Listen, Charlie, did your team come up with anything at all on that dress van?'

Blades chuckled. 'You are going to enjoy this, Sam. You really are. The chaps working on the van had a head-start. Almost finished. They found a nail-file and biro on the floor at the back, where the driver and his mate were tied up. Nothing fancy, just a disposable plastic pen and a metal Woolworths' file. Easy lost from a top pocket when you stoop. Anyway, there's smudged prints on the biro. No use. But quite a good set of prints on the nail-file.'

'Billy Catte!'

Blades chuckled again.

'They had a distinct look of some prints that we dusted down in his house. But no, Sam. Not Mr Catte. We got a bright little smart-arse working here. Ben Felix. Fresh from college. Mustard-keen. Sent him beetling to Canton Infirmary. Dusted down a cup used by the lovely Emma Catte. Spot on. Her prints on the nail-file in the dress van. No two ways.'

'Emma Catte? She was locked up in the infirmary when the van was done.'

'See?' said Blades encouragingly. 'I told you that you was going to enjoy this one, Sam.'

# THREE

# Nice Try

# Chapter Nineteen

The first centre of Ocean Beach had grown on the hill above Alexandra Gardens and the steamer-pier. Its tall villas dated from an era when even the name of the resort was a matter of doubt. The houses stood above what was known colloquially as 'the ocean beach' of the Canton coastline. The squares of grey Victorian mansions had taken their names from more distant ocean paradises: Madeira and Bermuda, Cape Rock and Tenerife.

No shippers or coal-owners lived there now. Most of the big houses were divided into apartments, some with individual entrances, many with communal halls and flights of stone garden steps. On a wet Sunday night of late February, these Atlantic squares were places of flapping branches and dancing shadows in the wind and lamplight. The tide was high and the breeze milder from the south-west.

The squat shape of an Austin Metro laboured on Atlantic Hill, where the lower road turned off by the pier and curved up past the railings of Alexandra Gardens. At the top of the hill, above the western darkness of the flooding tide, the car paused and moved a little awkwardly into higher gear. It turned into Madeira Square and then turned again into a cul-de-sac, running uphill at the far end. Where the founding fathers of the settlement had had their coach-houses, there now stood a row of a dozen lock-up garages.

The car stopped, facing one of these. The young woman who got out was in her late teens, wearing a blue nylon waterproof jacket and jeans. Her hair was combed tight round her head and trimmed at the length of her collar. There was a primness and a hint of freckling, narrowed eyes and tightened mouth. She spoke to a child of about four years old who was sitting in the back of the Metro. Then she turned towards the up-and-over door of the garage. As she pushed it up, turning it on its pivot, the young woman stopped and looked. The garage was already occupied by an empty car, its rear end towards her and the lid of the boot raised.

Rachel Wardle turned round again as two old men appeared behind her. They had stepped from the shadows at the end of the row of lock-ups. The stamp of their faces showed at once that the first was Funny Old Fellow and the other was Nice Old Boy with his crinkle-eyed benevolence. Had they been shorter, they might have been two of the Seven Dwarfs.

There was a struggle requiring such energy that she hardly seemed to have breath or presence of mind to scream. Once she managed to get a hand up and rake her nails across Nice Old Boy's face, the sleek armour of moulded plastic. She gave a harsh, tearing scream. Then her arms were behind her, turning her, until she bowed over the sill of the car boot. She screamed again, 'Get off! Get off me!' But the words came from her doubled body like a muted scream in a nightmare. Funny Old Fellow knotted a linen handkerchief round her wrists while Nice Old Boy kept his hand over her mouth and his lips to her ear.

'You don't want the kid smacked!' he shouted angrily. 'So do what you'll be made to do anyway. No one gets hurt. We're taking you into care, that's all. You know about taking into care! Let's see how you like a taste of it.'

His hand was drawn away and she drew breath deeply as a band of something strong and sticky was pressed over her face from the bridge of her upper lip to her chin. Funny Old Fellow and Nice Old Boy lifted her up bodily and she tried to jerk against them, without effect.

'You're only making things more difficult for yourself,' one of them called out, in a short breathless laugh. 'Isn't that what they tell the kids' parents? Lie still, act sensible, and you got all the air you need in there. Start acting up and it might be another story.'

In response to this rowdy interlude on a Sunday evening, a curtain corner twitched reprovingly here and there in the lighted windows at the rear of the flats.

There was a rug in the car boot as the two men lowered the girl into it. Nice Old Boy used a strap from the spare-wheel holder to pinion her ankles. There was a distant mewing, like a trapped cat, as he lowered the metal lid and locked it. Nice Old Boy had gone back to the Metro. He looked inside.

'Hello, Sunshine,' he called to the child in the back. 'You coming for a ride with us, are you? They're having a party down your dad's place. Your mum didn't want you to go. Still, we won't tell her. You come with us.'

A minute later Funny Old Fellow released the handbrake of the Metro steering it aside with his shoulder to the door-jamb. The headlights of the Granada came on with a full-beam brilliance. It started in a spurt of gravel across the lock-up yard. Despite Funny Old Fellow's wheeling of the Metro, the Granada thumped the other car's rear wheel-arch skidding briefly in its thrust.

After the shouts and the screams, Nice Old Boy drove sedately through the lamplit Victorian enclave of Madeira Square to Atlantic Hill. On a rainy February evening, full tide at Ocean Beach was no more than a slap and rush of water against sea-walls. In the damp air, a bronze sodium glare of street-lamps hung hazed by distance.

No one was on the Cakewalk to see them pass. The wide promenade lay black and wet, indistinguishable from the restless tide. The pier stretched out in winter darkness, closed until Easter, red navigation lights at its seaward end. Bay Drive was a place of windswept and boarded refreshment stalls. Municipal gardens lay in orange light, laurel bushes in black shadow. Down Rundle Street, the deserted Odeon steps caught only the light reflected from the carpeted foyer. Lamps behind the stained-glass windows of red-brick Holy Trinity evoked incense and Stations of the Cross.

On Sunday night, even the streets of the town centre were empty. One or two take-aways were open on the long low-rent suburban arterial stretch of Erskine Road. Its video libraries were well lit and busy. Space adventures and Electric Blue nudies, small-town American horror and heroines in leather. Young men with beer bellies and Mexican moustaches were ferrying home entertainment for all the family. The town had withdrawn behind closed doors.

Where the bow-fronted houses of the 1930s were set wider, the road forked, east to Canton, west to Sandbar. In the fork stood the Windsor, a roadhouse pub built between the wars with Tudor gables and leaded windows. Even here there were few vehicles in its car park. The red Granada turned on to the Sandbar fork, the darkness of the country road lying ahead.

'She be all right in there?' Funny Old Fellow asked the driver.

'Hard to say, Raz. We'll stop when we're clear of this lot.'

'I've had enough of this thing,' Funny Old Fellow said presently, as if to pull the mask off over his head. 'No one's going to see us now.'

'There's your little friend in the back seat with you,' Nice

Old Boy said sharply. 'Proper little chatterbox he'll be. Keep the thing on. What he doesn't see, he can't describe. And if he can't blab, he won't need quietening.'

'Won't be much left to tell,' Funny Old Fellow said with a snigger. 'I reckon there must be alarm-bells starting to ring all over this town about now.'

156

# Chapter Twenty

Monday morning ice patterns on the bedroom window would have made a glass engraver proud. The phone on Hoskins' pillowside table emitted a startled chirrup. He woke at the second ring and fumbled for the receiver.

'Sam? Gerald Foster. I'm down the *Western World* night-desk. Sam?'

Hoskins coughed and let out a gasp. His numbed fingers found the switch of the table-lamp.

'I was asleep, Gerald.'

'I thought you might be, Sam. And that's why I woke you.'

'What time is it?'

'Almost ten to six, Sam. Rachel Wardle didn't come home last night.'

'Ten to six! There's nights I don't come home, Gerald. Who's Rachel Wardle?'

'Daughter of Mrs Wardle. Canton social services. One of your posse that went to save Emma Catte from a maiden's fate.'

Hoskins pulled himself up on his elbow. Lesley turned away and drew the sheets round her again.

'Oh, that Wardle. I don't even know where her home is, Gerald.'

'Young Rachel's a mother's help for a woman called Belinda Zichy. Madeira Square, Ocean Beach.'

'I'm not following you, Gerald.'

'Listen,' Foster said. 'Half-past five this morning, when they're unloading the first lorries at Canton Covered Market, a driver sees this little kid wandering about. Four years old. He's got an envelope that says he and the envelope are to be taken to the *Western World* news-desk. One of our apprentices gets sent and brings him back. He's Joseph Zichy.'

'Is he?'

'And inside the envelope is a note from Billy Catte. He's taken Rachel Wardle into care. Seems he had to take the Zichy kid too. Rachel Wardle is going to remain in his care until he has proof that Emma Catte is released from the infirmary and reunited with her mother and sister in Germany. Germans don't extradite abused children. I put in a call about it to our foreign and legal desks in London when Catte's younger girl escaped there.'

'Bloody hell,' said Hoskins miserably. Still holding the phone, he slid down between the sheets to keep his shoulders warm.

'I phoned Ocean Beach divisional CID about half an hour ago. Not surprisingly, they've had Mrs Zichy screaming her head off all night. Thought the Wardle girl had done a bunk with her kid. Ain't so, Sam. Someone's done a bunk with Rachel Wardle instead. All getting to sound a bit nasty. I gather screams and struggling were heard near the Square about eight last night. The folks thought it was just another girl rowing with her boyfriend.'

'Has Forensic got the note?'

'All in hand, Sam,' Foster said quietly, 'but there's more to come. The note says that Catte wants his daughter back. But if he doesn't get response and action, then we'll start receiving Rachel Wardle bit by bit. Through the post. Hair torn out rather than cut. He reckons we'll notice the difference. One or two teeth, no doubt extracted with pliers by Mr Catte's own fair hand. Fingertip or two, took off with a heavy chisel. And there's one or two choicer items, which we'll keep until you stay-abeds have had your breakfast. He's offering to tape-record the proceedings and send 'em for broadcasting on the *Hit-Back Show*.'

'He's a bloody loony, Gerald. He's got to be. Or else it's a wind-up to see how far he can get.'

'I know he's a loony, Sam. You know he's a loony. Don't have to be CID to work that out. But if I was you, I shouldn't go into old Ripley and tell him it's just a wind-up. I phoned all this to Division the minute I got it. They're sending a bod down to look at the letter and a policewoman to chat up the kid. But I didn't get the impression that Tom Nicholls and company would take kindly to suggestions about it being a prank. There's aggravated assault and armed robbery already that they want to chat to Billy Catte about. And the feeling round the factory is that, alibi or not, he has to be accessory over Bob McPhail and Terry Cross.'

'What does the note say about it?'

'Nothing specific. The other thing he wants, by the way, is one hundred thousand in cash to start a new life.'

Hoskins snorted at the preposterousness of it.

'I need a hundred thousand in cash, Gerald, just to stay where I am. So why am I woken now with all this panic?'

Foster sighed. 'Friendship,' he said gently. 'You don't want to walk into the nick on a morning like this with feathers in your hair and your fly unbuttoned. You need this news when it happens, as it happens. That's my speciality.'

Hoskins put the phone down. As his feet touched the carpet, it rang again. This time it was Jack Chance.

'Sam?'

'I know,' Hoskins said. 'Gerald Foster just called.'

'Stan McArthur called me. They couldn't get you. Line engaged. There's a briefing at ten. Bloody hell, Sam, the bugger's kidnapped her daughter!'

'He says he has, Jack. Not necessarily the same thing. Could be Catte saying it when he hasn't done it. Could be someone else saying it for their own purposes. Could be the Wardle girl herself, on the try for a hundred thousand quid.'

He put the phone down. It rang again almost at once.

'DCI Hoskins, please?'

'I know. I know all about it.'

'There's a briefing, sir, at ten.'

'I know that too.'

Lesley turned over towards him and let out a shuddering groan.

'I might as well be trying to sleep in the middle of the headquarters briefing-room,' she said plaintively.

Hoskins got back into bed again and fumbled the warm sleekness of bare hips.

'In your present state, I don't think you'd get much sleep down the nick. Not with the likes of Jack Chance around.'

'Do something to that phone,' she said gently. 'I asked for a seven o'clock alarm-call.'

Hoskins took the receiver off and turned back towards her.

At ten o'clock there were a dozen of them sitting round a long table in the briefing-room. Ripley, with a pointer in his hand and a map of Ocean Beach on a board, was ready to begin.

'Right, people,' he said smoothly. 'You've read the handout. You know the details of the child's return this morning. Before we go back to that, I want to be sure that you have the details of Rachel Wardle's last known movements. We are told there has been a kidnap. There may have been. So far the child has confirmed part of the story. It is not unknown, however, for a young woman to use a fake kidnap as a means of disappearance.'

Chance looked at Hoskins in despair. Ripley went on.

'Mrs Wardle, the mother, is one of the social work team responsible for taking Emma Catte into care. She is divorced from her husband and living with a colleague, in the Marine Court flats at Harbour Bar. On Sunday she was visited by her daughter Rachel, nineteen years old and nanny to the Zichy child. Rachel Wardle and the child left about seven-thirty for Madeira Square. The car was a Metro, one of two vehicles owned by Belinda Zichy. The child says that they drove back without stopping and got to the lock-up garages at the rear of Madeira Square. Presumably that was about eight o'clock. Rachel Wardle opened the garage door. Two elderly men appeared and went in after her. One of them later came out and fetched the child. They put him in their car which was in the garage. He didn't see Rachel Wardle again. They drove him to a house, somewhere or other. He went to sleep. Next thing, he was in a car again. It stopped somewhere near the point at which he was found, probably near the Trading Street entrance of Canton Covered Market. The two old men were with him again. They told him to wait for his mother by the market gate. He was noticed a few minutes later. He did not, apparently, see Rachel Wardle at all after the incident at the lock-up garages. Yes, Mr Nicholls?'

'What about Mrs Wardle the mother, her companion, and Mrs Zichy, sir?'

'Mrs Wardle confirms that Rachel and the child left Harbour Bar at about seven-thirty. Mrs Zichy is a single parent of independent means. She was alarmed when Rachel Wardle and the child had not returned by ten o'clock. She phoned Mrs Wardle in Harbour Bar and learnt that the nanny and child had left there at seven-thirty. Then she phoned the police in Ocean Beach.'

'And that's it?' Nicholls asked.

'Almost, Mr Nicholls. We've questioned both Mrs Wardle and Mrs Zichy again. DC Asker and DS Williams are house-to-housing round Madeira Square. We've got three reports of residents hearing a row between a man and woman about eight last night. Shouts and a couple of screams. Then a car drove off. When they heard it go, no one bothered investigating. Mrs Zichy herself heard none of this. Two witnesses looked out and saw a girl and a couple of men by the garages. Assumed they were fooling about.'

'Anything to back up the child's story, boss?' McArthur asked.

'The lock-up garage was found open this morning and the car Mrs Zichy let Rachel Wardle drive, a cream Austin Metro, was parked by it. The car seems to have been abandoned rather hastily. Forensic are working on it and on the garage. That's about all we have for them at the moment. Except, of course, for the letter purporting to come from Mr Catte.'

Sergeant Tappin, tapered from broad shoulders to neat shoes, eased forward in his chair.

'Where's the press in all this, sir?'

'Co-operating,' said the Ripper with a self-conscious grin. 'Catte's letter was addressed to the *Western World*, of course. Both the *Western World* and its sister paper, the *Canton Evening Globe*, have agreed to an embargo on the story for the time being. We don't want to make fools of ourselves by a public appeal over something that turns out to be a private quarrel when Rachel Wardle flounces in this evening. But I'm seeing the CNT programme director, Radio Canton, BBC Television and Radio this morning. I'm sure they'll behave responsibly.'

'Just leaving the *Hit-Back Show*,' Chance said.

Ripley pulled a face.

'Yes,' he said, 'well, they're beyond our persuasive powers. In any case, they'd have to find out first. Even if they did and even if we don't put them out of business by then, their listening audience is fairly small.'

As the briefing ended, Ripley beckoned Hoskins.

'A word, Sam,' he said leading the way to his office. 'I didn't want to say so publicly, but it looks as if you're going to inherit this one from me. Billy Catte is on your caseload. The taking into custody of Emma Catte was supervised by you. Mr Clitheroe says, and I'm bound to think he's right, that this one is down to you. No point having two investigations now.'

Hoskins stopped, waiting for Ripley to unlock the door.

'Me and who else?'

The Ripper pouted in thought.

'If it looks serious, after all, and we have to start searching everywhere, you'll get all the man-power you need. We'll take that as it comes. For the moment, you'll have Jack Chance, since he's your skipper. Young Tappin for speed. Pargiter and Gosse in case it comes to shooting. And you'll need a guv'ner for your sergeants. Wallace Dudden, I think. It's time he was off traffic and into something that would give him experience in his new rank.'

Beyond Ripley's office window icy sunlight filled the heavens over Hawks Hill. The Superintendent turned and smiled ingenuously.

'What I wanted to say, Sam, is that no one blames you for what's happened. No one. No one takes the negative line that if Billy Catte was behind bars this wouldn't have happened. No way you could have caught him that day at the infirmary. No way at all. I don't blame you, in that respect. Nor does Mr Clitheroe. But now you're the one that's got to take the ball and run with it, Sam. I know you won't disappoint us. I don't think so for one minute.'

There was silence between them. Then Hoskins said, 'If I'm running this show, I want publicity. Large posters of Catte from his CRO photo and whatever we can get for Rachel Wardle. "Have you seen this man?" "Have you seen this woman?" A press embargo on reporting the case is useless. It saves face for us and the social services. That's all it does. It won't find Catte or Miss Wardle. I want everyone in the city on the look-out for 'em. Wider than that, if you like. I saw Catte at work in the infirmary. He's a nutter, Max. A fully paid up member of the rubber room.'

'I'll put the point, Sam.'

'And when do I get this letter from Catte?'

The Ripper's gill began to flush, making the moustache shine whiter still.

'The original is with Forensic. Copies to be issued here as soon as a list of authorised personnel has been drawn up.'

The cart-horse bureaucracy of the headquarters building had triumphed again. It was time to light a fuse under the Ripper.

'According to Gerald Foster, that letter contains a demand for money with menaces. One hundred thousand.'

Ripley waved it aside as incidental.

'Ransoms are immaterial, Sam. Find Rachel Wardle. That's what counts.'

'What I mean,' Hoskins persisted, 'is that someone could be having us on. Using Catte as a front. His own sons, for instance, if they want Emma out.'

'Then I imagine Catte will inform us his good name's being taken in vain,' the Ripper said smoothly.

'He might,' Hoskins said. 'Supposing his tongue's still attached to its root.'

Half an hour later Hoskins, behind his own desk, confronted Chance.

'There's nothing worse than a kidnap case, Jack, however you handle it. But I'm definitely the one in the barrel this time. If I sort Billy Catte and Rachel Wardle, the entire Division comes up smelling of violets. And if I don't, I get early retirement with the lads saying I always made a bog of things anyway.'

Chance's round flushed face seemed to swell with confidence.

'Bollocks,' he said. 'They're not all mean as Clitheroe and his lot. Who've we got?'

'Wallace Dudden, for a start.'

'Dudden? Ripley fallen out of his tree, has he? Dudden's never done anything but traffic offences and lost dogs! Even on traffic he couldn't change a car wheel when his crew got punctured. Who else?'

'Tappin, Pargiter, and Gosse. And you and me.'

'That's more like it,' Chance said. 'Tappin's nice and tasty on his feet, supposing there's any running to be done.'

But Hoskins was not listening.

'I want you here, Jack. Listen carefully when Rachel Wardle's girlfriend, the Zichy woman, tells her story. And listen to Mrs Wardle and her estranged husband and her new companion, too. Anything dodgy about 'em, I want to know. I'm going out the Beach. Have a word with Charlie Blades. See what Forensic might have on the Austin Metro and the rest.'

Chance yawned. 'You won't find Charlie up Clifton Hill. Nicholls reckons he's gone out to turn over Billy Catte's office at the Prize Bingo. Wants to find the typewriter that letter was done on. Thinks that's the quickest way home.'

Hoskins walked over to the window, his back to Chance, and gazed out across the raw February mist hanging like smoke over the flat alluvial landscape of the city.

'I want this case reported, Jack. I want pictures of Catte and the Wardle girl on every wall. I want pictures of his sons, Emma and the other girl if we can get 'em. For our own use, at present. I want people watching for them. If she's being held, it's somewhere round here. It has to be. They took her and the kid at about eight last night. He turned up at about five this morning. Nine hours. Part of that time he was in a house where he went to sleep. Knocks off a few hours.'

'Could drive a couple of hundred miles in six hours,' Chance said, unimpressed.

Hoskins turned round.

'No, Jack. Think about it. Suppose Catte drove to somewhere three hours off. You think he'd drive all the way back here the same night, just to dump that kid at the market? He'd hang on to the child. Or dump it somewhere nearer. Or even cut its throat. He's got to be here somewhere. You can hide a body in a city like this same as you can hide a twig in a tree.'

He took the Vauxhall Cavalier and drove alone to Clifton Hill. Charlie Blades was still out. The neon was dead above the Rundle Street Prize Bingo and the security locks were closed on the steel-framed shutters of the glass doors. In the lane at the back a patrol car was parked with hazard-lights pulsing. There was a police Transit van with its rear doors open. Hoskins went in, past the two uniformed men, and found Charlie Blades with his assistant in the little office.

'Morning, Sam. You remember seeing an Olympia portable typewriter down Dyce Esplanade?'

'Can't say I do, Charlie.'

'Nor do I. Can't find the bugger here either. That letter of Catte's was done on an Olympia Monica, according to the charts. There's a couple of things here that I'd swear we'll find were done on the identical keys. But of the machine itself there is – if you'll pardon my Swahili – not a fucking trace.'

'Took it with him, Charlie.'

'Course he took it, Samuel. Which means he has somewhere else to take it to. Which means in turn that you are going to have more grief than a month of funerals. He could be anywhere. And he's got friends.'

'You reckon it's his, Charlie? This letter?'

'Done on his machine, my friend. And our little dust-off showed the same prints on the paper as on his CRO file. Can't say fairer than that.'

'Nothing else?'

'There's a lot else, Sam. But not much here. Look at the mess! You reckon anyone runs a business in all this unwashed crockery and dog-ends and piles of junk? I found this specimen of reading matter, bit fruity in places. Never knew running a reformatory could be such fun.'

He handed Hoskins a copy of *Elaine Cox: A Well-Reared Tomboy*.

'Find your prints on the best pages, will we, Charlie?'

Blades chuckled. 'What I've got home, Samuel, I don't need rubbish like this. I had a fantasy this morning. It was her two little bleeders that got kidnapped. Never heard of again. Had to console her grief over and over.'

'And what else, Charlie?'

'I've got two going over the Austin Metro in the motorpool and two going over the lock-up garage by Madeira Square. If that's where it happened, we'll find something.'

Hoskins sighed and lodged himself against the edge of Billy Catte's desk.

'We don't know she's been kidnapped, Charlie. Just this note on Catte's typewriter.'

'If it's not Catte, you'll hear from him or his lawyer, Sam. Outraged voter. Innocent man wrongly accused.'

Blades whistled a little tune to himself and went through some papers on the desk. Hoskins turned the pages of Mr Catte's paperback fantasy, the words making no impact upon him. He had intended riding back to Area Forensic with Blades. But Blades was enjoying himself too much with what he had found. Hoskins decided to press on alone.

# Chapter Twenty-One

Hoskins drove to Madeira Square, leaving Blades to finish his examination of the Rundle Street arcade. He went out to the car and drove up the rear lane to Bay Drive. The early mist had cleared and Ocean Beach lay in February sun. The sea was a flat calm on which the sun played with a dull silver sheen, like the interior wrappings of cigarette packets in Hoskins' youth. It was a day caught somewhere between winter and spring, making the kidnap drama of the previous evening yet more unreal.

Above the pier and the gardens, the tall Victorian houses of Madeira Square were quiet as a Sunday. He drove round the north side to the row of lock-up garages in the cul-de-sac. The Austin Metro had gone but a patrol car was parked at one side. Hoskins pulled up and walked across to the open door. A young man with ginger curls and glasses looked out. He was wearing the white overalls of a garage mechanic.

'DCI Hoskins. Canton "A" Division. Anything that might help us yet?'

The young man shook his head.

'I'm Ben Felix. Not a great deal here. Didn't expect it. A few footprints from a woman's shoes. We assume that must be Rachel Wardle. Also two recent sets of prints from men's shoes. Probably from earth that was wet during yesterday's rain. Only one set of tyre tracks superimposed on the prints and it's not the Metro. Those shoes were here last night. We assume the prints belong to the two men whom the child remembers.'

'Anything about them?'

'Tall,' Felix said. 'Shoe-size nine or nine and a half. That indicates not much less than about six foot in both cases. Probably sharp dressers, rather narrow shoes, built for style rather than comfort.'

Hoskins stood on the threshold of the open lock-up. 'Two elderly men, the boy said.'

Ben Felix pulled a face and shook his head.

'They weren't wearing old men's shoes. Younger style. Another thing. Rachel Wardle's prints enter the garage and then stop. She never walked out again. Whoever grabbed her

166

probably lifted her into a car that was already inside. Doesn't
sound like an old man to me. And the Metro was definitely
shoved out of the way. We could see the marks the shoes
made in the dirt where he dug his toes in. Not an old man's
caper.'

Hoskins nodded. 'Draycott, the pharmacy van driver, talked
about masks. So did the one outside Madame Jolly Modes. I
daresay the kid took old men's masks for the real thing.'

'In the dark, he might.'

'No fingerprints? No dog-ends? Nothing like that?'

Felix smiled his regret. 'No, Mr Hoskins. I'd say they
knew their job well enough to wear gloves.'

'And only two of them?'

The young man shrugged.

'Only two got out of their car. Could have been someone
else inside. And here, just here inside the lock-up door, there's
a mess of shoeprints. At first sight you can't tell what. But a
struggle of some kind. Look where the chalk lines are and
you see the different angles of the feet. That's not someone
walking.'

'And this was definitely last night?'

'Defo,' the young man said. 'Since the rain started yesterday
afternoon that Metro hasn't been in here but another car has.
That other car's tyres and these shoeprints are on top of any
mark made by the Metro up to yesterday. The rain started in
Ocean Beach about half-past five, according to the Canton
Weather Centre. After that, there was an unidentified car in
this garage. A woman in Rachel Wardle's shoes walked in
here but never walked out. There was two men in here, on
foot, perhaps another in the car. There was some scuffling of
feet near the entrance. After that, the unidentified car drove
out with all of them in it. One of 'em previously shoved the
Metro out of the way to clear the path. I could be wrong –
but I'm not.'

Hoskins beamed at the earnest young face.

'Smashing,' he said enthusiastically. 'I'm going over to
Area Forensic to see what they've got on the Metro.'

'Not much,' Felix said. 'Except that someone had took
a slice of paint off the rear corner. Might tell us something
about the other vehicle that was here. Biggish car, anyway.
More than the Metro.'

Hoskins drove back to Bay Drive and up Clifton Hill,

past the little hotels, the petrol station, and the ice cream parlours. When he walked into Area Forensic there was still no sign of Charlie Blades.

'Afternoon, Mr Hoskins,' said Alec Crayle cheerily. 'Looking for Dr Blades?'

'Still down Rundle Street,' Hoskins said. 'Anything on the Metro?'

Crayle waved an arm and led him through thick double-doors to the workshop. Hoskins' ears were assailed by the scream of bolts being power-tightened as the Metro, on its ramp, received the attentions of Crayle's team. Crayle gestured at it proudly.

'That scrape on the back. Other chap left a flake or two of his paintwork on the car and on the ground. Plum-red top-coat, matching Ford standard undercoat and grey double-proof anti-oxide primer. Exact combination for T or W registration Ford Granada. Not a respray either. That primer is the original, unique factory job on an import from Spain. Not a scratch until last night, I'd say. One careful owner looking for his car this morning.'

Hoskins grinned. 'More like it, Mr Crayle. Anything else?'

Crayle took him by the arm and led him back from the shriek of power tools, the sharp breath of petrol and the enclosed air of vulcanised rubber.

'Someone pushed that Metro. Had his shoulder to the door frame while he did it. Caught some fluff from his coat and a short white thread, just like the whisker of a cat. We vacuumed the dress van and the pharmacy Transit very carefully. There was another cat's whisker thread in the Transit. Same material, if not same coat. Only thing is, it's a coat made for Marks and Spencer by the thousand. Greyish jacket. You know anyone that wears that sort of jacket, Mr Hoskins?'

'Not yet, Mr Crayle, but I'm hoping to be introduced before long. Supposing Charlie Blades shows up again this afternoon, you might tell him I've gone back to Division. One or two things that can't wait any longer. What I shall need is any keys that were found down Mr Cat's Prize Bingo, other than the ones to fit the Rundle Street locks themselves. Need to match them as soon as possible. If he could finish with them today, I'll have them picked up tomorrow.'

'Right-o, Mr Hoskins,' said Crayle cheerily. 'Watch out for any red Granadas coming after you.'

# Chapter Twenty-Two

A cold afternoon wind rattled the fifth floor of the head-quarters building. Hoskins and Chance stood together, looking down at the list on the Chief Inspector's desk.

'I want various things, Jack, and I want them fast. Ripley's taking it more seriously now he knows Billy Catte's typewriter produced the ransom note. This case needs sorting out before Catte or his friends come back about the hundred thousand pounds and how it's to be paid.'

'What's first?' Chance asked.

'Photographs. We've got Catte and Rachel Wardle for the posters. I want any photos that can be got of Mrs Catte and the other daughter. And the two sons, wherever the hell they are. And I want a WPC watching Emma Catte. I wouldn't trust hospital security to keep her under guard. She could walk out in a rubber mask for all they'd notice. But first, let's have a full set of pictures for everyone on the team.'

'I'll get Jenny Riley on that.'

'Then,' said Hoskins quietly, 'I want a list of every one of Catte's family, friends, associates, and all premises they might have access to. Use St Catherines House and the entries for births and marriages, if it helps. Get Interpol to check the German connection.'

'What about Allied Control Commission in Berlin?'

'Them too. Mrs Catte could have family there. And I want a proper inventory of all keys found in the search of Catte's home and office. Every one matched against a lock. Tappin and two DCs can handle it. Any that can't be matched are to be shown to every registered locksmith in the city, if that's what it takes. I need to know what premises he could open if he had to.'

'Right,' Chance said enthusiastically.

'And I want every joke-shop and toy-shop visited. Anywhere that sells masks. Full set of photos. See if anyone answering those descriptions bought masks in the last few months.'

'Pargiter and Sue Bennett could do that.'

'And this Ford Granada business . . . '

'I checked that,' Chance said, 'while you were at the

Beach. There's two reported stolen in a fifty-mile radius and not found. One went missing several weeks ago. Used by a surgeon's wife for taking the kids to school and so on. The other belongs to a retired ironmonger down in Barrier. Widower of almost sixty living with his sister. Lost it and reported it three nights ago. New tyres on front wheels. Forensic is sending a lad to look for tracks in the bloke's garage. Thinks it could well be a match for the tread they found at the Madeira Square lock-up. We'll know by tonight.'

Hoskins straightened up.

'Right,' he said. 'If it is his car, he's probably seen the last of it. After a caper like this it'll very likely have been through the crusher or into the dock by now. If it's not a match, we'll have to start checking ownership of Ford Granadas right through the city and the area. Where the man-power comes from, I don't know. What else does that leave?'

'The witnesses,' Chance said. 'Mr and Mrs Wardle, the parents, and Mrs Zichy.'

'Anything there?'

Chance sat down, uninvited, and stretched his legs out. The bright afternoon sun shone directly through Hoskins' window, heating the warm air of the office like a conservatory. Chance shook his head.

'I can't see it, Sam. Mr Wardle's about fifty, senior position in the housing department. He and his missus seem pretty cool about the whole marriage business. Split up twelve years ago. Young Rachel went her own way.'

Hoskins stared out across the domes of City Hall towards the distant glitter of the tidal anchorages. Chance broke the silence again.

'You reckon they'll pay this ransom if things get nasty, Sam?'

Hoskins yawned. 'Not if they can help it, my son. They don't want half Canton kidnapping the other half and writing to old Gerald Foster about it. As for Emma Catte, there's Jack Cam trying to get her made a ward of court today and out of social services' hands. If she gets out, there's nothing left but the demand for money.'

'You don't think Billy Catte might still go for the money?'

Hoskins shook his head.

'He's been in the business a long while. Small-time graft but a lot of footwork. And he's bigger now. Rundle Street amusement arcades. Naughty-naughty down the Realito. Got a lot to lose. Even if he thought about ransom, he's not daft enough to bank on being paid off. It's Emma he wants most. If Jack Cam can spring her, Billy might just let Rachel Wardle go. He could disappear. He's got cash and a roof over his head in Spain and Germany.'

Chance went out. Hoskins turned to the transparency he was preparing for his six o'clock briefing. It was the first of such importance that had fallen to him. Suspects. Families. Associates. Keys. Premises. Vehicles. Search patterns. He sat back at length, admiring the abstract design. Hoskins was a draughtsman, a model-maker. Diagrams spoke clearer than words. Then he began to calculate the man-power needed for the tasks. After several minutes he sat back in dismay, like a man finding his pocket empty at the arrival of the restaurant bill. It would take half the Division to cover the investigation this way. And even that offered no guarantee of success.

The phone rang. It was Jack Chance in the sergeants' room.

'Sam? There's some sort of rumpus going on outside the court building. Parents and well-wishers. They're trying to get their hands on social workers that've been giving evidence in this appeal case of Jack Cam's.'

'Who's covering it?'

'Tom Nicholls went down with a dozen of his uniformed detail to keep order. Thing is, I've got photostats of some faces we wanted. Not likely Billy Catte would show himself down there. Some of the others might. You want to go down and look 'em over?'

'See you at the car park in three minutes, Jack. We'll take the Cavalier.'


The Crown Court building stood on the far side of the Memorial Gardens, at right-angles to City Hall. Hoskins pulled into the parking bay at one end. Like the other buildings of the civic centre, the Crown Court was a pillared Edwardian survival in pale tide-washed stone.

Nicholls had closed off the side-road with wooden barriers. The pavement at the foot of the Crown Court steps was packed by eighty or a hundred men and women, most of the men dressed in anoraks or donkey-jackets, the women in jeans and wind-cheaters. Two or three posters proclaimed FAMILIES AGAINST CHILD-TAKERS and SET OUR CHILDREN

FREE. There was no sign of a television crew but a *Western World* photographer was standing by one of the newspaper's estate wagons.

'Hang on,' Chance said suddenly. 'There's no film loaded in the camera.'

He began to unbutton a Minolta X-100 from its case. Hoskins got out and walked to the front of the building. He crossed the avenue and watched from the far side. Nicholls had his dozen uniformed men down the court steps, the formation fanning out at the bottom. Chance came up to him with the camera.

'What'd'you think, Sam?'

'Looks like Tom Nicholls doing his "Now-now-move-along-there" routine. Let's have some snapshots anyway. And I want copies of any others taken by Gerald Foster's man. Can't see Billy Catte or any familiar faces here. This is strictly Mount Pleasant high-rise and Orient back-to-back.'

At that moment there was a shout from the leaders of the crowd. The youthfully concerned face of the Director of Social Services had appeared above them, between the pillars of the court entrance. At road-level, half a dozen uniformed police had begun trying to hold a space round a black Rover 2000 with a driver at its wheel.

The Director of Social Services walked tight-faced towards the first step. There was a howl from the front of the crowd. Several of the women began to scream with anger. Something larger than an egg rose in the air and smashed without effect on one of the upper steps. Another missile, the first stone, flew up, hit a column and bounced back down the steps. The six uniformed men at the car were pushed aside as the crowd thrust forward, leaving them in the rear of the action.

Tom Nicholls looked about him, realising that half his detail was now cut off from the rest. But the Director went down another step. The crowd paused. He took a third step down towards his car. A young woman with a scarf over her curled blonde hair ran up two steps and, as he lifted an arm to defend himself, she spat at his face. Several of them were almost on him now, a ululating anger filling the cold sunlit afternoon. Another arm went up and smashed down. Neither Hoskins nor Chance could see the effect.

At the foot of the steps, the six uniformed men moved away from the crowd and cleared a path up to the entrance in a tight bunch like a rugger-scrum. The two sides drew apart. The Director of Social Services, wiping at his face with a handkerchief, took a step or two backwards. Tom Nicholls turned round and picked up a loud-hailer. His uniformed men now formed a line across the top step, the Director of Social Services somewhere behind them. The driver of the black Rover 2000 moved off gently and drove round to the rear of the building. The loud-hailer screeched and whistled as Nicholls tested it. Then his voice rang clear across the avenue and the Memorial Gardens.

'This is a police announcement. You are committing wilful obstruction. That is a criminal offence. Clear the pavement. Please clear the pavement in front of the court building. If you have a legitimate complaint about the conduct of the social services department, there are proper channels for making it.'

This was received with shouts and cat-calls. But Nicholls talked them down.

'Those of you who persist in this obstruction will be arrested and charged. It can do your cause no good whatever. Your arguments are being put now in the court itself. Clear the pavement and go about your business.'

Someone shouted an objection that Hoskins could not hear.

'There is no more room in the public gallery,' Nicholls boomed at his interrupter. 'The number of seats is limited and they are full. I am asking you to disperse, to go and wait quietly— '

He broke off as someone appeared behind him. Hoskins glimpsed the fat tadpole-shape of Carmel Cooney, the large head and the melon-smile. He began talking energetically with Nicholls. The crowd waited quietly and the impassive blue line of helmeted police stared down at them. After some hesitation and reassurance, Nicholls handed Cooney the loud-hailer. By contrast with the Chief Inspector, Cooney was a master of the art. His public meetings were held in the boarded Vestry Road Baths or the Connaught Park Stadium where the rhetoric of pragmatic Fascism rang on tile and steel and iron-framed glass.

'My friends! Bear with me a moment, if you will. I understand your anger and frustration. Believe me, I know what your feelings must be. But I ask you, please, to do as Chief Inspector Nicholls requires. He is in the right and you will strengthen your position by doing as he tells you. If you use violence now, you play into the hands of your enemies in the social services.'

By contrast with Nicholls, Cooney's voice was strong and smooth as a silk choker. He smiled at them all, the teeth evenly set like a crocodile's.

'Your case is proceeding. Your cause is just. We may not see an end today. We may not see an end this week. But, God willing, we shall triumph soon. Justice will prevail. Those poor victimised children will be returned to you. Let them come safely home again. The people who have injured you and your little ones shall be called to account. Have no fear of that, my friends. We shall seek justice for the evil they have done. On that you have my word.'

There was sporadic and hesitant clapping. Nicholls stared at Cooney, helpless to correct his error of judgment in allowing the councillor to use the loud-hailer. The crowd listened hungrily. The uniformed line waited, braced and ready. Behind Cooney stood the outline of Jack Cam, tall and thin in his dapper fawn suiting. With watch-chain, hand-made tan shoes and neatly barbered grey-black hair, he had an air of the Edwardian stage-door dandy. But when he spoke his voice still betrayed a hard nasal edge of law learnt in Canton evening institute and Saturday-night police courts.

'I want you all to come with me now,' Cooney was saying, the smile flashing again. 'The Marina Suite of the Royal Peninsular Emporium stands open. I invite you all to be my guests for tea and to discuss your grievances.'

The tension seemed to fall away from the men and women below him. For the first time in weeks someone of importance had spoken to them kindly and with respect. Cooney handed the loud-hailer back to Nicholls and walked down towards his audience. He spoke to one or two of them. Then, like a teacher with a class of children on an outing, Cooney lurched to the front and led them down the avenue towards the open spaces of King Edward Square, Great Western Street and Atlantic Wharf.

At the end of the procession, the men and women wandered to either side, as if not quite able to decide on Cooney's invitation. Half a dozen of them were crossing the Square at one side of the court building when the Director of Social Services came out of a rear door to which his chauffeur had driven the car. Hoskins, walking across to where Tom Nicholls stood, saw the *Western World* cameraman framing the Director on the pavement. Perhaps it was this which attracted the attention of Cooney's last followers. They began to walk and then to run towards the Director. As the black Rover moved off, they ran after it down the middle of the road, brandishing fists and hurling a few small clods from the narrow flower border along the avenue. There was no chance that they would reach the Rover nor hit it with the clods of earth. But the *Western World* photographer, camera raised, caught a dramatic view of the common enemy being chased off the scene. Hoskins guessed that Gerald Foster's front-page on the following morning was going to do his readers proud.

At six o'clock that evening the briefing was a subdued one. Hoskins himself felt like a pupil transformed into a teacher. His place was usually among the rows of men shifting their large cramped bottoms on the little wooden chairs of the briefing-room. He was the one who caught the muttered ironies and scepticisms of Stan McArthur or Jack Chance as Ripley or Clitheroe held forth.

He looked at his audience now, outlining the search procedures and routine checks of keys and premises from his projected transparencies on the white hardboard screen. He thought they listened to him more intently and more seriously than they did to Clitheroe or Ripley. He was still one of them. But even as he thought this, Stan McArthur's lips moved perceptibly for the benefit of John Truman to one side of him.

'Time,' Hoskins was saying, 'isn't on Catte's side. In the folders issued to you, there are photographs of his family and known associates. He can't show himself without being caught. Even people who might take food to him are being looked for. Billy Catte or the kidnap-hoaxer is trapped as surely as the victim or accomplice. And that might be the greatest danger.'

Stan McArthur said something else from the side of his mouth.

Hoskins came out of the briefing alone and went back to his room. He stood at his window, staring out at night-time Canton, the yellow take-away neon and the New China supermarket of Orient Parade, the long sodium-lit stretch of Dyce Street to Pier Head, the showboat blaze of derrick-head lights on a container ship that waited its turn off the Railway Dock.

A put-up job. The most likely and easiest explanation of amateur kidnap. But Mrs Wardle had taken Billy Catte's child from him. Now Mrs Wardle's daughter had been taken in her turn. Catte had been prepared to kill Dr Underwood at the infirmary. The demand note had been typed on Catte's Olympia Monica. Hoskins had to assume that the kidnap was in earnest.

For the first time, he found himself at the dead centre of a major investigation, the point at which nothing moved. Other men were knocking on doors of Catte's family and friends, checking keys with locksmiths, compiling lists of disused buildings. The phone rang.

'Mr Hoskins? John Deacon, press office. Mr Clitheroe asked me to keep you informed on media coverage of the Billy Catte affair. No television report of the set-to outside the law courts this afternoon. BBC local news and Coastal Network are ignoring it. Editorial policy is to avoid coverage of parental action against social services until there's a result in court. There's a local BBC talk show featuring Eve Ricard on behalf of the council. I gather from the preview that she suggests parents who subject children to the ordeal of court proceedings in this way are guilty of a further form of child abuse.'

'Does she?' said Hoskins, awe-stricken. 'I bet Catte's glad he didn't kidnap her.'

Deacon chuckled.

'The press is going the other way. Lay-out of tomorrow morning's *Western World* has a front-page banner: "A Mum's Anger". Action photo underneath of the Social Services Director wincing back and a woman's head going forward at him. You can actually see the gob flying. Gerald Foster must think he's in for Pic-of-the-Year. Two Fleet Street features also using it. There's an inside shot of folks chasing the car with raised fists. Nice action.'

'Thanks, John. Incidentally, the embargo on reporting Rachel Wardle's kidnap comes right off tomorrow. I want the whole city looking for Billy Catte.'

'Right-o, Mr Hoskins. One other thing, by the way. Fred Salter on the *Canton Globe*. He got in with the mob that Cooney took to tea down the Emporium. Seems Cooney stood up there and talked to them all. His usual thing about the CNT and BBC being a bunch of sanctimonious hypocrites and run by poufs and lessies. Anyway, Salter reckons, Cooney said he's starting his own paper. Morning and evening editions of the same format. *Atlantic Morning* and *Atlantic Evening*. Going to report the news as people want it, not as some young fart in BBC editorial thinks they ought to get it.'

'A daily paper?'

'Salter reckons. Punchy reporting. Skin on centre page. Top-rate sport and crime. Tear the throat out of the city council and the Labour group. Cooney said something about a deal with a company that prints trade weeklies for the shipping and steel industries. That's James and Wadley. I'll try to find out.'

'You do that, John. I'm off home to bed.'

On the following morning Hoskins glanced at the first page of the *Western World* while the steam from the toast turned into smoke. The photograph from the original lay-out was still there, illustrating 'A Mum's Anger'. There was a sub-heading: 'Councillor Calms Riot'. On the inner page, as if it had no connection, a single column covered the Dock ward by-election. Following Cooney's television outburst, the paper had done a snap opinion poll. It favoured him by a majority of 5 – 4 in a ward that had never been anything but Labour. Hoskins closed the paper and attended to the toast.

He was in his office at half-past nine when the internal phone rang.

'Mr Foster for DCI Hoskins.'

'Put him on.'

'Sam? This is for you, officially. As officer in charge of an investigation. I've just got home and found a small package shoved through the letter-box. Sent by hand, not post. Somewhen last night. I've opened it but I'm not touching it. This is one for Charlie Blades and his team.'

'Can you see what's in it, Gerald?'

'Got that far, Sam. There's an item of ladies lingerie, to put it delicately. And there's a ring with a couple of stones in it. Unless I'm very much mistaken, you've got a message from Billy Catte about Rachel Wardle.'

'Stay there, Gerald. I'll ring Area Forensic and I'll have

someone with you. I've got a briefing to do, and the Ripper to see, so it won't be me in person.'

'There's something else,' Foster said.

'What's that, then?'

'Whoever these maniacs may be, Sam,' Foster said, 'they've got my home address. I don't fancy that, my friend. Not one little bit.'

'Try me at lunch, Gerald. Porter's Lodge at one, if I can make it.'

# Chapter Twenty-Three

Before the Porter's Lodge or even Superintendent Ripley, Hoskins kept one other appointment. Avoiding Jack Chance and the use of the motorpool Sierra, he parked his Vauxhall Cavalier in the narrow straw-littered bay of Navarino Street bonded warehouse, opposite the commercial library and newspaper reading-room. He walked down the rows of reading-stands where the old men sniffed close at the columns of print, the smell of unwashed flannel impregnating the very stone of the mottled floors. Even the sunlight through frosted glass seemed colder than lamplit evenings in such a place.

Jimmy Liddell was staring with a look of vague disapproval at a close-columned page of the *Steel Trades Journal*. He was trying to read without his glasses. A patina of violet oil shone on the water-buffalo sweep of his greying hair. He straightened up, suddenly on parade again.

'I guessed what it was, Mr Hoskins. The answer's "no". Not a dicky-bird. Nothing. Soon as I saw them two pictures in the case outside Monmouth Street nick, I knew it. There's been talk, of course. But hardly a soul down Peninsula ever heard of that woman Wardle, let alone her daughter. Only one or two that had their kids took away. And Billy Catte's gone as though he'd never existed. So's his wife and younger daughter and his sons.'

Hoskins pulled his gloves off.

'It's not what you know now, Jimmy. It's what you might hear. There's money riding on this. Other things apart.'

The old man shifted his feet and sniffed.

'Much money would that be, Mr Hoskins? Percentage of something, perhaps?'

'Quite a bit, Jimmy.'

Liddell shook his head. 'That's all very well, Mr Hoskins. I could do with the cash. But there's no point wasting your time with duff gen. Is there, now? If it was ordinary crime there might be voices talking everywhere. But this is personal. Family. Down to Billy Catte and perhaps his sons, they reckon. Not known as tearaways, though the one they call "Tom" Catte might be. Seventeen, eighteen.'

Hoskins clapped the old man on the shoulder of his scuffed suede coat.

'There's a shopping-list, Jimmy. Things I might pay for on their own.'

'Is there, Mr Hoskins? Such as?'

Hoskins looked round the skylit room. It was still empty.

'About a dozen videos missing from Billy Catte's place down the esplanade. Boxes there but tapes gone. One Ford Granada. VCL 492W. Cherry-red.'

'You don't want much, Mr Hoskins, do you?'

'And then,' Hoskins said, 'there's a typewriter. West German made. Olympia Monica portable. Grey base and off-white top.'

'That's it, is it?'

'It's just the start, Jimmy. I want Billy Catte and his helpers. And I want Rachel Wardle unharmed.'

Liddell drew lines across his forehead with a fingernail, as an aid to thought.

'A lot of people want that, Mr Hoskins. People that reckon this city won't be fit to work in until this is sorted out. The doors that's being knocked on! The places that's being turned over by your lot! No peace anywhere. There was road-blocks in Clearwater and Mount Pleasant last night, they reckon.'

'Routine, Jimmy. Nothing to what's coming next, if Billy Catte isn't turned up. You might let that be known.'

Jimmy Liddell closed the binder of the *Steel Trades Journal*.

'It's known all right, Mr Hoskins. Feeling is, Billy's spat in everyone's beer. Not got many friends just now. Other feeling is that you could have this case finished tomorrow, if you wanted to. Tell those stupid buggers to let Emma Catte go. She's not committed any crime. Billy's got no reason to hold on to that girl afterwards.'

'He might,' Hoskins said.

Liddell waved it aside. 'Too much to lose, Mr Hoskins. Ten, fifteen years ago, Mr Cooney was about where Billy Catte is now. Amusement arcades, gaming machines, skin-shows for the punters. Bit of punishment when necessary. Touch of razor here and spot of fisting there. But he stuck at it. Made money and ploughed it back. Now his skin-shows are all charity spectaculars or Blue Moon concerts. Gaming machines bought him a stake in the Peninsular Emporium. Took a high-class pony and made her Jolly Modes. See him now. On the telly, offering to give away a hundred grand. He wasn't much better than Billy Catte in the old days.'

'Kidnap, Jimmy. That's what I'm talking about.'

'Ah,' said Liddell scornfully, indicating the end of the discussion. 'Don't tell me an understanding couldn't be reached, if it would get everyone off the hook.'

At the headquarters building applications were made out to the stipendiary magistrate for warrants to hold William Catte and his sons, Steven and Kevin, for questioning in connection with the disappearance of Rachel Wardle. Hoskins left Ripley to arrange their presentation and went to meet Gerald Foster. The BBC and CNT newscasts might be fastidiously aloof from the antics of the Angry Mum and her allies. The press took the other side. On King Edward Square, placards for the lunchtime *Canton Globe* boasted GIRL HELD DOWN IN HOSPITAL ASSAULT – COURT STORY. The social moralists of the airwaves had been swept aside by public enthusiasm for the details of Emma Catte's ordeal.

Gerald Foster was late for lunch, the first time that Hoskins could recall such a thing. He slid into the high wooden booth of the Porter's Lodge opposite Hoskins and beckoned one of the waitresses.

'Sorry about this, Sam. I've been back at the office. Anything from Blades?'

Hoskins shook his head.

'I've been out all morning, Gerald. One thing, though. I'm putting two blokes to watch your flat from a parked vehicle. The next freelance postman that tries to shove a parcel through the door is going to find himself nicked.'

Foster brushed a hand over his bunched and greying hair.

'I'm the one that's about to be nicked, Sam. The paper's had writs from the city council. So have two of the Fleet Street lot who used our story of the parents' legal action to get their kids back.'

'Writs for what, Gerald?'

'Contempt of court,' said Foster sourly. 'By reporting what the parents said, apparently we might have indicated who the children were. And by showing that picture of the angry mum spitting at the Director of Social Services, we're held to have named her kids. That's the council's legal argument. A breach of the anonymity rules for juveniles. Seems we're allowed to report the council's concern at escalating child abuse but not to report the parents' denials. That's why the TV companies have only been telling one side, Sam. Their lawyers warned them off the other.'

The uniformed portress set down the glasses of Jupp's Special Brew and went back for sausage and mash.

'Council ought to thank you for carrying the Rachel Wardle and Billy Catte pictures. They can't object to him and his family being identified.'

'People that hold council appointments in this city, my friend, don't live in the real world any longer.'

Hoskins shook his head. 'So what happens next, Gerald?'

Foster's mouth tightened with vindictive satisfaction. 'Tomorrow morning, the bastards get it with both barrels, Sam. First the MORI poll findings that were twisted to make it seem like one in ten children were abused instead of one in two hundred and fifty. Then the report from the University Hospital at Leeds that re-examined fifty kids. First examiners couldn't tell the difference between cigarette burns and impetigo rash nor bruises and birth-marks.'

The two friends ate sausage and mash. Hoskins broke a long silence.

'You heard about Cooney starting a newspaper?'

Foster nodded, drawing mashed potato off a fork without looking up.

'Might not be a bad thing, Sam. He'd go ahead with a story like this and to hell with courts or consequences. I've got shareholders and directors riding on my back. Not to mention the Press Council.'

The meeting ended in unaccustomed gloom. Hoskins went to his car and drove back to the headquarters building. Ripley was standing in the glass-fronted reception room that opened off the main lobby. He was talking to a slightly built man with fair hair and a face like a wistful rabbit. Hoskins recognised Mr Wardle. Before he could slip past, Ripley saw him and beckoned him in.

'Chief Inspector Hoskins, Mr Wardle. I've shown Mr Wardle the sapphire ring, which he identifies as one that he gave his daughter on her eighteenth birthday. I've briefed him and brought him up to date. We know she's being held in this area and we think we know who by. We're checking a list of properties and movements, drawing the net tighter.'

Wardle ignored the Superintendent. He turned to Hoskins, his tone casual as if he might have been sedated.

'That ransom,' he said. 'I want it paid.'

Ripley edged round to get his attention again.

'Official policy is not to pay such demands, Mr Wardle.'

'I don't give *that* for any policy. I can raise the money. I want it paid.'

Hoskins put a hand on the visitor's arm. 'Sit down a minute, Mr Wardle.'

Rather to his surprise, Wardle sat down.

'Now,' said Hoskins, 'what do you suppose would happen to your daughter if the ransom was paid and Emma Catte was released?'

A flicker of uncertainty troubled Mr Wardle's blue eyes. 'They'd let her go, wouldn't they? No reason to keep her then.'

Hoskins stared at the copies of the *Police Review* scattered on the glass table-top of the reception booth.

'Mr Wardle, we're dealing with Billy Catte, a known villain, with two loyal sons. Look at it from their angle. If you pay the money and they let Rachel go, she could identify them. She could describe the place where she was held. She'd be a mine of information. Once they had what they wanted, there'd be no reason to keep her alive. A dead body can't tell as much as a live one.'

Wardle uttered an exclamation that was mid-way between a gasp and a laugh.

'But that's silly. Why?'

Hoskins looked up from the table.

'Mr Wardle, these are not people who keep their word if it suits them to break it. More to the point, I think that such a crime would be their third murder in the past few weeks. Not to mention a couple of armed robberies.'

Wardle stared at him. 'Who did they murder?'

'PC Terry Cross and PC Bob McPhail, in my opinion,' Hoskins said quietly. 'I shall be seeking warrants in respect of that charge before long.'

There was a pause.

'I want to pay the ransom,' Wardle said again. 'Is there any law to stop me?'

Hoskins shook his head. 'I doubt it, Mr Wardle. But there's certainly no law requiring me to assist you. You wouldn't find it easy on your own. I shan't assist you at the moment. To put it bluntly, Mr Wardle, the fact that her kidnappers haven't yet got what they want may be the only thing keeping your daughter alive.'

After Wardle's departure, Hoskins and Ripley went up together in the lift. At the fifth floor they walked in silence to Ripley's room and went in. The Superintendent turned round as the door closed.

'What kind of a bedside manner d'you call that, Sam? Telling him whether he pays the ransom or not, he's unlikely to see his daughter alive again?'

'It's the truth, Max, bedside or otherwise. I want to show Catte and his boys that they'll have more aggravation holding the girl than letting her go.'

'And the murder charges?'

'Work it out, Max. The robbery outside Jolly Modes was down to the Catte family. Catte's car was used in the attempt on Boots. Whoever did that left behind the gun that shot Terry Cross and probably stuck up the pharmacy van.'

'Billy Catte was with you, Sam, when Cross and McPhail were killed.'

Hoskins stared at the misty afternoon over the trees of Hawks Hill.

'And if he helped cover up, Max, he's still accessory. I can't see them going this far if it was just fear of the hospital finding out about Emma Catte's lost virginity. Being lively with boyfriends and step-father Billy. She's fifteen, Max. Foster home would have to let her go in a year. Much easier for Catte to push off to Germany until it all blows over or she joins him there. If he's got his wits about him, he's just done a bunk.'

Ripley sat down and stared at the framed photograph on his desk.

'I don't know, Sam.'

'I do,' Hoskins said sharply. 'They want Emma Catte free. Badly enough to kidnap. It's not her sex-life. They know she's held where we can get at her. They must be scared witless how much she could tell about Cross and McPhail. Four of 'em did the pharmacy van that morning. Three men and a girl, according to Draycott who was driving. McPhail reported several of 'em in the car before they killed him. That's two Catte sons, Emma, and one other boy.'

Ripley touched his ruler, as if for luck. 'I still don't know, Sam.'

Hoskins sat down.

'Listen, Max. You think a girl having a bit of nooky at fifteen – even with her step-father – is big news in Billy Catte's social circles? I doubt if it rates a mention. Armed robbery and two policemen dead is what this is all about. That's why they want Emma out of sight.'

Ripley made a little sound of exasperation. Looking more than ever like a weary grey-haired beagle, he got up and turned to the window.

'So we tough it out with them, Sam? Is that it?'

Hoskins nodded again, at Ripley's back. 'Warrants for the arrest of William Catte and his sons. Suspicion of armed robbery and murder of two police officers. The sons for doing it, Catte for complicity. We might mention moves for the extradition of Sonja Catte from the Federal German Republic. With that amount of aggravation following him around, Billy Catte's going to be as welcome in the criminal underworld of this city as a case of HIV positive. There's not a pimp or thief, not a bruiser nor a whore down Peninsula that fancies getting mixed up in police murders.'

The Ripper turned round.

'And Emma Catte?'

'No charges yet. I want it known that we're grilling her over the murders.'

Worry-lines deepened on Ripley's brow. 'Better check with Clitheroe. He's officially leading the murder hunt.'

'As for the search,' Hoskins persisted, 'I want every dog-handler we can spare searching street-by-street in the areas Catte's likely to hear about. I'd like a traffic helicopter doing sweeps over the city and areas surrounding, morning, mid-day and evening. In other words, Max, I'm sending a message to Billy Catte and his two boys. Their best hope is to forget Rachel Wardle and get the hell out of this city while they've still got the chance. Paying them a ransom won't get her back. Tightening the screws on them might. They're not going to worry about her identifying them as kidnappers if they know we already want them for police murder.'

Ripley took a deep and undecided breath.

'It's a hell of a risk, Sam.'

'So is trying to pay them off, Max. Put yourself in their

place. A hundred thousand quid and getting Emma is worth fighting for. But a murder charge already announced, money running out, no friends, dogs at the door, aerial surveillance? That means getting out fast. And getting out means being in the open. And that's when we might catch them.'

'And Rachel Wardle? Surely she takes priority.'

'Terry Cross and Bob McPhail,' Hoskins said grimly. 'That's my priority. And whatever Mr Clitheroe may be doing, I need them as my lever. If this kidnap means what it says, that may be the only way we'll see Rachel Wardle alive again.'

# Chapter Twenty-Four

From the outside the new University Hospital at the Crest might equally well have been a cigarette factory or the head-quarters of a bank. The long ten-storey block formed a white crescent against the spruce trees and firs of the first valley hill. Built for easy access from the ring-road, it had become a subject of complaint by out-patients and visitors who waited under tin shelters for the irregular bus services and a handful of taxis.

The secure wing, no more than a section of the third floor, seemed isolated from sight and sound of the outside world as Hoskins and Chance entered the quiet corridor. White doors stood solid and windowless either side, sheltering mania and depression, obsession and homicidal zeal. At the far end of the passageway a figure appeared, spruce and slim, neatly suited and exuding a scent of the Peninsular Emporium's barbering for gentlemen. Hoskins felt his heart sink. He had expected Claude Roberts at the worst.

'Morning, Mr Hoskins. Mr Chance.'

The Celtic twang of Jack Cam's voice had the resilience of a steel spring.

'Morning, Mr Cam. Locked you up too, have they?'

Cam's chuckling was a throaty intake of breath.

'This take long, will it, Mr Hoskins?'

'Better ask your client, Mr Cam. Give me straight answers to straight questions and it shouldn't take long at all.'

Cam looked as if he had just caught on.

'Ah, well, Mr Hoskins, that's a matter of how straight the questions seem.'

'You be taking an active part, will you, Mr Cam?'

The lawyer's glasses caught the light as he turned his head up.

'You wouldn't want it otherwise, Mr Hoskins. You wouldn't want it said in court that you'd come out here and terrorised a poor child in the absence of her adviser. A poor child that's been victimised enough already by hospital authorities and social workers. A girl that's been attacked and abused.'

'That's the line, then, is it, Mr Cam? And where's Mr Cooney in all this?'

'Very busy, Mr Hoskins, so much boot having to be applied to the council's social services' trouser-seat. Led a march to the infirmary yesterday. Very effective speech he made there. Still, you know Mel Cooney. Thrives on work.'

They entered a room lit by sunlight through the steel slats of Venetian blinds. But the same deadened silence prevailed. Emma Catte was at the end of the plain table, a uniformed policewoman standing by the door. Jack Cam sat next to his client. He indicated to his visitors two chairs on the opposite side of the table. Hoskins was not surprised to find that he had the sun shining directly into his eyes.

'When you're ready, Mr Hoskins.'

'I shall have to caution Miss Catte first of all, Mr Cam.'

'If you didn't, Mr Hoskins, you'd find me cautioning you. Carry on then.'

After the caution, Hoskins began.

'Is your name Emma Beata Catte?'

The girl brushed her fair hair nervously with her hand and looked at Cam. He nodded. Emma looked back again.

'Yes,' she said.

'Were you born Emma Beata Franz?'

Jack Cam leant forward.

'Miss Catte can't be expected to know, Mr Hoskins. Not a competent witness to her birth. She knows what she's called now. That's enough.'

'Are you William Catte's step-daughter and do you live at Eighteen Dyce Esplanade, Canton?'

Cam leant forward again.

'She can tell you where she lives, Mr Hoskins. Whether she's strictly step-daughter or not depends on documents. Without she sees them, she can't say.'

'Do you live at Eighteen Dyce Esplanade?'

'Yes.'

Hoskins took a deep breath.

'Were you with your step-brothers at eight o'clock on the morning of Wednesday the fifth of January this year?'

There was an air of pomade and perfumed shaving soap as Cam leant forward again.

188

'We're not having leading questions in here, Mr Hoskins. Not if you want my client to answer them.'

Hoskins felt his mouth tighten. A muscle twitched in his cheek.

'All right. Where were you on the morning of the fifth of January at eight o'clock?'

But it was still Jack Cam's nasal twang that answered him.

'Miss Catte has no reason to reply to an innuendo of that sort. And you've no cause to question her on such matters. My client is a private patient here, transferred to this ward under a physician of our choosing while the case against the staff of the infirmary is heard. Her counsel, Mr Raven, and I have agreed to this interview on the understanding that she is to be treated as a hospital patient. First sign to the contrary, I terminate this discussion and you don't come back. All right?'

Hoskins drew breath and swallowed his exasperation.

'Miss Catte is presumably aware that two policemen were brutally murdered on that afternoon by occupants of the same car that robbed the pharmacy van.'

'I daresay she can read the newspapers, Mr Hoskins. Not a crime.'

But the quick movement in Emma Catte's eyes, sideways and downwards, betrayed her.

'And I suppose she knows, Mr Cam, that warrants for the arrest of her step-father and step-brothers have been issued in connection with those deaths. That after a fourth attempt at robbery a nail-file with her fingerprints upon it was found—'

Cam held up his hand.

'You want to arrest her step-brothers or anyone else, Mr Hoskins, you go right ahead. But I won't have Miss Catte bullied. The one place she can't have been when that robbery outside Madame Jolly Modes took place was at the scene of the crime. She was locked up with witnesses. The one place she can't have been when Rachel Wardle disappeared was anywhere nearby. Again she was locked up here. Now, if you got something relevant to ask, you ask it.'

Hoskins ignored Cam and stared at Emma Catte. She was looking down at the table now, the fine blonde hair spread like an untidy wimple.

'I'd like to ask her this. I'd like to ask if she realises she could see her step-brothers and her boyfriend next time with their heads blown clean off.'

'No!' Emma Catte looked up, screaming at him her denial of the possibility. But she was scared now. Without Cam in the room, Hoskins knew he could break her easily.

'Mr Hoskins!'

'Listen!' said Hoskins furiously. 'There's something your client has a right to know. Something you haven't told her because you don't want to spoil your case against the social services. Emma Catte may be the only one who can save their lives.'

'Meaning?' Cam asked sceptically.

'Meaning this,' Hoskins said, 'I could talk about charging her with obstructing a police inquiry. But I'm not interested in that. I'll tell you what interests me. Her step-brothers, step-father too, are going to be arrested after this kidnap business. They've no money, no food and they're on the run. There's dog-handlers and aerial surveillance. No chance of 'em getting out of this city. They'll be taken before much longer. They'll be taken either by persuasion or shooting if necessary. Your client's co-operation might save their own lives. And even if she didn't drive the car or pull the trigger when those policemen were killed, she'll go down. If she covers up for the Catte brothers now, it won't do them any good. But it will make her an accomplice. And it might cost them their lives. Tell her that, Mr Cam.'

Cam looked at him expressionlessly.

'No, Mr Hoskins. I'd rather tell it to the Police Complaints Authority.'

'Well then, Mr Cam, I hope you have more luck than you did last time.'

Emma Catte had buried her face in her hands. A hooting sob came from between her fingers.

'I didn't want them dead! Not them, not anyone!'

Hoskins stood up, taking Cam off his guard.

'All right,' he said, 'then all you've got to worry about is this. What happens when the case against the social services is over? What happens when Mr Cooney's won or lost it and when Mr Cam's finished his job? You don't think they're going to take you on for life, do you?'

She looked up suddenly, the tears stilled.

'On your own is where you'll be,' Hoskins said gently.

'No cosy foster home. No going back to your mum. Locked up here or more likely a detention centre. Locked up by the people you've been slanging in the courts. I'd hate to wear your skin then. Very good your performance this morning. But a few months of what's to follow and you'll be begging someone to come and listen. Your step-brothers and their dad, even your boyfriend, could be dead by then. And I'll have lost interest. Think about that before you go to sleep.'

Jack Cam's hand was on his arm. Hoskins turned and walked out of the room with him. They went down the corridor with Sergeant Chance following.

'They gave you a bugger of a case with this kidnap business,' said Cam, trying to be friendly.

'You likewise, Mr Cam.'

Cam hooked a thumb under his waistcoat watch-chain and grinned.

'Rather enjoying the appeal court, Sam. Toby Raven made the infirmary medical officer produce his drugs register yesterday. There it was, black and white. Emma given a valium jab to stop her struggling while they had their wicked way with her. Arrogant bastards never bothered to cover their tracks.'

'I suppose that's hospitals,' Hoskins said vaguely. 'I wouldn't know.'

Jack Cam gave a grin that was scarcely distinguishable from a snarl, the Saturday-night salute of the Peninsula bravo.

'Take care, both,' he said, dismissing them with a wave and stretching his bony arms as he walked back towards his client's room.

Chance turned the Sierra on to the Northern Quadrant bridge, following the suburban arterial avenue of bow-fronted 1930s semi-detached Clearwater.

'Waste of a morning,' he said savagely. 'Bloody Jack Cam!'

Hoskins smiled. 'I wouldn't say that, my son. He likes to impress the client but he's grown up in this town. He knows that from time to time he'll have to trade with us over a case or do a deal over a client. Jack Cam's sharp as a ship's rat. But I reckon I can live with him. We got away with more than I expected.'

'Such as?'

'The dog that didn't bark.'

'Which was that?'

191

'Emma Catte's nameless boyfriend. Twice I coupled him with Billy Catte's lads as the fourth member of the gang. And twice she could have denied it.'

Chance braked sharply at a crossing.

'She denied the whole bloody thing.'

'Yes,' Hoskins said patiently. 'But she never denied that step-brothers and boyfriend and she went together. I'd like a word with Miss Catte's fancier.'

'So would social services.'

'And there again,' Hoskins said mildly, 'I planted a seed or two. Miss Catte protested enough. But she's not sure whether I might not be right after all.'

He took the *Western World* from under the dashboard. On the front page was a photo of a solemn procession. The staves and poles had an ecclesiastical look. But the dress was anoraks and jeans from Orient or Barrier. At the head, supported by two bruisers from the Blue Moon Club, was the lumbering and floundering shape of Carmel Cooney. The staves and poles bore squares of card with the names of children taken into care. Gerald Foster had played safe with a photograph that left the names indistinct. But the headline pulled no punches: 'Set Our Children Free! Councillor at Parents' Rally.' Lower down the column was a promise: 'Candlelight Vigil Planned at City Hall.'

Hoskins folded the paper. They were in the Mount Pleasant district. Several tower-blocks, built of sea-grey concrete in the 1960s, were coming down. The cleared sites between the remaining clusters of drab apartments were patched with wild grass. Rutted mud from earth-movers and diggers made a landscape of desolation. He saw with approval that one of the dog-teams had begun a search of the remaining blocks, the white van with its caged interior parked close by. Wherever they were, Billy Catte and his sons would hear the news.

A second dog-van pulled up by the Retreat, a neighbour-hood pub of new brick, the colour of carbolic soap. Beyond its shallow windows that resembled gun-slits, the comfort-less interior was upholstered in sticky plastic. Knife-cuts in the seats had been repaired with plain patches, smooth and shiny as a skin-graft. The dog-handler in black leather jacket got out of the van, whose rear was heaving with the energy of the trapped Alsatian. On what looked like the blast-wall protection of the Retreat, Tommo 2 had signed himself in black spray-paint, next to the exhortation, FUZZ IS SCUM! KILL A JACK!

Chance followed the ridge towards Hawks Hill. The surveillance helicopter rattled and chattered overhead.

'You reckon this could flush 'em out, Sam?'

'It might, Jack. It just might.'

He went up to the fifth floor with Chance and made an entry in his duty diary. The phone rang.

'Mr Hoskins? John Deacon, press office. There's a cassette in your mail. DTI investigators taped the *Hit-Back* broadcast last night. Did you hear it?'

'Better things to do last night, John. Why?'

'Might just have a bearing on the Catte inquiry. It's about foster parents.'

'I'll lend it an ear, John. Thanks.'

He found the cassette in his in-tray and slipped it into the player.

'Tonight,' said the quiet voice, 'we spotlight child-takers and child-keepers. Many children have been taken from home by the social services department lately, for no better reason than to make the department look busy. Keep those jobs. Earn that promotion. No prosecution of a parent has followed. Only condemnation without trial and without evidence. No child diagnosed physically or sexually abused by proper criteria. Have you been a victim of this harassment? Someone you know been victimised? Want to do something about it? Want to get even? The *Hit-Back Show* will help you.'

Hoskins sighed.

'The child-takers of the social services can only operate so long as they can find foster parents to hold children captive on their behalf,' said the voice pedantically. 'Even the social services have found that some of these foster parents have a rather unhealthy interest in other people's children. Yes, that's right, folks. The social services are providing your children for other people to abuse. We hope that listeners to our show will help to persuade foster parents that child-taking does not pay.'

There was a pause, as if the broadcast might have ended abruptly. Then a sheet of paper rustled and the voice was back.

'Children are often held in captivity in foster homes without their parents being allowed to see them or even to know where they are. We have been fortunate, thanks to a disillusioned member of social services staff, to acquire a list of names and addresses of current foster homes. Is your child held captive there? Are children of your friends imprisoned? Make a note of the addresses and go looking. Here are fifty-two names and addresses of foster homes. You'll find one near you. The first name is Alker and the address One hundred and thirty-four St Cyres Road, Connaught Park, Canton. The second . . . '

To Hoskins' relief, the phone rang again.

'Sam?' It was Ripley's voice. 'We've got a tape.'

'I know, Max. I'm listening to it.'

There was a pause.

'Video tape, Sam. Rachel Wardle. Left on the reception desk at Coastal Television. Didn't hand it in. Just left it. No one can remember who it might have been. Then comes a phone call. A man telling the receptionist to look. We'll have to get the Wardle parents. And you'll have to see it first.'

194

# Chapter Twenty-Five

At five o'clock that evening Hoskins watched the video tape a second time. This time it was on the monitor in Charlie Blades' office. Rachel Wardle's face was bleached and faded like a ghost but the prim line of the mouth, the shingled hair and the hint of freckling appeared as if through a dreamer's veil of mortality. The pallor and the straggling hair suggested a body retrieved from the sea. She spoke in the curiously flat and non-committal tone of the captive. There was urgency in the chosen words but she spoke them as if she did not greatly care. Perhaps she was reading them.

'Emma Catte must be returned to her mother in Germany. When that is done and my present companions are reimbursed for their financial loss, I shall be free to go. Please do as they ask. As the daughter of the social worker in charge of Emma Catte's case, I believe there was a cruel error of judgment. I condemn totally the manner in which the social services and medical authorities of this city have behaved. I have no excuse for my mother's conduct. If justice were done, the senior members of the department and of the council committee would be suffering instead of me.'

Blades shifted in his chair.

'She's been coached,' he said scornfully. 'What I hear, Emma Catte was screwed rotten by every man in sight. No doubt including step-father Billy.'

Hoskins scowled at the screen. 'Wardle may be trying to put herself on their side for safety, Charlie. It's early for her to have been conditioned.'

'You reckon they could?'

Hoskins nodded. 'With her type, they wouldn't even have to try. A few weeks more with them and she won't know salt from sugar. She's Patty Hearst writ small. Give Rachel Wardle another month and she'll be helping them with armed robbery.'

Blades shook his head, mystified. Across the roofs of the tile-hung department stores, the movie palaces of the Odeon and the Luxor, the Ocean Park funfair and the New Pier, the late winter sun was going down into the Channel with a glare like a blood-orange.

'Please do as I ask,' Rachel Wardle said, still in the same dull voice, as if she did not greatly care. 'Please let Emma Catte go free . . . '

The picture jumped and went out of focus. Hoskins braced himself for what ke knew came next. There was a scream, a wordless cry of disbelief. Then another, louder with the energy of pain. Then a third, which tailed off in a howl of despair. Then there was a whimper.

'Help me,' said Rachel Wardle's voice. 'Please help me.'

'The reckoning is,' Hoskins said softly, 'that they just told her to scream her best without doing anything to her. If they'd done something, we'd have pictures too. They wouldn't miss a trick like that. All the same, the Wardle parents weren't shown the last few moments of the tape. Mr Wardle already wants the ransom paid. That's being refused on the advice of Clitheroe as ACC Crime. So what've we got exactly, Charlie, on Mr Catte's home movie?'

Blades went across to a vertical cassette-deck.

'More on audio than vision, Sam. Our engineers enhanced the sound on the tape. They reckon from acoustics, the pattern of echo or sound reflection, that this was video'd in a fairly confined space. Couldn't hear much in the way of background noises, no roads, no traffic, nothing from other occupants in a building. Might be there but we can't hear 'em. Listen to this, though.'

Blades pressed a switch and there was a coarse shrillness like Rachel Wardle's first scream. He switched the tape off again.

'What's that, then, Charlie?'

'Not something you'd notice normally on the tape, Sam. Seagulls. Could be the coast or a rubbish–dump.'

'Could be anywhere from Eastern Levels to Sandbar. Further than that even.'

Blades shook his head and pressed the play-button. This time there was a subdued metallic screeching.

'They reckon it's starlings,' Blades said. 'A bloody great flock of 'em settling for the night. Gabbling and nattering. Not likely to be an urban area, unless it's a park of some kind or a building they could all get into – or on to. We're asking a couple of ornithologists to pin-point starling roosts in the area. Bit of a long shot, though.'

'Anything else?'

Blades moved back to the video recorder. He began to play the tape again with the sound turned off.

'That's all we've got so far on the audio, Sam. We blew up some of the images on the tape. She's sitting so the light from a window of some kind falls on her. We did our best with it. A very small window, if it's a room. It might be a caravan. Bloody cold in February but difficult to trace. Could be on a site or parked in someone's yard. Ben Felix checked the catalogues. He reckons it looks like a small caravan window. Probably a Sprite.'

Hoskins stared at the image again.

'Right, Charlie. That's definitely a nod and a smile down the drinker for you if this pays off. That the lot?'

'Angle of the light suggests that, at this time of year, it was video'd not later than four-thirty in the afternoon. And, if it's the window of a Sprite, the caravan's berthed lying north to south.'

The sun began to liquefy on the Channel horizon beyond the Cakewalk promenade. The domed kiosks and pavilions of the New Pier lay like a Turkish palace trapped in fire. A gun-metal grey of the sea deepened the shadows of Ocean Beach shopping parades. Hoskins stared at the video image.

'Thing is, Charlie, not Catte nor anyone connected with him has a caravan, so far as we know. Not his style. Villa near Malaga was his idea of fun.'

'Afraid that's it, Sam. They're ninety per cent certain of it.'

Hoskins stared down at the seaside rush-hour on Clifton Hill.

'Can I use your phone?'

'Help yourself. Nine for an outside line. Private, is it?'

'No, just Jack Chance.' Hoskins dialled the number. 'Sergeant Chance, please. Jack? Listen. That pharmacy van driver. Draycott. They took his keys, didn't they? Right. Does he own a caravan? How should I know where? Phone the bugger and ask him. And that ironmonger down in Barrier that had the Ford Granada nicked for the kidnap. Daniels. Ask him the same question. Ask it now. Also get the local branch of the Royal Society for the Protection of Birds. Is there a roost for a starling colony near the coast or a refuse-tip? Names of any likely ornithologists. And stay put. I'm coming back.'

Edging through Clifton Hill traffic, he took the Canton

Link and Northern Quadrant. He was in his office just after six with Chance on his heels.

'Nothing on ornithologists, Sam. And Draycott's not in. His wife says they've never owned a caravan. Never even hired one for holiday. Daniels wasn't home yet.'

Hoskins hung his coat up.

'Get back to Daniels. Wherever he is.'

Chance went out. Hoskins picked up the phone book. He ran his finger down a classified list of Camping and Caravan Sites. Sea Breeze, Ocean Rest, Sundowner. Fifty miles west of Canton, there were sites by the dozen along the twenty miles of 'unspoilt' Atlantic coastline through the Burrows from Minavon Bay to Mondragon Head.

He rang the sergeants' room. Stan McArthur answered.

'Stan? Sam Hoskins. We've got a nibble on the Rachel Wardle case. If I'm right, it's also armed robbery and the killing of Cross and McPhail. Get hold of the phone book. Yellow Pages. Phone every camp site along the Burrows. See if a Mr J. R. Daniels of Holt Street, Barrier, owns or rents a caravan there. Also our friend Draycott. His wife says they never had one but no harm in asking. The site offices should be open now for booking. Where you can't get an answer, make a list and phone Minavon Division. Names and addresses of keyholders.'

He put the phone down and then dialled another number.

'DCI Hoskins. Mr Clitheroe still in, is he? Then I shouldn't let him go home, love. He might only have to come back again. No, but what you can tell him is this. We might have a break in the Rachel Wardle case. Evidence on the video tape. I'll probably know more in the next twenty minutes, provided we can get Mr Daniels. It'll take longer if we have to go through a list of keyholders. Supposing I'm right, I'll need Mr Clitheroe's say-so. CID team with a view to making an arrest at dawn tomorrow. Fifty miles away.'

Chance had left the *Canton Evening Globe* on his desk. Hoskins turned to the classified advertisements for caravan hire. As he did so, he noticed that a 24-hour strike had been called by Canton social workers in protest at 'media bias' and the slanders of Councillor Carmel Cooney. Blood pressures were rising by the minute. He had listed a dozen individual owners of caravans, when Chance knocked and entered.

'That's it, Sam. Daniels. Him and his sister. A Sprite

caravan parked at Tudor Farm behind Minavon Bay. Farmer has about a hundred of 'em on concrete ramps. Permanent mobile homes. But no one goes near there in winter.'

'And the keys?'

'Spot on, Sam. Daniels left a key in the Ford Granada, with a spare ignition. Magnetic holder under the bonnet. First place a young car thief looks. And the caravan registration was in the car. Daniels' name and Tudor Farm, Minavon. I've got the local cop-shop there on red alert. They're going to have the site owner ready for us. Suggested rendezvous is in the car park of the Mondragon Hotel about three miles off.'

Hoskins was out of his chair.

'Right, my son. We'll go down and take a look. I'll put it to Clitheroe.'

'Who's going down? And when?'

'Too late for tonight. First light tomorrow, I should think. Positions at six. Go in at about seven o'clock. I'm not moving while it's dark. Not with the likes of Wallace Dudden blundering about. And one half of the Tactical Support Unit shooting the other.'

'So who's going?'

'Two carloads of CID. Two dog-teams. Four marksmen, just in case. They'll be at the back and they'll stay there until told otherwise. And Mr Daniels.'

'He'll love that,' Chance said sardonically.

'The two carloads,' Hoskins said. 'People we can get now. You, me, Tappin, Stan McArthur in the first. Dudden, Truman and two of the DCs in the second. And you'd better look after me, my son. If I stop a bullet, then Wallace Dudden takes over. As the only DI, he has to be next in line.'

'So far I was just worried,' said Chance winsomely. 'Now I'm scared bloody witless.'

Hoskins ushered him to the door.

'I'll see Clitheroe. Get the timetable done. Tell our lot. Canteen meal at ten, followed by briefing down there. Several hours kip and off about four in the morning. Phone Minavon again. Get surveillance on the gate of the site. Also any information about suspected intruders or unusual goings-on.'

They stood in the corridor. Chance put his notepad away. 'Anything else?'

Hoskins thought for a moment.

'Yes,' he said. 'Every caravan on that site may be empty.

But this may be where they've got her. If that's so, impress on our lot that the operation won't go wrong because of some stroke of genius by Billy Catte. It'll be because one of us took the wrong turning and landed everyone in the wrong caravan park. Or some oaf slammed a car door getting out and woke the neighbourhood. If anything like that happens on this outing, I shall personally revive the cult of the castrato voice. Single-handed.'

Jack Chance drew his bulk upright.

'Well, tra-la-la-la,' he said coyly.

By the time Hoskins came back from Clitheroe's office, Chance was waiting for him again.

'I reckon you might have scored this time, Sam. Minavon rang back. Inspector Brady. There's a chap called Andrews owns Tudor Farm caravan site. This time of year it's closed, even to punters who keep their trailers there. He doesn't go in much. Sometimes has to chase off yobs, not often. Thing is, he saw someone drive in and cruise round several days ago, after dark. As if looking for something. Went out to see what they wanted and they drove off.'

'Did he report it?'

'Phoned Minavon police. Seems there's been a bit of caravan theft. Harder to trace than cars. He reckoned this was a red car. And, I quote his words to Mr Brady, it could have been a Granada or something.'

Hoskins opened the door of his office and Chance followed him in.

'What about this merchant Andrews? Did he see anything before last week?'

Chance shook his head.

'Has to take his holiday this time of year, in his line of business. He was off for a fortnight. Someone using the place might have known that.'

'Right,' said Hoskins thoughtfully. 'This could be it, then.'

'Mr Clitheroe going to have everyone tooled up, shooters and the lot, is he?' Chance inquired hopefully.

Hoskins continued to stare out across the darkened civic centre.

'Not if I know it, my son,' he said quietly. 'Not if I know it.'

# Chapter Twenty-Six

Sleep was impossible. Hoskins was still sitting at his desk, staring at the opposite wall and trying to visualise the moment of impact, when Chance came in just before three. Mr Daniels had been fetched with his second key for the caravan. The site owner had been alerted to rendezvous with the team outside the Mondragon Hotel, where the single road into the village ended on the cliff high above Minavon Bay. There were to be six vehicles in the police convoy. Two unmarked cars would contain CID officers and Mr Daniels. Another car would take the four men from the Tactical Support Unit. In a second group of vehicles there were to be two dog-vans and a Land-Rover.

Down the long undulating suburban avenue of Clearwater, they headed for the ring-road. Half-way to the interchange, Hoskins noticed a group standing outside one of the gabled and bow-windowed 1930s villas. There was a police patrol parked in the bronze flush of the street-light, its radio emitting a sporadic bleep and squawk. A uniformed patrolman and a WPC stood in the gateway. Hoskins had just time to see the shattered edge of broken window-glass and the message in black spray-paint along the garden wall. SUPPORT MR CAT. At the end there was a two-circle drawing of a cat with ears and whiskers. The *Hit-Back Show* had claimed a victim. Out-raged parenthood – or playful Canton teenagers – had started to 'go looking'. Foster homes of children diagnosed as abused were about to undergo popular 'persuasion'.

The convoy picked up speed on the darkness of the Northern Quadrant, heading west. Chance, at the wheel of the first car, turned off behind Ocean Beach and Sandbar, the blue motorway rectangles promising destinations all the way to the Irish Sea. Hoskins noticed the head-lolling of Tappin and McArthur dozing in the rear of the car. Mr Daniels, a plump grey-head, was nature's wearer of floppy shoes and baggy trousers. He sat between the two sergeants in the back, upright and fidgeting. Chance drove without speaking. Hoskins was glad of it. When his back needed watching, he would trust the job to Jack Chance rather than anyone else on earth. But Chance had a habit of making light of danger by grotesque facetiousness, a mincing parade of bisexualism which was the reverse of his actual behaviour.

After forty miles the first car signalled to turn off the motorway at the next slip-road. Presently Hoskins watched the streets of an anonymous little market town, empty and cold in the lamplight. A place of livestock auctions and country antiques. Then they were down in country lanes, the hedges high on either side. He tried his radio.

'Moonbeam One to Minavon control. Do you receive me on this frequency?'

The voice that came back was clearer than Canton itself.

'Minavon control to Moonbeam One. Hearing you clear. Surveillance maintained on target. We reckon there's someone in there. Also we're sending out breakfast, on Mr Clitheroe's instructions. Arrangements with the Mondragon Hotel for it to be available in the Atlantic Bar from eight o'clock onwards.'

'Moonbeam One. Arrangements understood. Over and out.'

Chance began to accelerate up a narrow incline towards the village. 'Thank God for that,' he said, hearing the promise of breakfast. 'All this is giving me an appetite.'

The Burrows, twenty miles of peninsular cliffs and bays, was the scene of Hoskins' boyhood holidays. They were coming into Mondragon now, the village strung on half a mile of road, a dark ghost of August on a winter night. It was a place of white walls and pale grey slate, modernised in the holiday boom of the 1930s, over-run since by chalets and caravans. But the long firm sweep of the sandy beach was still what Hoskins thought of as the edge of the world. To him, it was this constant thunder and roar of Atlantic rollers that was real sea, not the billows of the south coast nor the tepid Mediterranean swell. This was the sound of early childhood, as natural to him as a heartbeat.

With Chance, Tappin and Stan McArthur, he got out in the darkness and looked down from the end of the cliff road, by the low white cottage-buildings of the Mondragon Hotel.

'Right, Mr Daniels,' he said cheerfully. 'Just point out the lie of the land, if you will.'

They were on a grassy rise above the fall of the cliff. Below them, a five-mile sweep of Minavon Bay ran from

Lion Rock to Minavon at the far end. A slight but bitter wind was coming in with the tide, the great part of the sand still uncovered. At the top of the beach was a pebbled slope and a low bank like a sea defence, though it stood above the high water-line. Behind it, a mile or so along the bay, lay Tudor Farm Holiday Camp. In the cold starlight Hoskins could make out the pale shapes of row upon row of 'mobile homes'.

'Over there,' Daniels said, 'where the first line is by the bank. Almost on the beach. Four along from this end.'

Andrews, the site owner, was there, anxious to be an expert in the matter.

'You can either go back and round the road to the camp entrance. In that case you'd have to come at it through the camp. Or else you can just climb the bank from the beach and come down almost on top of it.'

'I expect we'll do both, Mr Andrews,' Hoskins said reassuringly. 'Mr Daniels, if you sit here with one of my colleagues from Minavon, you'll see it all.'

He looked about him, the Atlantic night-breeze shuffling the dry cliff-top stalks.

Stan McArthur came back from a conference with the Minavon sergeants in the hotel car park with its low whitewashed walls.

'All set, boss.'

'Right,' Hoskins said, 'I want the second CID car to go with Mr Andrews to the main camp entrance. Also the Tactical Support Unit. No shots to be fired unless you see targets making a break for it and only then if they open fire first. If they've got Rachel Wardle with them, let them go. Follow but don't intercept. All right?'

'What about the dog-teams, boss?'

It was a leather-jacketed handler with slashed peak and Cuban moustache.

'Camp gates,' Hoskins said. 'We can't risk Rover starting to bark with excitement on the beach.'

Even in the darkness, he saw the man's face tighten with the distaste of the lion-tamer for the clown.

'He's called Viceroy, in case you should ever need him, Mr Hoskins. The other one's Khan. Last squad officer that called him Rover got bit.'

'And that wasn't even by the dog,' Chance said sidelong.

Hoskins took control again, the tension dispersed for the moment.

'The approach along the beach will have to be on foot. We can't get a vehicle down except at the Minavon end. And it's too risky to make that much noise. DI Dudden, DS Chance, DS McArthur, DS Tappin and I will take them from the beach. We need the rest of you in position as close to the Sprite caravan as possible by half-past six. Gives you over an hour. Ample cover behind the caravans and other vehicles. Take instructions from DI Jones of the Tactical Support Unit. You'll see us come over the bank from the beach and go into the caravan at seven, when there's enough light. It's all going to be very quiet. No sledgehammers and no warnings. We've got Mr Daniels' key to the vehicle. We'll be in there before they know what's happened. Unless, that is, someone on our side alerts them. Right? Any questions?'

'You going in without guns, boss?' It was Burden from the second car.

'Yes,' Hoskins said, aware of the Tactical Support group listening for a gaffe. 'We can open the caravan door with the key. If they're there, we grab them. We can't start shooting inside a caravan. Anyone could get hit. Or a bullet might go straight through the wall of the thing and hit someone outside. This way, if you hear a shot you'll know it's them and not us.'

It was still dark, just after six o'clock, when Hoskins and his party went down the roughly stepped cliff path at the side of the Mondragon Hotel. The mountain behind the shore rose long and tall in darkness. Cliff grass and the sand of the bay were flushed by pale starlight. The dawn wind now cut bitter chill, gathering strength with the flooding tide.

'Why's Dudden with us, Sam?' It was Chance too softly for the rest to hear.

'You fancy having him on the other side with a shooter, do you, Jack?'

'No,' said Chance reasonably. 'Not a lot.'

'Nor do I, my son. That's why he's with us.'

The ribbed sand was firm under foot. Hoskins kept his party close to the rocks at the top of the beach, less likely to be seen from the fields and holiday sites. As the sky grew light, the cold sea assumed the grey-green dullness of a razor-blade. The first black winter arrowheads of seabirds cut low and straight above the frothing tide, turning inland with the aerobatic skill of an air-show fighter.

Hoskins listened for sounds of the other party, driving inland to the camp gates. He heard nothing. And in that case whoever might be occupying the Sprite caravan had heard nothing. For the first time he began to regret not carrying a gun. It was instinct, not logic. At one moment he visualised the caravan interior empty, neat and swept in the last week of summer. Then he saw it with waiting figures, the gun-muzzles each like the black wound they inflicted. The shouted obscenities. The blasting roar. The pain and dark.

He forced his mind back to practical matters. By ten minutes to seven they were level with the first caravan, hidden from it by the pebbled slope and the brambled mound of earth at the top of the beach. He pulled his coat tighter and shivered a little in the wind as he turned to the others in his group.

'Right,' he said quietly. 'Wallace, if you stay on the mound there and keep contact with the others, Jack and I will go in first. Stan McArthur and Dave Tappin cover the rear of the vehicle. The main door seems to be at this end but they might be able to get out the other way. New safety regulations for trailers require another exit.'

There was a worried look on Dudden's heavy face.

'What happens if they get past you and Jack?'

'They'll probably run for the camp entrance. In that case they'll run straight into our other lot. If they go for the beach, they won't get far. We'll have everyone in pursuit. But the first sign of guns, get your head down and keep it down. You can't do anything about it, so don't try. That is definitely a job for the Tactical Support experts.'

He looked at his watch. It was four minutes to seven. Motioning the others to follow, Hoskins ducked his head and moved as silently as possible on the large pebbles above the sand. They were firmly set and wide enough. Beyond them, the brambles and bracken hung black and wet from the winter night. Chance was beside him, Tappin and McArthur immediately behind. Wallace Dudden followed at a little distance to keep observation.

Hoskins went down on one knee. Chance did the same. The caravan, fourth in its row, was about thirty feet from them. With its oval shape and single pair of wheels, it had an old-fashioned look. There was no immediate sign of occupation. The curtains, half-drawn across the little windows, might equally well have been arranged for a night's sleep or the months of winter. Beyond it, the lines of caravans stretched almost to the foot of the mountain with its white farmhouse and track above the sea. There was nothing to betray the presence of a dozen police officers, four of them carrying automatic weapons.

Hoskins took a deep breath. It was at this moment that he always had a split-second of gloom, having picked the wrong building or been given the wrong key. Chance moved his head closer.

'There's definitely someone or something in the far bunk, Sam. You can see through the curtains, on the left. Something heaped up with a blanket or cover over it.'

'Could just be bed linen, folded or stacked.'

'Daniels said the bunks were empty when he was describing the interior.'

'Perhaps he forgot. If there is anyone there, let's get 'em before they start moving.'

'There's someone there, all right,' Tappin whispered. 'And if it's just an old dosser, I shan't complain.'

Sideways, down the rough descent of the slope on the far side, Hoskins led Chance and the others to the curved shell of the two-wheeler. He motioned McArthur and Tappin, who ducked their heads below window-level and moved round the far end. Softly, as if laying the last ace on a twelve-storey house of cards, Hoskins slid the flat key into the lock of the door. He turned it gently and felt the rasp of metal disengaging.

Still there was no sound nor response. He drew a deep breath, his heart beating in his throat, and folded his fingers round the smooth metal oblong of the door-handle. He looked at Chance and nodded once. Then he drew a long breath and held it.

Hoskins turned the handle down, opened the door gently and took two steps into the half-lit interior. There was no one, except the shadowy figure in the bunk. At that moment, he let out his long breath and drew in air from the caravan itself.

The putrid sickliness came like a watering in the throat, welling up as nausea. He pushed Chance aside in the doorway and burst out into the open, coughing and spitting to clear his gullet of the taste instilled by foul air.

McArthur came round from the other side of the caravan. 'What's up, boss?'

Hoskins straightened up from his spasm and wiped his eyes. 'If I'm not mistaken, Stan, we've found Rachel Wardle.'

Tappin had gone in, handkerchief over nose and mouth, opening the two little windows and the other door. Just then, Hoskins would have given his pension to avoid going back. But it was not to be avoided. Allowing a minute or two for the worst of the stench to disperse, he braced himself to go and face the ordeal.

The body was lying on its back, covered entirely by a brown army blanket. Standing at arm's length, he took the coarse hem and turned it down from the head. He saw the dark corrugations of the hair. The worry-lines caused by the apparent weight of the skull. The eyes that bulged, as if with indignation. The glum flesh-folds and tired skin.

'That's crazy,' said Chance at his elbow. 'It's not Rachel Wardle. That's Billy Catte.'

Hoskins studied the quiet face, its shrivelled and waxy look from the mummifying blanket. Nothing made sense to him as he turned to Sergeant Chance.

'Right, Jack. Get over to the cars. Tell Brady and Minavon that we're going to have knee-deep Forensic from Ocean Beach. Put through an alert to Division as well. I reckon we can still be back there about mid-day. Get Greene or Jenkins here as scene-of-the-crime officer, soon as possible. Someone that knows enough about evidence not to walk all over it.'

Chance stood there, almost as if he had not heard.

'But what's he doing dead, Sam?'

Hoskins shook his head.

'More to the point, my son, what's Rachel Wardle doing now? And Billy Catte's two little boys?'

Breakfast in the Atlantic Bar of the Mondragon Hotel was a rather jolly occasion for everyone but him, so it seemed to Hoskins. The square functional summer room, added at one side of the old cliff-top house, felt achingly chill to him. It was a place of cement rendering patched by damp, metal windows spider-webbed and locked. The video game stood silent and unlit. A sellotaped handwritten notice on the wall advertised a Prize Draw that had been drawn months ago.

Chance and McArthur were playing darts, the board and its slate hanging on the rough white stucco. The rest of the team stretched out on the torn caramel plastic of the wall-seats. Despite the billiard table at the centre of the vinyl tiling, or the hint of summer campers singing along on warm evenings, the bar seemed as comfortless to Hoskins as a hospital waiting-room.

When Brady had taken charge, on behalf of the Minavon division, and the pathologist had arrived, Hoskins went back with Chance and McArthur. Dizzy from lack of sleep, he entered the Lambs Chambers apartment at lunchtime. The morning post lay on the mat, several bills and circulars. He tossed them aside unopened. Then, with the pale February sunlight flooding the closed curtains of the bedroom, he took off his jacket, pulled off his shoes, lay down on the bed and went to sleep.

# Chapter Twenty-Seven

Hoskins woke late in the afternoon. The quiet sunlight across the turf of Lambs Acre was beginning to fade. For a moment he felt disorientated, waking as the shops closed and the traffic mumbled homeward. It was like being an invalid or a traveller sleeping off jet-lag. His brain felt comfortably insulated from the world by a thick layer of cotton-wool.

Reaching for his glasses, he went through and ran a bath. At least the phone was quiet. From his bath he went to the kitchen. It was late enough in the winter for the fading afternoon sun to be accompanied by snatches of bird song. He thought about food and decided to prepare himself brunch in place of the breakfast that he had been too queasy to eat at Minavon. At six o'clock he turned on Coastal Television News, eating scrambled egg with a fork as he sat in the arm-chair and watched the day's events flick by.

It was a dark-haired man reading the news this time, his eyes staring glassily as he followed the prompter. Another smiling ingratiator, uninvited in the living-room. Hoskins finished his last forkful and was crossing the room to the sink when the voice from the television called him back.

'Windows were broken last night at three houses in Clearwater occupied by foster families of children in care. Slogans were also sprayed on several garden walls. A spokesman for Canton social services department declined to discuss details of the attacks in order to protect the anonymity of children and foster parents. The incidents have brought more calls from social workers for the 24-hour token strike threatened in protest at remarks made by Councillor Carmel Cooney in a *Coastline* discussion. Our reporter Alice Dean spoke this afternoon to CPSU area chairman, Jaye Swinton.'

Hoskins took a step back. Swinton's face filled half the screen, still large and flushed. For the first time in Hoskins' experience of him, he was not chewing gum. The young woman reporter asked her first question. Swinton replied with the patient sigh of a man seeking an answer from the world.

'People in this city have to decide whether they want social workers to do their job or not. Councillor Cooney doesn't, I think that's pretty clear. But these revenge attacks by people whose kids have been taken into care are something more. We're talking about thugs who're prepared to attack houses with their own children inside them. We've always assumed that people would give a certain respect to those who take these children into their families. But if these attacks mean nothing to people in this city, and even possibly attacks on members of the caring professions and their own families ... Well, all right, we'll have to start thinking differently about that.'

'But if a father is prepared to go to such lengths as these attacks suggest, isn't it possible that he's an innocent man frustrated by the system?'

'Look,' said Swinton, as if explaining the proposition to a five-year-old. 'No child is taken into care without reason. Physical abuse. Emotional abuse. Whatever. You've got social workers, doctors. You've got disclosure sessions with the kids and really traumatic experiences coming out.'

'But not convincingly enough to prevent parents appealing to the courts?'

Swinton's jaw moved sideways, teeth seeking the phantom ball of spearmint.

'Parents that're prepared to drag their kids through the courts in order to repossess them are guilty of abusing them further by doing it. That's established beyond doubt. It's totally traumatic for those kids. It has to be. I mean, I have to deal with kids who've been through these ordeals when their parents go to court. Picking up the pieces. And believe you me, what those parents inflict in the process is diabolical.'

'But better than taking the law into their own hands ... '

'Yes,' Swinton said, 'if you like. But I'd just like to say this to anyone who thinks they can intimidate us. We shan't stop taking children into care just because foster homes are attacked. In this city we've got a programme of social policing, if you like to call it that, and we'll stick with it. We have to for the sake of the kids. But if the goodwill dries up and there's no volunteers to foster these children, that won't stop us. I mean, there's no going down that road. What will happen is that kids will be in institutions instead of among families. That's something these thugs ought to consider ... '

Hoskins went through to the kitchen. As he was pouring coffee, he heard his own moment of fame.

'The body of a man was found early this morning in a caravan park near Minavon. His identity has not yet been disclosed but Minavon police say that he had been dead for several days. A police spokesman declined to comment on suggestions of a connection with the recent disappearance of Rachel Wardle outside an apartment in Madeira Square, Ocean Beach.'

The rush-hour was over and the civic buildings of Canton lay in a rosy-tinted sunset calm as Hoskins drove down the Mall past the first blossom on the trees in the Memorial Gardens. Ripley was on the fifth floor, waiting like a man who expects a lift home. He knocked and entered Hoskins' office.

'Wanted to catch you, Sam. They brought Catte back to the Path department at the Crest this afternoon. Cut him open stem to stern. Preliminary report is that he'd been dead some little while.'

'I don't need convincing about him being dead a while, Max. It was stuffy in there when I found him.'

The Ripper cleared his throat with a woofing cough.

'No, Sam. What I mean is that he may have been dead since before Rachel Wardle was kidnapped. He might have nothing to do with it. The note we received was on his typewriter and his prints were on the paper from his Rundle Street office. But he could have been dead when it was typed.'

Hoskins stood up and drew a curtain across the twilit window.

'Those two sons of his,' he said quietly. 'Those two little bastards. They were there in Mordaunt Lane when Cross and McPhail were shot. And so was Emma Catte. Bet my pension on it. Of course they wanted Emma Catte free. Scared of what she might say if we started on her. And Billy Catte was scared because of what the doctors might find he'd been up to with her.'

Ripley drew in a waggish sniff of air, as if enjoying the difficulties.

'Won't work, Sam. We had to send a message to Germany this morning, informing Sonja Catte that she is now a widow. Our friends in the Bundespolizei were most efficient in finding her. That's not all they found.'

'No,' Hoskins said. 'I know that. She took the younger girl with her.'

'And the younger son, Kevin,' Ripley said quietly. 'Which leaves Steven – the one they call "Tom" Catte. You reckon he could handle all this on his own? If he's alone, we'd better start considering the possibility that Rachel Wardle is dead. Suffocated on a gag, perhaps. Then there was panic and they scarpered.'

Hoskins thought about it for a moment.

'Or she's part of it all,' he said.

The Ripper's mouth tightened despondently.

'Either way there's going to be real pressure to scale down the search. We've given it a lot of man-power. No one's got cause to complain over that. But the way it is, Sam, there's no other lead short of going to Germany and trying to interview the younger son. I don't fancy it. If there's a body, it'll probably turn up.'

Hoskins sat down.

'Just think of this, Max. Rachel Wardle goes missing in company with Catte and his eldest son. Something goes wrong and Catte dies. Wardle and the boy do a deal. She stays with him. They go for the ransom and split it between them. You reckon she's so honest she wouldn't do it?'

'You think she's the type?'

Hoskins chuckled. 'When there's fifty thousand being waved under the nose, Max, you'd be surprised how many people are the type. And if Mr Wardle huffs and puffs long enough, someone might offer the money. As I understood him, he wasn't beyond raising the cash himself.'

'Yes,' the Ripper said. 'Well, we can't stop him raising the money. We can't prevent him giving it to anyone he likes. But we aren't going to make it any easier for him to show that kidnapping works, whether it's real or faked. If this one went wrong, he could be paying money for someone who's already dead.'

He went out and Hoskins dialled Ocean Beach.

'Dr Blades, please. Charlie? Sam. Do you know more than I know about Billy Catte?'

'I know more about Billy Catte than Billy Catte knew, Sam. I was there when they cut him up. Stacked his guts up on a little cake trolley beside the slab. I know about little pimples he never thought he'd got and funny blue blubbery inner tubes that he never dreamed of. All the time he was carrying them round closer than his wallet. And they're bugger-all use to him now.'

Hoskins drew a deep breath.

'If ever I want to stop eating and lose weight, Charlie, I'll just get you to talk to me about your work.'

Blades chuckled. 'You're getting soft, Samuel. Bit of sudden death makes me feel frisky, in a way. Don't ask me why. Must be the same reason as all these people who used to go to public hangings.'

'Did they say what he died of?'

'Well he didn't just pass away peacefully in his sleep,' Blades said. 'There was enough blood left in him to analyse. Carbon monoxide poisoning. Car exhaust. Not an easy way to murder someone and not usually an accident. I should say he topped himself. Must have done. Good advertisement for filling your tank with the old lead-free.'

Hoskins tried to make sense of it.

'In the caravan?'

'Two schools of thought at present,' Blades said. 'Either he did it in his lock-up and someone moved him after. Or he parked his limo next to the caravan and fed the fumes into it through a rubber tube. Died in bed. Bloody depressing whichever way you look at it. That punter had his Ford Granada pinched a few days before the Wardle woman went missing. So the Catte family had a key to the caravan then. That's what makes it possible Billy Catte croaked before she was grabbed.'

'Smashing,' said Hoskins miserably. 'That's a real help, that is.'

For two hours he composed his report on the events at Minavon Bay. When he looked at his watch, it was half-past nine. The Ripper had gone home. Clitheroe had gone home. Jack Chance had not appeared at all. Hoskins decided that his writing up of the morning's drama was strictly overtime.

He drove the long way round through the dockland terraces of Taylors Town. Then he turned on to the rough road by the reed-fringed foreshore with its warnings against flooding at high tide. The track followed the foot of Lantern Hill at the level of the tidal channel. By the promontory stood the derelict jetty from which Victorian ship-owners used to hail their captains returning to Canton with Brazilian coffee or

Canadian timber. Then the road ran into the muddy-shored esplanade of Harbour Bar with its Starlight Room dance hall at the end of a little steamer-pier. The short urban sea front was a modest row of Edwardian shops and snack-bars, their lights on and open for business, and a block of yellow-tiled flats.

Lesley was in paint-stained jeans and sweater, brush in hand, like an advertisement for someone's polyurethane gloss. From force of habit, he stepped inside before kissing her. She walked ahead into the new-paint smell of the kitchen.

'I'd had enough anyway,' she called back. 'Was that you this morning, by the way? Down at Minavon?'

'Yes,' Hoskins said softly to himself. 'That was me.'

He picked up the *Canton Evening Globe*'s final edition from the dining-table. A wintry photograph of Minavon Bay in varying densities of grey newsprint. BODY FOUND IN BURROWS CARAVAN. Billy Catte's name was not mentioned. The laws of inquest and libel required formal identification before that news was scattered abroad.

Lesley returned presently with two cups of coffee on a tray and the jeans over her arm. Hoskins had difficulty keeping his eyes off the pearly thighs and the hips encased in cotton web.

'I can't sit down in these,' she said, flourishing the jeans. 'Paint all over them. I need a bath.'

'We could have one together. I haven't had a bath since five o'clock.'

In the bath the water shone like oil on the sleekness of her pale flesh.

'It struck me today,' Hoskins said, handing back the soap. 'Even on a winter morning at seven, I like the Burrows. We could have a smashing time there in the summer. Really go native.'

'All right. Move that leg. You're too big for this.'

Hoskins was about to reply, but Lesley was out of the bath before he had even heard the phone ringing. Then she padded back, towelled and wet-foot.

'You,' she said, slithering back into the warm water. 'Gerald Foster.'

Hoskins surged out and stamped across to the phone.

'Sorry, Gerald, I was in the bath. And I'm off-watch. Definitely.'

'So's Jack Chance,' Foster said. 'Just thought one of you might like to know. We've had another message from Billy Catte.'

'Billy Catte's dead. Didn't they tell you it was him we found this morning? Been dead a couple of weeks, they say.'

'I know that, Sam, and you know that. But it seems Billy Catte doesn't know it. He's been on the phone to Mr Wardle. And Mr Wardle's been on to me. Seems he's disillusioned with the police investigation. Wants his daughter back. He's ready to pay.'

'Billy Catte? On Wardle's phone?'

'Listen,' Foster said, 'Wardle reckons his phone rang earlier this evening. He picks it up and hears his daughter screaming. Begging them not to do something to her mouth. Then a voice. The price is the same, however. Mr Catte still wants a hundred grand. There'll be another message about how it's to be delivered. And from now on we'll be getting bits of Rachel Wardle through the post until payment is made.'

'Thinking is, Gerald, she either died about the same time as Billy Catte or else she's now part of the game. Anything about letting Emma Catte go free?'

There was a pause.

'No,' Foster said. 'Now you mention it, that wasn't included. Still, your lot must be monitoring Wardle's phone-calls. Someone's bound to have a tape. And Billy Catte's still demanding ransom. If it is him.'

'Not in the past few days, Gerald.'

'The two sons, perhaps?'

'One's definitely in Germany. And kidnap isn't a one-man business. What worries me, Gerald, is that there has to be another joker in the pack. And at this moment I don't know who the hell it might be. Unless it's the girl. But she's not likely to agree to being cut up and sent through the post.'

Foster sighed a long breath of sympathy.

'You need to dial three nines, my friend. Ask for police assistance.'

# Chapter Twenty-Eight

Next morning Billy Catte's identity was released to the press. He was variously referred to as the owner of an amusement arcade and a bingo king. No more was said of the possible connection with the disappearance of Rachel Wardle. Jack Chance became knowledgeable but without offering consolation.

'Stands to reason, Sam. He'd been in the bin last year. Depression. This time he'd lost his wife and the two girls. Worse still, he'd be done for screwing young Emma. And possibly a bit of naughty with the younger one. Ten or fifteen years in gaol if he's unlucky. And you'd still have Fleet Street loud-mouths wanting the judge sacked for being soft on him.'

'Turn off by The Keep,' Hoskins said, 'I want to pick up some papers.'

'Ten or fifteen!' Chance said. 'And with Emma in the hands of the local Gestapo, he was right in it. When they'd finished, that'd be his lot. What could he do but have Rachel Wardle grabbed and then offer to do an exchange?'

Hoskins grunted. 'He was probably dead by the time that happened, according to the post-mortem. Can't be positive but they think so.'

Chance shook his head.

'I thought we all agreed Rachel Wardle was grabbed to trade for young Emma.'

'Yes,' Hoskins said, 'but not by Billy Catte and not because of Emma's colourful sex-life. Miss Catte was there when that pharmacy van was hit and when Cross and McPhail died. That's what she might start talking about and that's why someone wants her out. Her two brothers probably.'

'What's the hope of a good grilling?'

'Not with Jack Cam trying to get her made ward of court. Let's see if she's released, that's our best bet. Arrest her as she leaves the court.'

'I don't know,' Chance said doubtfully.

'I do, my son. There's a lot too much interest in under-age sex and not half enough in old-fashioned robbery. Robbery and murder, that's what this lot is all about. I keep saying it, if anyone would listen.'

Chance drove round King Edward Square, towards the tall Viennese belfry-tower and opera-house entrance of City Hall. Not until he saw the group of pickets with 'Official Dispute' placards did Hoskins recall that this was the day on which social services staff had promised a 24-hour strike. It was in protest at Cooney's slanders and to rebuke public indifference, while promising to maintain essential services. A television crew waited on the pavement. The cameraman swung his lens, trying to get an interesting view while excluding another group of protesters on the far side of the road.

This second group of a dozen was held back by several uniformed police. Hoskins caught the FACT placards on sticks. FAMILIES AGAINST CHILD-TAKERS ... POUFTAHS OUT! ... SUPPORT COUNCILLOR COONEY ... Neither BBC nor CNT had any intention of letting the viewers see that parents who had lost their children to the social services department were there to jeer the strikers.

'Keep going,' Hoskins said quietly. 'If these two mobs want to pitch into one another, let 'em get on with it so far as I'm concerned.'

Turning his back on Chance as they reached the fifth-floor corridor in the headquarters building, he closed the door of his room and entered his arrival in his diary. He stood at the window, looking down at the Mall. The first March sun caught a haze of pink blossom on the trees of the Memorial Gardens, long before their leaves. Every year of his life, this was where spring had begun, on the flat sheltered lawns that received only the south-west breeze.

Beyond the gardens, by the domes and flying chariots of City Hall, he could still see the two groups facing one another across the red tarmac'd avenue with uniformed police keeping a truce line. The social work strikers, lapel-badges and beards to the fore, were silent and glum. The protesting parents with their FACT banners had begun to hoot and jeer again. On this occasion, there was no sign of Carmel Cooney. So far as Hoskins could see, a good many odds might be shouted but there was no likelihood of a riot.

The clock on the Viennese belfry-tower of City Hall began to strike ten. He turned away to phone Charlie Blades for a forensic report on Billy Catte's clothing. There was a knock at the door. Jack Chance was back.

'One thing for us, Sam. You remember those two guards in the dress van that was hit outside Madame Jolly Modes? Seems one of them is brother-in-law to old Daniels who had his Ford Granada pinched and his caravan used.'

'What's his name?'

'John Short. Married the sister of Daniels' dead wife.'

'Anyone run him through the CRO computer yet?'

'Last night,' Chance said. 'Nothing against him. No convictions, no charges, no cautions.'

Hoskins walked towards his desk.

'Might be all there is to it, Jack. He had to be someone's brother-in-law. After all, if he was part of the hit, he'd hardly choose a day when they were only carrying fifteen hundred from Madame Jolly. Any other time, they might have had twenty thousand from the Blue Moon Club and the Winter Garden, as well as the Emporium. Doesn't make sense. No connection with Billy Catte?'

'Nothing showed up.'

Hoskins sat down. 'Leave it for the moment. Jot him down and leave it. Anything else?'

Chance looked puzzled. 'Not that seems to concern us, Sam. But there's a Dyce Vale carrier loaded with coke on the hard shoulder of the motorway near the Eastern Causeway. On its way from the Mordaunt Coking Plant to Atlantic Factors. Seems it had a blow-out in one of the tyres. Soon as that happened the driver pulled in. But then he jumped out, abandoned the tipper and did a runner across the fields.'

'Why?'

Chance shrugged. 'Up to no good. He had to be to behave like that. I mean, no one abandons a load like that if it's all legit.'

Hoskins fondled his chin and thought. Then he shook his head.

'Not one for us, Jack. I don't see a gang of armed robbers pulling another motorway hi-jack just to make off with a ton and a half of nutty slack or whatever it was. Has to be another of life's great unexplained mysteries.'

'And this was waiting,' Chance said. He put down a copy of that morning's *Western World* on Hoskins' desk. 'Seems they're committing the assault on Emma Catte to the Crown Court. And Jack Cam's set to get a result on his appeal against her place of safety order. Released into her mum's care, she could be.'

Hoskins shook his head.

'Released into my care, more like. If Jack Cam wins, I can nick her on suspicion of involvement in the murders of Bob McPhail and Terry Cross. I can do it the minute she sets foot outside the court. She's not a ward any more.'

Chance brushed back his flap of dark hair. 'Anything else?'

'Yes,' said Hoskins thoughtfully. 'I want a forensic examination of that tipper. Comparison with results on the pharmacy Transit, the Nissan Bluebird and the van at Jolly Modes. Not to mention the caravan.'

Chance stared at him to see if Hoskins was serious.

'Forensic examination? On a load of nutty slack?'

'That's right, my son,' Hoskins said quietly. 'Exactly that.'

'Bloody popular that's going to make us down the Beach,' Chance said glumly.

He went out and Hoskins picked up a report on the possibility that Billy Catte had died elsewhere and been moved to the caravan where his body was found. He preferred that. Such movement and secrecy constituted the crime of concealing a death. His phone rang.

'DCI Hoskins? Miss Cordell, for ACC Crime. ACC would like a word as soon as possible.'

'I'll come straight up.'

'ACC is in a meeting. He suggests you come up in ten minutes.'

Hoskins went up in ten minutes. There was a uniformed constable on guard outside the door that opened directly into Clitheroe's office. Hoskins walked past and went in through the main door of the ACC's suite. Miss Cordell, grey-haired and comfortable, sat at the ante-room typewriter.

'They're ready for you now, Mr Hoskins. Mr Clitheroe wants you to go straight through.'

With a feeling of foreboding Hoskins knocked at the internal office door and opened it. Someone was dead. Something had gone appallingly wrong. He knew it and the faces of Clitheroe and Ripley confirmed it. They sat beside one another on the far side of the desk. There was a clear plastic bag on the blotter. Hoskins saw the blood upon it and a curious root-like totem.

'Sit down, Sam,' Clitheroe said. 'We have to make a collective decision.'

Hoskins took a chair on the visitors' side of the desk, his eyes still on the bloody and misshapen fragment.'

'What's that?'

Clitheroe sat back, as if he might hook his thumbs in his merchant-banker waistcoat.

'If you believe the accompanying note, Sam, it's Rachel Wardle's tooth. Hence the screams on the phone to her father. Foster's at a Rockwell editorial meeting in London today. His side-kick called us to collect this an hour ago. The note is on Billy Catte's typewriter and paper. Either the ransom is paid according to instructions tomorrow, or Rachel Wardle will be returned bit by bit. Teeth, fingertips, tongue, and a list you can guess for yourself.'

Hoskins looked again, quickly and uneasily, at the bloody fragment.

'We know it's hers, do we?'

'Her records confirmed it as probable,' Ripley said. 'The note even gave her dentist's name. Carter, in Prince of Wales Road. That note also promises to feed the rest of this horror story to the media. The odd thing is that they still don't mention Emma Catte. All they seem to want now is money.'

Hoskins thought about this for a moment.

'What's our policy over paying the ransom?'

Clitheroe's thin black-moustached mouth tightened.

'Torpedoed is what it is, Sam. Mr Wardle got a note about this unsavoury little exhibit. Shoved under his secretary's windscreen-wiper in the City Hall car park. We've been watching his house, of course, but not his secretary's car. His note also contains a detailed account of how you draw a tooth with a pair of pliers. And also how you separate people from their other bits and pieces. He can raise the money, he says, and he's going to pay the ransom. He says it's family money. I think the press are buying the story. If we propose to sit by while these maniacs mutilate their victim, the Wardle family is going to the press and television. Either we let him pay or the Division will be in the eye of one of the biggest public storms this city has ever seen.'

Hoskins took another furtive look at the obscene and bloodied fork of the rooted tooth.

'Where does that leave us?'

Clitheroe looked at Ripley.

'One thing, Sam,' Ripley said, 'if that ransom is to be paid, we must do it. Wardle would be useless as a decoy. He might fail to make contact. He might get himself killed. The younger Catte boy is in Germany. But Tom Catte can't work alone on a kidnap. The Zichy child saw two men. Footprint evidence supports that. But we still know nothing about Tom Catte's confederates, apart from Emma Catte in psychiatric care and the younger boy in Germany.'

'So who recognises them? Who carries the money?'

'Billy Catte was your case, Sam,' Clitheroe said. 'So you get first refusal.'

From this height Hoskins could just see across the trees of Hawks Hill to the receding slopes of the valley and the toy-Gothic castle built for Lord Dyce by Giles Gilbert Scott a century before. He stared at the conical roofs of the fairy-tale towers and the warm perspective of wooded hills.

'I'll need the details,' he said philosophically. 'The sooner the better. Easiest thing in the world to make sure they don't get away with the money. The difficult bit is finding Rachel Wardle.'

Ripley smiled. 'I understand you thought she was part of the caper, Sam. Drop-out daughter rips off rich parents – or rips off the public purse.'

'Perhaps,' Hoskins said. 'But if it suited them, that young woman would be demoted from accomplice to victim in a split second. They've killed twice for less than this. Looking at that tooth, I'd say those screams might be real.'

Clitheroe folded the cloth over the exhibit and looked up.

'Two o'clock tomorrow afternoon, Sam, a message will be received on our PBX. It won't be long enough to trace the call. We follow instructions. You wear trousers and singlet. No microphone, no radio, no wires, no gun. Any tricks and Rachel Wardle will be dead. Any sign of any of us near you, the same applies. You carry the money on your own. You must be seen to be on your own. We have to assume these lunatics mean it. One foot wrong, Rachel Wardle is dead. She depends on you. Do as they say. Leave the clever stuff to us.'

The silver dart of a jet-fighter on a practice mission stitched the blue spring sky. It hit both sides of the valley horizon in a pulse of light, faster than any angel on the draw.

'To go back to my first question,' Hoskins said slowly. 'Do I understand that our policy is to pay them off? Even if they killed McPhail and Cross?'

The ghost of a smile hovered under Clitheroe's dark poisoner-moustache. He shook his head.

'Only one policy, Sam. Catch these little bastards and put them where they belong for as many years as possible. And tell the world we've done it.'

# FOUR

# Child's Play

# Chapter Twenty-Nine

Like a competitor stripped down for a carnival game, Hoskins stood in flannel trousers and cotton singlet. Clitheroe and Ripley looked him up and down. The plastic courier bags padded out with notes in £10 and £20 bundles lay in a canvas grip beside him.

'Do just as they say, Sam,' Clitheroe said gently. 'Leave the rest to us. We've got the best observation posts in the city centre. Top of the Sun Life Assurance Tower. City Hall terrace. Even the roof of the building here. We've got a dozen specials called in, monitoring every traffic-surveillance camera in the city and on the ring-road.'

Hoskins felt his stomach tighten with an involuntary spasm. 'What about patrols?'

Clitheroe shook his head.

'There's a chopper on standby behind the wall of The Keep, on the Army Recruiting pad. But putting something into the sky is too obvious, except as a last resort. We'll have back-up as close to you as we can. Jack Chance will be in the Sierra. Stan McArthur and Dave Tappin riding with him. There's a dozen other vehicles.'

Someone knocked at the door and Clitheroe raised his voice in a non-committal bray. It was DS Pargiter, breathless and holding a sheet of paper.

'It's what we've been waiting for, sir.'

'Was the phone-call taped or traced?'

Pargiter shook his head. 'It was made to the desk at the ambulance station. Message for DCI Hoskins to be forwarded to police headquarters at once. A man's voice.'

Clitheroe took the sheet of paper and read it.

'Amateurs, Sam! This is something out of a smart-arse cops and robbers film. You're to be at Webbs Bookstall on the top level of the covered market at two-twenty-five. That gives you twelve minutes. You're to be there alone. Ask for details of Box Thirty-eight and give the name of Wardle. Seems Webbs has a display-case of cards for people who want to buy and sell or get jobs done. You're not to be seen in a car or with anyone else. If there's any attempt by us to approach Webbs or the market, the deal's off. We get another bit of Rachel Wardle through the post. Perhaps the whole lot. You walk from here.'

'I suppose they could have someone watching the market,' Hoskins said. 'More likely to be bluff. Hard to say with the crowd in there. They could even have someone watching me as I leave here.'

'Do as they say, Sam. Leave the rest of this to us. We'll keep Jack Chance as close behind you as we dare. It looks as if they're going to lead you all over the city before you drop off the loot.'

Hoskins looked at his watch.

'Eleven minutes. Webbs Bookstall. Box Thirty-eight. Right now, what I want most of all is Rachel Wardle in one piece. Nicking these other scabs is a bonus.'

He went down in the lift, the canvas grip in his hand. He crossed the Memorial Gardens, short-cutting King Edward Square and heading for the pillared and skylit entrance of the Victorian covered market. It was almost twenty-five past two as he came out beyond City Hall. Time enough, at a brisk walk. Great Western Street was busy in the warmth of the March afternoon, candy-striped shop blinds drawn out over the payements for the first time that year.

Hoskins saw no sign of surveillance. A car passed that might have been a patrol but the face at the wheel would never see sixty again. At three minutes before twenty-five past two he turned into the Grecian loggia of the stone-pillared market, the oldest part of Great Western Street between the department stores. On one side the stalls were built up with ramparts of vegetables, only the heads and shoulders of stall-keepers visible. Opposite them was a seaweed stink of fish, the dull silver of dead scales, a massacre of feathered poultry, and an autopsy of skinned and flop-eared pigs.

Under the pitched glass roof of the long building, rows of ground-level dairy and vegetable stalls ran fore and aft. The alleyways between were packed with slow-moving shoppers. Somewhere in that procession might be Jack Chance or Stan McArthur. Somewhere might be one of Tom Catte's friends. Half of 'A' Division was probably parked round the adjacent streets, trying to be inconspicuous.

Hoskins strode up the old wood of the wide stairs to the sunlit cast-iron gallery that ran round four sides of the market. It was a narrow promenade of pet-stalls and sellers of birdseed.

There was a smell of sour meal and grain. Used records and spares for radio enthusiasts. Webbs Bookstall, consisting of cut-price and dog-eared paperbacks, stood half-way along. A man in his thirties with a sparse beard was warming his hands round a cup of soup.

Hoskins paused. There were no telephones in the market stalls. Any attempt at approach by Chance or the others might be seen at once. Tom Catte or his friends would start watching him somewhere along the route. He guessed that the market was where watching would begin.

A gold-figured clock, its four faces high above the stalls at the centre of the ground level, was just touching twenty-five minutes past two.

'Wardle,' said Hoskins quietly to the bearded young man with his thermos and soup. 'Box Thirty-eight. A message for Wardle.'

'Right,' the young man said, turning to a small ledger. 'Message from the gentleman about the FM tuner he's selling. The amplifier went yesterday. He suggests a word on the phone. Can't oblige you here, I'm afraid. I told him we nip in and use the Emporium when we want one. You're to go to the inquiries desk on the third floor of the Peninsular Emporium opposite the telephones. He'll contact you there at two-thirty, if you're still interested. That's four minutes. Hasn't left you long, has he?'

Hoskins turned and began to jog down the narrow gallery to the stairs. The way was clear to the stalls below. In Great Western Street he sprinted and dodged through the crowds, aware of a car moving slowly behind him and stopping. Jack Chance or Tom Catte? He ran on without looking round.

Under the blinds of the Royal Peninsular Emporium, he dashed through the first doorway and made for the escalator taking the moving steps two at a time to the third floor. The desks for 'Information' and 'Accounts' stood at one side. On the opposite wall, the four public telephones under their transparent acoustic hoods were unoccupied.

Hoskins looked about him and saw no one. He went across to the inquiry desk and the girl smiled.

'DCI Hoskins, Canton CID, "A" Division . . . '

At that moment one of the telephones rang and he turned back towards it.

'Let's have your name,' said a voice, young, male, sardonic. Hoskins' heart sank at the sound of it.

'Hoskins DCI. "A" Division.'

There was a pause and then the voice again.

'Right, Hoskins DCI. For a start, forget those clever ideas you was having a minute ago in the market. And don't even think of that carload of CID that's been shadowing you from King Edward Square. We got you well covered. That's money you're carrying, is it?'

'Yes.'

'Right. Start praying we let you hand it over according to plan. It's two fingertips next time. Took off by a hammer and chisel.'

With nightmare incongruity the cheerful sounds of department store commerce went on all about him. A voice over the public address system invited its listeners to try a new bra under the supervision of Diane, the store's lingerie consultant.

'Say what you've got to say,' Hoskins said flatly.

'I'll say it,' the voice said. 'Just once. Now, you leave this phone off the hook. Don't break the connection, if you want to see her again. You walk round the corner and into the gents toilet. You take the money from the bag and put it in the waste disposal for paper towels. It's like a metal drawer that pulls out of the wall and pushes in again. Left-hand side of the washbasin. Soon as you've done that, you come straight back here and pick the phone up again. I'll tell you where she is. Got it?'

'Yes,' Hoskins said.

'Then don't muck about. You've got sixty seconds from now. After that I put the phone down and you get two dinky little fingers in the mail. And if there is a next time after that, the price is going up.'

Hoskins put the receiver on its ledge and shouted at the inquiry desk.

'Don't let anyone touch that phone.'

He strode round the corner, through an outer entrance, and pushed open the door of the men's toilet with its relayed piano music and submarine warmth. There was no one else to be seen. The metal towel disposal was at one side of the basin, set in the wall like the night-safe of a bank. Despite all his instincts, this was no time for acting clever. Both Tom Catte and Clitheroe were right about that.

He opened the chute wide, stuffed the courier bags into it and closed it again. Then he strode back to the phone.

'Done it, have you?' the voice asked.

'Yes.'

There was a pause.

'Right,' said the voice at last. 'Then listen. I'm saying this once. So listen. First of all remember that even if you was to catch one of us, you'd still get bits of her by post till he was released. You'd be hearing her screams every night, all over the city, from the tapes on the *Hit-Back Show*. And if you was to catch us all, she'd have no one to see that she got food, nor water, nor even air. She's well banged up. Just the nostrils uncovered.'

'No one's trying to catch you,' Hoskins said. 'Rachel Wardle safe and well is the priority.'

There was another pause.

'What you do,' the voice said, 'is go back and get a car. You take the road through Orient and out by Lantern Hill. Follow on from there through Ocean Beach and up the hill at the far end to Highlands Avenue. Don't stop there. Turn inland round Sandbar and on towards Minavon and the Burrows. Got that?'

'Yes,' Hoskins said.

'Now, instead of going on to Minavon through the Burrows on the coast road, you turn off to Mondragon. Through Mondragon to the hotel. Right? You'll have to leave the car there and take the path towards the Lion Rock headland. When you get to the headland, you go all the way out, to the edge of Lion Cliff. Stand as close to the edge as you can.'

There was silence. Hoskins guessed what was coming.

'And then,' said the voice, 'you can toss yourself off.'

There was a constricted giggle of delight before the phone went dead.

Hoskins put the receiver down and ran back towards the men's toilets. There was still no one to be seen. He opened the wall chute of the towel disposal and found nothing. Releasing the catch of the main panel, he opened that and dragged out the black plastic refuse bag. It was empty except for a few crumpled paper towels. Of the packeted banknotes there was no sign.

In the lobby between the two doors there was a window with a fire exit sign. He opened it and saw a metal-railed walkway with steps down to a yard below. There was no one on the metal escape or in the yard. But a final length of iron ladder, hinged and chained up for security, had been let down. With a breathless expletive he headed towards the escalator. As he hurtled down the steps, he saw Chance and McArthur in the ground-floor Food Hall. He felt winded and blown.

'Car and radio, Jack! The money's gone. We've been seen off. They grabbed it from the third-floor toilets and went down the fire escape. Get this building sealed off and alert Division. They're not going to give us Rachel Wardle.'

Chance went out to the car. Hoskins pointed McArthur towards the Atlantic Wharf entrance of the store and Tappin to the arcade of Prince's Passage. Taking the lane to the delivery bay, he ran back towards the yard with the fire escape. The lane and the yard were empty. A fury of frustration gathering in his heart, he walked out to the street again.

Two more CID sergeants, Pargiter and Driscoll, were there with Burden, James, Manley and Plater from the duty crew. The Royal Peninsular Emporium was sealed off, for all the good it would do. Customers pressed at the glass doors trying to get out. Crowds began gathering on the pavement to watch them.

'They must be on foot.' Hoskins, sitting in the car on Atlantic Wharf with the door open, listened to the confusion of radio traffic. 'DCI Hoskins to control. The targets have disappeared taking the money with them. Somewhere in the region of the Royal Peninsular Emporium and Atlantic Wharf. We have no reason to believe that Rachel Wardle will be released. I suggest the helicopter should be airborne and sweeping the city centre. I repeat that there is no indication of Rachel Wardle's release or that she is still alive. Arrest of suspects should now take priority.'

'Sunburst to control. We have Atlantic Wharf in view from Sun Life Tower. Possible target, could be Tom Catte, crossing station forecourt to Metro-rail. Wearing jeans and a plaid shirt in white, grey and brown. Five foot ten or so, slim build, dark hair. Appears to be on his own. Not carrying a package.'

'Control to all units in area of Atlantic Wharf. Youth possibly answering description of Steven Catte entering Metro-rail booking hall on Atlantic Wharf. He is not – repeat, not – carrying any package. Follow if possible but do not arrest until instructed to do so. We want to see where he's going.'

Hoskins nodded at Chance. The motorpool Sierra drew out into the traffic, circling the wide square of Atlantic Wharf towards the incline of the station approach. To one side of the main terminus was the Metro-rail booking hall with its adjacent platform. Chance stopped the car.

'What d'you think, Sam?'

'Hand me your anorak and wait here.'

Oddly but anonymously dressed in the hooded anorak, Hoskins got out and entered the booking hall. Whoever the suspect was had gone ahead. Hoskins flipped his warrant-card at the barrier. There was a double platform for the Metro-rail, one side running west to Orient, Lantern Hill and Ocean Beach, the other north-east to Longwall, Parkland and Clearwater. Hoskins went cautiously up the steps from the subway as the Ocean Beach train rumbled overhead and the doors hissed open. He let it go, then walked up into the sunlight. End to end the platform was empty. He came back down.

'The man in the check-shirt. Where was his ticket for?'

'That one? Ocean Beach, boss,' the collector said.

Hoskins went out to the car.

'Bravo Four to control, DCI Hoskins. Suspect answering possible description of Steven Catte seen boarding Metro-rail with a ticket for Ocean Beach. Cover Orient and Lantern Hill stations as well. Also the north-east line, in case he's going to double back. Alert Ocean Beach and pass on his description. I'll be there as soon as I can.' He sat back and looked at Chance. 'Right, my son, here's what you've always wanted. Get me down the Beach before that train.'

Chance switched on full beam and the whooping crane siren. With an engine snarl that cleared the way more effectively than either, he left the curb in a spurt of chippings and steered out sharply into the traffic. Cars seemed to fall away at either side as the Sierra ate up the tarmac'd length of Great Western Street, shot the crossing into King Edward Square and keened towards Clearwater with a roar like sixth gear. Pedestrians drew back from crossings and family saloons tottered aside like old men on sticks. Jack Chance was doing seventy-five down the undulating suburban arterial of Clearwater and loving every minute of it.

A lorry ahead of them filled the windscreen with alarming speed. Chance crashed the gears and braked. The rear of the Sierra swung to and fro, then steadied. At the lights Chance pulled out, headlights blazing, and crossed against the traffic. They were on the Northern Quadrant junction, the longer but faster route, the only one that might overtake the Metro-rail train. Cars and freight-trucks hung back while Chance swung across into the outer lane. The Sierra accelerated with a supercharged snarl, the needle hovering above ninety. For five or six minutes, traffic peeled away in front of them as the Northern Quadrant gave way to Canton Link, the inland verge of Lantern Hill on the horizon turning into the bleak funfair beach of Ocean Park with its roller-coaster and sideshows.

'Bravo Four to control. DCI Hoskins. We're on Balfour Road, above Bay Drive. We should be at Ocean Beach Metro-rail with time to spare. Please tell Ocean Beach Division to keep out of sight. I don't want it to look as if there's a reception committee.'

'Control to Bravo Four. Understood. Will relay your message.'

Chance took the upper road, skimming the residential hills that ran down to Bay Drive. He turned at last into the final loop, where Bay Drive ran round Ocean Park and turned back on its tracks. Here, fenced by iron railings and tall grass from Canton Railway Dock, was the Metro-rail station for Ocean Beach. Only the width of Bay Drive divided it from the Whirlibirds and Horror House of Ocean Park Amusements.

Chance parked the Sierra forty yards short of the Metro-rail entrance below the railway embankment. It was a nondescript space in a line of cars left by morning commuters to Canton. He glanced at his watch self-admiringly.

'Four minutes before the train, I reckon. How's that for a bit of burn-up?'

'Bloody terrifying,' Hoskins said. 'Here it comes, across the embankment behind the dock. Keep your head down. I don't want to be seen.'

The light aluminium coaches of the train rumbled in. There was a pause. Two women and an elderly man came out of the booking hall. The doors of the train closed again. Hoskins' heart sank.

'He's off at Lantern Hill or Orient,' Chance said, plaintive at the injustice.

Between the figures coming down the pavement, Hoskins saw a patch of plaid shirt in the cold seaside brilliance.

'Hang on, Jack,' he said quietly. 'I think we've struck gold.'

# Chapter Thirty

The disembodied glimpse of plaid shirt hovered in the shade of the booking hall doorway and then moved clear of the other pedestrians.

'I don't believe in this amount of coincidence,' Hoskins said. 'It's got to be him. With or without the money.'

The dark-haired youth in the plaid shirt stood on the pavement looking across at the plaster casing of the soaring roller-coaster track.

'He's going into Ocean Park,' Chance said.

'No he's not, my son. Taxi office.'

'What the hell's he want a taxi for? And why's he empty-handed?'

Hoskins put the handset microphone to his mouth.

'Bravo Four to control. We're in position outside the Metro-rail station at Ocean Park. The man answering the description of Steven Catte, *alias* Tom Catte, who boarded the train at Canton Central station has just got off here. He's crossed the road to the taxi office by the station entrance to the amusement park. We're waiting for him to come out. If he takes a taxi, I shall follow him. I shan't detain him until we know where he's going.'

'Control to Bravo Four. Understood, Bravo Four. Message for DCI Hoskins from Superintendent Ripley. Second target believed sighted by Bluebird One but not carrying a package. Now driving alone in white Volkswagen Passat that crashed the barrier out of the Churchill Avenue multi-storey car park. No contact by mobile unit but Bluebird One has vehicle in sight, proceeding north on Clearwater Avenue. Presume vehicle's destination may also be Ocean Beach.'

'Bravo Four. Understood.'

Hoskins looked up from the handset. Beyond the promenade rails and the shuttered kiosks, the afternoon sea glittered at slack tide.

'Bluebird,' he said thoughtfully. 'They're using the chopper, Jack. Aerial surveillance. In other words, our mobile units have lost him, supposing they ever found him in the first place.'

'It's the one here that bothers me,' Chance said. 'If they've got a limo, why would he be going by train and taxi? And if they got the money, where is it? All this has a distinct feel of cock-up.'

Hoskins glanced at the taxi office.

'Keep your head down, Jack. He's got to reckon this is an empty car.'

A gust of Channel wind rattled the lanyards against the empty metal flagpoles of the deserted and unlit fairground. Two or three cars drove past, disappearing round the bend of the circle and down the sea front side of Ocean Park as they turned back on their tracks.

'I still don't get it,' Chance said. 'If he's on the run, why's he sitting round twenty minutes in a taxi office when he could have nicked a car and driven it himself? If that's Tom Catte, and the white Passat is his oppo, where's the loot? They'd hardly use three different getaways.'

Twenty minutes extended to thirty and thirty-five in the quiet afternoon.

'Taking their time to answer his call,' Chance said. 'They're supposed to get a car here in five or ten minutes. You reckon he's being naughty in there?'

Hoskins shook his head. In the mirror, he saw an Ocean Beach Radio Taxi with its black and cream livery coming up behind them as it responded to the office call.

'Bravo Four to control. I think we're off. Ocean Beach Radio Taxi, registration number D453 VLR. Don't try contacting the driver. He might be another suspect. If not, he could easily turn into a victim.'

'Understood, Bravo Four. Mr Clitheroe wants you to follow the car but not to intercept it.'

Hoskins watched two men, driver and plaid-shirt passenger, come out of the little taxi office to the waiting car. The black and cream Volvo pulled quietly away from the curb. Chance let it reach the bend of Ocean Park loop. Then he drew out after it. They rode the terminus circle of Bay Drive, round the high steel-mesh fence of the amusement park. Chance allowed another car to filter in, screening them from their target, as they came down on to the main length of Bay Drive. The Cakewalk promenade ran by the low seawall, the ice cream coloured hotels rising beyond the beach lawns.

They passed the pier-approach and the art deco modernism

of the Winter Garden. As the road began to climb, west of the promenade towards Highlands Avenue and the detached villas of Scottish Baronial or Spanish Tile, the radio brought news from Canton and Clearwater. The chatter of rotor-blades was clearly heard.

'Bluebird One. Bluebird One to control. Suspect vehicle now approaching junction of Clearwater Avenue and Northern Quadrant. Identify as white Volkswagen Passat, registration C4090 LMU. Repeat, white Volkswagen Passat, C4090 LMU. And he's signalling. On the Quadrant roundabout. He's turning east, east, east . . . '

'That's the wrong way!' Chance said furiously. 'If he's meeting up with this dumbo, he's going the wrong way!'

'Victor One to control. We almost got him at Connaught Park traffic-lights, boss. He was in the lane to turn right but went straight on. Left us stuck behind another car waiting to turn. What do you want us to do?'

'Control to Victor One and Victor Two. Do not, repeat do not, follow suspect vehicle towards Clearwater junction. Turn off and join ring-road east of Clearwater. Junction 7, north of Hawks Hill. Do not drive on to Clearwater. Delta Two and Delta Three, come off westbound surveillance lay-by and leave motorway at next junction. Turn back on east-bound carriageway and endeavour to make sighting of white Volkswagen Passat C4090 LMU.'

Hoskins listened to the developing chaos, stone-faced. Airborne observation broke the silence.

'Bluebird One to control. He's definitely east-bound on the Northern Quadrant of the ring-road. In the fast-lane in excess of eighty miles an hour. He looks as if he could be going all the way to London. This is Bluebird One, control. Please advise on surveillance. I'm bound to be conspicuous if I stay here, even if he hasn't noticed already.'

The radio messages began again. This time it was Ripley's voice.

'Control to Bluebird One. Stay where you are. Maintain surveillance. As soon as mobile units join the ring-road at Hawks Hill, break contact and return.'

Hoskins looked up. They were on Highlands Avenue now, heading west towards Sandbar. The large detached houses stood behind rhododendron hedges that had grown tall and thick as a fortress wall. On the far side of the road, the ground fell away in pine-shaded slopes and ravines to a glitter of sea below.

'Watch it, Jack,' he said quietly. 'He's pulling too far ahead.'

Chance accelerated towards the next bend and then slowed down once more. Ahead of them was a row of neighbourhood shops among the leafy avenues of the rich. Chance let another car pull out to screen them from the taxi.

'We need a change of cars, Sam. One of the Ocean Beach mobiles parked down a side road. He's bound to spot us if we keep this up much longer.'

'No time, my son. Any case, with this amount of radio traffic there'll hardly be room for the six o'clock news, let alone a call to Ocean Beach.'

As if to prove him right, the voice of helicopter surveillance came urgently across the airwaves.

'Bluebird One to control. White Passat approaching the Park Hill tunnel and the Mount Pleasant turn-off. He's not turning off. Going through the tunnel in the east-bound nearside lane. He can't turn off the ring-road now before Market Cross. Could be going back into the city centre.'

'He's just come from there!' Hoskins said hopelessly. 'What the hell's Ripley's lot playing at?'

Chance ignored him, watching the black and cream taxi. He pulled out suddenly round the car ahead, closing the distance as the taxi picked up speed. The avenues of Highlands and the Links were now giving way to open country. Sandbar with its green hill rising behind the little harbour lay six or seven miles ahead.

'Bravo Four to control. Following Ocean Beach Radio Taxi D453 VLR on A4850 Ocean Beach to Sandbar road at junction with B342. If there's any hope of a change of cars, we'd appreciate it.'

He sat back and heard an outburst from somewhere above the three hundred yards of motorway tunnel that burrowed through the northern spur of Mount Pleasant, a dozen miles away.

'Bluebird One to control. Bluebird One to control. White Passat containing suspect is no longer in sight.'

'Don't be fucking ridiculous,' Hoskins said furiously to the imagined pilot of the helicopter. 'You're right above him!'

'Bluebird One to control. White Passat has not exited

from Park Rise tunnel. He must still be in there. Alert police mobiles and emergency services, in case there's been an accident in the tunnel.'

'Control to Bluebird One. Maintain your surveillance on the eastern end of the tunnel . . . Control to all eastern-bound units on Northern Quadrant. State position.'

'Delta Two to control. I reckon we're the nearest, boss. We've passed Clearwater junction. About half a mile from the Park Rise tunnel and the Mount Pleasant turn-off.'

'Control to Delta Two and Delta Three. Possible accident in Park Rise tunnel. Investigate and report.'

'Understood, control. There's a lot of vehicles tailing back from the tunnel but traffic still moving in the outer lane.'

Chance was almost racing the taxi now, the coastal hedges of the country road flying past. Hoskins stared at the radio.

'I don't believe I'm hearing this,' he said forlornly.

They were clear of Ocean Beach now, a yellow fire of mustard fields to either side, the first dandelions of spring scattered like stars in the verges. A Gothic lodge was all that remained of Lord Dyce's country seat at Clifton Park. The fine dust of a cement works had settled over the site, rusty roofs and tin chutes, the rattle of churning stone. The old road to Sandbar was dotted by red-brick farm houses of Georgian style rising from flat pasture. Early clouds of smoke-white blossom hung against pearl-misted sky, where the old farm houses had become cream-tea cafés or conifer-perfumed garden centres.

'Victor Two to control. White Passat C4090 LMU has been abandoned in the Park Rise tunnel, east-bound nearside lane. No sign of occupants. No evidence of collision. Looks as if whoever was in it must have been following another car that stopped in front of it in the tunnel. Driver of Passat must have gone off with the other car. That's about it, boss. We'll need a recovery truck to get the tunnel clear.'

'Marvellous!' said Hoskins scathingly. 'Bloody marvellous! A couple of teenage villains can organise a change of vehicles better than the entire city police. That leaves us as the only people still possibly in touch with a hundred thousand quid and whoever's going to start chopping Rachel Wardle into little pieces. Whatever you do, Jack, don't lose this bugger. Not even if he sees us. That's a risk we'll have to take.'

They were almost in Sandbar, a flat coastal strip against a

hinterland of steep green hills and overhanging woods. White cottages and a turreted Victorian mansion stood among the trees on a hillside ledge. At the far end of the road, sheltered by the curve of the hill, was a stone quay with its café, bed and breakfast, and souvenir shop. The sea itself was an infinite expanse of quietly rippling tide, grey-blue in the sunlight except where the green hill coloured the calm of the little harbour. In summer, Sandbar was packed to suffocation with day-trippers and pleasure-craft. At present it was empty.

The taxi was parked opposite the high sea-wall dividing the beach from the road. On the inland side the flat coastal strip was occupied by Sandbar racecourse, developed by Blue Moon Leisure on the site of the old Ocean Front dog-track. It had brought money into Sandbar, in exchange for a long ten-foot high wall of prison-grey stone with spikes upon its ridge. Beyond this, several majestic horse-chestnuts had survived from the days of Lord Dyce's planting.

Chance drew off the road into the beach car park, from which the taxi could still be seen over a low wall.

'What's he doing, Sam? There's nothing here.'

The taxi was by a high wooden gate with the sign 'Tattersalls' above its brown paintwork. Tom Catte got out and walked back towards the public entrance, dominated by a concrete blockhouse with a row of empty flagpoles. The signs pointed to Members Entrance, Club Offices, Owners and Trainers. He seemed to look for something there. Then he walked back.

'Bit previous for the flat-racing season,' Chance said.

The course itself was visible beyond the wall, the white big-windowed buildings and the expanse of turf giving it the look of an old-fashioned aerodrome. Only the white rails curving along the lower slope of Sandbar Hill gave Blue Moon Leisure a hint of Ascot and Epsom. The old dog-track stands had been there fifty years, like open-sided barns, their paintwork rancid from ocean sun and cold squalls of rain.

Tom Catte appeared from the far side of the taxi, carrying a duffel-bag.

'He didn't have that before,' Chance said indignantly. 'Where the hell did it spring from?'

'I think we're going to have to ask him, Jack. Nice and easy.'

They got out of the Sierra and closed the doors quietly. Tom Catte was at the racetrack entrance again, beside a square white building of the 1930s, inset with a black panel and the name SANDBAR in silver-grey letters several feet high. He walked in past it without being challenged.

'You reckon they've got her here, Sam?' Chance asked.

'I don't reckon anything, my son. And that bag could be full of oats. He might not even be who we think he is.'

Despite the high wall and the barbed wire, there was no security patrol in sight as they followed him at a distance through the opening for Members and Club Office. Above the grandstand ahead of them the perches of the television cameras and the tall well-heads looked like the superstructure of a spy-ship. From the rear, the stands were a panorama of towers and hoists that might have done credit to a light-engineering works. To one side there was white shingled wood and picture-windows, where the Turf Grille at the back of the stand looked out across the sea.

'Billy Catte,' Chance said suddenly. 'He was a member here. His style. He'd have to be. Cooney owns it. All his paying guests, like Billy Catte and Horse-Parlour Pruen, must have had privileges here.'

The youth carrying the duffel-bag on his shoulder crossed a yard towards a row of lock-up garages with up-and-over doors. Hoskins edged round a corner and watched.

'If I'm right, Jack, Billy Catte could have died here.'

He heard the metallic slither and rattle of the lock-up door and looked again. The front of a red Ford Granada was just visible.

'Bloody hell,' said Chance, impressed at last.

'I want him, Jack. Nothing spectacular. Nice and quiet. He could still have a sawn-off shotgun, by my reckoning.'

They walked to one side, round the edge of the yard, backs to the wall of the Club Office, the afternoon shadow of the grandstand darkening the scene. Hoskins had almost reached the first of the garages when he heard a movement. It was not in the garages but somewhere behind them. He motioned Chance back and round them.

Alone now, Hoskins moved forward. He drew level with the open garage door, his back against its post. Edging round it he saw the concrete shell with the red bulk of the Ford Granada in it. Billy Catte, loyal protégé of Carmel Cooney, was not only a member at Sandbar; he was probably a director with personal parking and seating in the grandstand. Hoskins reminded himself that he must find out why in hell that had not been followed up.

There was no one in the garage. The window in the rear wall was open.

'You bloody asked for this! You been asking for it all the way from the Beach!'

He turned and saw the boy with the duffel-bag. Almost before he recognised the mat-grey of stunted barrels and the polished grain of the stock, Hoskins threw himself into the shelter of the garage. He heard a hot bark of powder, an impact like flung gravel. The windscreen of the Ford Granada shattered.

'Get clear, Jack!'

But it was Tom Catte's feet he heard, a dull rubber plop of his strides on the tarmac. Hoskins saw the young man reach the roadway entrance. He ran towards the shelter of the adjoining wall with Chance behind him. They paused then risked a dash towards the entrance itself. The taxi was empty, its driver sitting by the slipway to the beach. He walked forward, saw Tom Catte sprinting towards him with the gun, then stopped.

'The car!' Hoskins shouted to Chance. 'Get to the car!'

He had no doubt what Tom Catte would do. A hundred-to-one the driver had left the key in the taxi ignition, having the vehicle in his sight. It was pointing in the wrong direction for a fast getaway, towards the cul-de-sac of Sandbar quay. But it was the one hope of freedom for Tom Catte. He tugged open the driver's door, threw the duffel-bag and shotgun inside, then started the engine.

Hoskins, ignoring the ache in his chest, jumped a low wall of the beach car park as Tom Catte fumbled the gears of the black and cream taxi. McPhail and Cross had died trying to confront Tom Catte face to face. There was a better way.

Chance scrambled behind the wheel of the Sierra as the taxi lurched towards a wide slipway running to the sands. With the wheel locked tight, Tom Catte used the space to turn on his tracks towards Ocean Beach. He brought the taxi round as Chance accelerated across the car park in a cloud of stone-dust.

'There's another barrel still loaded, Jack,' Hoskins said quietly. 'Don't let him use it. Ram the bugger.'

But there was not going to be time. Tom Catte was

gathering speed on the Sandbar road, hurtling towards the point where he would be past the car park entrance and clear of them. With a feeling of desperation, Hoskins saw it about to happen. Then, for the first time in weeks, fate changed sides.

Tom Catte, unused to the taxi, skidded on the wind-blown sand that eddied across the tarmac. He recovered almost at once and set the nose of the black and cream saloon straight towards Ocean Beach. But though Chance had missed the engine and driver's door of the taxi, the Sierra shot from the car park entrance, airborne for a second as it leapt the low ramp, and hit the taxi squarely in the rear passenger door. There was a crunch of pressed metal and a grinding sound of the Sierra's bumper trailing on the roadway. Hoskins, thrown up rather than forward by the impact, came to rest in his seat. At first it seemed as if the two vehicles were locked in a zany slithering dance as they spun through a half-circle. Like a fluke at billiards, Chance had scored a hit at just the point to spin the Sierra on to the road and the taxi into the dressed stone of the sea-wall.

Hoskins dived out and over the Sierra's bonnet. The cars were not entangled after all. The impact had locked and then thrown them apart. The bonnet of the Volvo taxi was forced up and the driver's door burst open. Tom Catte began to fumble for the weapon on the seat beside him. Then, seeing Hoskins too close, he tried to get out.

Jack Chance's door was jammed. For what seemed several minutes Hoskins grappled with Tom Catte on the dry scattered sand of the beach road. He felt the warm breath in his face and the fingers locked in his hair. Alone, he was probably no match for his adversary. Then Chance was with him. Struggling and lunging, Tom Catte was pulled up and back, so that he sprawled across the front seats of the wrecked taxi. He began to curse and utter a breathless keening. Hoskins fumbled and found the handcuffs that he had taken from the Sierra. While Tom Catte tried vainly to wave his arms clear, Hoskins managed to lock one cuff over the boy's right wrist and the other over the taxi's steering wheel. At last the struggling ceased.

Hoskins drew breath. It felt like the first time in several minutes. Then he drew back and found himself looking at a small notice, level with the taxi's driving-mirror.

'Thank you for not smoking,' it said.

242

# Chapter Thirty-One

The first fly of spring was a deep-voiced bluebottle, lured from the darkness by warmth and light. Among blue-grey coils of rising tobacco smoke in the narrow room, it bumped and grumbled against the metal shield of a fluorescent strip.

Tom Catte's face at eighteen had the chin cleft and solidity of a middle-aged man. From tight dark curls to canvas shoes, he was his father's son. The uniformed constable by the door eased his shoulders with a whisper of serge. Tom Catte drew an ashtray across the table and tapped his cigarette.

'You sit here all night, if you want,' he said to Hoskins. 'I'm going to bed.'

Beyond the metal slats of the window shutters the Mall was in rainy darkness, the floodlights darkened on City Hall domes and War Memorial pillars. Another breath of smoke drifted upwards in the narrow cream-distempered room.

Hoskins shook his head.

'Police and Criminal Evidence Act, my son. You don't go anywhere for thirty-six hours, if this nonsense keeps up. There's a duffel-bag next door. They're still counting the banknotes in it. There's a key to a caravan at Minavon taped under the engine cover of that Ford Granada.'

'So what's the charge?'

'Driving without a seat-belt, if necessary,' Hoskins said grimly.

Tom Catte sprawled waggishly back in his chair. He was smart, and he knew it.

'If you'd ever read the law on the subject, Mr Hoskins, you'd know that seat-belts aren't compulsory when driving a taxi. That was a taxi I was driving when you tried to kill me. Case you hadn't noticed.'

Hoskins controlled his rage with bitter quietness.

'Don't piss me about, my son. I want answers.'

Tom Catte was unimpressed. His forehead creased with the effort of drawing smoke from the last inch of cigarette.

'And I got questions. My dad had a director's garage out Sandbar racetrack. I went out to start clearing it. Not been there for a year. He left his old shotgun there. I'm confronted by you two thugs about to attack me. Nothing said about being the police. Self-defence, I fire overhead and run, you after me. Could be someone with a grudge against my dad. I run to the taxi and the driver's not there. So I try to get away. And you two try to kill me. And then there's this business of money, which certainly wasn't there when I looked last. Nice bit of plant, that.'

Hoskins stared at him. 'And that's the best you can do, is it?'

'It's all I have to do. I'm not saying anything more.'

Hoskins watched the boy light a fresh cigarette from the stub.

'In case you hadn't heard, my lad, this money is connected with a kidnap and the murder of two policemen.'

'I read about those two,' Tom Catte said casually, 'in the papers. Not down to me. As for kidnap, you need to have a think. If I did that, then the worst thing you could do is keep me here. If I'd got friends, they'd be giving her a night to remember now. If it was me alone, she'd be sitting tied to a chair, gag in her mouth, waiting to die.'

'You think you can't get a life sentence at eighteen?' Hoskins said quietly. 'For this lot, life could mean life. You need every friend you can get, my son.'

'Nothing to say.'

The door opened and Chance beckoned him. They stood in the corridor.

'How's it going in there, Sam?'

'It's not going anywhere, my son. He's acting dumb.'

'I got the taxi driver's story,' Chance said. 'Apparently Mrs Catte has an account. They get a message this morning and a key through their mail-box. Key fits a left-luggage locker at Canton Central. Mrs Catte's left a parcel in a duffel-bag to be collected from the locker at three and taken to their Ocean Beach office.'

Hoskins stared. 'If the taxi driver had the locker-key how could our young friends use it to stash the money they'd just picked up at the Emporium?'

Chance shook his head. 'They have copies cut by a bent locksmith while hiring the key and locker in the normal way. They could have keys to open every locker in the station at any time. This time, they had the money taken out by a taxi that no one suspected. When the driver arrived out the Beach, there was Tom Catte waiting for his lift to Sandbar. Seems he used his mum's account quite a bit.'

'Marvellous,' said Hoskins miserably. 'Forget the taxi driver for the moment. I think we'd better have a solicitor for young Catte.'

'Asked for one, has he?'

'In a manner of speaking. I'll give Jack Cam a ring.'

'I thought Claude Roberts was Billy Catte's brief.'

'Billy being dead and Jack Cam acting for Emma, I'd say that points to him.'

He walked off down the corridor with Chance in pursuit.

'Sam, you're not going to let that bugger Cam walk all over this inquiry?'

'Can you think of a sharper legal brain to look after our customer?'

Chance stood in front of Hoskins' door.

'For fuck's sake, Sam! Whose side are you on?'

'I'm on my side, Jack, which is more than can be said for Tom Catte. But Mrs Catte's still in Germany and someone has to look after the lad's interest.'

'I don't believe it,' Chance said helplessly.

Ten minutes later, Hoskins was back in the interview room.

'Now then, my son,' he said to Tom Catte. 'You have the right to silence and I have the right to detain you on suspicion of murder. You'll have your brief here in half an hour. Mr Cam.'

'What for?'

'I understood you'd want your solicitor. Mr Cam's acting for your step-sister. We'll also be questioning her. Don't want different briefs, do you?'

Tom Catte looked at him, the dark eyes betraying their first uncertainty.

'You're pulling a bloody stroke, Hoskins!'

Hoskins shrugged. 'Have a word with Mr Cam. Then, if you want to lodge a complaint on the grounds that I've protected your rights for you, go ahead and do it.'

Jack Cam, in a narrow-cut old-fashioned dinner-suit with a starched shirt-front, was there at half-past ten. Hoskins went out to his room and found Clitheroe in the corridor. The poisoner-moustache was tight on the upper lip.

He followed Hoskins into the Chief Inspector's room.

'Ten seconds, sir,' Hoskins said, picking up his phone and dialling Chance in the sergeants' room. 'Jack? I want the most senior member of social services you can raise. Quick as possible. Any means necessary. I'll take Swinton, if I have to, but no one junior to him.'

He put the phone down. Clitheroe was staring as if hypnotised.

'Do I understand, Sam, that you've brought Cam in as young Catte's solicitor?'

'Yes,' Hoskins said firmly.

'Jack Cam? Have you any idea what that means?'

'Yes,' Hoskins said again. 'I've got a very fair idea of what it means. He'll be too busy to do anything else tomorrow.'

Clitheroe flapped a fist up and down in the air, as if looking for something to hit.

'He won't be too busy to tell that little thug to keep his mouth shut.'

'He's not opening it anyway. Jack Cam might even talk some sense into him. Young Catte won't listen to me. I'm the enemy. He might listen to the best criminal defence solicitor in this city, who's already on Emma Catte's side.'

'How long have you been a CID officer in this Division?'

'About fifteen years before you first set foot in it,' Hoskins said.

Clitheroe's dark eyes gleamed with a promise of insubordination charges and suspensions from duty. Then he checked himself. It was only when he had reached the door that he looked at Hoskins again.

'I hope you know what you're doing, Mr Hoskins. For your own sake, I hope you do.'

Hoskins sat down and stared at the wall. Ripley knocked and entered. The blueberry flush had gone and he was pale from exhaustion, an old moose with the antlers bowed.

'What the hell did you say to Clitheroe, Sam?'

'Just discussed progress with Tom Catte, Max.'

'And Jack Cam. What's all this about Jack Cam?'

'Tom Catte needed his brief,' Hoskins said. 'I don't fancy this investigation being held up because we've bent the rules.'

'But Jack Cam!'

Hoskins sighed. 'It's possible that Tom Catte is the only one who knows where she is. He's certainly the only one here to tell us. As he describes it, she's sitting tied in a chair, a gag stuffed in her mouth, trying harder and harder not to choke. He might listen to Jack Cam. He won't listen to us.'

'I hope . . . '

'You hope I know what I'm doing, Max. Clitheroe's exact words. I know what I'm doing, all right. I just hope it works.'

Ripley turned to the door, tired and beaten by it all. Then he looked back.

'Oh, a message from Ben Felix, by the way. Charlie Blades' side-kick working late at Area Forensic. Those keys under the lid of the Ford Granada. Fitted the car and the caravan all right. But no one had ever used them.'

'That's nice, Max.'

'I hope so, Sam,' said the Ripper gloomily. 'I do hope so. See you in the morning.'

Hoskins poured himself coffee from his thermos and unwrapped a sandwich. He dialled an outside line and heard Lesley's voice answer.

'Just wanted to talk to someone nice and normal,' he said. 'Well, I think you're nice. I'm not sure what's normal any more. What're you doing now? Try the film on the other channel. Tell me about it tomorrow. Well, what're you wearing in bed? Take it off. Go on, just for me. Course it's not ridiculous. Just making an old man very happy. Hang on, I think I'm wanted. Tomorrow. Definitely.'

Chance was in the doorway.

'Mr Swinton,' he said with a faint tone of apology at having brought the second best.

Swinton, the youthful red face shining and humid, the beard bristling, looked excited and eager to hear.

'Developments, I understand, Mr Hoskins.'

Hoskins waved him to a chair. Chance took the other one.

'We've caught Tom Catte. He's wanted for questioning over the deaths of two policemen, as well as the disappearance of Rachel Wardle. He has at least two accomplices. One was seen by aerial surveillance this afternoon. The other picked him up in another car, somewhere in Park Rise tunnel on the ring-road.'

Swinton fondled his beard as an aid to thought. 'Was the ransom paid?'

'Paid and recovered, while in the possession of young Mr Catte.'

Swinton beamed at him. 'That's great! I mean, that's really great! Shows these other thugs their trick won't work. So we're really getting somewhere.'

Hoskins shook his head. 'No, Mr Swinton. We're at a brick wall. Tom Catte's stopped talking. Not a word. He's given an explanation as to what he was doing when arrested. He hinted to me privately that they left Rachel Wardle somewhere until they know the money's safe. Left her tied to a chair and with a gag in her mouth. If that's true, she must be suffering the torments of the damned by now. She'll probably die, almost certainly by choking and suffocation, somewhen tomorrow.'

Swinton stared at him, as if not understanding.

'But that's deliberate murder! I mean, they'll lock him up and throw away the key.'

'They'll do that anyway, Mr Swinton. Two police officers were murdered back in January. I don't suppose he thinks Rachel Wardle can add much to that.'

Swinton continued to stare.

'He could be interrogated.'

'He's been interrogated, Mr Swinton. And now he's got his brief, Jack Cam, with him.'

'Cam's a rotten little fascist! You can't just leave Rachel Wardle to die.'

'I've no intention of leaving her to die, Mr Swinton. I don't even think she's likely to die. But I'm not taking chances. That's why you've been brought here. How much authority do you have in the case of Emma Catte?'

'Emma Catte? Why?'

'Who's above you?'

'There's the director. Depends what you want.'

'Do you have enough authority to get the place of safety and the care orders on Emma Catte set aside? To do what Jack Cam's been after in the courts?'

'No!' It was a high-pitched cry of resentment. 'That girl's been emotionally and physically abused. She's fifteen, for pity's sake. Read the medical reports sometime. She has been abused. No two ways.'

'Probably by her step-father, Billy, who is now dead. Possibly by her elder step-brother, who's next door facing a long prison term. I want an agreement between you and Mr Cam. The case dropped by social services. Emma Catte transferred tomorrow morning to an open hostel, free to come and go. Released into her mother's custody, if Mrs Catte returns from Germany. Or flown out there as soon as arrangements can be made. You could swing that, could you?'

Swinton moved spearmint around his teeth and looked at Hoskins again.

'In other words, give these bastards what they've been asking for. Make it look as if we've given in.'

'That's it,' Hoskins said. 'They still think Tom Catte's loose with the money. If Emma's free, they've got all they want. No need to hold Rachel Wardle.'

'Complete bloody surrender.'

'Loss of face,' Hoskins said. 'Cam may win his case anyhow. This way, you might save Rachel Wardle. Anyway, you lose Emma Catte once she's sixteen. You really think a few months of professional pride is worth a woman's life?'

Swinton sat in silence for a moment. Then he looked up.

'Tell young Catte we'll let her go if he'll say first where Rachel Wardle is.'

Hoskins shook his head.

'I put that to him a couple of hours back. He's facing two life sentences for the murders of police officers. That's what he'll bargain over in the end. Your case with Emma Catte is a stone-cold loser. And he knows it.'

'There's no way of baiting the other hook?'

'An investigation where two policemen have been murdered? I wouldn't be allowed to soft-pedal that, even if I wanted to. Forget Tom Catte. See if we can persuade the ones that are still holding Rachel Wardle.'

'What if Tom Catte's the only one that knows where she is?'

'That's a risk we have to take, Mr Swinton.'

Swinton's chair creaked. He looked down at his shoes and then looked up.

'Can I go somewhere and use a phone?'

'Mr Chance will show you where.'

Chance came back alone. Hoskins was studying a paper from his in-tray.

'Here's an odd one, Jack. You remember Mr Short that was driver's mate when the dress van was hit outside Madame Jolly Modes? The one that was brother-in-law to Daniels who had his Ford Granada nicked and caravan used?'

'What about him?'

'That load of coke abandoned on the motorway. He should've been driving. Contract driver for them at weekends. Been off sick after the robbery at Jolly Modes. Someone else was driving the lorry. And they don't know who.'

'Sod that,' Chance said intently. 'What about this lark of letting Emma Catte go in the hope of getting Rachel Wardle back? That's just what they want, Sam. These bastards are getting exactly what they want.'

Hoskins shook his head.

'No, my son,' he said thoughtfully. 'They're getting exactly what I want.'

# Chapter Thirty-Two

Hoskins woke at seven o'clock next morning and decided to strike the first blow. He dialled the *Western World* news-desk and heard Gerald Foster's voice.

'Gerald? Sam. We're questioning a man about the disappearance of Rachel Wardle. You won't get a word out of the press office but you might hear from other sources. The opinion on high is that if a word of this finds its way into your columns, it is definitely you over the barrel. Thought you might see it that way, Gerald. TV and radio are co-operating. Nope, not even a name. The minute it's cleared, I'll phone you. Cheers, Gerald. Talk to you soon.'

His arrival in the headquarters car park coincided with Jack Cam's. Cam had exchanged caramel suiting for informal cream blazer and flannels, an air of Henley regatta. Though it contrasted with the sharp whiskered face, the outfit hardly suggested a day in court. Tom Catte was a new full-time preoccupation.

'Morning, Mr Hoskins. Didn't know you were setting up a legal aid service.'

Hoskins shook the proffered hand and they walked in together.

'You know how it is, Mr Cam. Like to see the prisoners' rights respected. With you acting for young Emma, I naturally thought you'd be the man for Tom.'

'His name's Steven, actually, Mr Hoskins. And it's Mr Cooney's instructions I'm acting on in the other case. "In *re* an infant", as they say.'

'Then you could have declined Steven Catte, Mr Cam.'

'Never decline business, Mr Hoskins. Matter of principle. Any case, those social services wooftahs are caving in. Not the fighting kind. Never were.'

The lift doors opened on the fifth floor.

'Think your client might have something more to say this morning, Mr Cam?'

'I hope my client will do as I bloody well tell him,' Cam said with a friendly leer. 'You must let me buy you a canteen coffee at lunchtime.'

Hoskins went into the sergeants' room and called Chance.

'Leave young Catte for the moment. What's happened with Emma?'

'She got the news. She's moving from Colditz about now. Cleared it with Cam's partner, Todd Brown. There's a hostel overlooking Connaught Park, on Lake Drive. We've got a van there. Dave Tappin and two plain-clothes WPCs.'

'What about CNT and Canton Radio?'

Chance grinned. They walked into Hoskins' room.

'Miss the radio news this morning, did you, Sam? City council withdrawing a care order imposed on a teenage girl. First of the cases to reach settlement. Order withdrawn, as a goodwill gesture, after the death of her step-father. Department not admitting an error or a misjudgment. The girl to remain in hostel accommodation until her mum gets back from abroad. Seventeen other appeals continue tomorrow. That goes out on every news broadcast up to six o'clock this evening. Should make sure Tom Catte's friends hear it.'

'Young Catte say where he's been living?'

Chance shook his head.

'Dyce Esplanade, he reckons. But no one's been living there since before Billy Catte died. He could have been anywhere.'

'Anything more about the lock-up garage in the directors' yard at Sandbar?'

Chance sat down. 'Forensic reckon Billy Catte died in that car. Tests on evidence of what's politely called body-fluids.'

Hoskins read his post. The Police Federation assisted by Coastal and Metropolitan was offering him life insurance on favourable terms.

'Anything else on Billy Catte?'

'He was a depressive. That's why he always looked so bloody miserable, even with his dancing-girls and two-way mirror. Then he was caught screwing his step-daughter. He reckoned on going down for a long time. He'd be like an animal in the nick. Rule 42 for his own safety. Ten years solitary. Warders snarling and villains sneering. A bath in scalding water while they looked the other way. That's why there was that daft attempt to get her by holding a doctor hostage at the infirmary. He was too far gone to care about a few more years. When that went wrong, he'd had it. So he went out to Sandbar on a quiet afternoon. Closed the garage door. Turned on the engine. Lay back and took a weight off his mind. That's the reckoning down Area Forensic.'

Hoskins looked out across a glitter of cool sun on deep-water anchorages.

'Concealing a death. Let's add that to Tom Catte's charges. He and the others must have found the body. Couldn't leave it in the lock-up. Moved it to the caravan at Minavon. After all, it's only twenty-five miles away.'

'Where's that leave Billy Catte?' Chance asked.

'In the deep freeze, waiting for his inquest. And it leaves me nostril-deep in the constabulary cess-pool.'

'What for?' Chance asked suspiciously.

'Because, my son, I've been doing the same as every other stupid bugger on this case. Goggling like a punter at all the teenage sex, while there's two policemen dead and armed robbery breaking out like chicken-pox.'

'So where's that leave the kidnap?'

'Not down to Billy Catte,' Hoskins said. 'It was young Tom and his friends wanted Emma back before she told her story. I reckon they knew Billy Catte was dead. But he still had his uses in covering the murder motive.'

Chance stretched. His full red face was tight-skinned with fatigue.

'If you think that's what it's about, Sam . . . '

'It's always been about that, my son. Armed robbery and murder. But social services and Cooney between them stirred up the under-age girl business. And these young ruffians used it to their own advantage.'

When Chance had gone out, Hoskins phoned Area Forensic again.

'Dr Blades, please. Charlie? Sam. Things are boiling up here. Anything on the Mordaunt Coking Plant truck? One extra set of prints to match one set in the pharmacy van? That's all right, Charles. I reckon I know who it is. And one other extra set from the pharmacy van to match the Ford Granada and the caravan? I know who that is as well. Smashing, Charlie. I'm a happy man. There's two more villains that no one ever thought of. Not big-league crime. Not teenage tearaways. But I think that's nailed the kidnap and the murders of Terry Cross and Bob McPhail. All I need now is Rachel Wardle.'

Alone in the room he allowed himself a moment to admire the cool March sunlight on the urban mass of Canton's foreshore. After weeks of civic uproar and sexual scandal, reformatory novelettes and skin-videos, gangland and club-land, hostage-taking and ransom demands, the truth was pleasingly simple. In his blood, Hoskins felt it all coming right. Thanks to something as mundane as an abandoned load of what he called 'nutty slack'.

# Chapter Thirty-Three

At twelve o'clock Hoskins considered Jack Cam's offer of a cup of canteen coffee. But when the phone rang it was Chance again.

'Sam? A call from Dave Tappin. We've got the "off". Emma Catte's left her lovely new home – alone. She's at the bus stop on the corner of Lake Drive and Connaught Road. They gave her spending money at the hostel.'

'Right, Jack,' said Hoskins softly. 'Get the car started. I'm on my way. Take Stan McArthur and Jock Craigmiller in the back seat.'

It was almost too easy. Emma Catte had caught the bus from Connaught Road to Atlantic Wharf. The only problem was to drive slowly enough to remain behind the lumbering custard-yellow double-decker without seeming conspicuous. Two plain-clothes policewomen, comfortably dressed in mackintoshes and headscarves, followed the girl into the Royal Peninsular Emporium.

Hoskins, binoculars in hand, rested his elbow on the low concrete wall of Churchill Avenue multi-storey car park. With Chance and the other two sergeants, he was on the upper level, opposite Canton Central railway station and the Metro-rail. He had a wide view of Atlantic Wharf at the lower end of Great Western Street.

Chance came across from the car.

'Message on the radio from Jilly Barnes, Sam. Emma Catte's using one of the public phones in the basement of the store. Jilly can't hear what she's saying. She doesn't want to get too close and be recognised again later on. Apart from which, Emma's not talking very loud anyway. We don't know what number she dialled but it was only six figures. That means it's in the city.'

Hoskins nodded. Like swirls of white meringue, the torn cloud-scraps were pluming and thinning across the blue sky of the windy day. Beyond the railway bank and the long scar of its tracks, he could see the squat funnels and wide hulls of container vessels in Prince of Wales Dock. A shiver of light caught the chop of waves across the cold sheen of the deep-water anchorages beyond Harbour Bar. He turned his binoculars back on the striped canvas shop-blinds and the Great Western Street entrance of the Royal Peninsular Emporium.

'Boss!' It was Stan McArthur beside him. 'We're off again. Jilly Barnes reckons that girl's walking to the Atlantic Wharf entrance, where the buses stop. Looks like she's going to meet someone but phoned ahead first.'

Hoskins straightened up.

'Right, Stan. Everyone back in the car. We'll drive round and pull in by the station approach.'

Craigmiller was by the car door. 'She's in the queue for the number forty bus, Mr Hoskins. East-bound.'

'What's the route?'

'Taylors Town to Barrier, running just inland from the wharves and shoreline. It goes past the railway station, down Churchill Avenue, through the high-rise blocks round the Tidal Basin, then along the old Sea-Wall Road into Barrier itself. Stops in Ferry Road, the one with the shops that runs inland.'

'Then let's get on with it.'

Chance brought the Sierra down the spiral of the car park and out on to Churchill Avenue. He pulled in by the white concrete tiling and green neon of the National Ice Rink.

'Control to Bravo Four. Bus passenger on service number forty. Vehicle number D859 FDW.'

'Bravo Four to control. Understood. Will proceed when vehicle is in sight.'

'He's in the mirror,' Chance said. 'Here we go.'

The bulk of the custard-yellow bus rumbled past, followed by several cars. Chance joined the end of the procession. Hoskins caught sight of Jilly Barnes' headscarf near the door. In the rear window of the upper deck there was a glimpse of fine blonde hair. Emma Beata Catte, *née* Franz. Chance hung back far enough to avoid overtaking the bus at its stops in Churchill Avenue and along the high-rise apartment blocks built on the land-reclamation site of the old Tidal Basin. Then they were in Barrier, Sea-Wall Road running just inside the protective bank built by Dutch engineers against the tide a century before.

The flat terraced streets of Barrier had no horizon but their own rooftops and chimneys under a limitless sky of Atlantic blue. It was the last land before the ocean, mudflats drained by Victorian enterprise. There was brine in the air and the soil was sand or silt. Mop-headed acacias along the pavements of residential roads were almost the only trees in this area of coastal Canton.

Chance hung back, letting the bus turn down Ferry Road towards its terminus. Beyond a small Methodist chapel of cream corrugated iron with a wooden spire, there were half a dozen shops in a shallow parade. Emma Catte stepped down into a quiet area of grey stone houses. After so much drama, she was a slight and rather frail figure with her length of fine pale blonde hair blowing in disorder. Jilly Barnes glanced at the Sierra and moved off, her surveillance completed. She walked back up Ferry Road towards her lunch break.

Emma Catte turned a corner, just by the little shops. Chance drove slowly, crossing the end of the road where she had turned. There was no sign of her.

With a clenched expletive, he took the corner and accelerated towards the next junction. But the streets were empty under a blue lunchtime sky.

'Take it easy, Jack,' Hoskins said gently. 'This is either too good to be true or too true to be wrong. Reverse up Holt Street fifty yards and hide round the corner in Brunswick Avenue.'

'What for?'

'Because, my son, we've got an old friend living in the second house along.'

Chance did as he was told, parking the car round the corner from a pair of semi-detached stone houses of the 1890s. There were narrow front gardens and pathways of cracked yellow tiles leading up to each front door.

'What now?'

'Get reinforcements, including a couple of WPCs. There's back gates and rear lanes behind these houses. Keep an eye on 'em, Stan. I don't want anyone leaving this house without being shadowed.'

Chance looked uneasy.

'You reckon she's in there, Sam?'

'I'd bet money on it, my son.'

'You going in alone?'

'I reckon I can handle this without the Tactical Support Unit and telescopics peeping over every garden wall. It's only a driving offence.'

'A driving offence? You fallen out of your tree, Sam?'

But Hoskins was out of the car and walking slowly up the path to the front door. As he rang the bell, Chance began to call for back-up.

The front door of Gothic glass panels opened. Hoskins smiled. He spoke with amiable apology, sharing a joke at the extent of his own incompetence.

'Good morning, Mr Daniels. You must be thinking you'd never see your Ford Granada again. Nicked by car thieves and then impounded by the law. Almost got it sorted now. Convenient to come in and have a word, would it be?'

He scuffed his feet on the doormat and entered. The door closed behind him. Jack Chance stared.

'Bloody hell!' he said awe-stricken.

The dark hallway and the overstuffed sitting-room with its flower-pattern chintz on settee and arm-chairs was much as Hoskins had expected. Daniels was still the baggy-trousered and canvas-shod veteran of small business. Of his sister there was no sign. Hoskins sat down.

'I thought you'd like to know we've made progress, Mr Daniels. Forensic have almost finished with the car. Then it's back to you. We've caught the chap who pinched it. Steven Catte. Son of the Billy Catte that we found at Minavon Bay.'

Daniels betrayed himself by the slightest movement of dark eyes in a tired hang-dog face.

'That so?' he said, sitting down with a little sigh of effort. 'Good.'

Hoskins tightened his face in a perfunctory smile and adjusted his glasses. He tugged a notepad from his pocket.

'Just formalities really. Got your driving licence to hand, have you? Saves us getting through to Swansea on the computer.'

Daniels looked just a little grimmer as he drew the green plastic from his back pocket. Hoskins looked and returned it.

'Good,' he said, as if relieved. 'Still do a lot of HGV driving, do you?'

'Do what?'

'Your licence. Authorises you to drive a heavy goods vehicle. Still do a lot of it?'

'Why?'

Hoskins shrugged. 'The shop going out of business. You being short of retirement age. The Ford Granada and the caravan at Minavon having been paid for by your sister. You living here with her. Not surprising if you went back on the road to earn a bob or two.'

Daniels dismissed it with a breath. 'That was bloody years ago. You fancy hauling an articulated truck from here to Milan or Rotterdam at my age. Would you?'

Hoskins smiled and shook his head.

'Nothing like that, Mr Daniels. I was wondering if you happened to have a blow-out on the Northern Quadrant the other day, while driving a ton and a half load from Mordaunt Coking Plant to Atlantic Factors?'

Daniels stared as if the words meant nothing to him.

'No,' he said at last.

'All right,' said Hoskins gently, 'but for someone who never did, you took a while to make up your mind, didn't you? I don't want to make too much of it, Mr Daniels, but if someone asked me whether I was driving a ton and half of coke last week, I don't suppose I need to think twice about it.'

'I thought you'd gone loco for a minute, that's why.'

Hoskins gave another quick smile, as if at the justice of the rebuke.

'All right,' he said. 'Fair enough. One thing I would like to know, though. When did you last drive for Mr Short? He should have been on that tipper.'

Daniels stared at him again. The metal shutters were coming down and the bomb-proof doors closing.

'Or for Mr Draycott?' Hoskins asked.

'That's it,' Daniels said. 'I'm not having this. You come about the Granada. Anything else is well out of order.'

Hoskins nodded agreement.

'I'm not here to question you about a crime, Mr Daniels. But your little ironmonger's shop down Ferry Road went bust, didn't it? Principal creditors were the Inland Revenue and VAT, I should think. Nowadays it's all Do-It-Yourself chain-stores and stupid people hammering nails through their gas-pipes. Don't seem to want real ironmongers any more. I'm on your side there.'

Daniels stared at him. 'Then why the questions?'

'Look,' Hoskins said, 'I'm not Inland Revenue. I'm not VAT. I couldn't care less about them. But I can see how a man in your situation might take to driving again to earn a living. While drawing a bit of dole at the same time. If I had to investigate your circumstances, which I hope I won't need to do, you'd be hard pushed to show me where else the money comes from.'

Daniels' expression remained the same but his voice was quieter. Hoskins recognised the slipping of the first pebble to start an avalanche.

'What do you want?'

'Not you, Mr Daniels. I'm not trying to bring a charge against you. But I can see how you might want to work – to drive – for cash-in-hand. No point knocking yourself out just to hand it all to the creditors – in your case the Inland Revenue and the VAT. Cash in the claw and not a word said.'

'I'm not discussing it.'

'Of course you're not,' Hoskins said reasonably. 'That's why I know you were up to it. If you weren't, you'd be discussing it for all you were worth.'

Daniels took a deep breath and let it out again. 'What do you want, exactly.'

Hoskins smiled to reassure him.

'It's not the newest game in the business, Mr Daniels. Someone with the say-so over transport or contract driving for a big outfit can do it. Either a fictitious name gets hired as self-employed with no tax stopped from the money and no insurance paid. Or else a known name works for a couple of outfits at once and pays part of the wage to someone to do one lot of his driving for him. There's half a dozen ways it can be done.'

'You tell me,' Daniels said sourly. 'I wouldn't know.'

Hoskins gave him a kindly smile.

'I think you would. For example, there's a driver phoning in sick to the firm that pays his wages. While he's on the sick, he draws state benefit if his wages stop. But he's actually hauling a load for someone else. If you never heard of things like that, my friend, you must have led a sheltered life.'

But Daniels was not done for yet.

'What's it to me?'

'Just this,' Hoskins said, 'I reckon your brother-in-law, Mr Short, was working two at once. While Blue Moon Enterprises thought he was taking a little longer over his deliveries for them, he was actually earning as contract driver.

Only he was off sick last week and someone who shouldn't have been driving that wagon got in a panic when it had a blow-out. Still, we reckon it wasn't you, don't we.'

'Course it bloody wasn't,' Daniels said miserably. 'So what's all this about?'

'Mr Draycott and the pharmacy vans for Atlantic District Health Authority. Remarkable man, Mr Draycott. Able to be in two places at once. Drawing wages from the authority, while driving piece-work for someone like Mordaunt Coke. Sometimes had to cover his tracks by getting a mate to take the delivery Transit out. And that person was also pulling in forty quid a week from social security, being unemployed. A bit naughty, Mr Daniels, but not the crime of the century. So Mr Draycott puts ten quid in someone's claw for an hour or two on the Transit, while he takes half the day off and does a contract drive, being paid Health Authority wages at the same time. Everyone ends up smiling. Except, of course, the Health Authority and social security. I think you've done a bit of driving for him. In fact, I know you have.'

'You think what you like.'

Hoskins shook his head, as if in sympathy.

'Your prints that had to be eliminated when we examined your caravan. Matched one set on the pharmacy Transit. And there was a set in that coke tipper that was a dead ringer for Mr Draycott's on the Transit. Fair enough?'

'A couple of times,' Daniels said helplessly. 'That's all.'

'But not on the fifth of January this year?'

Daniels stared, as if clearing his head after a punch. Then he remembered.

'If you want to waste your time looking, you'll find I was being examined in court over my bankruptcy. From ten in the morning until afternoon. And I was with my solicitor, Mr Anthony Gray, from nine in the morning.'

Hoskins emitted a sigh of satisfaction.

'And so you couldn't drive for Mr Draycott that morning, could you? Which is why Mr Draycott had to drive the van himself.'

But Daniels had taken fright now.

'I'm not saying any more.'

'You don't have to, Mr Daniels. And so far as I'm concerned, there's nothing against you. Whether or not you're fiddling the social, the tax and VAT is up to you. I haven't got time to go chasing on their account, even if I cared.'

Daniels creased his brow in an effort to comprehend.

'You sure?'

'Quite sure,' Hoskins said, getting up. 'What interests me next is the key to your caravan, the one taped under the bonnet of your car.'

'You said it was still there.'

'It was, Mr Daniels. Forensic examination showed it had never even been in the lock. None of the tiny little marks that the lock might leave. So how did these thieves get into your caravan?'

Daniels' flaccid face woke into sudden inspiration.

'I could have forgot to lock it when I came away in October. Easy done.'

Hoskins smiled.

'So it is. And how did these intruders manage to lock it when they left.'

'It's a Yale,' Daniels said plaintively. 'It . . . '

He stopped at the edge of the precipice.

'Exactly, Mr Daniels,' Hoskins said gently. 'It locks automatically. Even in October with all the rush of getting away. I reckon they had to use a key. Your key.'

Daniels put his hands to his face, moving his head slowly to and fro.

'I knew it,' he said quietly. 'I bloody knew it.'

Hoskins watched him for a moment, then resumed in the same gentle voice.

'Don't upset yourself, Mr Daniels. But if you see your son, tell him to contact me. We have to speak to him. The sooner, the better.'

There was a pause. Then Daniels spoke without looking up. 'How long've you known this?'

'More or less since the first time we heard about your caravan at Minavon.'

He stood up. Daniels followed suit, avoiding the Chief Inspector's gaze.

'Where was your ironmongery business by the way, Mr Daniels? Can't remember seeing it.'

Daniels paused. Hoskins smiled.

'Just interest, Mr Daniels. If I wanted to know for police purposes I could have it off the computer in thirty seconds.'

Daniels nodded. He was no trouble now.

'Ferry Road. Not the shopping parade up here. Down the other end by the laundry. All up for sale now. Premises, freehold, goodwill.'

Hoskins stared, trying to imagine the nature of Mr Daniels' goodwill.

'And what's happened to the family, the kids?'

'Tried it here,' Daniels said. 'Didn't work out. No good, not living with the sister. They made their own way. Comes a point where you can't look after 'em for ever. I got a basinful to contend with here.'

Hoskins nodded. 'I'm sure you have, Mr Daniels. Anyway, I'll get in touch about the Granada. Shouldn't have to keep you waiting much longer.'

He walked slowly to the front door, down the dark narrow hallway with its faded prints of old cottage scenes on the wall. A smell of boiled vegetables drifted from the kitchen. He sensed the eavesdroppers behind its door.

Daniels stood in the interior porch. His face, harshly lit by the sun, had the look of drowned flesh, pallid and crumpled by immersion. He managed a brave farewell.

'Right. I'll hear from you, then.'

'That's a promise,' Hoskins said.

# Chapter Thirty-Four

The four bulky men sat in the parked Sierra, hidden from view of the Daniels house by the corner of Holt Street and Brunswick Avenue. Unseen officers of CID had moved into other positions to cover the rear lane and road junctions.

'Nothing,' Chance said gloomily. 'No sign. She could be long gone. Supposing she ever went in there. If this goes wrong, Sam, I reckon you'll be wearing a cork backside, courtesy of Mr Clitheroe.'

'She went in there,' Hoskins said. 'The first time she spreads her wings, she comes straight out to Barrier. Not exactly Las Vegas, is it? Vanishes outside the house of a man who drove that pharmacy van on a freelance basis. Drove it often enough for his family and friends to know the drill. Not driving it the Wednesday of the hi-jack, because his bankruptcy case was on. Convenient, that was. And then the Catte family nicks his car. Mr Daniels has a taste that starts my mouth watering just thinking about him. And I'll bet Emma's little ears were pressed to the door all the time I was talking to him.'

McArthur and Craigmiller began a desultory and irrelevant conversation.

'Shut it!' Hoskins said suddenly. 'Something's up. Foot patrols have stopped calling in.'

'Not before time. It's gone three!'

'Shut it!'

The radio bleeped into life.

'WPC Lucas to control. Girl answering description of Emma Catte, leaving Twenty-three Holt Street. Walking back towards Ferry Road . . .'

Hoskins sighed.

'If I'm right, she's going to turn down the Ferry Road towards the laundry. Go straight across here, Jack, parallel to her. Down the rest of Brunswick Avenue. We'll go to the bottom and then drive round across Ferry Road lower down.'

Chance moved off slowly, past the semi-detached houses in grey stone, their narrow gardens nodding with lilac and prunus. It was quiet as a Sunday. He turned left at the next junction, moving slowly over Ferry Road and disappearing into the opposite street. Craigmiller tapped Hoskins' shoulder.

'She's there, boss. Coming down the nearside.'

'All right,' Hoskins said soothingly. 'Take us up the next parallel, Jack. Then we'll turn into Ferry Road higher up and park a long way behind her.'

Chance did as he was told. They drew in by one of the mop-headed acacia trees, the long quiet perspective of Ferry Road ahead of them in the cool sun.

'She's going down past the laundry,' McArthur said.

'No she's not. She's stopped. Turning in.'

Hoskins put the lapel microphone to his mouth.

'Bravo Four to control. Female target, reference 102, seen trying to enter lock-up shop, believed to be former business premises of Daniels Ironmongery in Ferry Road. We'll need to surround and survey until she comes out. If she goes in, I shall follow in about five minutes.'

Chance eased the car forward and stopped fifty yards short of the shop. By the low wall at one side a board stood flag-like on its post announcing the sale of the freehold premises by Western Commercial Properties.

'She's not come out,' McArthur said. 'They have living accommodation over these little shops, what used to be the top floor of a house. I lived in one when I was a kid. Flight of metal steps at the side to an upstairs door. We had a door and a hallway where there used to be a bedroom one time.'

Hoskins glanced and saw that McArthur's description was accurate.

'Let's pay 'em a call. Someone's living rough in there while it's unoccupied.'

'They could have Rachel Wardle,' Chance said doubtfully. 'Not to mention guns.'

'Then let's do it quietly, Jack. They lost the Eley revolver at Boots. They lost the shotgun at Sandbar. And they lost Tom Catte as their marksman. If she's in there, the last thing I want is loud-hailers and heroes in black berets waving M-16s in the air.'

'So what's the plan?' Chance asked. 'They could still have Rachel Wardle.'

'I'll ring the bell and inquire,' Hoskins said, putting his mouth to the microphone. 'Bravo Four to control. Female target has entered premises at One Hundred and Eighteen Ferry Road. I'm putting three officers to cover exits and taking a look.'

Five minutes later Chance was standing in the doorway of the empty lock-up shop, its windows to either side blanked out by white polish. Craigmiller was concealed under iron steps leading up from the little back garden. Hoskins and McArthur went up the main steps at the side. The doorbell produced no sound. Hoskins took a deep breath and beat twice with the knocker.

There were footsteps, loud on bare boards. The door opened and he saw a tall youth of about seventeen with fair curls and a dimpling 'sonny boy' face.

'Hoskins,' Hoskins said. 'Western Commercial Properties. All right to show a gentleman round, would it be? Not now necessarily but later this afternoon.'

The boy hesitated. He shifted a little. Petulance filled the 'sonny boy' face.

'Not exactly,' he said. 'We're moving gear now. It'd have to be tomorrow.'

Hoskins nodded. 'Right,' he said. 'I'll tell them. You'd be Mr Daniels' son, I take it.'

'For what it matters . . .'

The girl's face appeared, dim in the shadows by contrast with the sunlight round the open doorway. Hoskins dropped his glance. It was too late.

'That's them, Raz! That's the police!'

The door slammed half-way but not before Hoskins could put his shoulder to it, forcing the metal tongue of the lock just clear of its bolt-hole. For a long moment there was a breathless struggle, the two men on one side pressing against the boy and the girl on the other. The defenders were close to their goal of shutting it but the weight of Hoskins and McArthur began to tell.

Young Daniels gasped something to the girl. The door gave suddenly. Hoskins saw a dim image of the boy flying down the hallway and into one of the further rooms. But Emma Catte was struggling and clawing at the two men to gain time for him. Then McArthur had hold of her and Hoskins pushed past. He moved quietly to the doorway through which the boy had vanished.

It was a large tiled kitchen of the shabbiest kind. A tin of food stood open and half-eaten on a rusted draining surface. There was enough refuse in the plastic bin to keep the lid from closing. A scent of rotting pulp hung in the sunlit air. Putting out sacks for refuse collection might have betrayed young Daniels' presence. The boy was standing with his back to an old-fashioned sink with brass taps, a wide and deep trough of pitted porcelain that reminded Hoskins of outside wash-houses in slum tenements. The light fittings had been stripped from the kitchen and the floor was bare.

Young Daniels was an amateur. The knife in his hand was a kitchen-carver. Good to look at but useless in a struggle. Even a Vestry Road warrior after a football match would prefer the sharp little triangle-blade of a Stanley knife.

'It's too late, my son,' said Hoskins quietly. 'Too late for that. Tom Catte's packed it in. That's how we knew where you were.'

'You get fucking stuffed! You followed Emma!'

Spittle flew from the boy's lips with the desperate energy of resistance. The shout was hard enough to flush his cheeks. Hoskins sighed.

'Don't be a prat all your life, Raz. How do you think we knew Emma was your girl? Certainly wasn't your dad that told us. It's down to Tom Catte.'

'No!' But there was uncertainty in the spoilt blue eyes.

'Well,' Hoskins said, 'you'll have plenty of time to talk it over between you, where you're going. Twenty years and more, if this keeps up.'

But Sonny Boy Daniels held the ace.

'You nick me now and you've seen the last of Wardle. There's no one else knows where she is. Not even Emma. She's going to die, cuffed to a radiator pipe in a room on her own. You got that?'

Hoskins took a step forward.

'I hope not,' he said gently. 'I hope not, for your sake. If that happens, you'll say goodbye to the world until you're a quiet middle-aged man of forty or fifty. Even if Emma's still available, you'd be bent as a butcher's hook.'

'Fuck you!'

But there was despair in the shout. Hoskins took another step and a risk with the truth.

'Tom Catte told the lot, my young friend. It wasn't you that ran down McPhail. It wasn't you that shot the other policeman. You happened to be there. That's not a crime, though concealing it is. But it's not murder nor anything like. As for this silly lark trying to rob vans, that's small-scale. And even Rachel Wardle might be seen as no real harm done. Still, if you want a go at murdering another policeman now, you'll be away for a long, long time.'

There was no movement.

'Give your ears a chance,' Hoskins said reasonably. 'There's a dozen or two officers round this building. Some of 'em armed. You don't think you're going to walk out through them just because you're carrying a carving-knife, do you? You'll be shot dead first, my son. Where's the point to that?'

Like water flooding down a drain, the fight went out of young Daniels. His arm dropped. Hoskins stepped across and took the carver away.

'That's better,' he said gently. 'You might have hurt yourself with that.'

McArthur and Craigmiller took the boy to police head-quarters in another car. Hoskins and Chance examined the echoing uncarpeted rooms above the ironmonger's shop and the dusty shell of the shop itself. The upper floor was where Daniels, the father, had lived before his bankruptcy. There were remains of meals, a mattress in the back room and a makeshift curtain over its window. But of Rachel Wardle there was no sign. Hoskins went out to the car.

'Bravo Four to control. No evidence of missing person on premises at One Hundred and Eighteen Ferry Road. We're still looking for accomplices in her disappearance.'

'Control to Bravo Four. Mr Clitheroe for you.'

Hoskins waited, then heard Clitheroe's voice.

'We're getting nothing from your friend, Sam. Nothing. Solicitor requested. Nothing more.'

'I'll be back presently. Meanwhile, I'd like all surveillance ended here. There's no point to it.'

'That's already been done, Sam. You're on your own.'

He went back and found Chance.

'Take the car, my son. I'll call in when I want to be fetched. Meanwhile, I'm going to have a quiet look round here. And a think.'

'On your own?' Chance said uneasily.

'Just that. I'll be safe from harm, supposing that's what's bothering you.'

Left to himself, Hoskins went through the building again. A musty roofspace, warm from sun on tiles, smelt of stale sawdust. Rooms of the empty apartment rang hard as he walked them. On the lower level the shop was box-like and bare. Only the wooden counter, the fitted shelves and the electric points remained.

He went back up to the kitchen. The late afternoon turned to a mackerel cloud-pattern over the slack tide beyond the sea-wall. An hour later the sky was a deeper and darker blue as the street-lamps came on.

He tried to imagine what it must be like to die, locked to a radiator pipe by a metal cuff. Would there come a stage of emaciation where the hand was little more than bone, slim enough to slip the cuff? Probably not. Such images belonged to a world beyond reality. The Wardle parents were to be tormented by thoughts of their daughter summoning the desperate and terrified resolve of the vixen in the trap, gnawing through a trapped limb to gain freedom. But the images in Hoskins' mind were of two patrolmen, lying dead in a muddy winter lane. That case was almost at an end.

Young Daniels was the last of the four in the car when McPhail and Cross died. Tom, Emma, Kevin and Raz. Other accomplices to the kidnap were still at large, no doubt. One at least, perhaps more. But not for much longer.

The sky had gone now, its clouds indistinguishable from the dark vault above the city. Red and yellow panel-neon came on above the Tandoori Take-Away in the little shopping parade at the seaward end of Ferry Road. Atlantic Video Hire was brightly lit and busy. The traffic-lights at the inland junction of the road lit the darkness of the room very faintly in a sequence of red, amber and green. It was no more than the illumination of a face in the night by the glow of a cigarette. Hoskins stood up from his chair by the window and eased his cramp in a leisurely stretch. Then he sat down again.

He had not been listening to the footsteps. Now that they had stopped he knew they had been in his consciousness all the time. They began again, not on the pathway but with a twanging resonance of metal stairs at the rear of the building. There was a pause and then a key scraped in a lock. Hoskins sat still. The darkness turned dimmest amber as the traffic-lights changed.

The footsteps reached the half-open door of the room. Hoskins stood up again. His dimly perceived movement prompted a response.

'Sorry,' the voice said. 'Took longer to get fixed up. Mandy's boy ran short last week.'

Hoskins moved forward.

'Miss Wardle?' he said gently. 'Miss Rachel Wardle? My name's Hoskins, DCI, Canton "A" Division. I think you and I ought to have a little talk.'

In the gloom of the traffic-light turning green once more, he saw her draw back, as if to run. But she had hesitated too long. Hoskins was blocking the doorway, even before she could get through it.

# Chapter Thirty-Five

Tom Catte lounged back in his chair beyond the stained wood of the bare table. A bleak fluorescent glare caught him at an angle that again showed him tired and old beyond his years. But there was a self-confident and sardonic line in his face, a crispness of dark hair. Had circumstances differed, he might have been a young Jack Cam. He blew out smoke and drew breath through his teeth.

'You can have it either way,' he said casually. 'No odds to me.'

Even the tailoring of the suit had a narrow and snappy look of Jack Cam.

'And you can have your brief,' Hoskins said. 'You've only got to say.'

Tom Catte lifted an end of his upper lip, the sneer of a movie gangster.

'I don't need a brief for this. None of it was ever said. Right?'

'We'll see.'

Tom Catte drew another lungful of smoke and seemed not to care.

'Well,' he said philosophically. 'You'd sound a prat repeating it anyway. The choice you've got is whether I plead guilty to this lot or not guilty.'

The night sky through the window behind him shed starlight on the domes of City Hall and the dark shop fronts of Great Western Street.

'So what's your proposition?'

Tom Catte pulled a face.

'I could plead not guilty. Doesn't matter whether I am or not. But with the evidence there is, I'd probably lose. Don't need Jack Cam to tell me that. On the other hand, I could plead guilty, which leaves Raz Daniels having to do the same. You can choose which you want.'

The first fly of spring was performing aerobatics again in the metal shade of midnight fluorescence, bumping and fizzing.

'It's your choice,' Hoskins said quietly.

Tom Catte tightened his mouth, drew smoke, and let it out again.

271

'If I plead guilty, Mr Hoskins, it's to this. Me and Raz Daniels held up Draycott in that pharmacy van. Two of us. Me and Daniels was there when those two policemen got topped. Just two of us. Me and Daniels and the Wardle girl set up the kidnap. And that's it. Emma and young Kevin knew nothing about any of it. Right?'

'It's not up to me,' Hoskins said. 'You know that.'

Tom Catte stubbed out his cigarette and leant back again.

'Then here's the story if all four of us goes up the steps. That pharmacy driver, Draycott, is a tow-rag. Even you know that. He's been on the fiddle for years. Drivers that done a legal maximum get work from him. They don't pay tax and he takes a cut. Grafters that want to earn without it showing. False names. So-called contracts. Not just hospital vans. He's got fingers in half a dozen places. You try putting him up as a witness and he'll be in the dock with the rest of us. I'll see to that. And he's your only witness. Right? Shoot a bloody great hole right through the middle of your case.'

'And that's it, is it?' Hoskins asked sceptically.

'No,' said Tom Catte, 'it isn't half of it. Even if you could prove there was two more at the pharmacy van, you couldn't prove it was those two. Nor when those policemen were topped. As for Boots the Chemists, someone stole my dad's car with my shooter in the glove compartment. If it was me, d'you think I'd leave a Colt forty-five behind? And when that Jolly Modes business happened Emma was in care and Kevin in Germany. I had her nail-file in my top pocket. Fell out when I stooped. So far as they're concerned, you've got Draycott's evidence against them and nothing else. And even he never saw them. If they go down, Draycott goes too. You'd better tell him.'

Hoskins nodded and watched Tom Catte light another cigarette.

'So where does that leave Rachel Wardle?'

Tom Catte shook his head, admitting a mistake at last.

'That was Raz Daniels' idea. She's a stupid little cow with a habit to feed. Sniffing the white stuff. Mainlining, for all I know. Needs some sense belting into her. That Zichy woman she worked for was blind as a bat. Raz used to screw the Wardle girl sometimes. Just for exercise. After Emma was taken into care, he gets a bright idea. Rachel Wardle had a thing against her parents, her mother being a self-righteous old bag and her father's family having money. So there's a suggestion we stage a kidnap. She doesn't even have to be hurt.'

'Whose idea?'

'Theirs,' Tom Catte said dismissively. 'I told 'em to stuff it. Next day, Dad went out the infirmary to get Emma. I kept the motor warm. When I saw him come out with you lot after him, I drove across the lawn and picked him up. But it was losing Emma tipped him over. Them social services slags got a lot to answer for. She was practically sixteen and they weren't blood related.'

Hoskins nodded, as if he understood.

'And what about Sandbar?'

'He'd got business to do. Couldn't use his own car after the infirmary nonsense. Raz said he'd drive him. Dad couldn't go back to Dyce Esplanade that night either. There was police outside. He said he'd got a place to stay at Sandbar, where he wouldn't be found. Quite calm about it all. He took the red Granada that was Daniels'. Borrowed it off Raz. We never saw him after. Next evening we went down to Sandbar. No red Granada anywhere. I thought he'd leave it in the lock-up. So he had. I thought he'd leave a message. So he did. He was dead in the front seat.'

'Concealing a death,' Hoskins said. 'That's an offence as well.'

Tom Catte almost sneered at him.

'Hounding a man till he's nowhere to go! Treating him like an animal and taking his girl away! That's an offence in my book. I saw what those dogs in social services were like. So then I told Raz we'd pull the kidnap stroke. All I wanted was Emma out of that DHSS kennel. We had to put Dad somewhere. Raz's father had this caravan down Minavon. We took Rachel Wardle there and did the video with Dad's camera. Then we drove the Granada there and left Dad's body. I knew he'd be found and buried proper. First thing, I had to look after Emma and Kevin.'

'Who did the ransom notes?'

Tom Catte shook his head.

'I did some on the old portable that Dad had in the car. I gave them to young Daniels. I was away three days, getting young Kevin to Germany.'

'How?'

Tom Catte looked down at his hands.

'That's for me to know and you to find out, Mr Hoskins. Still, he's there now, so I must have done it.'

'All right. Why?'

Tom Catte looked up with a pained expression, as if Hoskins had gone suddenly stupid.

'Because Dad was gone,' he said simply. 'I told you. What happened to the family was down to me. I wanted them all out of this poxy country.'

'Who took out Rachel Wardle's tooth?'

The young man shrugged.

'A dentist. We never planned things. Just made use of what happened. She'd got this dodgy tooth. Almost everything about her was dodgy, come to that. Mind you, for a hundred grand a lot of people wouldn't mind losing a healthy tooth even. She went to this place in Orient. Gave another name and said she was on holiday here from the Channel Islands. Not registered under the Health Service. Gave the name of a cousin of Daniels that really does live out there. All too bloody easy. Said she'd keep the tooth as a souvenir to claim off her health insurance there.'

'So what was the rest of the plan?'

Tom Catte looked surprised.

'We didn't plan,' he said simply. 'The things just happened. If they hadn't done, other things would have happened. We'd have done it some other way. Of course, we planned things like Rachel Wardle picking up Raz in the motorway tunnel. That was small stuff. Mostly, we just waited to see how things went and made use of what happened. And you have to admit, if you hadn't got to Ocean Beach and Sandbar that afternoon, I'd have shafted the lot of you.'

Hoskins nodded. 'You don't believe in making crime easy to solve, my son,' he said gently. 'Did Rachel Wardle agree to have a finger taken off, if the tooth didn't work?'

Tom Catte attempted a grin of boyish frankness.

'She didn't even know it was mentioned. Until you meet her, you don't know what a real stupid little cow she can be. And she's not family. Nor's Raz, come to that. But me and him agreed. The minute we needed to, she'd be kidnapped for real. I don't know if I could do the finger bit. If it was life or death, yes. For Emma, yes. And the money was only so we could get clear. That's the family. Us against the rest. It's how Dad always saw it.'

'So Rachel Wardle might have lost a finger and young Daniels shares a life sentence with you,' Hoskins said wearily. 'All on behalf of the family.'

Tom Catte brightened up. He came forward in his chair, elbows on the table.

'How long do you think I'll be away for, Mr Hoskins? Just a guess.'

'Not up to me,' Hoskins said. 'A long time.'

Tom Catte nodded eagerly. 'Only what I thought, watching Mr Cam, I'd like to take up the law, if I can. I could really go for that. Just to watch him working! He's beautiful! In prison, for instance, there's nothing to stop you studying, is there?'

'Not that I know of.'

'That's something I could do,' Tom Catte said thoughtfully. 'I really could.'

'Mr Cam is dropping the case against the hospital for assaulting Emma,' Hoskins said.

Tom Catte's dark eyes glinted as he turned his head.

'But I'm not, Mr Hoskins. I reckon I'll be seeing some of them scumbags in due course. I've got their names in my head. Little bit of unfinished business for later on.'

It was on the following morning when Hoskins and Ripley discussed Tom Catte's offer. They were in the Ripper's office. Almond blossom sprouted like shell-bursts on the garden trees of Hawks Hill.

'ACC's advice,' Ripley said cautiously. 'If Catte and Daniels plead guilty, they'll make a statement from the dock, saying they were there alone when Cross and McPhail died. Even if they weren't, there's no sufficient case against Emma or Kevin Catte. We'd at least have to show that the same four robbed the pharmacy van. Our only witness is Draycott, who turns out to be a petty swindler. Paying grafters who don't declare earnings, collecting overtime himself and doubling up on contract work.'

'So what's the thinking?' Hoskins inquired.

'The thinking, Sam, is this. If we bring murder charges against Emma and Kevin, we'll lose. If we bring armed robbery charges against them, we might well lose. And suppose they were acquitted on the judge's direction, early in the trial, for lack of evidence. And then they went into the witness box and offered an alibi to young Catte and Daniels as well. The whole thing might go bad. The jury is sitting there with the judge telling them that two of the four are innocent. Then those two say the other two are innocent as well. Mr Clitheroe doesn't give a toss about Catte and the social services. But he's worked hard on the murders. He doesn't want to end up losing the lot.'

'So we accept Tom Catte's offer? We let him dictate terms?'

Ripley shook his head. 'We let him and young Daniels plead guilty to murder and armed robbery. We settle scores over Cross and McPhail. We get the bastards who drove the car and pulled the trigger. We lose two juveniles who happened to be there. That's acceptable. It's not Clitheroe pulling rank by giving his inquiry priority over yours. The murder of police officers has to come first. If that's not cleared up, we breed despair among the law abiding and give comfort to the law breakers.'

Hoskins stared down at Ripley's desk. Where the brochures for Bournemouth had once been, a sheet of paper just failed to conceal a confiscated paperback copy of *Elaine Cox, A Well-Reared Tomboy*, stamped in mauve with the legend 'Property of Her Majesty's Treasury'. The Ripper followed Hoskins' gaze. His gill coloured a little and he shifted the papers on his desk. Elaine Cox vanished as if by a conjurer's skill. Hoskins returned to the attack.

'And the rest is off, is it? Everything else to do with the Catte family and Draycott, not to mention Daniels?'

Ripley sighed. 'That suggestion of Tom Catte's, Sam. Did it never occur to you that he'd been put up to it by Jack Cam?'

Hoskins looked surprised.

'No, Max, it didn't. He doesn't need Jack Cam. Tom Catte's a bright boy. A psycho, perhaps, but bright enough to think this one out all on his own. So where does all this leave Rachel Wardle and the so-called kidnap?'

Ripley stroked his chin.

'Down to you, Sam. Definitely a feather in your cap. It wouldn't have looked very clever, losing a hundred thousand quid. We'll be charging Miss Wardle, along with Catte and Daniels. We owe you that.'

'Charging them with what?'

The Ripper smiled a gentle far-off smile.

'Something nice and old-fashioned,' he said wistfully. 'Money with menaces.'

Stan McArthur took Tom Catte's statement that afternoon with Hoskins sitting back. When it was finished, Hoskins said, 'I don't understand. Why? Why kill them?'

Tom Catte looked suddenly embarrassed, as if he had hoped to avoid such a question. Then a frown of curiosity creased his forehead.

'I don't know, Mr Hoskins. It was like a film or something. Even when it was happening it was like watching someone else. I thought, it's not real. And the minute it was over, I thought, you bloody fool. You bloody fool. It was like it didn't matter because it hadn't happened. If someone asked me, ten minutes before, would I do anything like that, I'd say not in a million years.'

Jack Cam got up from his chair next to the young man.

'Right, we'll leave it there, Mr Hoskins, if you don't mind. I'll have a word with Mr Raven before deciding if we need a medical assessment of our client.'

They walked out together.

'Not very pleasant this sort of case, Mr Hoskins,' Cam said. 'Two colleagues dead. Still, I suppose you got a result.'

Hoskins stopped and looked at the spruce barbered face.

'Not me, Mr Cam. This is down to Mr Clitheroe. Mine's the appended charge.'

'What's that, then?'

'Money with menaces.'

Cam smiled at the absurdity of it.

'That's something for a sprog DC on his afternoon off.'

Hoskins reached for his door-handle.

'I don't qualify, Mr Cam.'

'Course not,' Cam said. 'You being a DCI with twenty years on the slate.'

'Not the rank, Mr Cam. It's just that I don't get afternoons off any more.'

Alone in his office, he dialled Minavon.

'Mr Andrews? DCI Hoskins. Not about the case, no. Private matter. They tell me you do cottages as well as caravans. Right the far end of Minavon beach, miles from anywhere. Is it? Two miles? Well, I suppose I'd bring enough supplies for the fortnight. That sounds smashing, Mr Andrews. Two weeks in June for preference. Two people. No, a hundred and ninety quid isn't a problem. Can you hold that for me till four o'clock? Just long enough to confer. Much obliged, Mr Andrews. Ring you back then. Cheers.'

Beyond his window, the cool March sun gleamed on the civic marble of buildings in the Mall. Petals were coming down in pink drifts from the wind that blew across dockland Peninsula from deep-water anchorages. But Hoskins saw only the wide sweep of warm Minavon sand, the glittering brilliance of midsummer sea, Lesley walking naked from the tide towards the whitewashed cottage. He could smell the tang of fish cooking and see the dull gleam of light on a dark wine bottle. The sun was dipping and the sheets were cool.

There was a knock at the door. Jack Chance.

'Give me a minute, Jack,' he said. 'Something important just came up.'

She was closer on the pale sunlit sands, a seawater gloss on a sheen of pearly thighs. Hoskins drew the telephone across his desk and dialled her number in Lantern Hill.

>>> If you've enjoyed this book and would like to discover more great vintage crime and thriller titles, as well as the most exciting crime and thriller authors writing today, visit: >>>

# The Murder Room
## Where Criminal Minds Meet

**themurderroom.com**